I0611961

Dark Poison

Corrupted Coil Series: Book 3

Theo Mann

The Invisible Publishing Company

Corrupted Coil Series

Contents

Chapter 1

E liska swerved to avoid a fountain of rock ejecting out of the cliff to her left, but she didn't get clear in time. Gravel pelted her in the head and made her scream.

Yann Dilnao and the Barbarian Servant Anríq closed on either side of her, but they couldn't protect themselves, either.

Eliska stuck her staff in the air and fired a jet of magic over their party. Her protective field sure felt small, now that it only covered herself, Anríq, Yann, and Marine trailing along behind.

The stone cliffs flanking this canyon blasted out of position and rumbled higher and higher to the skies. They kept on growing without stopping and the landscape closed in from all sides.

Broken rock tumbled out of cracks to rain on the party. Eliska's shield caught most of the rubble, but that wasn't the worst of it.

The travelers should have raced out the end of the canyon into open country by now, but the cliffs kept building new walls in front of the four friends.

The walls jutted up in two parallel lines running away around corners and veering at intersections. The canyons twisted into a maze of confused channels leading nowhere.

"We gotta get out of here!" Yann yelled.

Eliska tried to look around for some way out. She almost tripped over her own feet when one of the nearest cliff walls started to change.

It morphed in strange shapes and then reformed into a giant creature.

She didn't recognize it as any kind of Darkling. It looked more like one of the monsters from the Layer where she and Marine got trapped alone.

The monster roared, arched the spikes on its curved back, raised massive, jointed arms to the skies, and brought them down on top of the travelers.

The monster's fists smashed into the canyon floor with brutal force and created another earthquake.

The travelers wheeled away to save themselves only to almost get pulverized by another monster coming at them from the right.

The cliffs kept growing and transforming everywhere Eliska looked. They all came after the travelers and stomped and punched into the ground trying to smash the friends.

She took her staff down to fire at the monsters, but that meant removing the shield of protection.

When she did hit the monsters, they exploded in hurricanes of revolving debris that put the travelers in just as much danger.

The monsters stepped on each other, kicked each other, and fought each other trying to get close to the group.

The monsters roared at each other, but instead of turning on each other, they all suddenly seemed to come to a decision to work together to capture or destroy the group.

Eliska spun backward to plant herself in their path. At least she could guard her friends' retreat.

She unloaded on the monsters and shielded herself at the same time, but the whole mountain range came alive and more monsters burst out of every ridge and peak.

They detonated in the beam of her magic, fell down in piles of rubble, and other monsters climbed over their fallen comrades to close on the party.

Anríq sprang over to her side, hauled back his club, and pounded one monster after another. His booming thumps disintegrated the rock monsters.

Clouds of flying shards sprayed Marine. She screamed and ducked under her arms. Yann grabbed her and pulled her away.

"Come on, Marine!" he yelled. "Keep moving!"

Eliska didn't turn around to see how sane Marine was acting right now. Eliska kept up a constant barrage of magical blasts to shatter the rock monsters as fast as they would come.

Anríq had to keep spinning one way and the other to hit them all. He launched himself off the ground to hammer them closer to their faces.

Eliska caught a glimpse of movement out of the corner of her eye and glanced behind her. More of the same kind of monsters shot out of the mountains all around here. How were there even mountains here anymore?

She turned to confront these new monsters, but those facing her circled to box her in.

She also caught a glimpse of the cliffs. They towered over her and Anríq in a complete ring. The friends couldn't get out of here. They were trapped.

"Hold on, Anríq!" she yelled. "I'm going to shatter the Island!"

"Do it now!" he roared from high above her head. Every strike of his club exploded another rock monster.

She swiped her staff in a circle, jammed it down into the earth at her feet, and detonated the bedrock under the surface. The Layer exploded and threw everyone into mayhem.

Marine screamed again. Eliska caught sight of Yann holding onto Marine as they both cartwheeled off into space.

Anríq hurtled past Eliska falling way too fast. She dove for him, but she couldn't catch him in time.

She fired her staff at him, magnetized her to him with a binding spell, and his bulky body slammed into her way too hard.

She grunted in pain, but she managed to pull Yann and Marine to her, too, before they all plunged through a curtain of fire into another sky full of storm clouds.

Icy rain whipped everywhere and lightning crackled back and forth around the travelers. Gravity yanked them sideways and the four friends hurtled between thunderclaps.

They burst out into another howling tornado tearing the Layer apart.

"Do you see any land?!" Yann yelled in her ear.

"I don't see anything!" she hollered back.

"Can you get us anywhere—before we crash into the ground somewhere?"

She raised her hand to create her Coil projection to see where they were, but she didn't want to take her eyes off the storm.

At that moment, a colossal force slammed down on the four friends from above—or what Eliska thought was above. She couldn't be sure which direction was up.

The impact flattened all four of them onto a hard stone surface and knocked the wind out of Eliska's lungs. She gasped and spluttered trying to orient herself….and then she saw where she was.

She pried herself off the floor in a neat room constructed of grey stone. The four stone walls met up with a heavy timber ceiling.

The room even had nice furnishings in it. An ornately carved wooden lectern stood in the center of the room with a high, three-legged stool topped with a red velvet cushion. A massive book lay open on the lectern.

A wooden bench sat under one of several tall, thin, pointed cathedral windows in all four walls. Colorful embroidered tapestries hung from the walls between the windows.

More desks stood against the opposite wall between the windows. A strong wooden door with iron fittings exited the room to the left.

Eliska peeled herself off the floor and pushed herself up onto her knees. Those windows looked out into a cold grey sky, but a cheerful fire crackled in a massive stone fireplace to one side. It made the room toasty and comfortable.

"Where are we?" Yann choked.

"I don't know. At least we're on solid ground again." Eliska looked out one of the windows. "It looks like we're in an Island somewhere."

Another gasp cut them off. "I know where we are!" Marine shot to her feet. She acted awfully sane all of a sudden. "This is the Temple—the Temple of the Guardian Templars!"

"Are you sure?" Yann asked. "How can you be sure just from seeing one room?"

"You don't understand!" She raced around the room looking at everything and touching all the furniture. She dashed from desk to desk and tapestry to tapestry. "This is more than just any old temple. This is *my* temple! This is the Temple where I did my training! This is the temple that got destroyed in the other Layer—Brother Matherus's Temple!"

"How is that possible?" Eliska asked. "You saw the ruins. Brother Matherus died when the Temple got destroyed."

"Maybe it didn't get destroyed," Yann suggested. "Maybe it just moved when the landscape shifted."

Marine was too busy feasting her eyes on everything. She rushed to the lectern and actually screamed when she saw the book. Her hand flew to her mouth.

"What's wrong?" Eliska got to her feet and took a step forward, but she didn't want to go over there to see what made Marine so distressed.

Marine pointed at the book with shaking fingers. "This proves it! This was the book Brother Matherus was working on when I left the Temple."

"That proves that it *couldn't* be the same Temple," Eliska pointed out. "You left the Temple long before it got destroyed. He couldn't have been working on the same book."

Marine's eyes shot up and skimmed the room. She didn't see her three friends standing right in front of her.

"Do you realize what this means?!" she whispered. "It means we can access the whole Temple library! We can look up everything we need to know about the Voyant!"

"You said your order didn't know about the Voyant," Eliska reminded her. "You said that was the reason you went into the Dark Layers and communed with Darklings."

Marine pointed at her. "Aha! I gotcha! I said I went into the Dark to find out the Voyant's plans. The order already knew about the Voyant. Anyway, the Brothers and Masters didn't tell me everything they knew about him."

"Then you could find the bolus of knowledge," Eliska suggested. "Or you could use the library to find out the information that the order put into the bolus of knowledge."

Marine touched her forefinger to her lips and cocked her head to look off into space. "Theoretically—yes."

"Why didn't they tell you everything?" Yann asked. "Why would they keep it from you if you were going into the Dark to get information for them?"

"That's the thing, see? I was barely an initiate to the order. My father sent me here to receive my education and to train to use my magic. I wasn't even planning to join the order when all of this happened."

"I don't understand," Eliska replied. "Why does that mean they would keep important information from you?"

"Because I was just an initiate. I was never a full Templar and I was never going to be one. No one under the rank of Brother has access to the library. Even the lower-ranked Brothers aren't allowed access to everything in the library. The order reserves most of their more closely guarded records for senior Brothers at the very least and some of it only for Masters."

"Which one was Wesh?" Eliska asked.

"I don't know. I never asked him."

Yann looked around. "So where's the library?"

Marine turned to the door to leave the room. "I'll show you."

Chapter 2

Yann went over to one of the peaked cathedral windows and looked out at the sky surrounding the Guardian Temple.

"We're in a tower—and I can't see the ground. We might not be attached to any solid ground at all. We might be stuck in an air Layer."

Eliska crossed to his side to take a look. "This room might be an Island all by itself. We might not be able to get to the library. It might not even exist."

"I'm going to find out." Marine pulled the door open.

The others followed her outside onto a stone landing leading to a wide spiral staircase.

"How are you so sane all of a sudden, Marine?" Eliska asked. "I still have my magic which means you and Anríq must have yours, too."

"I do," Marine chirped over her shoulder. "The Temple's magic protects me from the Dark—which means the Temple's magic is still intact."

"So you'll lose your sanity if we ever leave here?" Yann asked.

She grinned at him over her shoulder. "I guess so. Some things are more important than keeping your sanity."

"What's the point if you don't ever get any useful information out of the Darklings?" Eliska asked. "You've been communing with them all this time and you haven't found out anything we can use."

"I can only keep trying." Marine kept climbing down, stopped at another landing, and pulled open another equally sturdy door.

This one led into a towering chamber with massive, crisscrossed timber arches rising overhead. Porticos and carved stone colonnades led into other halls on either side.

Desks stood in rows in some of these halls. Others contained long tables lined with chairs.

Lively fires burned in the fireplaces in each room, but the whole Temple echoed with an ominous silence.

"Where is everyone?" Yann whispered.

"They should be here!" Marine breathed. "There should be thousands of people living and working here—servants, household staff, Templars, students—even local villagers worked here." She peered into each room as the group passed. "I don't understand."

"Maybe the Temple is under a spell," Eliska remarked.

"Or maybe the upheaval moved the Temple and left the people behind," Yann suggested. His eyes flew open. "I know! Maybe this is the bolus of knowledge! Brother Matherus said he and the other Templars hid the bolus in the Layers. What better way than to transport the whole Temple somewhere else? That would distract the Voyant into killing all the Templars. He wouldn't know where the Temple was."

"I don't think so," Marine replied. "We didn't do anything special to find this Temple. We would have had to use powerful magic to break whatever concealment spell the Templars used to hide the bolus. We wouldn't have just accidentally fallen into it."

"Don't you think it's a little too convenient that we did just accidentally fall into it?" Eliska asked. "Don't you think it's a little too coincidental that we were falling through random Layers and we just magically happened to fall into the one place in the whole Coil that could give us the information we've been looking for? Sorry. I don't buy it."

Marine cocked her head again. "You might be right."

"I am right. We didn't wind up here by accident."

"Then how *did* we wind up here?" Yann asked.

"I don't know. Maybe the Templars did something so that members of the order would be able to find it if they needed it."

"But I'm not a member of the order—not one of any rank," Marine pointed out. "If they did that, wouldn't they reserve that for Brothers and Masters?"

"You were a member of the order even if you were only an initiate," Eliska countered. "You're on a mission for the order and you're looking for information to carry out that mission. Maybe that had something to do with it."

Marine shrugged that away. "Maybe."

"So where's the library?" Yann asked again.

"Over here."

Marine led the way through a bunch of different corridors—all of them completely deserted.

Every room radiated with warmth. Not a speck of dust marred the windowsills or the furniture. Everything looked like the people living here just stepped out a few minutes ago.

The group passed another hall full of long tables lined with chairs. This one actually had plates and cutlery sitting at each place.

"I'm hungry," Yann murmured.

Marine giggled. "I'll take you to the kitchens after we check the library."

The group came to another staircase, climbed it, filed down some more corridors, and took another spiral staircase into another tower.

Eliska studied Yann on the way. He didn't show any further sign of distress over his father's death—and Rien Dugas's death—but they must have still bothered Yann under the surface.

Eliska made up her mind to keep an eye on him, but she didn't bring it up. She didn't want to dredge up painful memories. Getting over his father's loss would be hard enough.

Marine finally came to a massive set of double doors. The Templars had carved the heavy wooden planks with all kinds of bizarre figures, scenes, and undulating patterns.

Marine pushed open one of the doors and the group stepped into a gargantuan library.

The chamber rose out of sight with countless bookshelves loaded with books. Multiple levels, landings, and staircases connected them to each other.

"How do we find anything about the Voyant in here?" Yann whispered.

"We have to use magic." Marine crossed the hall and stepped up on another raised lectern near the door.

Eliska didn't see any other desks or lecterns in the place—just miles and miles of books.

"If you aren't allowed to see the books because you aren't highly ranked enough, won't the library block you from seeing them now?" Eliska asked.

Marine only shrugged again. "We can only try, right?"

She raised one hand, shut her eyes, and a bright white light glowed from her palm. Nothing happened at first...and then a large book materialized on the lectern in front of her.

"Wow!" Eliska breathed. "How did you do that?"

Marine opened her eyes. "That's the way the library works. Anyone can come in here and request the book they want—or they would come in here if they were allowed in here." She made a face over her shoulder. "Which I'm not. I wouldn't dare to come in here if any of the Brothers were around."

"So how do you find out what you want to know?" Yann stepped onto the lectern next to her and looked down at the book. "This thing is huge. It would take us weeks to read this and it might not even contain the information we want."

"That's easy." Marine extended her hand over the book and created the same glow.

The book floated open, laid itself out on the lectern in front of her, and the pages rustled. They stopped at a certain page.

Yann and Marine bent over it. Eliska and Anríq stayed where they were.

Marine ran her finger down the columns of written text. "Here it is. This lists the names of the previous Voyants....their birth and death dates....and which Islands they originally came from."

"Does it say anything about them having an order of members?" Eliska asked.

"Here. Take a look at this," Marine called without looking up. "This says the Voyant serves the King in the White Spire." She frowned to herself. "Hmm."

"I thought you said the Voyant lives in the White Spire," Eliska pointed out.

Marine studied the page in front of her and then waved Eliska up to the lectern. "Come up here. I need you to help me figure this out."

Eliska shuffled her feet. "I...uh....I don't know how to read."

Marine blinked at her. "You don't?"

Eliska looked away. "I never learned. No one ever taught me."

"I don't know how to read, either," Anríq interjected.

Marine looked back and forth between them. Eliska cringed when she saw the wheels turning in Marine's head. Now the cat was out of the bag.

Marine finally waved that away. "Well, come up here anyway. You're making me nervous standing down there like a couple of ghosts."

She turned back to the book. Eliska and Anríq exchanged glances. Then they both climbed up on the other side of the lectern.

Yann and Marine went on studying the book as though Eliska and Anríq not knowing how to read meant nothing.

Column upon column of microscopic script covered every page. Marine ran her finger down the columns.

"Oseon Yuanov.....Borio Hateras.....Zatrevis Mirini...." Marine muttered.

"What does that mean?" Eliska asked.

"Those are the names of the previous Voyant Mendicats," Yann explained. "This lists all their births and deaths—so I guess that means they all started out as normal human beings."

"Oseon Yuanov was born in 9351 in the Lake Country," Marine read. "He died in 9397....in the White Spire."

"So he did live in the White Spire," Eliska pointed out. "How could the Voyant live there at the same time as the King?"

"We don't know they lived there at the same time," Yann reasoned. "Maybe the Voyant acts as some kind of regent."

"Borio Hateras was born in 17395," Marine interjected. "That's more than six hundred years after the previous Voyant's death."

Eliska gasped. "Why so long? That must rule out any kind of continuous succession or recruitment or whatever method they're using to hand down their power."

Marine frowned. "The same goes for Zatrevis Mirini. He wasn't even born until a hundred years after Borio Hateras's death. Something fishy is going on here."

"Can you find out any other information about the current Voyant?" Yann asked.

Marine ran down the whole list of names. Her shoulders slumped when she got to the bottom. "He isn't here. The last entry is listed more than five hundred years ago."

"Maybe that's the point," Yann remarked. "Maybe the Voyants only come out during instability cycles."

"Is there a way to find out?" Eliska asked. "Can we correlate the Voyants' lifespans with the instability cycles?"

"I have a better idea." Marine straightened up and raised her hand to close the book. It floated back into the enormous stacks.

"What are you going to do?" Yann asked.

"I'm going to find out about the King in the White Spire. It doesn't make sense that the Voyant would be there and the King would be there. There must be some connection. I mean....there is a connection—the spire itself."

She used her magic to bring out a different book. This one looked newer and not so big.

"What is it?" Eliska asked.

"This will show us the genealogies for the Kings in the White Spire. It will tell us who they are and any other information the order has on them."

She opened the book to a random page—except that it wasn't a random page.

"Holy crap!" Eliska breathed. "These are the same auras we saw in the tunnels!"

"These must be the Voyants," Yann pointed out.

"They can't be. Look." Marine pointed at the glowing figures' heads. "They're all wearing crowns. These must be the kings."

"Then why are they glowing—and they have that purple glow in their chests," Yann observed.

Marine turned page after page covered in the same figures. The same combination of couples covered every page.

Some of the couples were one man and one woman. Others were two women together or two men together. Some were old or young or a combination of both.

"Look at that." Eliska pointed to a pair on the third page. "This one is wearing a crown and this one isn't. What do you think it means?"

"Let's find out." Marine extended her hand over the book. A bunch of pages flipped to more lines of text.

She bent over and started reading. "Here we go. This lists the birth and death dates and the...." She trailed off.

Yann cocked his head to read over her shoulder. "Oh, I get it now! The kingship is passed down from father to son."

"Wait a minute," Marine interrupted. "Something doesn't add up here." She flipped a bunch of pages without using magic and came to the end of the list. "Here it is. The last king was Yimichi Ocuron. This says the Noleron Kupuro was the king's chief advisor until the king's death. Then Kupuro became the Voyant Mendicat and became Ruler in the White Spire—but it doesn't say he became King."

"He couldn't become King," Yann pointed out. "Kupuro wasn't the king's son."

"Yimichi Ocuron and Noleron Kupuro are Barbarian names," Anríq interrupted.

Everyone whipped around to stare at him. "Seriously?!" Yann gasped.

"Are you sure?" Marine exclaimed. "How could Barbarians become King?"

"I don't have an explanation for it, but I'm certain they are both Barbarian names," Anríq replied. "I know people with those names. The Ocuron and Kupuro tribes are famous in the Barbarian world."

Marine bent over the list. "What about Goneneus Aeka?"

"No," Anríq replied.

"This lists Goneneus Aeka as the King in the White Spire before Yimichi Ocuron. So they weren't father and son, either."

"So why did the Voyant become Ruler in the King's place?" Yann asked.

"It must have been because the King didn't have a son who could take the throne after him," Marine suggested.

"Maybe that's why the Voyant is doing this. Maybe that's why the Voyant is coming after us—to find the person who would be next in line to take the throne."

"We don't know that the Voyant *is* still coming after us," Yann pointed out. "He hasn't come after us since we left Tenby."

"You're still alive," Marine pointed out. "You could be the one he wants."

"But I'm not any king's son. Eliska is the only person here whose parentage is unknown. If he was looking for someone, it would be her."

"We don't know who your mother is, Yann," Anríq interrupted.

Yann snorted. "Are you telling me my mother was a princess—and she got together with some imp on the backstreets of Middleborough, had a child out of wedlock, and then vanished into the Layers? I don't think so."

"We know the Voyant is after someone even if it isn't one of us," Marine pointed out. "We have to find the person in order to stop the Voyant."

"Well, it can't be me," Yann went on. "I don't have any magic to control the Coil the way the Voyant does. All these kings and rulers are shown with this magical aura."

"True," Marine replied.

"Now what do we do?" Eliska asked. "This doesn't get us any closer to finding the person."

Marine raised her hand and put the book back. "I think it's time we visited the kitchens. We won't be able to think on empty stomachs."

Chapter 3

Yann, Eliska, Marine, and Anríq climbed down dozens of staircases through the Temple to its lowest levels.

"All the levels look like they're intact," Marine remarked. "If the Temple did get transported to another Layer, the whole thing got transported undamaged."

"Let's go outside and see if we can find out which Island we're in," Eliska suggested.

They agreed on that. Marine led the way down, down, down into the Temple's cellars and eventually came to a long tunnel.

It ended in another cloud bank. The group halted at the edge and looked down at a vast sky full of clouds. It surrounded the Temple's lowest walls and didn't seem to have any bottom or land underneath i t.

Marine sighed. "This tunnel should have ended in the stable yards. I guess we're on an Island in the clouds." She turned back. "At least we're safe in here for now."

She wound her way back through the Temple's corridors to the kitchens. The party raided the pantries and loaded up baskets of pastries, fruit, cheese, and sweets.

"Enjoy yourselves while you can," Yann remarked. "We'll probably never get a haul like this again."

The friends took everything back up to the little tower room where they first started and settled down by the fire to eat.

"It doesn't seem possible that one of us could be the heir to the Kingship," Eliska remarked.

"I'm not," Marine pointed out. "I already know who my parents are and my father is definitely NOT the King in the White Spire."

"I'm not the heir to the Kingship, either," Anríq added.

"You might be if the previous two rulers were Barbarians."

"I know who my father is and he was not the King," Anríq replied.

"It doesn't make sense that I would be the one, either," Yann chimed in. "Even if my mother was related to the King, I still wouldn't be the heir because my father was an imp Watchman from Middleborough."

"You might be the next closest male relative," Marine suggested. "You might not be the King's direct son, but maybe you're the heir anyway because there is no one else to take the throne."

"Why can't the Voyant keep ruling?" Yann countered. "He's already there."

"But don't you see?" Marine exclaimed. "You could bring peace to the Coil if you took the throne away from him. Then he wouldn't be able to inflict all this chaos on everyone."

"You don't know that," Anríq corrected. "The Voyant is the one who controls the Coil. The records didn't say anything about the King in the White Spire controlling the Coil or having anything to do with the stability cycles."

"But we've seen these drawings of both the Voyants and the Kings with these halos—the same halos the Voyant has now," Marine argued. "Both the King and the Voyant must have the power. Maybe the Voyant gets the power when the King dies without an heir."

Anríq shrugged. "That does seem to explain it better."

"Then that rules me out as the heir," Eliska added. "I'm not a male relative and you didn't say that the lists included women as Kings—or Queens or whatever."

"No, they didn't," Marine agreed.

"But we did see women with halos—and wearing crowns," Yann pointed out. "So you might have something to do with it."

"Then why did the Voyant go after Middleborough?" she asked. "The Voyant went after Middleborough before I got there."

"We don't even know if the Voyant is still after us," Marine repeated. "The person he wanted could have been one of the Watchmen."

"It couldn't have been Omer," Yann reasoned. "It doesn't make sense that the King in the White Spire would be a Corsair."

"It doesn't make sense that the King in the White Spire would be a Barbarian, either," Eliska added.

"We don't know that the King or the Voyant were Barbarians," Marine returned. "They might just have the same names."

"My money is on Anríq," Yann interjected. "If he says they were Barbarians, I believe him."

Marine looked into the basket nearest her and pulled out a box of sweets. "Who wants to make themselves sick?"

"I think we already are," Eliska replied. "I haven't eaten this much in...well, forever."

Marine cracked a grin and pried the box open. "Then be prepared to spend a week in the hospital. These things will stick to your guts and take a month to digest."

"I'll skip it," Eliska muttered. "Thanks anyway."

"What are we doing after this?" Yann asked.

"I don't know about the rest of you, but I'm going back to the library," Marine replied. "I want to get more information about the Kings in the White Spire."

"Do you mean you've never heard of them before?" Eliska asked.

"I've heard of them, but I didn't know anything about them. I didn't know they had any kind of magic." She cocked her head. "That's strange, isn't it?"

"What's strange?" Yann asked.

"It's strange that he's called the King in the White Spire—and I knew that the Voyant lives in the White Spire—but I never connected the two." She shook that out of her head. "Anyway, we know now. They're connected one way or the other. We just have to find out how."

"How does them being connected help us stop the Voyant?" Yann asked.

"It helps if the instability cycles have any correlation to the King's death," Eliska pointed out. "If the King dies without an heir and the Voyant takes over, the Coil becomes unstable."

"How does that work?" Yann asked.

"I don't know, but what other explanation is there?"

"Let's go find out." Marine got to her feet and held out the box of sweets. "Unless anyone wants to eat anything else."

The other three all yelled, "NO!!"

She snickered, put the box of sweets back in the basket, and picked it up to take it with her.

"We should take these downstairs with us to the dormitory. We'll need somewhere to sleep tonight and we might get hungry. We won't want to trek all the way back to the kitchen every time."

"Now you're speaking my language," Yann replied.

She laughed and blushed at him.

The others stood up and helped her carry the remaining food down to the library. The friends left their goods outside while they went back to the lectern.

"What book are you going to get out this time?" Eliska asked.

"I don't know all the books in here, so I'll just make a request for something that tells us whether the instability cycles correspond to the King dying without an heir—or any other time a Voyant has to step in as Ruler because there is no King."

She raised her hand and the glowing orb brightened on her palm. She shut her eyes, but right at that moment, another light flashed between the giant stacks of books.

The Voyant's halo flared in the shadows and a shockwave of hurricane wind hit the library. It blasted outward from the radiant beams of his halo.

The disruption tore all the books off the shelves and sent them whirling in mayhem.

Eliska dove for Marine to catch her, but the blast slapped Eliska away, stripped her off her feet, and pitched her backward.

She tumbled across the floor and then another catastrophic flash sent her wheeling off into space.

She lost sight of everyone and everything—except a whole ton of books flying through the chaos.

Their pages fluttered open in the tempest and bizarre shapes, people, landscapes, and creatures erupted off the pages.

Some of these shapes tore the books apart. Others got sucked back into the pages when the wind blew the books shut.

Masses of debris and shadowy vapors whipped all around her and she could no longer deny anymore that it all deliberately came after her this time.

Shadows formed in the Dark and gruesome faces and creature shapes appeared in the Layers. They lunged for her only to dissolve in the whirlwind a second later.

Others pulled their Layers toward her and slashed across her face. They tore her clothes and tried to pummel her into revolving tornados of shrapnel.

The debris itself formed different shapes. Curtains of shards or walls of spikes assembled themselves in her path.

She rotated her staff one way and the other trying her hardest to bombard them all out of her path.

She succeeded in plastering her way through some of them. Others came at her too fast, hit her, and shredded her skin before she had time to stop them.

She screamed. She wouldn't survive this mayhem much longer, especially not with Dark forces trying to actively destroy her like this.

None of them turned into Darklings, though. That was the strangest part.

She looked, but no Darklings came out of the Layers around her.

The stuff whirling all around her didn't assemble into Darklings, either. The clouds of Dark vapors didn't take any permanent shape.

She didn't understand it, but she couldn't stay here tumbling alone in this void. Yann, Marine, and Anríq were nowhere in sight.

She grabbed her staff in both hands. This Layer had no floor, walls, ceiling, or any solid surface. She would just have to shatter the Layer another way.

She thrust out her staff at the hurricane of debris around her and smashed her magic into it full force.

It shattered and gravity yanked her down way too fast. She screamed again, but before she could fall very far, she hit the ground, and rolled to a stop in a bed of long, dry grass.

Chapter 4

Eliska clutched the grass and the earth groaning in relief for something solid to hold onto. She was on the ground, thank the stars.

She gasped and panted...and then she tasted blood. Blood dripped
into her mouth from wounds all over her face and blood soaked her
clothes.

Before she could move even to sit up, Anríq walked over to her from
somewhere. He went down on one knee behind her and laid his hand
on her back. "You got hurt. Lie still a minute."

A rush of warmth flooded her from his hand. It spread through her
body and closed all the wounds.

She flopped on the ground and let her head fall on her arms. "Thank
you!" she choked.

He flexed his fingers against her back and then rubbed it in a comforting motion. "Do you feel all right now?"

She nodded.

"Stand up," he told her. "I need you to help me."

She pried herself off the ground. She didn't know what he meant
about needing her help. She got to her feet and looked around.

The two of them stood in another vast grassland spreading in all
directions. Low swells covered the terrain. That was it. She didn't see
any rivers, streams, trees. or any other vegetation.

A distant line of blue mountains looked tiny on the farthest horizon. They might have been a thousand miles away.

"I don't see Yann and Marine," Anríq told her. "Can you find them?"

Eliska opened her Coil projection and he added his magic to make it bigger. The golden lines traced Eliska's and Anríq's route from the cloud layer to this Island.

"It's strange, " she remarked. "The cloud Layer is still there. It's perfectly intact."

"The Voyant didn't destroy the Layer. He only came after us."

"That must mean he's after Yann," she pointed out. "He's the only member of the Watch still alive who was in Middleborough when the attacks started."

"Yann and Marine are in that Layer there," Anríq pointed to the lines separating from his and Eliska's.

"I don't see anything strange about it," Eliska remarked. "It looks like a stable Island....but it has magic—and Dark forces. Marine will probably be crazy there. Yann will be alone. We should rejoin him. He'll need our help."

Eliska looked around at the surroundings again. She found it difficult to accept that nothing in this landscape was trying to attack her the way it did in the chaos Layer through which she just passed.

From what she could tell, the Voyant or maybe even the Coil itself were trying to destroy her or at least hurt her.

She didn't want to destroy this Island. Stable landscapes were becoming increasingly difficult to find and they were too precious.

The Coil would take the Island back soon enough. She didn't want to destroy it before then.

She opened her mouth to suggest that she cut a hole in this Island to send herself and Anríq back into the Layers.

She cut herself off when she saw Anríq scowling at the horizon. "Is something wrong?" she asked.

"I know this Island," he muttered.

"You do? Is there something here that could help us?"

His nostrils flared. He didn't stop glaring at everything. "This is my home Island—or it was. It smells the same. I traveled in the Coil for years and never smelled anything like this anywhere else."

She brightened up. "That's great! Do you want to...." She trailed off again when she saw the look on his face.

She had been about to suggest that he visit his family while he was here, but that might not be the best idea after all.

He went down on one knee, dug in the dirt, and pulled up a handful of the soil.

He smelled it and clenched his jaw. "It is the same Island. It was part of the Ancestral Empire....but it's here now. The Dark river must have fractured it and now this Island is floating separately in the Coil."

"Do you want to leave? Do you want to get out of here before you meet someone you know?"

He compressed his lips once and turned away, but there was nowhere to turn away to. He only wound up glancing over his shoulder at the terrain behind him.

Eliska didn't dare to interrupt his thoughts. She didn't know the circumstances that caused him to leave home. He intimated when he first joined the Watch that the circumstances hadn't been anything good.

She didn't say anything even to ask if he wanted her to shatter the Layer and take them somewhere else. She stood in silence and waited for him to decide what to do.

He didn't seem aware of her existence. He became so engrossed in the landscape that he forgot she was there—or he acted like it.

She would have liked to go over to him and maybe touch his arm to bring him out of it—or at least to show him that she cared.

Anríq took off walking across the grasslands in no particular direction. She didn't understand why.

Eliska didn't want to leave Yann on his own with no one but Marine to talk to. He wouldn't survive for long by himself and she wouldn't be able to help him once she lost her mind again.

She did say she could commune with the Dark whenever she wanted to or come out of it whenever she wanted. Could Eliska trust that? She would be trusting Marine with Yann's life.

Eliska hoped and prayed Marine stayed out of the Dark for Yann's sake. Marine better not leave him unprotected.

Eliska didn't want to take that chance, but she couldn't exactly leave here without Anríq.

She could have, but something told her not to. She followed him.

He walked for a long way—much longer than she expected.

She kept opening her Coil projection to check on Yann.

She couldn't see the golden lines without adding Anríq's magic to the image, but she did see the Island where Yann landed. The Island stayed stable. It didn't collapse. She just hoped he was safe there—for now at least—just long enough for her to find him.

She considered more than once if she should let Anríq walk away. He would be fine. She never doubted that. Yann needed her more right now.

Anríq climbed a rise and stopped at the top. Eliska climbed up and stopped next to him. She would tell him now that she was going to get Yann. Anríq could make up his own mind about what to do and where to go.

As soon as she got into that position, she saw what he was looking at. A caravan of nomads crossed the grasslands a few miles away.

These weren't Barbarians or gypsies. They were just scruffy poor people trekking across the countryside.

They wore tattered clothes and they didn't take care of their hair. Frizzy mats of disheveled hair stuck out from their hands. Dust covered their faces.

They lead heavy, lumbering pack animals loaded with bundles of goods. Some of the pack animals pulled wagons. None of the nomads rode on the wagons or on the animals. Everyone walked.

The pack animals' shaggy pelts swayed with their lumbering gate. Their big, bony heads hung almost down to the ground.

They had horns, but the animals followed the nomads in docile submission. None of the nomads had to do anything to control the animals or make them go in the right direction.

The nomads were too far away to see Anríq and Eliska watching them. What was so important about these people?

She'd seen these nomads a hundred times. They didn't have magic. They didn't have anything. They were just poor people wandering through their Island trying to stay alive.

Eliska inhaled for the second time to ask Anríq about catching up with Yann. She opened her Coil projection behind Anríq's back.

Her heart sank when she saw Yann's Island collapsing into another Layer. She couldn't see the golden lines to show her Yann was going or if he was even still alive.

She shut her hand and clamped her eyes shut. Yann would just have to take care of himself until she caught up with him—if she caught up with him.

She glanced around at the landscape one last time. If Anríq didn't agree to come with her, she would just have to leave him here.

She shook her hair out of her eyes while she summoned the nerve to break the silence...and then she saw them.

A line of Barbarians climbed a hill in the distance on the other side of the nomads' route.

The Barbarians brought fifty men each as powerful and frightening as the men who attacked the Black Watch.

Chapter 5

The nomads definitely saw Barbarians moving in on them. The nomads' caravan stopped in the middle of the field and closed together in a protective cluster, but they wouldn't be able to fight this many Barbarians.

Ten men from the nomads' group brought out weapons to confront the Barbarians. This would be a slaughter.

The Barbarians started walking down the far hill to intercept the nomads. The nomads swiveled in their direction and raised their weapons to defend the rest of the party. The women and children tried to hide behind their pack animals, but it wouldn't be enough.

The men moving into position triggered the Barbarians. They burst into a run and charged the convoy. Shrieks, roars, and war cries echoed across the grassland to Eliska's ear.

Anríq took his axe off his back. Eliska saw him about to walk out there and confront the Barbarians, but he wouldn't be able to get there in time.

She lunged forward, grabbed his hand, and magicked both of them into the Barbarians' path to block them from the nomads.

Eliska didn't know what she would do once she got there. She only knew she couldn't let the Barbarians wipe these people out.

She swiped her staff across the ranks of Barbarians and took down ten of them in one pass. Anríq swung his axe as the Barbarians surrounded him.

A deafening boom blasted outward from that sweep and leveled another nine Barbarians who tried to encircle him.

Eliska got caught in the heat of battle. She couldn't pay attention to what Anríq was doing or if the Barbarians were attacking the nomads yet.

She pivoted her back to Anríq so her assault wouldn't put him in danger.

Barbarians rushed her, but they never got near her. She laid down swipe after swipe with her staff and fired blasts at the biggest Barbarians to knock them to the ground.

She tried not to kill them, but she might have done it anyway without meaning to.

Without warning, another magical explosion pelted her across the side of the head. She thought at first that she and Anríq might have drifted too close together.

The shot hurt, but it didn't harm her. It just infuriated her.

She spun around and all her rage erupted when she saw two Barbarians magic-users closing from her left. They fired magical bursts from their bare hands to bombard her.

She deflected the shots with her staff and even ricocheted a few back at them.

Their attack ignited her fury and she stalked toward them to take them down. She could squash these puny upstarts with one blow if she wanted to.

She didn't even try to shoot at them. She hardened her resolve and stormed across the field. She deflected all their shots easily. They couldn't touch her a second time.

Her reaction unsettled them and they started to back away They split apart to flank her. That was their last move.

She held up one hand to protect herself, jammed her staff down into the soil with the other, sent a jet of magic through the earth, and opened a hole under one of them.

He screamed when he dropped through it into the Layer below. She closed the hole over his head and his screams died away.

The other magic-user stopped shooting when he saw his friend disappear. Eliska turned to face him and the guy's eyes darted to her face. She glared at him....and he spun away and bolted.

She let him get ten paces before she curled her fingers upward in a grasping motion. The grass under his feet twined out of place and snaked around his ankle.

The grass brought him crashing down on his stomach and then all the grass around him came alive. It sprouted upward, laced over him, and formed a solid mat of vegetation.

He thrashed and screamed, but he couldn't get away from the grass. It completely covered him, but it didn't kill him. It just held him there so he couldn't get away.

He tried more than once to use his magic to break the restraint, but Eliska's magic overpowered his.

Yelling voices drew her attention back to the fight—but it wasn't a fight anymore.

Anríq and the men from the nomad group faced off against the last ten Barbarians. Anríq held his axe in one hand and his club in the other.

The Barbarians all stood across from him with their weapons pointed at him, but they didn't attack.

The nomad men kept yelling for the Barbarians to back off. The Barbarians yelled curses and threats at the nomads.

Eliska strode over to them and planted herself next to Anríq. He was too nice not to destroy all of them with one thump of his club. They had no idea who they were dealing with.

She pointed her staff at them, sent a crackle of magic down it, and the end started to glow. She didn't have to make it glow. She just wanted to threaten them.

"Get out of here before I kill you all," she snarled. "Take your magic-user and leave if you want to live at all."

The biggest Barbarians pointed at Anríq. "I know who you are. You're Taitus's son. You won't get away with this. The Dinu Tribe will pay for this."

"I don't think so," Anríq murmured back.

The biggest Barbarian pointed at him as he backed away. "This isn't over yet. We'll see you again and then we'll finish this."

"It is over," Eliska interjected.

The Barbarians backed away. Eliska waited until they got to a safe distance before she shot a stream of magic at the Barbarian wizard lying under the grass. She released him and he hustled to catch up with the rest of his friends.

"Don't kill them," Anríq murmured out the side of his mouth.

Eliska spun around. "Huh? What do you mean?"

"Don't kill them. Neutralize them and let them live."

She frowned at him. "What do you mean? They're walking away."

He started to shake his head when another bloodcurdling shriek echoed across the field.

The Barbarians started out by backing away. Then they turned to walk the rest of the way up the hill.

Without warning, they spun around and charged.

Anríq didn't react right away. He raised his club, but he didn't do anything with it. He just stood there and waited for the Barbarians to close with him.

The nomad men stepped forward to meet the assault, but Eliska had seen enough.

She grabbed her staff with both hands the way she did in the Layers, thrust it forward, and delivered an almighty thump in the Barbarians' direction.

The shockwave flattened all of them in a split second. These idiots just did not learn.

They floundered, scrambled, and fell over themselves on the ground trying to stand up straight. A few of the biggest, spikiest Barbarians stumbled to their feet.

Just to make her point, she stepped in front of Anríq, blocked him from them, and faced the Barbarians alone.

"We can keep doing this all day long if you want to," she breezed. "I could have killed you just now, but Anríq told me not to. If you're smart, you'll walk away while you still can. Go back where you came from—and don't let me see you around these people again."

She planted her staff on the ground at her feet and twisted the knife by studying her fingernails.

The Barbarians snarled and cursed her. They hurled a few more threats at Anríq, too, and against his tribe.

She made sure to keep a close eye on these fools when they finally walked away for the second time.

They paused on the far hilltop where they started, but they didn't come back. After a few minutes, they dropped behind the hill and disappeared.

Eliska waited another minute and consulted her hand window just to make sure. Then she turned around to find Anríq behind her. He'd already put his weapons away.

"Are you okay?" she asked. "Those men knew you."

He nodded. "They belong to the Ula tribe. They live in the adjoining territory next to my father's territory."

"You should have let me kill them. They're scum."

"If you killed them, the Ula Tribe would have blamed the Dinu tribe for their deaths. It would have sparked a full-scale war."

Eliska snorted. "I really don't want to get mixed up in Barbarian tribal politics if it's all the same to you. Let's get out of here and go find Yann."

"I can't leave now, Eliska," Anríq replied. "Yulo threatened to retaliate against my tribe for this. I have to stay and answer the challenge. I can't leave the tribe unprotected."

Eliska smacked her lips in exasperation. She opened her mouth to tell him that he would have to stay alone because she couldn't leave Yann unprotected.

Right then, three of the nomad men rushed over. One of them grasped Eliska's hand and shook it way too hard.

"Thank you so much! We're so grateful!" The same man turned to Anríq, but the other two were already surrounding him and telling him about how grateful they were. "We have some food...and goods. Please....help yourselves to whatever we have....anything you want..."

"We don't want payment," Eliska told him. "We're just glad you're safe."

The first guy shot a glance toward the hill where the Barbarians disappeared. "We'll never be safe from them. They'll just wait and ambush us somewhere else. That's the way they do it."

"We'll stay with you," Anríq offered. "We'll travel with you to make sure they don't come back—or to defend you if they do."

The man's eyes dipped to Anríq's clothes....and his tattoos. "You 're....you're a Barbarian."

"He's a Servant," Eliska interrupted. "You saw the way he defended you just now. He's offering to protect you from them."

The man turned to her. "Are you a servant, too?"

"Me? I'm nobody. We're just traveling together."

"Oh." The man turned back to Anríq, but the sight of him must have been too intimidating.

The guy walked off, rounded up his people, and the nomads got their pack animals moving. The nomads didn't introduce themselves to Eliska and Anríq.

The nomads set off across the countryside heading in the direction they'd originally been traveling.

Eliska used her hand window to keep an eye on the Barbarians, but they didn't come back.

They returned to a camp a few dozen miles away. Eliska couldn't see it from here with the naked eye.

Anríq didn't look into her hand window to see what the Barbarians were doing. He walked straight ahead with his eyes locked on the horizon. He cast occasional glances around the terrain to make sure no one was coming.

Eliska didn't interrupt his thoughts and the nomads didn't try to talk to either Eliska or Anríq.

They might have understood the Servant's vow well enough to know he wasn't supposed to talk to people, but she doubted that.

They didn't recognize him as a Servant. Even if they did, they could have talked to her.

The nomads retreated from the pair as far as possible without outright walking away in the other direction.

The convoy traveled all day and didn't stop until nightfall.

The nomads unloaded their pack animals and left the creatures to graze in the open grasslands. The nomads didn't tether the animals to stop them from wandering off—but they didn't wander off. They stayed near the group.

The nomads pitched tents and built fires. Their camp scene reminded Eliska of the gypsies, but without their finery—and without their magic. The nomads did everything by hand.

Anríq stood guard over them while they unloaded. Then he walked off to a different swell thirty feet from the nomad's camp.

He squatted down behind it, pulled some handfuls of grass out of the ground, bunched them into knots, and used his magic to ignite them into a fire.

"Why don't you camp with the nomads?" Eliska asked. "They said they would be happy to have you—I mean us. Why are you settling down out there?"

He stared into the flames without looking up. "The Servant's path is a solitary one. I will serve by protecting them. I don't belong over there....but you can go if you want to."

She glanced at the nomads. They brought out food and started preparing it over their fires.

Her stomach tightened when she saw the food, but she didn't want to leave Anríq alone.

He didn't exactly need company or comforting. He traveled alone all the time.

She squatted down next to him and then sat all the way down. The fire warmed her.

"You stayed with the Watch," she pointed out. "You camped with them, ate with them, and even talked to them."

"That was different," Anríq replied.

"How? If your mission is to protect these nomads, then how is that different from your mission to help the Watchmen?"

"The nomads won't give me any information about how to protect them or what the Voyant is doing or anything related to my service. The Watchmen did give me that. I could only find out how they needed me to serve them by listening to their conversation—and by being part of their group."

She hesitated to say it. "I'm worried about Yann. Maybe we should go find him."

Anríq looked up. "Where is he?"

She opened her Coil projection. Anríq added his magic to expand it.

The gold lines got lost in the mayhem of swirling Layers. The Layer where Eliska had seen him before completely disintegrated and then the lines vanished in the confusion.

She shut her hand with a sigh. "I guess he's gone, too."

"He might not be dead—just lost." Anríq looked down at the fire again. "I sense that he's still alive."

She gulped. She wanted to believe that.

Long experience in the Coil told her not to hope for it. She didn't know where Yann was or how to find him.

"If he is the one the Voyant is looking for, then he'll need help even more than before."

"I'm going to help these people first," Anríq told her. "You can go if you want to, but I don't want to leave this Island yet. I can't leave it when people are in danger."

"What do you know about the Ula Tribe?"

He shrugged. "They're typical Barbarians. They've been carrying on a territorial conflict with the Dinu tribe for as long as I can remember. Both tribes try to take the other's territory and drive each other out. It never stops."

She opened her mouth to ask if that had anything to do with him leaving home, but she stopped herself in time. She shouldn't ask.

Chapter 6

E liska sat up and scanned the countryside. The sun was coming up over the grasslands. The nomads packed up their camp and loaded everything onto their pack animals.

The creatures stood in one place and waited. No one had to restrain them. They didn't wear halters or bridles or lead ropes. They just did everything the nomads wanted them to.

The animals started walking along with the rest of the group when the nomads moved out. They continued in the same direction as yesterday. Eliska didn't see where they might be going.

She kept a sharp eye on both the landscape and her hand window. She searched the surrounding countryside.

She didn't see anything until close to midday. So many hours of silence and stillness passed that she almost forgot to check.

She glanced into her hand.

The nomads stopped at one of the very few rivers in this grassland. It wound between the low swells. No one could see the river unless they looked right down on top of it.

Dense water plants choked the banks on both sides. They soaked up the water and prevented taller trees from growing.

The nomads settled down for an extended break. Anríq and Eliska both drank from the stream and then squatted on one of the swells to keep watch.

Eliska glanced into her hand window again, but she didn't expect to see anything. She only looked from force of habit.

She froze when she saw Barbarians coming closer. These came from a different camp twenty miles away.

The nomads had already passed too far away from the Ula Tribe for them to come after the nomads again.

Eliska bumped Anríq's elbow and showed him the Barbarians in her hand window.

They came heavily armed and brought a lot more men. They looked like they had emptied their camp of every man of fighting age.

He took one look and turned away with a grimace.

The nomads didn't notice anything. They finished eating and drinking, packed up their animals, and started back on their endless migration.

Anríq and Eliska dropped behind to follow them. Eliska kept a close eye on the Barbarians getting closer.

She barely took her eyes off her hand window to see where she was going.

The Barbarians climbed one of the distant hills. A solid mass of armed fighting men spread out across the field.

Their hair spikes gave their heads a strange, inhuman outline from this distance. The sun glittered on all the studs and spikes on their clothes.

The nomads armed themselves and the men moved to the rear, but the Barbarians never came any closer.

They only advanced when the nomads got far enough away. Then the Barbarians crossed the field to another stopping place at a respectful distance.

"What are they doing?" Eliska asked. "Why don't they attack?"

Anríq turned around to face the Barbarians. They were in the process of approaching again. They took a position across a series of swells five hundred yards away.

The nomads stopped to face the Barbarians, too. "Keep going," Anríq told them. "Don't stop. "

"What if they attack us from behind?" the same man asked.

"Eliska and I will protect you. Don't worry. Keep going. Leave the Barbarians to us."

The men took a long time before they accepted that. Anríq relaxed visibly when the nomads finally rejoined their convoy and kept going.

They put more and more distance between themselves and Anríq and Eliska. Eliska watched both parties. She didn't worry about her and Anríq being able to protect the nomads from the Barbarians.

Anríq narrowed his eyes at the Barbarians in the distance. They stayed on their ridge of swells a lot longer this time. They didn't try to flank the pair to get near the nomads.

Eliska used her hand window to watch the nomads getting farther away. The Barbarians didn't move to intervene. They must have come here to confront Anríq.

The silence dragged for another long, ominous minute before the Barbarians stepped forward. They all carried weapons, but Anríq didn't take down his axe or raise his club this time. He faced them empty-handed.

Eliska tightened her grip on her staff, but she didn't raise it. She could do that at a moment's notice.

She braced herself to defend Anríq if she had to. He might not want to fight his own people, but she sure as hell would.

She wouldn't let these heathens do anything to him even if he was one of their own. All the more reason to protect him from them.

The Barbarians kept the same shoulder to shoulder formation as they crossed dozens of swells. Their hair spikes, horns, black eye paint, tattoos, and spiked clothing made them look even more intimidating up close.

They stopped in a long line facing Anríq and Eliska. Anríq still didn't move to touch his weapons.

Eliska scanned up and down the line of fighting men. They covered so much of the area that they could get behind her easily. She wouldn't be able to stop all of them. Then they would go after the nomad's convoy.

They might have wanted that in the first place, but they must have changed their minds. The Barbarians could have done that already if they really wanted to.

They must have magic-users with them, too. The magic-users could tie up Anríq and Eliska while the other Barbarians ran around them and assaulted the nomads.

The Barbarians didn't attack. One huge guy with giant hair spikes jerked his chin at Anríq. "You have to come back with us."

Anríq dipped his chin once. He didn't close his eyes or hold his hands together nor did he bow. "I will serve," he growled.

The Barbarian guy snorted. "You better not talk like that around the Chieftain. He'll kill you."

Anríq only nodded. "Let's go."

The Barbarians didn't move for a second. That one guy studied Anríq like the guy couldn't figure out why Anríq was being so accommodating.

The guy finally slapped his knuckles against the bicep of the man standing next to him. The big leader swiped his finger at Anríq.

The Barbarians advanced out of line, surrounded Anríq, and took his weapons. He didn't fight them. He raised his arms out to both sides and waited for them to take everything, including his bags.

The Barbarians glared at Eliska, surveyed her up and down, and left her alone. Maybe they didn't realize that her staff was magical.

"Come with us," the first man ordered again and the party broke up.

The men who disarmed Anríq went in front. The rest of the Barbarians' formation surrounded Anríq and Eliska at the center. None of the Barbarians seemed to realize that Eliska was still armed.

They wouldn't have been able to disarm her.

She studied them on the way, but she studded Anríq a lot more closely. She would have liked to ask him who these men were and what they wanted from him, but she didn't break the silence.

He contracted his face into a solid wall of ice all the way back to the Barbarians' camp. He glared at the horizon in front of him, clamped his mouth shut, and refused to look right or left at anyone. She'd never seen him so furious.

She kept an eye on her hand window all the way back to the camp where this group of Barbarians started. They didn't stop even once to rest.

She observed the camp on the way there, too. Some boys spotted the party coming. They ran around and told everyone.

Then practically the entire camp rolled out to stare when the men escorted Anríq and Eliska into the area.

The Barbarians camped in large tents made out of animal hides stitched together and spread over wooden frames. The camp actually looked more like a small village with families living in each permanent dwelling.

The Barbarians didn't use domesticated animals for anything. They hunted and marauded for what they wanted.

The tents showed plenty of decoration of stolen trinkets and even some gold-plated armor, shields, and finery stolen from the Barbarians' victims.

The Barbarians in the camp watched in silence until the party got a few hundred yards away. Then some of the children rushed out and accosted the men with questions.

That set off all the others and everyone moved in talking at once. The women wore the same combination of leather studded clothing, partially or completely shaved heads, and as many decorations of beads, coins, shells, and other trinkets tied to their clothes and hair.

The women also wore the same black eye paint on their faces and just as many tattoos as the men.

The children wore their hair the same but without as many decorations. The youth started to get tattoos around the age of twelve or thirteen. Then they dressed and acted the same as the adults.

People surrounded Anríq bombarding him with questions and exclamations. Eliska couldn't hear what they were saying over the noise of so many voices.

The crowd escorted the men back into the camp. Anríq and Eliska got swept along with the mob.

Most of the men were already in the traveling party, so the women surrounded everyone talking.

The men talked back, but they didn't move out of position all the way back to the camp.

Those in front entered the camp first. By the time Anríq and Eliska got there, a massive throng of people packed around the two prisoners.

Eliska couldn't think of her and Anríq as anything else. Why else would the Barbarians disarm him to bring him here?

He showed no sign of concern over them disarming him. He didn't resist in any way. He could have used his magic to fight these people, but he complied with everything.

The crowd stopped in the middle of the camp with everyone still talking a mile a minute. The noise built to a seething tide of voices all exclaiming, pointing, and questioning.

No one asked Eliska anything. Everyone made a huge deal over Anríq.

Without warning, dead silence fell over the crowd. The Barbarians parted and cleared the way to one extra-large tent at the center of the camp.

The onlookers moved aside in time for Eliska to see two of the biggest Barbarians step out of the tent.

They threw back the door flap and their eyes hardened when they saw Anríq and Eliska standing there. These men stood five or six inches taller than Anríq and much bulkier.

They moved aside and a much older Barbarian man stepped out of the same tent.

He wore all the same black studded clothing as the others. Tattoos covered his arms, chest, stomach, and half of his face.

He wore more jewelry and decoration than any of the others and kept his head shaved completely bald.

He stopped there outside the tent and skewered Anríq with a hard glare. Eliska clamped her hand around her staff ready for anything.

She would have to cast a shield of protection around herself and Anríq to protect them both from a crowd this size. The Barbarians could rush her from inches away before she or Anríq had a chance to defend themselves.

The older man strode forward, stopped in front of Anríq, and inspected him from head to toe.

Then, in one sudden move, the man burst into a huge smile, clasped both hands on Anríq's shoulders, shook him once, and pulled him into a hug.

The man laughed and pushed Anríq back still smiling from ear to ear, but the man's cheeks spasmed with emotion. "Son..." the man croaked. "You came back!"

Anríq burst into a matching grin and his lips trembled. "It's good to see you again, Papi."

The man laughed, crushed Anríq's neck in one meaty hand, and glanced at Eliska. "Who's this? Who did you bring back with you?"

"This is Eliska. She's a friend of mine." Anríq turned to Eliska. "This is my father, Taitus. He's the Chieftain of this branch of the Dinu Tribe."

Taitus held out his hand to shake Eliska's. "It's a pleasure to meet you...and thank you for bringing my son back."

Eliska didn't tell this man that she didn't have anything to do with it.

Taitus put her completely out of his mind and grabbed Anríq again. "You must come and stay in my tent. We'll hold a feast for you. This is a great day."

Taitus threw his arm over Anríq's shoulders and pulled him toward the tent out of which Taitus just exited.

"We have so much to discuss," Taitus went on in Anríq's ear. "I sent people out to search for you, but you traveled through too many layers. I was hoping I would see you again to talk to you about everything going on here."

They vanished inside the tent. The three biggest Barbarians glanced around and their eyes hardened when they saw Eliska standing there, but they didn't do anything. Then they both went inside, too.

The rest of the crowd dissolved in talk. Everyone exclaimed over and over again about Anríq coming back and how much the chieftain valued him.

Chapter 7

The Barbarians eventually drifted back to whatever they'd been doing before the search party brought Anríq and Eliska here.

All the men who went out to escort Anríq and Eliska here wandered away. None of them tried to guard her. No one even spoke to her.

She checked in all directions, but they left her completely alone. Maybe now she should leave and go look for Yann, but she wouldn't be able to locate him in the Coil projection without Anríq's magic.

Just then, he came out of the same tent and crossed to her side. "Come inside," he told her. "My father wants to honor us as his guests."

"He wants to honor you, you mean. Maybe I should...." She waved behind her.

"No," he insisted. "You have to come. He wants you to. I want you to." She opened her mouth to argue, but he only shook his head. He took her arm and led her toward the tent. "My brothers want to hear what you know about the instability in the Coil."

She checked herself. "Your brothers...."

He pulled her inside the tent.

A long, low table stood on one side of the tent's interior room. The table only stood two feet off the ground.

Elaborately decorated cushions surrounded it on all sides. Taitus sat in the center of the table with the other three huge Barbadians on his left side.

"These are my brothers, Hoch, Esegan, and Baoco," Anríq told Eliska. "Here. Sit down here."

He gestured toward a cushion two places away from Taitus. Anríq sat right next to his father.

The instant they sat down, a bunch of people other people entered the tent. Men and women started laying out huge gold and silver platter piled with food.

Some of the food consisted of extravagant pastries dusted with white sugar. Other dishes looked like bizarre kinds of fruit.

Eliska couldn't imagine where these Barbarians could have gotten any of this.

The Barbarians couldn't have gotten any of this from hunting. They must have stolen int, but she didn't know anywhere nearby they could have stolen it from.

The servers laid out platters on every inch of the table with each platter displaying a different delicacy. Eliska didn't recognize half of them.

The servers backed off and left the food there. As soon as they cleared out of the way, more people entered the tent.

They took up every other cushion around the table. Anríq didn't introduce these people.

They all started eating and then the servers set up more table to fill the whole tent. The servers went around the room laying out more and more food.

Eliska even saw people sitting on the ground outside. They packed the camp. The servers served them, too and kept bringing more food out of nowhere.

Taitus talked to Anríq nonstop about everything going on in the Dinu Tribe's territory and outside it.

"The Alara tribe has been encroaching on the Ula tribe west of here," Taitus was saying. "They've had a few battles. We think the Alara plan to come for Dinu territory next, but we'll wait and see. The Ula want us to ally with them to drive the Alara off, but I plan to let the Alara weaken the Ula first. That way, when we finish off the Alara, the Ula can't use our alliance to turn on us."

Anríq didn't answer. His father must have been waiting for him to offer some insight into the strategic value of his decision.

Taitus looked up. "What do you think of that, son? Do you agree with my strategy?"

"I don't know anything about it," Anríq replied. "I'm a Servant. I don't get involved in wars unless it's to defend the defenseless. I don't think you want me to believe the Dinu tribe is defenseless, do you?"

Taitus scowled at him. "You aren't going to persist in this Servant nonsense, are you?"

"Yes," Anríq replied.

Taitus's expression went back. He turned away, grimaced, and helped himself to the food.

Anríq's brothers ate plenty. He finally took a piece of fruit.

Eliska didn't know what to do, so she copied him. She didn't see why she should hold back on eating any of this food as long as Taitus was throwing this feast for her and Anríq.

She didn't feel right about splurging as long as Anríq was eating modestly. She owed it to him to help him make his point—whatever that was.

"The Thora Tribe waged war against us two years ago," Hoch added from farther down the table. "We finished them off and drove them out of the area. You would think the Alara would get the message and back off."

"Maybe they already have," Esegan added. "Maybe they only want to take the Ula tribe's territory and leave us alone."

"That's ridiculous," Taitus fired back. "The Alara would only plan to take the Ula tribe's territory to strengthen themselves before they attacked us. They must be trying to take additional territory. That's the only reason they would wage war in the first place. As soon as they established themselves as our neighbors, they would amass their forces to encroach on us the same way."

"Why don't you ally with the Ula?" Eliska asked. She should have stayed out of it, but her curiosity got the better of her.

"Oh, I will," Taitus exclaimed. "I'm already negotiating with them. I'll just make sure the process takes longer than expected. Then the Ula won't be in any position to pose a threat to us after the war is over. They'll have no choice but to bow to us as the superior tribe."

She let the matter drop there. Taitus turned back to Anríq and started talking to him at length about a bunch of other people Eliska didn't know.

Anríq faced front and chewed his fruit slowly while he listened. He didn't make eye contact with his father nor did Anríq offer any comments on what Taitus was saying.

"Now that you're back, we can divide our force into four instead of three," Tatus went on. "That will give us better coverage our perimeter to the north and the west. Then no one will be able to encroach from there, not even the Ula."

"I won't participate in any of the tribe's raids or the force," Anríq interrupted. "I'm a Servant. I told you I won't get involved in any fighting unless the tribe itself is in danger."

"That's nonsense," Taitus fired back. "The tribe *is* in danger. We're in danger from the Alara—and the Ula."

"You said the Alara are attacking the Ula first," Anríq countered. "The Alara don't have any designs on Dinu territory yet."

"I just told you the Alara plan to attack Dinu territory!" his father snapped. "What are you doing here if you don't plan to help the tribe?"

Anríq compressed his lips and his nostrils flared again, but he didn't express any other sign of annoyance. "I told you I'm a Servant. Do you see this?" He pulled his vest open. "I didn't come back here to forsake the Servant's path."

"Why did you come back, then?" Hosh asked. "Did you come back to rub in in our faces that our brother is a spineless coward?"

The tension in the room spiked off the charts. The other guests pretended to keep talking, but most stopped to listen.

"I came back here because I'm on a mission to save the Coil from the instability," Anríq replied. "I came back here because the Layer we were traveling through collapsed and we fell into this Island. I didn't know your territory survived when the Ancestral Empire collapsed. I wouldn't have come if I knew you were here."

"That's rich," Tatus countered. "You wouldn't come back here to visit your own family?"

"You were the one who told me never to come back," Anríq replied. "You were the one who threatened to kill me if I ever showed my face here again."

Silence fell over the table—at least it fell over Anríq, Taitus, and his brothers, and those sitting closest. Everyone else in the tent pretended to go on feasting.

Eliska finished her fruit and didn't take anything else. Now she understood why Anríq didn't help himself to the food.

Taitus didn't break the silence, either. After a while, the people on the other side of the table left and different people took their places. Eliska recognized one of them as the magic-user she tied up with grass.

She was beginning to get a clearer picture of the political landscape around here. The first band of Barbarians to attack the nomads—those Barbarians belonged to the Ula tribe.

This magic-user had been with them. He'd been helping the same band that threatened to retaliate against the Dinu.

Now here was this young magic-user sitting right across the table from Taitus and helping himself to Taitus's food. Was this young magic-user a traitor—or a spy? Was he playing both sides of the field?

Taitus came out of his trance and waved across the table at the four men sitting opposite him.

"You remember Birino....and this Waro, Liffi, and Rechner."

Anríq nodded. "I remember."

"They're good magic-users—very useful in locating wealthy wagon trains and travelers for us to raid. Maybe they could show you around."

"I know my way around," Anríq replied. "I remember everything. I didn't forget when I left."

"Well! You must be tired!" Taitus clapped Anríq on the back. "Lanara will show you a tent where you and your companion can stay as long as you're here. I'm sure we have a lot to discuss. We can decide what to do later."

Anríq straightened up, squared his shoulders, and faced his father. "I won't give up the Servant's path, Papi. I'm sorry that disappoints you, but I didn't come back to stay."

His father's features darkened all over again. "I don't believe you came here by accident. You could have left this Island the minute you realized where you were."

Anríq shrugged. "I had an encounter with Yulo out on the planes. He threatened the Dinu tribe because I intervened to stop him from a attacking some nomads. I stayed to answer his challenge and to make sure he didn't threaten the Dinu. That's why I came back....and then Hoch and Esegan came out to bring me in. That's why I'm here. I'm still a Servant. Papi. I'll always be a Servant. If you don't like it, I'll have no choice but to leave."

"I don't believe you," Taitus snarled again. "I don't believe any son of mine could be so cowardly as to turn his back on his own Tribe...and for what—to go alone in the Coil and help a bunch of strangers? Don't you have any loyalty to your Tribe? I raised you better than that."

"You raised me to be a marauder and a murderer. My path lies elsewhere. You threatened kill me if I ever came back, but I warn you, if you persist in this, you'll have to try it if you want to stop me from continuing on my path. I'll defend myself by any means necessary—including fighting your magic-users here. I won't let you tie me up the way you did when I was just a boy. I'm a man now and I make my own way. I can accept you calling me a coward. I've been called worse."

Taitus jerked away and refused to look at Anríq again. "We'll discuss that later. Go to your own tent now. I don't want to talk about it anymore."

Anríq got to his feet. He cast a side look over his father and brothers before he walked out the door.

Eliska scrambled to get to her feet, grab he staff, and follow him. She didn't say anything, not even when they got outside.

She never imagined Anríq would be coming home to this.

He stopped outside and glanced around the camp. Would he walk away right now?

She didn't understand the rules of him answering Yulo's challenge or even what that meant.

Just then, a young woman rushed over to him, grabbed his arm, and pulled him forward. She had lighter hair than most Barbarians—almost as light as Anríq's.

Her fine features made her one of the most beautiful girls Eliska had ever seen.

"This way, Anríq! Your father assigned you a tent to stay in while you're here." The girl beamed up at him. "If you need or want anything, you only have to ask."

"Thank you," Anríq mumbled.

The girl stopped outside a random tent. She kept blushing up at him and her bright blue eyes sparkled. "Do you need or want anything?"

"No, thank you," Anríq replied. "Tell my father I'm grateful for his hospitality."

He pulled back the tent flap and disappeared inside. That left Eliska standing there facing the girl.

The girl burst into a big grin, stepped forward, and shook Eliska's hand. "It's very nice to meet you. I'm Lanara."

"I'm Eliska."

"How did you come to be traveling with Anríq?" Lanara asked.

"It was really just an accident. Our paths crossed and we started traveling together."

Lanara beamed at her like that was the most salient answer imaginable. "That's wonderful! Do you need or want anything—or does Anríq need or want anything?"

"I don't need anything and he said he doesn't—so I guess that means we don't."

Lanara split in another grin. "Of course he would say that. That's why I'm asking you."

Eliska didn't understand, so she just said. "Thank you anyway," and entered the tent.

Chapter 8

E liska couldn't tell if Taitus fitted out this tent especially for Anríq or if the tent had already been standing here beforehand.

A bunch of cushions covered one corner of the floor and another low table crossed the one room on the other side, but this table wasn't as big as Taitus's fest table.

Anríq flopped down on the cushions to one side and threw his arm over his eyes.

Eliska hesitated to get his attention, but the conversation with his father wouldn't leave her alone.

She squatted down next to him, hesitated a second time, and then let her hand fall on his other arm where it lay on the ground. "Are you okay?"

"I never should have come back here," he groaned. "I should have left this Island the minute I realized where we were."

"You can't blame yourself for wanting to see your family again."

"I didn't want to see them again," he snapped. She'd never heard him speak so harshly.

She sat down next to him on the ground. "Do you want to leave now?"

"I can't leave now," he mumbled. "Not until Yulo tries to make good on his threat....and now Birino, Waro, and Liffi will never leave me alone."

Eliska frowned at him. "The magic-users? Why would they bother you?"

"They hate me. They won't want me coming around threatening their positions."

"But you already said you weren't here to take anyone's position."

"They don't care. They don't understand the Servant's path. None of them do."

Just then, the tent flap whisked back and Lanara came in carrying another platter of food.

Two more girls her age entered carrying two more platters, laid everything out on the table, and smiled at Anríq and Eliska.

At least, the girls smiled at Eliska. Anríq didn't see them. He kept his arm over his face the whole time.

Eliska did her best to force a smile back. "Thank you," she repeated.

The girls waited for her to say something else. Then they all looked down at Anríq. He didn't take his arm down.

The girls hesitated and then rushed out of the tent. Eliska went to the table and took one of the trays.

It had some bread, cheese, more fruit, a few pieces of meat, and other ordinary food—not the delicacies Taitus served at his feast.

She carried the tray back to Anríq and put it on the ground. "You can eat something now," she told him. "They're gone. No one will see you."

He did take his arm down then. He propped himself on his elbow and helped himself a piece of meat. "Thank you," he mumbled.

She found herself chuckling. "You're quite the celebrity, aren't you?"

"Only because they think I'm something I'm not. None of them understands."

"Did our father really tie you up and threaten to kill you?"

Anríq nodded down at the food in his hands. "My brothers did a lot worse than that. They act all friendly now, but they can get downright vicious when they want to be—especially if they think someone is a coward and a traitor to the tribe."

"That's terrible," she exclaimed.

"It doesn't matter because nothing can change it now. I'm a Servant whether they like it or not. If they try anything, I'll just leave."

He stretched out on the cushions while he ate, but just then, the three girls came back with Anríq's weapons and his bags. They put everything on the floor next to him.

He looked up when they came in and they all blushed and grinned and batted their eyes at him.

He didn't move. They lined up across the tent like they were waiting for him to do something.

"Thank you," Eliska repeated for the twentieth time. "Was there something else you wanted?"

"Don't you want to....?" Lanara glanced back and forth between Anríq and the pile of weapons.

"We have everything we need for now," Eliska replied. "Thank you anyway. You can go."

"Um.....Taitus said to tell you that he's holding another feast for....for you....and Anríq...tonight....in his tent."

"Thank you," Eliska replied. "You can tell him that we'll be there."

The girls took way too long to leave, but they finally made themselves scarce.

Anríq waited until they left before he got up. He went through his usual slow, methodical routine of hanging his bags over his shoulder, his axe on his back, and hooking his club and his blade to his belt.

He didn't stop until he got back into his old usual comfortable state fully armed.

Eliska found herself watching him. The Servant's mark showed clearly on his chest between the two sides of his vest. Anyone could see it.

She'd found it easy to ignore the mark these last few weeks. She didn't even see it most of the time. Now it meant something much more serious.

Anríq's father must have considered that mark the worst possible insult.

She considered offering again for them to leave now, but she didn't say that. Anríq already said he couldn't.

He sat down on his cushions and went back to eating. He didn't lie down or cover his eyes.

"You don't have to go to the feast tonight," he told her. "You don't have to be here at all."

"I couldn't find Yann without you," she replied. "And something tells me you need me here right now."

He looked down at his hands. "I do. I'm glad you're here. I would hate to do this alone.

"Then it looks like I'm staying. As long as I'm here, your father would probably take offense if I didn't go to the feast."

"He might—or he might not even notice. He might be too busy paying attention to me."

Eliska smiled at the bitter tone in his voice. "Do you think he'll try anything—like violence, I mean—to make you change your mind?"

He bit off another piece of his meat. "Anything is possible. I would have thought he'd drop it after all these years, but apparently not."

She leaned back on the cushions. It felt good to talk to him—like they did when they escorted the children to the orphanage.

"Why did everyone have so much a problem with you becoming a Servant?" she asked.

"You heard them. They say I'm a coward. I don't go raiding and I turned my back on the Barbarians way of life."

"Don't they have other Servants?"

"All Servants leave the Barbarians. They don't come back for the same reason." He sighed down at his hands. "I suppose something like this was always bound to happen sooner or later. I would have stumbled on this Island eventually. Then I was bound to come to another confrontation. I couldn't hide from it forever."

"You didn't leave to hide. Did you?"

"No, not at all. I would have stayed longer, but I had to leave."

She cocked her head to study him. She would have liked to ask why he became a Servant, but she didn't want to pry.

"What will the other magic-users do?" she asked instead.

"They might try to kill me."

Her head shot up and she gasped. "They will?"

He nodded. "Or they might try to kill you. You'll have to be careful, Eliska. Those four can be vengeful when they think someone is threatening them."

She gaped at him in shock, but he only started back into her eyes as if he just told her it was raining outside.

She shut her mouth with difficulty and went back to eating. No one had ever tried to kill her—not out of spite.

She took a few more bites of cheese and opened her hand window to see where the Barbarians magic-users were.

"You better be extra careful of Birino," Anríq told her. "He'll want to get his revenge on you for defeating him—not to mention sending his brother to another Layer."

She didn't look up. The plot just kept thickening.

She located the Barbarian magic-users in the camp. They stayed in Taitus's tent eating and talking at his table.

The four magic-users passed the time with Taitus's other sons. They all laughed and joked together, but Eliska saw the magic-users talking amongst themselves plenty of times.

Were they plotting against her and Anríq? Were the Barbarian magic-users planning right now how to attack and maybe kill Anríq and Eliska?

She would have to think of a way to deal with that. She couldn't spend all her time looking over her shoulder for a bunch of idiot magic-users who wanted to come after her.

She sent out a pulse of magic to scan the other three. She already knew she could defeat Birino with one hand tied behind her back.

None of the other three were powerful enough to do it, either, but they might be if they combined their magic. Did they even know they could do that?

Anríq distracted her by stretching out on his cushion. "You better get some rest this afternoon. Night feasts can run late. You'll be up half the night if you do decide to go."

He got comfortable on the cushions, but he didn't go to sleep. He kept raising his arm to put food into his mouth.

She stayed where she was and thought the matter over. She would have liked to watch the Barbarian magic-users' every move, but that would be taking this a little too far.

She flatly refused to consider them a threat no matter what Anríq said. She could defeat them all easily. She didn't doubt that.

Chapter 9

A different Barbarian woman stuck her head through the tent flap, but she didn't enter right away.

She glanced around and took a minute before she realized that Anríq was lying down and Eliska was sitting on the floor next to him.

This woman was much older. She looked about Taitus's age.

Anríq looked up and made eye contact with the woman, but she didn't speak.

She blinked and glanced at Eliska before the woman dared to tiptoe further into the tent. "Um.....if you don't mind....if you aren't too busy..."

"We aren't," Eliska replied. "What can I do for you?"

"Um....I....just.....wanted to ask you...."

The puzzle pieces clicked in Eliska's mind. "Do you need someone healed? Is that what you need? Did you come to ask Anríq to heal someone?"

"Yes!" the woman gasped and tried to smile in relief, but her cheek spasmed instead. "I don't know where else to turn. Liffi and Rechner have already taken a look at him and they can't do anything."

Eliska stood up. "Who's the patient?"

Anríq stood up, too. The woman looked back and forth between them. "Um....he's my grandson....Urio....Um....which one of you is going to heal him?"

"We'll both come," Eliska replied. "Show us where he is.

The woman lunged for her, grabbed Eliska's hand, and kissed her knuckles. Then she did the same thing to Anríq. "Thank you so much! I've been at my wits end! I'm Lyka. You don't know how relieved I am that a Servant is here!"

"Just show us where your grandson is," Eliska told her. "We'll do what we can for him."

Lyka led the way out of the tent talking a mile a minute about her grandson's symptoms.

"He took sick last year and he just keeps getting worse. First he's hot, then he's cold. First he's too weak to stand. Then he's going crazy tearing the house apart. We don't know what the problem is."

"How can he have been that sick for so long?" Eliska asked. "Does he get any worse?"

"Just when we think he's getting worse, everything changes to a completely different sickness. I don't know what to think."

"What did Liffi and Rechner think?" Eliska asked.

Lyka cast a petrified glance behind her at the Barbarian camp. "I....I wouldn't like to tell you what they thought."

"But they couldn't heal your grandson," Eliska pointed out. "What did they try?"

Lyka gulped and her voice shook. "They....they said he belonged to the Dark and no one could heal him."

Eliska shut her mouth and gritted her teeth to stop herself from saying what she really thought. She was going to have enough trouble with the Barbarian magic-users as it was.

Lyka led the way to a different tent and stood back for Eliska and Anríq to enter first. Four other women hovered around a bed in the corner.

The boy lying there couldn't have been more than ten. A ridge of black hair ran down the center of his scalp, but no one had formed the hair into spikes.

He lay on the bed completely unconscious. The other women moved out of the way so Anríq and Eliska could get near the bed.

They both stopped there staring down at the boy. Neither of them moved.

"Can you help him?" Lyka choked. "Please…you're our last hope."

"Liffi and Rechner were right," Eliska murmured. "Your grandson is carrying a Dark curse."

"How can he be?!" One of the other women burst into sobs. "He's just a little boy!"

"He didn't turn to the Dark. Someone cursed him."

Eliska stopped herself from saying that one of the magic-users might have done it to make themselves look better.

Then the same magic-user would swoop in and save the day by healing the boy.

These four magic-users obviously didn't understand how much more powerful the Dark forces kept getting every single day. Now the magic-users couldn't take the curse back.

Eliska shook that off. She didn't know that the Barbarian magic-users cursed this boy. Anything could have caused the curse—although she couldn't think right now of what that might be.

She extended her hand over the boy, but Anríq snatched her arm away. "Don't, Eliska."

She glanced up at him. His blue eyes went hard, but they also swam with a depth of sympathy and understanding that twisted her heart.

She would have taken this boy's curse and added it to the growing well of poison inside her. A little more Darkness wouldn't make any difference to her.

Anríq pulled her away and took her place next to the boy's bed.

Anríq went through a long process of marking different symbols on the boys' skin, placing different to objects on the boy's body, and then Anríq bowed his head and shut his eyes.

He laid his big hand on the boy's head and the boy started to shake. Sweat broke out all over his body.

He jolted hard enough to shake the blankets off himself. One of the women screamed.... and then everything stopped.

Anríq doubled over and propped his hands on his knees while he caught his breath. Eliska touched his shoulder. "Are you all right?"

He nodded and turned back to Lyka. "He'll sleep for a while, but he should be fine now."

"Oh, thank you so much!" she quavered. "Bless you both!"

She kissed Anríq's knuckles again and he and Eliska turned away to return to their own tent.

They only made it two steps before the tent flap stripped back and three of the Barbarians magic-users stormed in. One of them was Birino, the young man Eliska tied up with grass.

He snarled through gritted teeth and curled his lip at her. "What are you doing here?"

"Anríq just healed this boy," Eliska replied. "You should be thanking him."

"Get out of here!" Birino snapped. "You have no business here!"

"Are you talking to me or to Anríq—because it sure sounded to me like his father wants him to have business here—more than you three, I would say." She waved to Anríq. "Come on. Let's go."

The other two magic-users dodged in front of Anríq. "You don't come into our tribe healing everyone like the long-lost hero when we know you're a coward and a traitor. If anyone in this tribe needs healing, we do it, not you."

"So you would let this boy die?" Eliska cut in. "That doesn't sound like you care very much about your own people."

"You stay out of this," Birino fired back. "You aren't part of this."

Eliska lost her battle to keep her cool. She sidestepped in front of Anríq and got right in the Barbarian magic-users' faces.

"Anríq is too polite to say this, so let me say it for him," she snapped. "If anyone comes to us for help—anyone at all—we'll give it. I don't care who it is and I sure as hell don't care about offending a bunch of useless idiots like you. We'll heal anyone who asks. If you have a problem with that, maybe you fools shouldn't be out there pretending to be the healers for this tribe. Maybe you belong out in the Coil by yourselves—far away from decent people. Now get the hell out of our way. We're leaving."

She glared at them all fuming in barely suppressed rage. How dare these jackasses interfere when Anríq was trying to help someone?

The three magic-users must have sensed already that she had more power than all of them put together. Birino already knew.

They glared right at her, shot a few death stares over her head at Anríq, and then stormed out. The women hung back not making a living sound.

Eliska waited until the magic-users left before she let herself relax. She touched Anríq's arm again. "Let's go."

They returned to their own tent where Anríq collapsed on his cushions with a groan.

Eliska sat down next to him, placed her hand on his chest, and then on his forehead. He was already spiking a fever. "It was worse than you made it out to be, wasn't it? Rest easy. I'll take care of it."

He grabbed her wrist and pried his eyes open to stare up at her. "Don't take it, Eliska. Don't take it on yourself—not again."

She had to smile at him. He really was the most caring person she'd ever met. "I won't. Now lie down. You have to show your father and everyone else that you're at your strongest tonight."

He sank onto the cushions. She put her hand back on his chest—right above the Servant's mark. She actually envied him for carrying it. She wished she could be good enough to carry it.

She shut her eyes and flooded him with her magic, but she didn't take the curse. She could have. She could have taken it from Urio in the first place, but Anríq didn't want her to.

She couldn't throw his concern back in his face, so she did what she could to heal him.

He tensed when she sent her magic into him. Then he gritted his teeth, spasmed a few times, and wilted with his eyes closed when she stopped.

He fell into a sound sleep and didn't wake up. She sat over him keeping watch until the sun started to go down.

Chapter 10

E liska came out of the tent and looked around the Barbarians' camp. Lanterns hung from every tent and lined the walkways between them.

The Barbarians had all tied their tent flaps open and more golden light streamed from every doorway. Voices bubbled all over the place and an air of excitement infected the camp.

Laughter, talking voices, and music drifted from Taitus's tent. People came and went from there and Eliska saw the servers carrying food to everyone.

Anríq stepped out of the tent behind her and stopped at her side. "You don't have to go," he told her.

"I should at least make an appearance. I'll stay a polite amount of time and then drift away in the confusion."

He faced front. "You're lucky. I wish I could."

"It's nice that your father is happy to see you again," she remarked. "Your family obviously loves you."

"He isn't happy to see *me* again—not the person I really am. He's happy to see something that isn't real."

"I'm sure he'll get the message soon enough."

He gazed across the camp toward his father's tent. "And then it will start all over again. He'll attack and try to destroy the Servant to save me from it."

Eliska didn't know what to say, and the next minute, he started toward his father's tent entrance.

She went with him as far as the threshold, but as soon as they got there, a bunch of Barbarian warriors from the search party surrounded the pair.

The men swept Anríq to another part of the tent, talked to him at length about a bunch of things Eliska didn't hear over the noise, and then escorted him to his father's table.

Eliska paused there trying to decide what to do with herself. She could have elbowed her way through the room and taken the seat next to Anríq. Maybe she should have, but something stopped her.

He sat down. His father had been talking to Hoch, but Taitus immediately broke off and turned to Anríq instead.

Dozens of people crowded the tables feasting, talking, and laughing way too loudly. It was a repeat of the earlier scene with no sign of ending anytime soon.

Taitus started talking into Anríq's ear the way he did earlier. Anríq kept staring straight in front of him and only answered when he absolutely had to.

He caught Eliska's eye across the tent. Anríq didn't insist or gesture or in any other way imply that she should come in and join him.

She took a step backward. Enough lantern light illuminated this part of the camp. Anríq could still see her, but she backed away from the feast.

He held eye contact with her in between those times when he glanced at his father and nodded.

Anríq wouldn't care if Eliska walked away right now. He told her a million times she didn't have to go to this feast. He wouldn't go if he could have found a way to get out of it. He wouldn't mind if she vanished into the woodwork.

Just then, the same three girls from earlier swept into view and surrounded Eliska.

"There you are! Lanara exclaimed. "Aren't you going inside?"

"I was just about to," Eliska lied.

"How did you catch him?" the second girl asked. "Did you use magic to bewitch him?"

"Um..." Eliska stammered.

"You must have," the third girl interjected. "He wouldn't look sideways at a girl without a magic spell to make him fall."

Eliska opened her mouth, but she couldn't think of anything to say.

"You're making her nervous, Nitera." Lanara gabbed Eliska's hand. "This is my friend, Nitera...and this is Deopra."

She pointed to one girl and then the other. Deopra had long, straight brown hair shaved up the sides into a ridge like the men's but longer in the back.

Nitera had a small, slight, almost childlike build with witchy black hair, bright green eyes, and pointed, elfish features.

"I'm Eliska," Eliska announced.

"So how did you do it?" Nitera asked again. "I wish I was born a magic-user. Then I could get any man I wanted."

Eliska started to say, "I didn't....."

"Everyone wanted Anríq before he left," Lanara interrupted. "Every girl in the whole camp was fighting over him day and night."

"But...he was only twelve then," Eliska pointed out.

None of the girls paid any attention. "He was completely oblivious—and now look at him." All three girls turned to stare though the tent flap at Anríq sitting next to his father.

"He's so much bigger than I thought he would be," Nitera breathed. "They said he was a coward, but he's bigger than half the men in the tribe."

"He's better looking, too," Deopra murmured. "He's beautiful."

Lanara turned to Eliska. "So how did you do it? How did you bewitch him?"

"I didn't," Eliska blurted out. "We aren't together. I thought... you know....he's a Servant. They don't get with anyone. They dedicated themselves to healing and serving humanity. We're just friends. We travel together. We aren't ...you know.....a couple or anything like t hat."

The three girls blinked at her in shock. Eliska didn't see how what she said could have such a profound effect on them.

Didn't everyone know about the Servants? They wandered alone. Even Anríq said the Servant's path was a solitary one.

They didn't get married or settle down or raise families like regular people. The Servants dedicated everything to others.

Without warning, the three girls gasped, turned to each other, grabbed each other, and burst into excited giggles and talk.

"Do you realize what this means?!" Lanara exclaimed in a breathless whisper. "It means he's still free! One of us can get him."

"Which one should it be?" Nitera asked.

"Whoever turns his head first," Deopra replied. "Each of us will have to use her best charms and may the best woman win."

Eliska opened her mouth to remind them that Anríq was a Servant and wouldn't fall for any of their charms.

Nitera grabbed Eliska's hand on the other side. Now both girls held Eliska from both sides.

"Could you use your magic to help us?" Nitera asked. "Could you bewitch him to fall for one of us?"

"I ....um....for a start...."

"She couldn't do that! It wouldn't be fair!" Lanara exclaimed. "If she helped one of us, she would have to help all of us and that would even the odds as if she didn't do it at all. You can't ask her that."

"Um..." Eliska went on. "He's a Servant. He won't go with any of you."

Lanara waved that away. "That doesn't mean anything." She turned back to her friends. "I have an idea. Nitera, you'll ask Liffi to create an enchantment for you. Deopra will ask Rechner and I'll ask Birino."

"That isn't fair, either," Nitera countered. "Then it would be a contest between three magic-users, not between us. I say we make a pact right now that none of us is allowed to use magic. We have to rely on pure feminine wiles, charm, grace, and animal attraction. That's the only way we can be sure that the best woman actually gets him."

The other two exchanged glances. Then Deopra nodded. "I agree. " She stuck out her hand. "Shake on it and may your word be your bond that you won't cheat."

The three girls shook on it.

Eliska stood back watching in fascinated horror. These women really planned to throw themselves at Anríq. They were all setting themselves up for heartache.

They turned shoulder to shoulder and gazed through the tent flap at him.

Lanara sighed. "He's stunning."

"He's mouth-watering," Deopra added.

"Look at those shoulders," Nitera breathed.

Eliska bit back laughter, but she didn't interrupt. She would definitely have to warn Anríq about this—not that he couldn't take care of himself.

The girls murmured a few more expressions of lust and admiration before Lanara threw back her shoulders. "I'm going in there to talk to him. You two make yourselves scarce. It would be too obvious if you all tried to talk to him at once."

"Why do you get to talk to him first?" Deopra demanded.

"Because I thought of it first. Now get lost, all of you." Lanara clasped Eliska's hand one last time. "Thank you so much, Eliska. You're the best."

Lanara burst into a bright smile and sailed off into Taitus's tent.

"That witch," Deopra muttered.

"She doesn't stand a chance," Nitera murmured. "She's too forward. Anríq will appreciate subtlety—not blatant flirting in his face. Come on, Nitera. We have plans to make."

Deopra pulled Nitera away and they left Eliska standing there in the dark.

She watched through the flap as Lanara crossed the tent and sat down next to Anríq, but she never got a chance to talk to him.

Taitus would not stop talking Anríq's ear off on his other side. Lanara didn't dare to interrupt.

She sat there for almost half an hour before she got tired of waiting and left.

She made it halfway across the tent before some other young men surrounded her. She wound up talking to them instead.

Eliska smirked at the whole scene and then headed off to her own tent.

Chapter 11

Eliska stretched out on her cushions to wait for Anríq to come back. She kept snickering to herself thinking about the three girls trying to capture him.

They were right. He was as stunningly mouth-watering as they said he was.

They would get a rude awakening when they finally figured out just how untouchable he really was.

There never was a Servant more dedicated to his calling. He wouldn't give that up for some girl just because she threw herself at him.

Eliska must have fallen asleep. She woke up when the tent flap whisked aside. Anríq ducked under it to enter.

It must have been late because no more lantern light shone through the tent walls from outside.

Eliska sat up. "You made it back. I wasn't sure if you would."

"Why wouldn't I? I was just down the way. I wasn't in danger."

She chuckled. "Little do you know."

"What are you talking about?" he murmured. "Did the magic-users do something?"

"No, not them. Some of the local girls are after you. They're planning to catch you and drag you back to their lairs where they can have their way with you."

He snorted in the dark. "Stop joking around."

"I'm not joking. They told me all about how they plan to get you. They're having a contest to see which of them can spin their feminine wiles to turn your head."

Anríq groaned and flopped down on his cushion. "That's ridiculous."

"They even asked me to use magic to bewitch you on their behalf—but first they thought you and I were together."

"Of course they did. My father put us in the same tent."

Her head shot up. "What does that mean?"

"He put us in the same tent because he thinks we're a couple. He probably thinks that's why I brought you here—to introduce you to the tribe."

She turned bright red, but the dark hid it from him. She wound up looking away.

"So did you agree?" he asked. "Did you agree to use your magic to bewitch me?"

She forced a laugh. It didn't sound like so much of a joke now.

"I told them.....I tried to explain to them that your path as a Servant prevents you from getting together with anybody, but they didn't listen. They only took it to mean that we weren't together, so you were free for one of them to get you instead."

"You didn't answer my question. Did you agree to bewitch me?"

"Of course not! How can you even ask that?! Besides, they realized that I couldn't bewitch you to like all three of them at the same time and it wouldn't be fair if I helped one of them and not the others."

Now it was his turn to laugh. "Eliska! I'm disappointed in you.'

"Then they decided to recruit Liffi, Rechner, and Birino to each cast a spell on you to make you like a different girl, but they decided not to do that, either, because then it would be a contest between the three magic-users and wouldn't actually determine which of the girls was the most charming, enticing, and the best. So they agreed to fall back on pure feminine art and may the best woman win."

He laughed some more. "Thank you for the warning. I'll be sure to keep watch on them. They'll be more dangerous than the magic-users."

He curled up on the cushions on his side so he wouldn't lie on top of his axe. He curled his arm under his head like he usually did.

She saw him about to go to sleep, but she couldn't settle down.

"So.....did you tell your father that we aren't together?" she asked.

Anríq didn't raise his head or open his eyes to look at her. "I didn't tell him and I won't tell him."

"But...he'll keep thinking we are together. He'll think...."

She broke off when she realized what Taitus must think. He thought Anríq and Eliska were wandering the Coil as a couple—like actually together. Maybe he thought they were spending every night together under the stars or something like that.

A confused torrent of images, fantasies, and emotions collided in her mind....and in her stomach. She would never get together with Anríq. No one ever would.

Which would be worse—a girl throwing herself at him and getting her heart broken when he inevitably left the Tribe to continue on the Servants' path—or spending every day and night with him, camping with him, talking to him, healing each other's sicknesses and injuries—and never being able to share a life with him like that?

The second one sounded like the worse torment imaginable—much worse than one of those girls getting her hopes dashed when she realized just how out of reach he really was.

Eliska was probably the closest person to him in the world. She knew him better than everyone in this camp—including his own family.

She knew how wonderful he was—and she also knew that he was completely unavailable. He was hands down the most unavailable man she'd ever met.

She never let herself think of him enough to want him—because she knew she could never get him. She would never be anything more than his friend—and that was enough. She didn't need anything more.

He needed a friend. He needed someone who knew him, supported him, and defended him. That was her role as the Servant in his life. She protected him in ways he couldn't protect himself.

She finally stretched out on the cushions across the tent. She lay awake staring at the ceiling and listening to him breathe. None of those girls had the first clue what a prize he was.

Being his friend and traveling with him was more of a prize than getting together with him could ever be.

None of those girls would ever know him the way Eliska did. That on its own was reward enough. She would never ask for more than that.

Eliska woke up with a start when she heard Anríq talking nearby. His voice didn't wake her up. His tone did.

"I already told you I wouldn't go out to war against anyone," he snarled. "How many times do I have to say it?"

"This your own Tribe we're talking about!" Taitus fired back. "Would you shame your own father in front of the whole Tribe? I didn't raise any coward."

"I'm not a coward," Anríq countered. "The Tribe isn't in any danger...."

"We're going out anyway!" Taitus snapped. "You're either coming with us or you'll suffer the fate of all cowards and traitors."

"You tried that once already," Anríq muttered. "I'm a lot bigger and stronger now. You won't get away with it a second time."

"Well see about that," Taitus shot back.

Eliska got up and went outside. Taitus and Anríq stood nose to nose right outside the tent.

Anríq's brothers and a bunch of other Barbarians surrounded the two men listening to their conversation.

"Are you threatening me?" Tatus hissed through gritted teeth.

"You're the one threatening me—as usual," Anríq fired back. "I'm not a boy anymore. Go on. Try it. Send my brothers after me to beat me up and then throw me in a pit and keep me there without food for three weeks. See how long that lasts."

Taitus clenched his jaw even tighter. "You'll push my patience too far, boy."

"You've pushed my patience a hundred times farther," Anríq returned. "If I was a normal Barbarian instead of a Servant, I would have killed you long ago for calling me a coward and a traitor. You know I'm a Servant. You wouldn't dare to talk to me like this if I wasn't."

Taitus leaned in extra close and snarled under his breath in a dangerous murmur. "You'll go out with your brothers and do your part or you're no son of mine."

"How many times have I heard that before?" Anríq snapped. "You've already turned your back on me and told me I'm no son of yours. You've left me nothing to lose."

The two men glared at each other. Eliska considered whether she should step in before the confrontation turned violent.

She would have to use powerful magic to stop the other Barbarians from attacking and probably killing Anríq. She didn't trust him to defend himself against his own people. His compassion would stop him from killing or maybe even hurting anyone.

Taitus broke eye contact first, spun away, and swiped his hand at his sons. "Let's go. We're moving out. Get your men in formation. We've wasted too much time on this already."

The other men broke up, but before they could go anywhere, a deep, booming voice bellowed from the other side of the camp. "Taitus! Taitus of the Dinu Tribe!"

Everyone froze and then the crowd parted to reveal the Barbarians who attacked the nomads on the open planes. They stormed into the camp in force and they all came armed.

Chapter 12

The Barbarians of the Ula Tribe halted a dozen yards away from Taitus. Eliska recognized Yulo, the leader who threatened Anríq.

Yulo leveled an accusing finger at Anríq. "This man attacked my band outright and killed my men! This is a declaration of war against the Ula Tribe! Hand over the offender or we'll wage war against your entire tribe!"

Yulo rotated his finger to point at Taitus.

"You pretended to negotiate an alliance with us, but you sent your son to attack us and destroy us. You're a traitor. Hand him over or we'll exact retribution against everyone here without mercy."

Taitus took a step forward and pivoted in front of Anríq. "I will not hand over my son to any murderous cutthroats. Go back where you came from and crawl into your holes—if you can even defend yourselves against the Alara Tribe. I did you a favor by even considering an alliance with you. You won't be able to fight a war against two tribes at once. You have no business coming here hurling threats and accusations. My son never attacked you or your tribe. He's been here the whole time."

Yulo opened his mouth to argue, but Anríq cut him off. He stepped around his father and held out both hands, one to Yulo and the other to his father. "Stop. We don't want war between our tribes. I stayed to answer your challenge, Yulo, and I will answer it. I'll turn myself over to you...."

"No, you won't!" Taitus snapped. "This punk is toothless. We'll take him and his men...."

"No," Anríq interjected. "Don't fight him." He turned to Yulo. "I'm here, Yulo. Do what you want."

Eliska stepped away from the tent, stopped next to Anríq, and faced Yulo. "I'll turn myself over, too. I fought your men the same way Anríq did. Whatever you plan to do to him to settle your grievance, you'll have to do to both of us. I wish you good luck with that."

"This is outrageous!" Taitus swiveled in front of both of them and cut between them and Yulo. "I demand a one-on-one challenge to settle this dispute. You say you want him to answer for attacking you. You'll do it man to man—right here in front of all these witnesses."

Yulo changed his expression in a hurry. His eyes darted to Anríq. "He's a magic-user. It wouldn't be a fair fight."

"I promise I won't use magic," Anríq replied. "If I use magic, I'll be declared the loser. All these people will be your witnesses."

Yulo raised his eyebrows. "So you won't use magic even once?"

"Not even once. Do you accept?"

Yulo glanced at Taitus. Taitus didn't intervene.

"I accept," Yulo finally replied.

The assembled Barbarians broke apart immediately, backed off, and cleared a space between the tents. Yulo's men took their places in the ring along with everyone from the Dinu Tribe. No one treated anyone else as an enemy.

Anríq strode over to the tent he shared with Eliska, stopped by the flap, and started taking off all his weapons.

"Are you sure you can beat him?" Eliska murmured.

"I'm sure," Anríq murmured back without turning around. "I wrestled him when we were boys. He's my cousin and I know all his weaknesses."

Eliska squinted at Yulo over Anríq's shoulder. "He's a lot bigger than you are."

"He's slow—and predictable." He took off his bags and pulled off his vest. "This won't take long."

"Don't get killed, okay? I wouldn't want everyone to expect me to act the grieving widow at your funeral."

He burst into a huge grin and his eyes twinkled at her, but he straightened his expression and went back to looking murderous when he turned away and entered the ring.

Yulo disarmed himself and took off all his studded leather harnesses.

He also took off his gauntlets. Anríq kept his on, but his didn't have any spikes.

He paced back and forth across the ring in front of Yulo. Anríq seemed to swell in size when he faced his opponent.

Yulo definitely had size and weight on his side, but Eliska realized Anríq was right.

He had a compact, crazy kind of energy that sent a shiver of tension through the crowd.

Yulo shook out his arms and jogged from one foot to the other. He didn't wind himself up with tension the way Anríq did. Yulo really was slower and dumber.

Anríq puffed out his cheeks inhaling deep breaths through flared nostrils. His father and brothers called encouragement to him and told him how best to tear Yulo apart.

Eliska didn't see how the fight could start.

At some silent and unseen signal, the two men rushed each other and collided in the middle of the ring.

The crowd went nuts and everyone started yelling at once. The Barbarians pumped their fists and elbowed each other as the two men battled for dominance.

Yulo got the upper hand first. He and Anríq met in a whirlwind of flying arms as each tried to consolidate his grip on the other. Yulo overpowered Anríq by hooking one muscular arm around Anríq's neck.

Yulo wrenched Anríq over at the waist and head-locked him there. Anríq struggled, but he couldn't break free.

He grappled to get hold of Yulo by any available body part.

In the end, Anríq grabbed Yulo by the leg, wrenched him sideways, and ripped the much bigger Barbarian off the ground.

Anríq hurled himself backward and body-slammed Yulo into the dirt right on the back of his neck.

Yulo's head hit the ground and the fall stunned him enough for Anríq to get away.

He didn't try to stand up. He flipped onto his back and brought his foot down on Yulo's face with brutal power. Yulo's head bounced again and Anríq scrambled away.

He got to his feet and went back to pacing at the other end of the ring while he waited for Yulo to stagger upright.

Blood dripped from his nose and he had to blink hard to get the stars out of his eyes so he could focus on Anríq.

Yulo's eyes didn't track right when he followed Anríq's movements back and forth across the end of the circle.

The noise coming out of the crowd grew to a deafening surge of voices. Eliska even spotted Lanara, Nitera, and Deopra cheering from the sidelines.

Anríq saw nothing but Yulo. Yulo waved him forward and the two men rushed each other for the second time, but they didn't collide.

Anríq charged Yulo just as fast, but at the last second, Anríq dodged and let Yulo blunder past him.

Anríq snatched Yulo by the back of his belt, yanked him off his feet, and brought Yulo crashing down on his face.

Anríq pounced on him from behind, grabbed Yulo by the head and smashed his face into the dirt a few more times before Anríq sprang away and retreated to a safe distance.

Yulo took longer to get up this time. He stumbled around facing the wrong way before he could focus well enough to locate Anríq.

Anríq kept pacing on the opposite side of the ring—the side where Yulo originally started.

Yulo took a few steps and tripped over his own feet. He could barely keep his eyes open.

His face swelled up in a mass of bruises with blood coming out of his nose, mouth, and one of his ears.

Without warning, two of Yulo's men sprang out of the crowd and grabbed Anríq from behind.

They caught his arms, restrained him between them, and one of the men waved Yulo forward to attack.

Anríq struggled. Eliska took a step into the ring and raised her staff. No way in hell would she let these bastards hurt Anríq.

Before she could move, Anríq's three brothers barreled out of the circle, charged straight past Yulo, and bombed in to attack the two men holding Anríq.

Yulo never got closer to them before Anríq's brothers fell on their opponents with punches, elbows, and kicks. The brothers stripped the two Ula warriors away from Anríq and pounded them into the dirt.

The rest of Yulo's men moved in to break up the fight. The Dinu Barbarians saw Yulo's men about to overwhelm Anríq's brothers.

The whole crowd surged inward and the place disintegrated into a bare-knuckle brawl with everyone against everyone else. Even the women and children got involved.

The Barbarians crushed around Eliska. She barely ducked out of the way to escape flying fists and elbows that would have split her head open. Then the weapons came out.

She fired her staff to create a ball of protection around herself. No one could get near her.

She forced her way into the crowd and worked her way through dozens of jostling bodies until she found Anríq in the confusion.

He grappled with three of Yulo's men. They pulled him to the ground and the four of them wrestled in between dozens of kicking, stamping feet, and bodies dropping all over the place.

Eliska lunged for them, hit the three Ula warriors with her magic, and pulled Anríq inside her shield.

"Are you okay?!" she bellowed over the noise.

He nodded fast, but he had a black eye and multiple bruises all over his face.

She fought her way to the sidelines and used her magic to heal him. Then the two of them turned to watch the situation dissolve into a knockdown-dragout fight.

A few flashes of magic went off in the confusion, but Eliska couldn't see the Barbarian magic-users under the dogpile of bodies.

Chapter 13

E liska bent over a pile of cushions. Anríq's brother Esegan lay on it.

She barely recognized him with his head swollen up in a mass of black bruises. A faint, strained wheezing sound came out of the hole where his mouth should be.

She placed her hands on either side of his head, shut her eyes, and sent her magic into him to heal his injuries.

They were extensive. He had stab wounds to his abdomen and lengths of fabric tied around leaking wounds in his legs, arms, and even his neck.

She reduced the swelling in his head, knit all his bones together, and closed the wounds to stop all the bleeding.

It took her a long time to repair all the damage—and he was only one person.

She finally finished and he collapsed into a sound asleep.

She stood up and took a deep breath before she dared to look around Taitus's tent. Dozens of wounded lay all over the place. Yulo and his men all lay injured on the floor. They couldn't go home. None of them could even walk.

Anríq knelt next to a different pile of cushions across the tent. He bent over Yulo, laid his hand on the man's chest, and Anríq closed his eyes, too.

Eliska went over to him. Yulo's glazed eyes started up at the tent ceiling. They didn't even register that Anríq was healing him.

A pool of blood stained Yulo's bare chest. More blood seeped from a stab wound right through the center of his chest.

Anríq wouldn't be able to heal that in time before Yulo died.

Eliska knelt down next to Yulo and placed her hand on top of Anríq's. His eyes popped open when she sent a flow of magic through his hand, added her magic to his, and used the flow to heal the wound faster.

He looked over at her and their eyes met. His eyebrows came together in the center to question her and then his expression softened.

She smiled at him. If Yulo died here, that would definitely trigger a war between the Ula Tribe and the Dinu Tribe. Eliska couldn't let that happen.

She placed her other hand on his forehead and used more of her magic to heal the injuries Anríq inflicted on Yulo's head. Anríq and Eliska worked together to pull him back from the brink.

His eyes drifted closed before they finished. Anríq slumped back on his ankles and his chin dropped onto his chest.

"Thank you, Eliska," he husked. "You don't know what this means to me."

She squeezed his shoulder. "Of course I do. Come on. Let's split up and heal the rest of the Ula men. Some of them are pretty bad."

She went through the tent healing one man after another. Anríq worked steadily on the other side of the room.

People from the Dinu Tribe kept coming in to deliver water, food, blankets—anything the newly healed patients needed.

Eliska worked her way around the room to where Taitus sat in the corner. He wasn't injured badly enough for either her or Anríq to heal Taitus before now.

He pushed her away when she tried to take care of him. "Bring my son here. I don't want anyone but Anríq."

She glanced over her shoulder. Anríq was still working on the Ula warriors.

She didn't want to argue with the Chieftain, so she picked her way between all the beds and laid her hand on Anríq's shoulder again. "Your father wants to see you. He doesn't want anyone else to take care of him besides you. I'll finish up here."

He got to his feet. He already looked tired with dark circles around his eyes.

She would have to make him go lie down and rest after this. She couldn't let him make himself sick by exhausting himself.

She worked her way through the Ula warriors healing them all.

She stopped when she came to Birino lying in a row with the other Ula warriors. None of them was conscious.

She bent over Birino, laid her hands on his torso, and found all the broken bones in his chest. His magic had faded to a low ebb. He wouldn't survive without her help.

She healed him and swiveled over to Liffi's bed, but he was already dead.

She paused there to stare down at him. She couldn't be happy about him dying—not like this.

She started to turn away. Plenty of Dinu men had suffered minor injuries—enough to keep her and Anríq busy for a long time. She might have to send him back to the tent to sleep before they finished healing everybody.

Just then, Rechner and Waro barged into the tent, stormed over to Eliska, and took one look at Liffi's dead body.

"You killed him!" Rechner snapped. "You're a snake! How dare you pretend to come in here healing anyone?! Get out of here!"

"I didn't kill him, you dimwit," she muttered. "He was already dead. If you're so worried about healing these people, maybe you should have come earlier instead of leaving everything to me and Anríq."

"You're an outsider," Waro countered. "How dare you lay hands on our men?"

"I don't see you doing it," she fired back. "The Ula Tribe would have declared war against the Dinu if Anríq and I didn't save Yulo."

Both magic-users spun around and saw Yulo lying there asleep. His face had returned to its normal size and shape. He didn't have a scratch on him now.

"You healed Yulo?!" Rechner practically bellowed. "How dare you?!"

Just then Anríq came over with his father. Anríq must have healed Taitus's injuries. The Chieftain acted much more cheerful now.

"Is there a problem?" Taitus asked.

"This Coil rat healed Yulo's injuries!" Waro snapped. "You're a traitor and an enemy of our people."

"I healed Yulo's injuries," Anríq interrupted. "Eliska only helped me. If you have a problem, you can address me, not her."

Rechner spun around, but he shut his mouth when he saw Anríq.

"Some of these men are still injured....and they're your own people," Eliska interjected. "Do you want to heal them or do you want me and Anríq to do it?"

Rechner opened his mouth to make another cutting remark about her being nothing but a traitorous coil rate, but the Chieftain interrupted.

"Rechner, you and Waro go outside. You're only getting in the way here. Anríq and Eliska are healing everyone. You would only make yourselves a nuisance. Why don't you go outside, organize the men to patrol our territory, and make sure no Ulas are out there crossing our perimeter? Go, Rechner—now!"

Rechner gave Eliska another dirty look, but he stopped himself from doing the same thing to Anríq.

"Continue with your work," Taitus told them. "And please make sure all the Ula men survive to go home to their own tribe. We don't need a war any more than they do."

He walked away and left Anríq and Eliska alone.

She took a few steps to his side and lowered her voice to a low murmur only he could hear. "You should go lie down. You're tired. I'll finish here."

He curled his lip at the surroundings. "I hate this life. We should leave as soon as we finish here. I answered Yulo's challenge. What happens to these people now is none of my concern."

"All right. If you're sure...." She found herself touching his arm again. "Seriously. You need to go lie down before you make yourself sick."

His eyes swiveled up to meet hers and she saw for the first time how bloodshot they were. He was a lot more exhausted than he let on.

"I couldn't do this without you, Eliska," he whispered. "You're a lifesaver."

She squeezed his arm and pushed him away. "Go on. Go get some sleep. I'll come see you later."

He gave her a half-hearted smile and returned to his own tent. She continued to work her way through the Ula warriors healing them one after the other.

Their minor injuries took no time or effort to heal. Then she finished with the minor injuries amongst the Dinu warriors and a few women and children who got hurt in the scuffle.

Lanara and the other girls brought in food for the patients by the time Eliska finished. She ate some, but not much. She was starting to feel drained and exhausted, too, but not from healing so many people. She needed sleep.

She took some of the food back to the tent she shared with Anríq. He lay on his side in bed with his eyes closed.

She planned to go lie down without waking him, but he stirred when she crossed the room. "Oh, you're back," he breathed when he saw her.

"How are you feeling?" She went over to him and laid her hand on his forehead. She didn't detect any illness, injury, or even any Darkness in him.

"I'm fine," he replied. "How are you? You shouldn't push yourself so hard."

"I feel okay. I'm just tired. Here. I brought you some food."

Chapter 14

Eliska set the food down in front of Anríq and sat on the floor next to his bed. She didn't want to go to sleep just yet—not when she got this opportunity to talk to him.

He twisted onto his side to eat. "Thank you," he exclaimed. "You take good care of me, Eliska."

She beamed at him. "When do you want to leave?"

"As soon as I explain to my father that I am leaving. I can imagine how that will go."

"He better not try to tie you up and throw you in a pit," she muttered. "I'll have to intervene if he does."

"He won't because I'm stronger than he is. If he sends my brothers after me to do it, I'll have no choice but to use my magic to defend myself. I was too young last time."

She took a chance and asked the question that had been burning a hole in her mind for weeks now. "What did happen last time?"

"Just what you've already heard. It's the same thing all over again except that I'm bigger....and I can articulate myself better. "

"So...all that stuff about calling you a coward and a traitor and saying you aren't his son and all that....?"

He nodded. "I spent years believing him and trying to make him like me. I tried not to be a Servant just so he would accept me, but it didn't work in the end."

"Did he really threaten to kill you?"

"Many times. ...and he threatened to kill anyone who encouraged or helped me."

"And he really beat you up, tied you, and kept you in a pit for three weeks without food?"

"That was nothing. He sent my brothers after me more times than I can count. He told them to make sure to beat the idea out of me no matter what. I would have died, but....." He broke off.

She didn't want to pry and he shook off the memory. "Anyway, I can protect myself now and they all know it. I never dared to turn my magic on any of them before, but I won't hesitate to do it now. I never even argued with them before. I thought there must be something wrong with me that I wanted to betray everything the Barbarians stand for."

"Why did you? Why did you become a Servant in the first place?"

"This life...it's nothing but mindless violence. There's no reason for it. They talk a lot about protecting the tribe and holding our territory from all these other tribes who want to invade us, but it's never that. Even if the tribes were totally at peace with each other, the warriors would still go out raiding defenseless caravans and travelers on the road. You know what they're like."

Eliska nodded.

"I couldn't live like that. Being a Servant is the only thing that gives my life any purpose or meaning. I wanted to die when I thought I'd be stuck here raiding and warring for the rest of my life. I tried it a couple of times."

She spun around to stare at him. "You tried....to end your life."

"Maybe five times. I would have succeeded if I had known how to use my magic better."

She gulped hard. In all the years she'd spent wandering the Coil, it never once crossed her mind to end her own misery.

She could have. She could have finished herself off and ended her ordeal in seconds if she really wanted to. Her magic was definitely strong enough and she knew how to use it well enough.

She'd been so mindlessly consumed with surviving everything that threatened her from the outside. Her every waking thought went toward finding a way to survive. She never thought once about becoming her own worst enemy that way.

He read her mind. "Anyway, everything got better as soon as I realized I could become a Servant."

"How did you realize it?" she asked. "What changed?"

"A different Servant came through here. This Servant came from this tribe and I realized I could do the same thing. Everything changed for me after that. I wanted to live so I could go out and help people. I didn't want to die anymore, but I still tried way too hard to get my father's approval. After a while, I realized I couldn't and it all went downhill from there—kind of like you've seen here these last few days."

She started at him in wonder. He'd never talked about himself this much before.

She saw him in new ways—not just because of what he said but more because of the way he acted since he came back here.

She saw it all in his interaction with his father. Their traded threats spoke of decades of conflict.

She could definitely see how Taitus used his power to influence young Anríq to change his ideas. Taitus knew how to throw his authority around, especially with his sons. He bit off more than he could chew when it came to Anríq.

Eliska looked down at the food in her hand. She pretended to eat while she thought it over. She didn't know what to say to restart the conversation.

Out of nowhere, his hand came to rest on her shoulder. "You should sleep now. You took over while I rested. Now it's your turn. You're tired. Go lie down. I'll take care of things out there."

She looked up and found him smiling at her. His hand on her shoulder sent a wave of pure blissful relief through her.

Nothing bad could happen to her as long as he was around. He protected her in ways no one else could—exactly the way she protected him.

She smiled back at him and dragged herself off to her bed. He crossed the room to stand by her side, rested his big, warm hand on her head, and sent a rush of his own magic into her.

He must have been able to feel the depth and power of the Dark poison still lying inside her. No one knew about that better than he did.

He didn't try to take it from her. He gave her just enough of his own magic to completely relax her and send her plunging into a deep, dreamless sleep.

She woke up to darkness, but lantern light shone through the tent walls the way it did the night before. Voise rose and fell outside. Anríq wasn't around.

She sat up. She felt much better after sleeping. Anríq had been right. She didn't realize how tired she really was.

She went outside. Lanterns lit up the whole camp and another tide of talking voices, laughter, and music bubbled from Taitus's tent.

She advanced through the camp. No one came out to accost her.

She stopped outside the flap and looked in.

Anríq sat next to his father as usual. Lanara sat on Anríq's other side talking to him, but Eliska could already tell it was going nowhere.

She did all the talking. He barely answered her. He held eye contact and let her rattle on in his ear about God only knew what. Poor girl. She had no clue.

Yulo and his men sat opposite Taitus, Anríq, and Taitus's other sons. Yulo sat directly across from Taitus and the two men talked.

Then Taitus said something to Anríq to draw him back into conversation with Yulo. Anríq had to turn away from Lanara to answer his father.

Lanara once again got stranded there with no one to talk to.

She squirmed in her seat. Some of the Ula warriors across the table tried to talk to her, but she didn't engage with them. She didn't know what to do with herself without Anríq's attention.

Eliska found herself gazing at him in admiration and affection. She didn't have to hide from herself how she felt about him because how she felt about him was purely innocent.

Any woman would be lucky to get together with him, but no one of them ever would. His calling demanded everything from him. What a shame.

She couldn't even call it a shame because it wasn't. The whole world was better off with him as a Servant instead of just another Barbarian breeding other little Barbarians to maraud and lay waste to the countryside.

Chapter 15

Eliska woke up in bed, glanced across the tent, and stiffened when she saw Anríq sitting up. He hadn't put his vest, weapons, and bags back on when he woke up this morning. He sat there bare-chested and stared at the floor in front of him.

She sat up, but she didn't dare to speak to him just yet. Something was wrong—very wrong.

She crawled over there next to him, but she couldn't touch him. "Anríq?" she asked. "What's wrong?"

"I was just thinking...." he mumbled.

She waited for him to say something else. She scrambled through her brain trying to imagine what he was thinking about.

Then she remembered and sat down on the floor next to him. "Are you ready to go talk to your father about leaving?"

He nodded. "I'm ready. I was just thinking."

"Do you want me to do anything....to help you?"

"You don't have to. I'll talk to him. ...and I don't think you should get involved. He needs to hear it from me. If you talk to him, it will only make him more defensive."

She nodded back at him even though he wasn't looking at her. "I understand. I'll do what I can to help you."

"Thank you," he mumbled. "I'm really glad you're here."

She finally let her hand fall on his bare shoulder. He felt so small and fragile like this. This must be so damn hard for him. "You should get dressed."

He heaved a massive sigh. "No, I'll go unarmed. Then he won't think I'm going to battle against him."

"Um..." She glanced around. His weapons, vest, and bags lay on the floor by the bed. "Do you want me to bring everything for you so you'll be ready to leave?"

"You don't have to. I'll just take everything when the time comes."

She didn't know what else to say. He sat there with his eyes downcast for a long time.

She couldn't fathom what was going through his mind. Did he question whether to continue with the Servant's path? He sounded awfully certain about it last night.

She eventually got too hungry to wait any longer. She brought over one of the plates of food from the table. "Eat something before we leave. You don't want to travel on an empty stomach."

He didn't look up while he picked up a piece of bread and chewed it. He did everything in a dull trance.

She really wished he would at least take his weapons. She didn't know what to expect from Taitus or his sons when they realized Anríq planned to leave for the second time to follow the Servant's path. They might try anything.

She sure as hell wouldn't go unarmed. She mentally rehearsed how she would handle it if they did attack him—or her.

She would just magick his weapons to him—like he needed them. He would be able to use his magic against them the way he said. He could defend himself as easily as she could even barehanded.

She stayed near him and didn't break in on his thoughts. She sure wished she could do something else to make this easier for him, but like so many other people she knew and cared about, nothing would ever make this better.

Anríq lost his father and his whole family exactly the way Yann and Barsali did. What a tragic waste.

Taitus could have been the father Anríq needed—like Yvan was to Yann. Taitus could have been Anríq's greatest ally instead of his worst enemy.

They weren't even enemies because Eliska already saw the love between them.

Both of them ached for the other. They just couldn't get over this one obstacle blocking them from each other.

Maybe it would have been like that for Yann if he left the Black Watch the way he said he wanted to. She could understand his reluctance to do that, but now he suffered a fate so much worse. His father was dead.

Which would be worse—having a father who pushed you away and said you weren't his son anymore—or a father who was no longer there at all?

Which would Eliska rather have? She never had to think about that because Yvan never disapproved of her. She never did anything to cause any rift in their relationship.

Now he was gone. She could preserve him in her memory in his most perfect state—in the state where he supported her, comforted her, protected her, and approved of her more than anyone else in the world—even more than Yann did.

She would always remember Yvan like that. She couldn't have survived anything getting in the way of that relationship and he wasn't even her father.

Now Yann didn't have to worry about his father's disapproval, but he would probably wish for his father's disapproval just to have his father alive again.

She shook those thoughts out of her head when Anríq got to his feet. He didn't look at her when he walked out of the tent.

She magicked his axe, club, machete, bags, and vest into a pile right outside the tent door. She wanted everything on hand in case the whole situation fell apart in front of her eyes.

Taitus and his older son stood across the camp talking to all their fighting men. The chieftain went through the crowd assigning different men to his sons' command.

"We'll come at the town from all four sides at the same time," Taitus explained. "That will overwhelm the Black Watch. They'll have to spread their numbers thinner and we can overcome them. Oh, you're here, my boy. Excellent. You can take the western wall...."

"I'm leaving the tribe, Papi," Anríq blurted out. "Eliska and I are leaving, so I won't be able to go with you on the raid."

Taitus spun around fast. "You're...what?"

"I told you. I'm a Servant and my place is out there following the Servant's path."

"Give it up," Baoco muttered. "Your place is here with us."

"You said you have to protect the defenseless," Esegan countered. "You'll be protecting all our women and children."

Anríq hardened his features and didn't back down at all. His empty hands and bare chest somehow made him look even more dangerous than if he had come armed.

"The camp isn't in danger from any immediate attack," he growled. "I already told you I'm going to continue on the Servant's path. That is the only place I will ever belong. I won't wage war against a town, a band of traveling nomads, or even another tribe of Barbarians. The

Black Watch defends the defenseless. I won't fight them so you can bring home your loot. You can do that without me."

"Then you're a coward," Taitus snapped.

Anríq shrugged. "Then I'm a coward. I'm going now to be a coward in the Coil. Thank you for your hospitality, Papi. I hope it's a successful raid."

Taitus narrowed his eyes at his son and clamped his lips shut.

Eliska used that moment to very casually bring her staff forward. When and where would the first strike come?

Who would be the first to attack Anríq to stop him from leaving?

He leveled his father and brothers with a brutal stare of outright challenge. They could all see he was unarmed. They would be the cowards if they attacked him now.

They waited, and when none of them made their move, he turned on his heel and crossed the camp on his way toward Eliska. Now at least he could arm himself. She wouldn't feel comfortable until he did.

She stepped sideways to give him a clear path to his weapons. Then she stepped behind him to guard him while he put everything on.

He kept his back to the camp. Taitus and his sons pretended to ignore Anríq.

He pulled on his vest and hung his bags over his shoulder. He strapped on his axe, his club, and his machete. Now everything was back to normal.

He turned around and advanced to her side. They were ready to leave.

He cast one last look around the camp. His father ignored him and went on talking to the other men as though Anríq wasn't there. Maybe it was easier this way.

Anríq nodded at Eliska and they turned to leave the camp by the same road they used to enter it.

She didn't ask where he wanted to go. They would have to wait until they got out of this area before they broke through into another Layer.

Then they would have to search before they met up with Yann again—if he was even still alive. He better be. Eliska couldn't stand it if he wasn't.

She withdrew her awareness from this Barbarian tribe. They were already part of her past the way they were a part of Anríq's past.

She turned away. She couldn't even see the Barbarians anymore. What a relief.

The tension went out of Anríq's body at the same moment. What a relief this must be for him, too. She wanted to smile at him, but that could wait.

She stopped in her tracks when she saw another group of Barbarians approaching the camp from that direction. She didn't recognize any of those men.

She'd become familiar with Yulo and his party while they recovered from their injuries and afterward when they made peace with Taitus and Anríq. These men approaching didn't belong to the Dinu tribe. They didn't belong to the Ula tribe, either.

Anríq unhooked his club in one swift movement and dropped the tip onto the ground. A deep boom went off from the point of impact.

That sound alerted all the men behind him. They all turned outward in time to see a whole different pack of Barbarians bearing down on the camp from three sides.

A long curved line of men all running abreast burst out of the surrounding hills. Eliska kicked herself for not keeping an eye on her hand window, but she didn't expect an attack to happen here.

The attackers let out a collective war cry that set her hair on end. She swung her staff forward and Anríq wound back his club to defend the camp.

Eliska sprang away from him to cover more of the advancing assault front.

The Barbarians plunged in before any of the Dinu warriors had a chance to prepare themselves. Some of them got caught completely unarmed.

The attackers swarmed in and raised their weapons to strike down Anríq and Eliska.

She blasted her staff in all directions to take down as many as she could. She didn't even try to avoid killing them. She didn't know who these bastards were, but she didn't have to worry about sparing them.

Even if they belonged to the Ula Tribe, they made themselves the Dinu's enemies by attacking an unprepared camp like this.

She got lost in the fog of battle. Anríq's club pounded and boomed a few feet away from her, but she couldn't see him with so many Barbarians rushing all around her.

A few enemy magic-users came out of the crowd, but she finished them off, too.

She cleared a space around herself and turned backward to storm through the camp.

Barbarians surrounded everyone from the Dinu tribe. Taitus fell on one knee fighting five giant Barbarians all attacking him at once.

Other attackers cornered Hoch to one side and pulverized him with their clubs and blades.

Esegan lay on the ground in a pool of blood. He didn't move.

Eliska fried at the attackers surrounding Taitus. Then she went after the enemy pulverizing Hoch, but he was already going down fast.

Anríq flattened his opponents in no time, but it still took way too long to clear the rest of the attackers out of the camp. Some of them made it all the way to the other side and went after women and children before the enemy ran off and vanished into the countryside.

Chapter 16

Eliska finished working on Taitus. She healed all his injuries, but he didn't regain consciousness when she finished.

She left him asleep and passed down the line of injured Barbarians healing anyone who still needed it.

She eventually made it to Hoch. Rechner and Birino had stabilized Hoch, but they didn't finish the job.

She placed her hands on his chest, found the internal organs still damaged in the assault, and healed them the rest of the way. He didn't wake up, either, but he would sleep now.

She stopped at the next bed. Anríq had been working his way through the tent all day the same way she had.

Now he stood in silence next to Esegan's bed and stared down at his brother's dead body.

"We never should have let this happen," Anríq murmured. "We never should have let our conflict stop us from keeping watch over the perimeter Now he's dead and nothing will bring him back."

She squeezed his arm, and then, just because, she let her hand slip into his. "None of this is your fault. Who's responsible for keeping an eye on the perimeter? You aren't even a member of this Tribe. You haven't been for years. You're a guest here. Your father should already have people for that."

"He does. The magic-users....."

He broke off and didn't finish. She heard what he didn't say.

The Barbarian magic-users should have used their magic to monitor whether someone crossed the Dinu perimeter.

Dozens of dead Alara warriors lay out in the middle of the camp. The able-bodied members of the Dinu tribe worked to carry the bodies out into the grasslands to rot.

No one saw this coming. Taitus never once considered that the Alara might have designs on the Dinu this soon.

Maybe he shouldn't have been so quick to screw over the Ula to weaken them. Maybe he should have sealed an alliance with them sooner.

She didn't say that out loud—not over Esegan's dead body.

"You should go back to the tent," she told him. "You're no good here. I'll handle this."

He nodded, but right then, Taitus's voice carried across the tent. "Where my son?" he demanded. "I want to see my son."

Anríq and Eliska turned around to see Taitus fighting off Deopra. She tried to both help him sit up and put him back in bed at the same time. She stammered excuses, but she couldn't help him.

Anríq and Eliska crossed the tent to the Chieftain's bedside. "You should rest, Papi. You're still weak."

"I will not rest!" the chieftain snapped. "I wanted—Aargh!" He tried to stand and collapsed back on his bed.

Anríq watched his father writhe in pain for a minute. Anríq glanced over at Deopra. "Leave him with me. I'll take care of him."

She bolted. Whatever idea she had about seducing Anríq went straight out the window.

Eliska hung back while Anríq moved in. He helped his father arrange himself on the bed in a comfortable position.

"You can't get up just yet, Papi," Anríq murmured. "You need to heal."

Anríq placed his hand on his father's chest and sent a wave of magic through him. It relaxed Taitus, but only slightly.

"You can't leave, my son," he choked. "You can't leave me...."

Anríq compressed his lips, but his face spasmed. "I have to, Papi. I already told you that. I can't stay here."

"Why?!" Taitus practically wailed. "What did I ever do to make you betray me like this?"

"I'm not betraying you, Papi. I would be betraying myself if I stayed."

"I don't understand." Taitus's voice cracked. " I lost you once. I can't lose you again."

Anríq's voice trembled just as much "You will never lose me, Papi, I'll always be yours."

Taitus let out a pathetic whimper of pure misery and his hand flew to Anríq's where it rested on his father's heart. Taitus pressed it tighter into his skin. "Please stay, my son. Please....You have no idea...."

Anríq didn't move for a minute. He stared down into his father's convulsing face. Was Anríq second-guessing his decision at last?

"I never told you...." Taitus stammered. "Your brothers....they're all good Barbarians...."

"I know," Anríq murmured.

"But don't you see?!" Taitus exclaimed. "That's their weakness. They do what they're told. They aren't leaders—not like you. They don't see the wider picture. I need you! You're the only one of the four worth making my heir. I can't hand over the tribe to any of them...."

"You have to—or chose someone else," Anríq murmured. "My path lies elsewhere."

"No!" Taitus shrieked before he fought himself under control.

"You told me all of this last time," Anríq went on in the same undertone. "You already offered to make me your heir. Nothing has changed. The same reason you want to make me your heir is the same reason I can't be. I'm sorry, Papi. I would do anything to make you proud of me, but maybe this is the way I can make you proud of me. It's the only way I have left."

"I am proud of you, my son," Taitus croaked. "I am prouder of you than you can know."

"Then why do you keep threatening me and calling me a coward?" Anríq murmured.

"Because I need you!" Tears leaked out of Taitus's eyes and streaked down the sides of his head. "I can't stand you leaving me."

"I don't want to leave you, Papi. I have to. I wouldn't leave if it wasn't absolutely necessary."

"It isn't necessary!" Taitus countered. "You could stay...."

"No, Papi," Anríq breathed. "I've already told you why. You just don't listen—or you refuse to believe me. Sometimes I think you haven't heard a word I've said. You think I'm a leader, but you don't listen to my recommendations. I could never be your heir."

Taitus wrenched his head away and choked on his own anguish. Anríq didn't stop sending waves of healing magic into his father through their whole conversation.

Eliska's chest tightened watching them. No one knew better than she did what it felt like to have Anríq heal that stabbing pain in her heart.

Now he was doing it to his own father—to the man who called him a traitor and threatened to kill him.

Anríq worked in silence for another fifteen minutes. Taitus kept his head turned and didn't look at Anríq again.

Eliska waited, and when nothing else happened, she walked away. She had too many other injured people to take care of

She went through the tent one person at a time. She spent considerable time healing Waro and Rechner. By the time she finished, her own exhaustion was catching up with her.

She went back to the tent. Lanara brought Eliska a tray of food, put it on the table, and left without a word.

None of the three girls said anything anymore about bedding Anríq. Maybe the three of them really had made up their minds that Anríq and Eliska were a couple after all.

Eliska just accepted that. At least the girls would leave him alone if they thought that.

She ate and was just stretching out on her bed to get some rest when he came back.

He buckled onto his own cushions, his shoulders slumped, and his eyes cast down to the floor.

She crossed the room and sat down next to him. "How is he?"

Anríq nodded at nothing. "He'll be fine—physically at least."

"He loves you. You know that, don't you?"

Anríq nodded again. "I know."

She rested her hand on his shoulder and then, for no reason she could think of, she put her arm around him and rested her head on his shoulder instead.

She didn't know why she did it. She just wanted to be closer to him and give him some comfort. She couldn't imagine anything harder than what he must be going through.

"You should go to sleep," he mumbled. "You must be tired after today."

"I am and I will. You should sleep too.

"I will," he mumbled. "I just need to think."

"It doesn't change anything, does it?" she murmured. "Nothing ever changes."

"No, it doesn't." He heaved a broken sigh. "I'll leave. I have to. Nothing can change that. It's only a matter of time."

She sat up and ran her hand down his hair just to express her affection for him. It didn't mean anything except that she cared about him.

She pulled the tray of food forward and put it on the floor in front of him. She took a piece of fruit and he took a piece of cheese.

They ate together in silence. She didn't need to make it better because nothing could. She could just be glad she was here to go through this with him. He wasn't alone. Someone understood.

They would leave here and go back out into the Coil. Then someone would know.

If they ever found Yann again, she would carry Anríq's secret the way same away Anríq carried her secret about the children. They both knew the worst about each other. They protected each other in that, too.

Chapter 17

Anríq and Eliska stepped out of Taitus's tent. The Barbarians who got injured in the Alara raid were all back on their feet. Eliska and Anríq had no more reason to stay.

Taitus's cheek spasmed and his lips trembled when he faced his son. "Is there anything I can do to convince you to stay?"

"No, Papi," Anríq murmured. "Knowing you love me would be enough to convince me to stay if there was any way I could possibly do it."

"I do love you." Taitus started to break down again. "I love you more than anything—and I'm proud of you."

Anríq barely spoke above a whisper. "I love you, too, Papi."

His father clasped him in a deep hug and then kissed him on the cheek. Taitus clamped his lips shut to hold back emotion.

Anríq's brothers stood back watching. Did they even know the things their father said about them to Anríq? It didn't matter now because Anríq was leaving for good.

Anríq stepped away. Taitus approached Eliska and clasped her hands. "Take care of my son, young one."

"I will, Sir," she replied. "I promise.

He compressed his lips and nodded once before he turned away. "Let's go. Separate into your companies and let's move out."

Anríq and Eliska migrated farther toward the opposite enough of the camp. Taitus, his sons, and all the Dinu warriors divided into the groups they planned to use to assault the town where they would fight the Black Watch.

Eliska considered suggesting that she and Anríq go to that town to support the Black Watch, but she didn't say that.

She wanted to get Anríq as far away from his family as possible. She and Anríq turned their backs on the tribe in more ways than one.

She went through the same process as before. The Barbarians slipped into the past. It was over.

Now Anríq could start the long, slow painful process of moving on—if that was even possible.

The two travelers crossed the camp to its far end....and she stopped again. The countryside ahead disintegrated before her eyes.

She took a second to realize it really was happening.

The grassland two hundred yards away evaporated in a swirling chaos Layer falling away into a void.

"LOOK OUT!!" Anríq bellowed over his shoulder, but it was already too late. The instability closed around the camp from all sides.

Eliska sprang away. If this had been any other random Island collapsing, she would have shattered the ground to send everyone pitching through the Layers to whatever Island of stability they could find.

She couldn't do that now—not with men, women, and children trapped on this one piece of solid ground. Their lives depended on this one scrap of land still left intact.

She thrust her staff into the air and ejected a torrent of magic. She poured all her effort into it and channeled magic from somewhere deep inside herself.

She spread a net of crackling energy around the camp to surround it, but the Layers pounded against that net with such force that they came close to overcoming it. She couldn't hold it off much longer. "Anríq!" she screamed. "Help me!"

He snatched his club and pounded it into the ground. That thump vibrated through the soil at her feet, but it didn't shatter the Island. It stabilized it—just a little bit.

He raised his club a second time, smashed it down with almighty force, and another shockwave of bone-crushing magic detonated outward from the point of impact. His magic collided with hers and flowed into the net to make it stronger.

Every muscle in her body quaked and shivered from the effort of holding her staff in the air. She felt herself weakening, but Anríq's magic stabilized her along with the rest of the Island.

The Barbarians screamed and ran in all directions, but they couldn't get away. Chaos surrounded the camp in a solid curtain of swirling vapor and hurricane chaos.

Landscapes wheeled past just inches beyond the last tents. The Layers shifted and morphed faster than Eliska could keep track of them.

The vapors cleared for a minute and reformed into a snowy blizzard world full of jagged mountains, cold grey-blue. Then the Layers collapsed that snow Island and the surroundings went back to a tumbling cauldron of instability.

It formed and reformed again and again—first into a land scorched with walls of fire, then into a peaceful grassy valley full of cows and horses and sheep, then a scorched wasteland with a few bleached bones rotting under a blistering sun, and then another grassland exactly like the one the Barbarians just left.

None of those landscapes stayed intact for more than a few seconds before they disintegrated in mayhem.

Torrential, howling wind tore through the camp and ripped tents apart. It snatched them off the ground along with cushions, utensils and anything not nailed down.

Mothers had to hold onto their children. People smashed their bodies together all holding onto each other for dear life.

Eliska and Anríq stood at the center of everything. He kept hammering his club into the ground again and again. She wouldn't have been able to hold off the chaos without his constant help.

Sweat broke out all over her body. She felt her strength about to give out. "Anríq!!" she screeched. "I can't hold it any longer!"

He dropped his club and rushed her, grabbed her in his arms, and crushed her against him.

He held her so tightly that she couldn't breathe, but at that moment, his magic cascaded through her in a blistering flood. He added his magic to hers and it all rushed up her staff in an epic starburst.

Her net exploded stronger than ever. She collapsed in his arms, but she didn't stop pouring her magic down that staff. She couldn't stop until she got these people to safety, wherever that was.

All at once, the camp dropped out from under her and Anríq slammed down on his knees still holding onto her.

They both collapsed and sprawled on the ground. Her strength completely failed her and she dropped her staff.

Her net blinked out, but she didn't need it anymore. The camp bobbed on some watery surface.

Anríq pushed himself up on his arms, looked around, and then glanced down at her. "Eliska!" he panted. "Are you all right?"

She nodded fast and felt how weak she was when she rolled over. She wouldn't be able to do that again anytime soon—not before she had a chance to recharge.

She trembled all over again when she saw where she was.

The section of land where the camp had been....it bobbed and floated on an undulating sea surrounded by a tall, towering night sky. Stars and revolving galaxies sprayed across a midnight sky.

She forced herself to sit up. She didn't trust herself to stand.

None of the tents remained. All the same people huddled on the bare ground where the camp had been. She and Anríq saved most if not all of them.

They cowered together in groups with their arms around each other. Parents hugged their children.

Entire groups huddled under that vast, sky spread out above them. None of these people had a scrap of shelter, food, water—nothing.

Eliska scrambled to pick up her staff in case this Island collapsed, too.

The camp really was an Island now...or more of a floating raft of soil held together by grass.

Birino and Wado huddled nearby with some of the women and children. She didn't even ask them to do anything to help her and Anríq cope with this situation.

Taitus, his sons, and the men who'd been about to go on the raid cowered to one side. Taitus's tent wasn't there anymore. Nothing was.

Anríq started to stand up, but he stopped when the raft wobbled underneath him. He wound up crawling over to his father.

"Papi!" Anríq gasped. "Is anyone hurt?"

"I don't know, my son," Tatus choked. "You...you saved us all."

"Not yet." Anríq turned back to Eliska. "Can you find out where we are? Is there anywhere more stable we can take these people?"

She opened her Coil projection in her hand. "Help me," she told him.

He added his magic to it. Chaos Layers surrounded this ocean on all sides. She didn't dare to shatter it to take the tribe somewhere else.

She did see two golden lines entering another stable Island several Layers away. Yann and Marine must be there together.

A matching charge of tension went through Anríq when they both saw the lines, but she didn't mention them out loud. She shut her hand.

"We'll just have to stay here," she decided. "If the Layer collapses, we'll have enough to do getting the tribe somewhere safe. We shouldn't hasten the process before we absolutely have to."

They both looked up to find everyone nearby watching and listening to their conversation.

Eliska became aware that they all saw her use her Coil projection. Did they even understand what it meant?

Anríq turned back to his father and then all the other people. "We're going to spend the night here. We have no choice. Eliska needs to rest....."

"What did you do?" Birino blurted out. "How did you hold the camp together like that?"

"Eliska did it," Anríq replied. "She has powerful magic. All of you should settle down. Stay as low to the ground as you can. Don't stand up or you might tip the Island over."

A few people sat down on the ground, but everyone already crouched as low as possible. Anríq sat halfway between his father and Eliska, but in a little while, he turned to face her.

"We'll wait until morning," he suggested. "Then you can check the projection and see about finding a safe Island for us."

"I don't think this place has any morning." She looked up at the stars. "It doesn't have a sun."

"Then we'll wait until you're rested enough."

Her hand flew to her head. "You're right. I feel like I'm going to fall over."

"Lie down here." He pulled her toward him and guided her down on the ground.

She lacked the strength to fight back and she didn't want to.

He positioned her with her head closer to him and rubbed back in between stroking her hair. Anyone watching would think they were a couple, but she knew better.

He wrapped her cloak around her to keep her warm. Her eyes drifted shut.

His fingers trailing through her hair helped her relax and the exhaustion overtook her, but she didn't fall asleep.

"Nowhere will be safe as long as the Coil continues to collapse," she mumbled. "You know that, right? We can go to another island, but that will only collapse, too.

"Then maybe the solution is to find out what the Voyant wants—either to defeat him or to give him what he wants."

Her eyes snapped open. "What do you mean—give it to him?"

"He wants this person—the magic-user who will replace him," Anríq went on.

She shot off the ground in an instant and stared at him in the dark. "Are you seriously suggesting....?"

"He wants to find this person. If that could bring stability to the Coil—or at least stop him from attacking everything and everyone—wouldn't that be worth it?"

Her jaw hit the ground. "Are you suggesting....?"

He only stared back at her. "I'm just saying it would be worth it. Don't you think?"

She gulped hard. "It isn't me. I'm not the one he wants."

"But if you were, wouldn't you think it would be worth turning yourself over to him?"

She shut her mouth with an effort and turned away. Her eyes darted everywhere.

If she was the person the Voyant wanted.....

"You could potentially save millions of lives," he murmured in her ear.

"What are you talking about?" Taitus interrupted.

"Nothing," Anríq replied.

"We don't know that I am the person," Eliska blurted out.

"No, you're right," Anríq replied.

She looked away, "Anyway, I'm not."

He didn't answer. She didn't want to think about whether she was the person the Voyant wanted or how she could defeat him or stabilize the Coil if she was the person.

Right then, she heard whimpering and sobbing coming from the people sitting nearest. The children cowered against their mothers and some of the women started crying.

They cast petrified glances at the ocean surrounding the raft and also at the galaxies and stars wheeling in the dark.

Some of the children looked eerily similar to the children she lost at the orphanage.

Without thinking about it first, she fired her staff into the center of the raft. A jet of magic spouted from the staff end. She didn't think about what she would create until she did it.

She sent out a spray of sparks at first, but their flashing colors and starbursts startled the Barbarians too much. She wanted to put them at ease, so she changed the patterns to flowers.

She morphed them into pictures of animals and then made the animals dance around, make funny faces, and do silly antics. Laughter and a few amazed gasps went through the tribe.

The tension eased, but not completely. Marine put the Watchmen at ease by singing to them, so Eliska made some of the images coming from her staff sign songs.

She made the songs humorous at first and then changed them to gentle lullabies.

The magical flashes lit up all the faces surrounding her. The Barbarians forgot to look at the surroundings and her magic distracted them from their circumstances.

She could have kept going, but Anríq got her attention by putting his hand on her wrist. "You need to rest."

She looked around at the people nearest her. She didn't want to stop.

He pressed her arm a little harder. "Eliska......you need to rest."

She would have kept it up all night, but he was right. This raft would need all her magic if it got swept up in another Layer collapse.

He took hold of her arms by the wrists and pried her fingers away from her staff. She found it impossible to let go until he took it out of her hands.

He didn't take it away from her. He laid it on the ground in front of her—right where she would be able to pick it up the minute she needed it.

The flow of magic cut off when she lost contact with it. She could have created the pictures with her bare hands, but she gave in to his guidance and let the display end.

"Lie down," he told her.

He steered her back down onto the ground next to him. How many times had he done that?

Her display worked to ease everyone's anxiety. The children stopped crying. Their mothers guided them to lie down on the ground, too. She couldn't help but notice how much the parents acted like Anríq.

He wrapped her cloak around her, squeezed her shoulder, and rubbed her back a few times, and then turned to his father and brothers.

They talked in low murmurs. They were still talking in a hushed whisper when she fell into a deep, dark, exhausted sleep.

Chapter 18

E liska woke up in darkness and felt the raft bobbing on the waves. The ocean undulated and swayed in a gentle rocking motion.

She sat up and looked around. Everyone in the Dinu tribe lay asleep around her—everyone except Anríq.

He stood a few yards away looking out at the stars and galaxies. He told everyone to stay low, but he stood straight upright. Something must be wrong.

She got to her feet and tiptoed over to him, mainly so she wouldn't tilt the raft too much.

"Is something wrong?" she whispered.

He glanced over at her, went back to looking at the stars, and pointed in front of him. "Look. I just noticed it about an hour ago."

She looked at what he was pointing at. Stars studded the sky from one horizon to the other. Nothing interrupted that solid carpet of brilliance up there.

Only one spot in the whole sky showed an area without start. It only looked about a foot wide from here.

It started out as a small, barely distinguishable spot in the distance, but it swelled slowly while Eliska and Anríq stood there watching. It expanded and no more starts appeared inside it.

"It's been getting bigger since I've been standing here," he went on. "I guess it will swallow this Island when it gets big enough."

"You should get some sleep," she told him. "You need your rest as much as I do. Have you been standing here watching it the whole time?"

He glanced over at her again and smiled this time. He didn't answer. He didn't have to.

Of course he would have stayed awake to watch that spot. He wouldn't want to take his eye off something that could endanger his tribe.

"Lie down," she told him. "I'll keep watch for a while."

They returned to the same place. He stretched out on the ground and she sat down next to him.

She would have touched him, but now of all times didn't feel like the right moment.

He made eye contact with her once before he shut his eyes. "Thank you for everything you're doing, Eliska," he murmured. "I'm beyond grateful."

"Just take care of yourself," she murmured back. "I'll need you when it gets here."

He folded his arm under his head and fell asleep immediately. So she was right about him being exhausted, too.

He didn't wake up. She watched the spot. It did keep getting bigger. It widened to cover almost a third of the sky.

Whatever passed for night in this place eventually came to an end and the sky lightened, but she had been right. This Island didn't have any sun.

The sky just expanded and changed color to brilliant crystal blue. The stars disappeared and day spread over the ocean in their place.

The spot didn't lighten. It stayed impenetrably black with nothing inside it. It blocked out half the sky by the time the first Barbarians woke up.

Then tiniest children started crying first and that woke up everyone else, including Anríq.

The agitation spiked off the charts when everyone saw the Dark Layer sweeping toward the party. No colored vapors swirled inside it. Anríq scowled at it.

"I think we should shatter this Island and take the tribe somewhere else before the Layer gets here," she told him. "We can't risk the tribe getting taken into the Dark."

Just then, Taitus and his sons scooted over to Anríq. "What are we going to do about this?"

"Eliska and I were just talking about it. We couldn't stay here even if the Dark wasn't creeping up on us." Anríq squinted at the sky and then nodded at Eliska's hands. "We have some time before it gets here. Let's find out where we are and locate another Island we can take the camp to."

She created her Coil projection and he added his magic to it. Waro and Rechner came over to watch.

Eliska revolved the projection in circles until Anríq pointed to a different Layer. "We have relatives there in another branch of the Dinu tribe. Let's go there."

"It's too far away," Waro interjected out. "We don't have the magic to hold the raft together through all those Layers."

"We'll just have to make it work." Eliska picked up her staff and started to get to her feet.

"You have to be careful, Eliska," Anríq told her. "You'll exhaust yourself again. If you keep pouring all your magic into this, you could make yourself sick and die."

"I won't die." She saw him scowling at her.

She didn't want to think about how this might affect her. She wouldn't be able to do anything else because there was no way in hell she would let these people fall into a Dark Layer. "You'll just have to help me. Put your hands on my staff."

"Wait a minute." He crossed the camp to exchange a few words with his father and brothers. Then Anríq went through the tribe giving everyone instructions.

"Everyone gather at the center of the raft. Come over here." He herded everyone to the middle. "Get down on the ground so your weight is at the center. Hold onto each other. This is going to get bumpy."

It took him a long time to get everyone into position.

The children sobbed and some of them screamed when their parents tried to move them even a few inches on the tilting raft.

The adults didn't respond much better. They hesitated to move at all. Some of the braver relatives had to pull their family members into position.

Eliska stood back and waited. Watching the Barbarians reminded her of just how experienced she was with everything related to the Coil.

Most people spent their lives in safe, stable Islands somewhere or other. Not many people had seen as much of the Coil as she had.

This was all normal to her. Traveling to different Layers and getting herself out of danger came second nature to her.

This wasn't even a dangerous Island. She could have gotten herself out of it in a few seconds.

Trying to protect so many people complicated things, but it didn't make it impossible. She didn't see why these people would be so scared about it, but she didn't tell them that.

Anríq got everyone into position and came back over to her. "We're ready to go."

"What are you going to do?" Taitus asked.

"We're going to take everyone out of this Island," Anríq replied.

"Is that safe?"

"Staying here definitely won't be." Anríq turned back to Eliska. "I'm ready. You'll have to direct it. I'll just send you my magic. You do what you want with it."

"If you're sure you want to do it that way...."

"Of course," he told her. "You know what to do and where to go."

She didn't argue. She did know where to go and what to do.

She didn't feel one hundred percent comfortable taking his magic from him to make it happen, but he sure seemed one hundred percent certain about it.

He clamped both his powerful hands around her staff, shut his eyes, and bowed his head. He clamped his jaws shut in deep concentration and his magic flowed into the staff.

Nothing happened until she sent her own flow into it and let the power build. The staff vibrated in her hands.

She let it cycle higher and higher and then blasted her magic out of the staff in all directions.

It whirled around the raft in a pounding tempest. Her magic crackled in the air and spread outward to form a rapidly revolving cylinder of air around the raft.

She dug deep and dumped more and more power into the funnel. It lifted the raft off the waves. The Barbarians screamed as the storm caught the raft and it started to spin.

The funnel extended higher and lower above and below the raft. The sky blurred in swirling vapors shot through with Dark forces.

The Dark Layer nearby burst out of position and swooped down on the raft. It struck Eliska's cylinder full force and then the world outside her funnel detonated in chaos.

She tried to shut her eyes so she could concentrate the way Anríq did. He never opened his eyes once.

He crushed the staff in a white-knuckle grip and his lips shivered away from his teeth in from the effort of adding all his magic to hers.

Her eyes snapped open in time to see Islands, Layers, shadows, and Darklings whipping past the field. They bombarded it from all directions and deafening explosions went off all around the raft.

People screamed and then pitched head over heel as the raft tumbled through one Layer after another.

Eliska had to divert some of her magic to holding herself and Anríq in place. She couldn't let this funnel collapse.

She blasted the raft into the wild Layers and then crashed through a dozen Islands one after another.

Landscapes erupted in her path and morphed into shapes that came after the tribe, but the raft fell too fast until it smashed down into a forest of tall trees. The raft crashed through the branches and then slammed down hard on the ground.

The blow knocked Eliska to the ground and she folded into a limp pile at Anríq's feet.

Chapter 19

Eliska drifted back to consciousness and felt Anríq's hand on her forehead.

She groaned and tried to roll over, but she lacked the strength even to do that.

"Lie still," he murmured. "You need to rest for a minute before you get your strength back."

She tried to look around. The raft was definitely on the ground in a lush jungle forest. Animal and insect sounds throbbed in the air.

Taitus's voice boomed out right behind Eliska's back. "What's wrong with her?"

"She exhausted herself by using her magic to save the tribe," Anríq murmured.

"Is she dying?" Taitus asked.

"She'll recover," Anríq replied. "She just needs rest. Tell Hoch and Baoco to scout the area and see about finding food and water for these people. We have some miles to cover before we meet up with the local branch of the Dinu tribe. Everyone will need to eat before we leave."

Eliska shut her eyes. She really felt awful, but she started to feel better when Anríq sent a flow of healing magic into her. It revived the trace of magic she still had left after pouring all her own power into that funnel.

He took his hand off her forehead, rubbed the side of her arm, and bent over to peer into her face. "How do you feel?"

"Tired," she croaked.

"Stay down. We aren't leaving for a few minutes. This Island is as stable as we're likely to find." He stroked his hand down the side of her hair. "You did it. You saved the tribe."

She tried to look away. Saving the tribe was nothing more than her doing her job.

She still didn't like to call herself a Servant, but she considered herself the non-Barbarian equivalent of one. Her life wasn't worth spit if she was anything else.

The Barbarians spread out. She didn't see any women and children sitting around whimpering in terror anymore. Maybe everything really was okay.

She must have passed out again because she woke up a few hours later to see the Barbarians sitting at a distance from her. Families sat around a bonfire with some animal roasting on the spit.

Anríq, his brothers, and his father stood off to one side talking.

Eliska dragged herself off the ground. She still felt bruised and fragile, but at least she could move around now. She raked her hair out of her eyes and picked up her staff.

Anríq saw her right away and came over to squat down next to her. "Do you feel better?" she asked.

She nodded. "Thank you."

"We're the ones who should be thanking you for getting us here. Everyone thinks you're an angel."

She snorted. "Don't tell them the truth, okay?"

He only smiled at her and put his hand on her forehead. That feeling of him touching her, checking on her, and sending his magic into her—it made everything all right.

"I'm okay," she told him. "We don't have to stay here any longer."

"We would be camping here even if you weren't down. Everyone needs to get their feet on the ground after that trip. Come on over and get something to eat."

Her knees wobbled when she stood up. She had to readjust her balance to account for being on solid ground.

She inched toward the Barbarians sitting around the fire. They moved aside to make room for her.

She became aware of everyone giving her strange looks. She really hoped they didn't start treating her like something special.

They divided the food between everyone. Anríq sat down next to her while they ate.

The Barbarians talked about their own business. The fighting men kept leaving, coming back, and giving reports, but the men didn't give their reports to Taitus.

The men always came over to Anríq. They told him whatever they'd found out about the surrounding terrain and the direction the party had to travel to meet up with their relatives.

Taitus and his sons hung back and didn't get involved.

Eliska ate in silence, and after another hour, Anríq stood up and started giving orders to all the men. "Form a column heading west and stay ready in case we meet anyone we don't know. Women and children stay in the center."

He pointed to his brothers.

"Take a scouting party in front of us and find places along the route where we can stop for water and rest. We have a long way to go. We'll need to break up the trip into more than one day."

The men obeyed him without a word of protest. Then he eventually gave the order for everyone to move out.

The women and children obeyed his orders, too. They crowded toward the middle of the column while the men flanked them.

Anríq and Eliska walked on the outside. "Maybe you should go in there, too," he told her. "You aren't back to full strength."

"You'll still need me to help defend the group if anything happens."

He compressed his lips, but he didn't argue.

The party set off across the countryside, left the jungle, crossed some open hills, and reentered another forest. The trip took a long time—a lot longer than Eliska realized.

Her fatigue caught up with her within a few hours. The rest of the Barbarians kept walking, but she couldn't take another step.

She didn't know how much longer they would have to go, so she veered aside, went off by herself, and collapsed under a tree.

She must have fallen deeper asleep than she realized because she woke up to Anríq bending over her again.

"I told you you shouldn't have tired yourself out," he murmured. "You've been doing way too much."

She lacked the strength even to open her mouth to tell him she had to. She no longer had a choice about that.

He scooped her up in his arms and set off with her. Her head fell on his shoulder.

She saw him acting toward her the way he would a lover or a child, but she couldn't even assign any special meaning to that.

He would have to carry her like this or else sling her body over his shoulder like a sack of potatoes.

He carried her back to the tribe and laid her on the ground by another fire. The tribe camped under some trees along a riverbed.

He covered her with her cloak and poured some scalding hot soup down her throat before he left her to fall asleep again.

She woke up in darkness. Fires crackled all over the area with different clusters of Barbarians sitting around them.

She tried to sit up. "Where are we?"

"We're in the Sojourner's Sanctum," Anríq replied. "We're only a few miles from our relatives' camp. We're staying here while you recover."

She would have liked to tell him again that she was okay, but he could already see that she wasn't.

She caught the Barbarians casting furtive glances in her direction. None of them tried to talk to her.

Anríq hovered over her in between taking reports and telling his brothers what to do. She even heard him telling his father what to do.

She stayed lying down near the fire for a long time. The Barbarians talked much more cheerfully here. They knew where they were, where they were going, and that their relatives would welcome them when they got there.

The Barbarians even laughed and joked with each other and a few other people sang.

The night wore on much more casually, now that everyone knew they were safe. Parents bedded down their children and then everyone dropped off one after another.

Anríq didn't stay up keeping watch. He curled up next to Eliska and fell asleep, too.

Her fatigue didn't keep her awake. Anríq posted watches to guard the tribe overnight. She shut her eyes and fell asleep again.

Chapter 20

Eliska woke up feeling much better the next day. She joined Anríq and the other Barbarians on the march westward. He kept receiving reports from the scouts and the warriors escorting the convoy across the countryside.

Hoch and Baoco started acting like Anríq's lieutenants and came back to tell him about a herd of waterbuck crossing the area to the north.

"We should hunt some of them so we don't roll up on our relatives empty-handed," Baoco suggested.

"Good idea," Anríq replied. "Take some of your men and go get as many of waterbuck as you can. We aren't that far out. We'll need the animals skinned and cleaned when we get there. The Chieftain will throw us a feast, so we'll need something to contribute."

The brothers left. Eliska found herself studying Anríq on the side. He sure had changed since he wound up with his people again. Now they saw what his magic could do for them.

She didn't comment on how confident and authoritative he'd been acting lately. Everyone else noticed it, too.

Taitus came over to them halfway through the morning. He started out by talking to Anríq about the terrain, the scouting parties, reports, and the personalities of the Dinu chieftain and his entourage that

Taitus and his sons would have to deal with once they met up with their relatives.

"You should negotiate with them, my son," Taitus insisted. "You know more about this situation than we do."

"I don't think so," Anríq muttered. "You can negotiate with them yourself. You're the Chieftain here, not me."

"I'm grateful for everything you and your companion are doing for us...."

"You don't have to be grateful," Anríq told him. "We just want to help you. You know that."

"You should be at my right hand when I negotiate with them," Taitus went on. "They'll need to talk to the person in charge."

"I'm not in charge," Anríq growled. "I told you that. I'm a Servant. I'm not a Chieftain and I'm not your heir. If you want to take someone, take Hoch."

"My son...." Taitus began.

Just then, some more scouts came back. "The Dinus are sending out an armed party to meet us," they told Anríq. "They might think we're hostile."

"Bring all our men to the front," Anríq told him. "Get ready to meet them, but keep your weapons down. Don't threaten them."

"The hunters aren't back yet," the scout pointed out. "We don't have our offering."

"We'll just have to make the best of it." Anríq waved his arm. "Get everyone into position."

The Barbarians hustled to carry out his order. Even Taitus went forward to join the men.

"Are you sure you don't want to stay?" Eliska asked as soon as the others passed out of earshot. "You could do these people so much good here."

"I couldn't be a Barbarian Chieftain," he muttered. "I'm a Servant. That's the only thing that qualifies me to lead anyone."

"You could be the leader they need you to be. You could get them to turn away from all this violence."

"Then they wouldn't be Barbarians anymore. They need a leader who is a Barbarian and I'm not one."

She studied him, but she didn't say whether he was or he wasn't.

He wasn't a Barbarians the way they were. Everyone else in the Coil shunned him for being a Barbarian. His own people shunned him for being a Servant.

It trapped him between the two and left him alone, but that was basically the point, wasn't it?

Eliska didn't have that problem, but she wasn't really a Servant. She was just pretending to be one.

What would happen if she really became a Servant? Would she have to wear her hair the way they did—and change her clothes—and get a bunch of tattoos?

The Servant's mark was a tattoo. She would have to get that, but no one would be able to see it if she didn't change her clothes. How would people know to come out and find her?

That would never happen because she would get all wrapped up in this war against the Voyant.

As soon as she finished getting these people to safety, she and Anríq would try to find Yann and go on trying however successfully to stop the Voyant from destroying the Coil.

She got lost in her own thoughts, but she had to come back to reality when an army of powerful Barbarians came over the hill in front of the tribe.

The Dinus sent hundreds of warriors to meet this one small band. All those Barbarians came armed to the teeth. Taitus's band wouldn't be able to defend itself against a horde this size.

Eliska could have taken them, but she didn't want to.

Taitus and his sons wound up in the central position of the men Anríq ordered to the front. The two groups stopped a few hundred yards away from each other.

Anríq and Eliska stopped side by side apart from the main column. No one would mistake Anríq for being involved in this.

Taitus and his men stayed where they were when a cluster of fifteen huge Barbarians advanced out of line to meet them.

The two groups didn't attack each other. That was a step in the right direction. The two groups met in the center of the field and talked. Eliska couldn't hear them from here.

They were still negotiating with each other when the hunters showed up with six skinned, gutted waterbuck carcasses. Taitus waved at them and the tension dissolved even more.

Eliska relaxed. It was done. These Dinus would take in the stragglers from Taitus's camp. They were with their own people now.

She felt the tension drain out of Anríq standing next to her. He did his duty to his people. Now he could leave.

She didn't look forward to another moment of parting between him and his father, but maybe now Taitus would understand what Anríq was and what he was trying to do.

She let out a shaky breath and turned to him to ask if he was ready to go.

The Barbarian chieftain on the other side waved to his men. They started to turn away to lead Taitus's party the rest of the way on their journey.

At that moment, a crack thundered across the sky. A forked line of black fractured the blue dome above the landscape. The crack kept spreading and lacing its jutting fingers all over the landscape.

"NO!" Anríq yelled, snatched his club, and raised it into the air.

Eliska saw the disaster about to strike and stabbed her staff upward to try to grab.....well, everybody.

She didn't get a chance to save anyone. Before she could move or activate her magic at all, the whole Dark web of cracks up there blasted apart into a million pieces.

The sky shattered and dozens of shards of solid blue erupted in all directions. Chaos pelted down on top of the exposed Barbarians.

Anríq struck his club on the ground and let off a deep boom of magic, but nothing could save an Island and a crowd this big.

Eliska fired into the Layers, but another burst of cracks raced through the soil under her feet. The Island exploded unbelievably fast and tossed everyone into the air.

She ejected a shield of protection around everyone near her—except that no one was near her. She and Anríq stood too far away from everyone.

The explosion threw both of them out into the wild Layers with rubble and even whole sections of landscapes smashing against her magical barrier.

He hurled himself away from her and flung himself into the barrier trying to break through.

"NO!!" he bellowed, but Eliska couldn't even see anyone out there or any sign of anything solid where the Barbarians might have taken shelter.

The next instant, they both broke through another Layer and crashed down, down, down through dozens of different surfaces, obstacles, and forces tearing them apart.

An almighty boom plastered Eliska's field and it burst. The impact tore her and Anríq away from each other.

The same blast also stopped him from getting back to anywhere he might have been able to find his family.

She fired her staff at him to magnetize him to her. Their bodies collided, and the next minute, they both landed hard on something solid.

Wet sand compressed around Eliska's face and she smelled salty waves. The cold air bit into her skin.

"NO!!" Anríq roared.

She looked up. He was just staggering to his feet and stumbling around a long, deserted stretch of beach.

Smooth, gentle waves curled onto the sand and hissed back into a vast, empty ocean. The steel-blue surface vanished into a rim of brighter blue on the horizon.

He staggered all over the place and looked everywhere, including up at a towering blue sky. It rose all the way out of sight with not a wisp of cloud anywhere.

NO!!" he roared one last time and buckled onto his knees.

He slumped there and his chin fell on his chest. His shoulders heaved and his breath came out in strained gasps.

Eliska peeled herself off the sand. She hesitated to go over to him, but she had to do something.

Her heart sank when she opened her Coil projection.

Dozens of Layers all collapsed on top of each other to destroy the Sojourner's Sanctum. She didn't see how anyone could survive that, but anything was possible.

She inched up behind him. He didn't look up, not even when she stood right behind him.

She didn't say anything. The wide beauty of this beach gave it a haunted air.

The empty landscape only seemed to drive a nail into the coffin of Anríq's hopes—into the Barbarians' coffins. Were they all dead?

She took a chance, let her hand fall on his shoulder, and squeezed. What could she possibly say to make up for this? There were no words.

"Let's keep moving," she murmured. "They might still be alive somewhere. We might find them."

He didn't respond except to make a choking noise in his throat.

Which was worse—getting thrown out of your own tribe or finding your way back to them only to have them yanked away from you at the last second?

His father had just been telling Anríq how proud he was of him. Anríq finally won the respect of his brothers and all his people—and now they were all gone, too.

She didn't say anything else because there was nothing else to say. She waited until he pushed himself to his feet. He didn't look up or check the landscape. She did that for him.

She considered taking his hand, but she didn't want to intrude on his grief even to offer him that flimsy little comfort.

She took a few steps and he fell in with her on their way down the beach.

Chapter 21

The beach ended at a rocky headland sticking out into the ocean. Eliska didn't see anything here that could give her and Anríq any shelter, fresh water, or any animals they might be able to hunt for food. She and Anríq couldn't stay on this beach.

She studied her hand window to find a path leading up to the top of the headland. Then she struck out inland heading for some trees in the distance.

She and Anríq walked all day without a word. Anríq didn't break the silence and neither did she.

She didn't really think about how to bring him back from this. She would have hated for anyone to try to bring her back from something like this. Trying to bring him back would only make him think didn't understand or didn't care enough to understand.

They made it to the trees as the sun touched the horizon. He threw himself down at the base of a tree, rested his elbows on his knees, and stared at the ground between his feet.

She left him there and went to scout the countryside.

The trees turned out to be a patch of woods with a paved road running behind it.

She didn't see any towns or houses. She hiked into the trees before she opened her hand window.

She couldn't track down Yann without Anríq's help and she didn't want to ask—not yet.

His mission would bring him back soon enough. He wouldn't be able to do anything else.

Then he would ask her to locate Yann so they could all meet up. She could wait until Anríq came back enough to be ready for that.

She switched her hand window and hunted a long-tailed gar. Then she found a small stream and fashioned a bowl to carry water back to Anríq.

She found him sitting in the same place. He didn't move or look up at her while she built a fire, skinned the gar, and started cooking it.

She sat down next to him not expecting him to interact at all tonight. She could live with that.

He surprised her by snapping out of his trance, picking up the bowl she left on the ground next to him, and draining it.

He glanced around with the bowl dangling from his fingers. "Where did you get the water? I'll refill this for you."

She smiled at him. "I'll get it. Here. Eat something."

She handed him another bowl full of food while she refilled the bowl. She drank one for herself and took the full bowl back to the fire.

She found him taking the gar off the spit and serving some of the meat into his own empty bowl to give to her.

She studied him across the fire. He acted the way he usually did. He went through every motion with his usual deliberate attention.

"Are you okay?" she asked.

"I am..........okay." He pronounced it in an exaggerated way that sounded strange. Was he trying to be ironic?

She frowned at him, but he didn't seem to notice. He went on with what he was doing.

She sat down, picked up the bowl he left sitting there for her, and started eating.

She was just licking the juice off her fingers when she happened to glance up. He stared at her across the fire with a different expression on his face. "Um...is something wrong?" she asked.

"Nothing's wrong," he told her. "Nothing you don't already know about."

She waited, but he didn't look away. "Why are you looking at me like that?"

He cocked his head to one side. "You need healing."

She snorted and tried to concentrate on arranging the fire. "Tell me something I don't know."

"I don't mean that. It's something else. You needed healing before you took Barsali's Darkness."

She made a face. "I already knew that, too. I don't have any family. I don't have anything."

"No, this is something else."

"What is it, then? What do I need healing from—apart from all the things we already know about?"

"I don't know, but you do. There's something else.....Something we don't know about. I'd say it's even bigger than all the things we do know about."

She found herself studying him again and he didn't break eye contact. He kept staring straight down into her soul. She couldn't remember anyone ever looking at her as intently as this.

She got the impression as she often did that he could see everything about her. He didn't need words to explain it. He saw the smallest detail of everything she was thinking even when she wasn't aware of it herself.

His attention made her squirm. "Are you saying you need to heal me for something?" she asked.

"No, I can't heal you from this. It's too big. Whatever it is, it isn't in my power to heal. I don't know what it is or how to heal it or if it even can be healed at all." He looked away. "I wish I could."

Those words twisted her guts. She already knew how messed up she was. She didn't need him to tell her.

She also already knew that he would heal her if he could. He would give anything to make her whole.

Nothing would make her whole—not from all the crap she'd gone through in her life. If he couldn't do it, no one could. It was too much for anybody, even herself.

She couldn't tolerate this feeling of being so damaged beyond repair. She had to change the subject. "Do you need healing?"

"Yes, I do."

Her head shot up and she gaped at him. "You do?"

He nodded. "Very much."

"Um...." She floundered trying to think of what to say.

She always considered him so perfect and untouchable. It never crossed her mind that there might be anything wrong with him—ever.

"What's wrong with you?" she asked. "Do you need healing from me? If you tell me what it is, I'll try to heal you."

His eyes locked on her with unimaginable power. "*Do* I need healing from you?"

"I don't know that. I don't have your healing power. I don't know if I have the power to heal you. I can't tell what's wrong with you or even if you need healing at all."

He inclined his head the other way. His eyes fell on her with brutal force. "*Do* you have the power to heal me?"

"I don't know," she replied.

She would have repeated again that she didn't know what he needed or even if he did need healing, but his eyes silenced her.

She didn't understand what he was asking—or if he was asking. He didn't actually come right out and ask her to heal him of whatever the hell he thought was wrong with him.

Everything about him impressed her as being so pure and right and true. He definitely didn't need healing from anything physical.

He went through every event of his life with calm certainty that he knew where his own path lay. He never questioned it, not even when his father tempted him with all the approval and honor Anríq could ask for.

She finally couldn't take his intense stare anymore. She tore her eyes away, fiddled with the sticks in front of her, and mumbled, "You talk more since you came back with Yann."

"I learned something when I was with him. I learned that some people need to talk to heal. Some people need me to serve by talking."

"Did you heal him by talking to him?"

"I don't know if I healed him or he healed himself or if he healed at all, but he needed my service. I served him by talking in the way that he needed me to. It isn't the Servant's way, but it was necessary for healing and service, so it must be the Servant's way. I didn't know that before. Silence isn't always necessary or even the best thing for service and healing. Sometimes they can even prevent service and healing. It's strange. Things change and yet I keep becoming more fully a Servant by discarding these rules."

She stared at him in amazement. He'd been talking so freely lately. She never thought he would open up as much as this. "What did he need to talk to you about?"

"He needed to ask me questions and to hear me answer them."

"What did he ask you about?"

"He wanted to know about my life with the Barbarians before I became a Servant....and why I became a Servant." He looked up at her again. "Would it heal you to hear me talk about that?"

"I....I don't think so. You kinda already did talk to me about it.... back at the camp. Remember?"

He nodded and looked away. "You're right. It didn't change anything. It isn't in my power to heal you, not even with that. I wish it was."

She thought a little longer before she decided what to say. "If it was in my power to heal you, I would do it."

"I know you would. You have served me and defended me from the beginning. I'm grateful for all you've done for me. I should have thanked you back then. I was too silent before." He broke off and then blurted out, "Thank you."

"Wow," she breathed. "It is....healing to hear you say that."

"It is healing to say it—finally."

She experienced another heart-wrenching rush of affection and almost painful devotion to him. She thrust out her hand and squeezed his arm just above his wrist.

That touch sent a charge through her hand and she didn't take it away. Touching him felt too good.

He burst into a beautiful smile and clasped his hand over hers. He pressed her hand deeper into his arm and another flood of warmth and blissful relief washed over her. She didn't have to hold back from him anymore.

This connection between her and Anríq—it really did feel like healing—as healing as serving those children....and everyone else.

It gave her some reprieve from the Darkness. This was one of the very few things she'd found that actually made her feel better.

They broke apart at the same time and went back to their usual comfortable routine.

After a minute, he said, "Let's see if we can meet up with Yann."

She opened her Coil projection and Anríq put his hand under hers, but this time, he actually laid his palm against her knuckles from underneath. She shivered at his touch, but the next minute, he sent a flow of magic into her hand.

The image expanded, but the lines showing where Yann was got blurry between multiple collapsing Layers.

"At least we know he's still alive....and look." She pointed at the second line next to his. "It looks like he and Marine are still together."

"That's good, but we won't be able to find them if we can't trace them to any specific Layer."

"Their route has gotten blurry before," she pointed out. "We should keep an eye on them. When they come to a more distinct Layer, we can intercept them."

He nodded. "So what do you want to do in the meantime?"

"Don't you already know that? Don't you need to wander until someone asks you for help?"

"I wasn't sure if you wanted to do the same thing."

She smiled up at him and found her cheeks burning. "I have nothing else to do."

Chapter 22

Anríq and Eliska came to the road and headed down it in no particular direction.

She fell in step next to him and another wave of relief eased the tension in her middle. She was traveling with him as a Servant.

She knew that now even if she never said it out loud. They were going to look for anyone who needed help—or anyone who asked them for help.

It felt good. It felt like the right path to take. It was the only path she could take from now on.

He didn't ask about her decision. She would have been surprised if he hadn't already figured it out."

They barely talked all day even when they sat down under a tree to drink some water and eat the last of their food.

She didn't need to talk to him about anything—maybe ever again. This must be how it was for the Servants.

The pair kept going until the sun started to go down. They didn't discuss where or how they would camp.

Eliska started to look around for a place to spend the night when another traveler hustled over the hill in front of them.

Anríq and Eliska had been hiking toward it and the surrounding hills all day. Eliska couldn't see what she and Anríq would find beyond those hills. It didn't really seem to matter anymore.

The traveler walked fast and even broke into a few bursts of jogging. A second later, two more people came over the hill behind him at the same pace. Were they chasing him?

The first traveler looked middle-aged. One of the followers was a woman. The other was a young man barely in his twenties.

They all wore nice clothes—as nice as the clothes people wore in Tenby, but these had a different style.

The middle-aged man wore a tailored black suit, a thin ribbon tie, and a black waistcoat over his starched, pristine white shirt.

A gold watch chain hung across his midsection and the hard heels of his polished black boots rang on the pavement.

The woman wore an expensive dress with tons of lace, but it didn't have all the bunched ruffles in the back like the Tenby women wore.

This one hung almost to her ankles with long, smooth skirts, a tight corset around her ribs, and puffed sleeves attached to a scooped bodice.

She also wore a gold necklace with a carved broach hanging in her cleavage and a white lace strip around her throat.

Elaborate brown curls bunched around her head and covered her shoulders in unnaturally luxurious tresses.

The young man wore a more modest suit of brown tweed without a watch chain. His curly brown hair bounced when he hurried up the road. He kept extending his arm toward the woman to support her even though she could walk just fine on her own.

The middle-aged man rushed up to Anríq and grabbed his hand. "You're a Servant! Please—please come to our city! All our people are stricken with a plague and it keeps spreading by the day. We don't know where else to turn. Our own healer died from the same plague. No one will come near our city so we haven't been able to get any other healers. Please! You have to come! People are dying every day."

Anríq studied him while the man poured out his request. The woman and the younger man caught up with him while he was still talking. They crowded around and all looked up at Anríq with the same pleading look.

Anríq didn't take his hand out of the man's grasp. Anríq shut his eyes and bowed. "I will serve."

"Oh, thank you!" The man kissed his hand. "Thank you so much! You don't know how grateful we are! Please come! The sun will be going down soon. You don't want to get caught out here on the road. Follow me and I'll show you where to go. We have a place for you to stay. We just thought....." The man's eyes darted to Eliska.

She read his mind. "Don't worry about it. You don't have to go to any trouble for me."

The man frowned at her. "Who are you?"

"I'm Eliska. Anríq is a friend of mine. We're traveling together. I'm a magic-user, too, so I'll come with him and help him heal your people. You can put me up in a barn if you have one. I don't care where I stay."

The man's expression cleared. "That won't be necessary. We heard a Servant was coming this way, but we assumed he'd be traveling alone. The house we planned to offer to the Servant has more than one room. Follow me." He turned back to Anríq. The man didn't let go of Anríq's hand all the way up the road. "My name is Quentienne Teofil. I'm the Mayor of Symphorian. This is my nephew Ogost Fournier and his mother, Odael. Ah! Here comes Brother Arsenault."

Right then, a third man rushed over the same hill coming from the same direction. He wore a full-length black cassock down to his feet.

A line of black buttons ran from his tightly buttoned collar all the way to the ground. He wore no other decoration.

"This is our parish priest," Quentienne explained. "He's been supervising what poor healing efforts we can give our people, but it isn't nearly enough."

Brother Arsenault charged forward and seized Anríq's other hand. "Oh, thank God you found him! Please come to our city! We're on our last legs."

"I already explained everything to him, Brother," Quentienne explained. "He's already agreed to come—along with his traveling companion here."

"Oh, thank you!" Brother Arsenault kissed Anríq's other hand and tried to tow him down the road faster.

Eliska stood back out of the way while these people started explaining everything to Anríq.

They all fell silent when the party crested the same hill and looked down the other side.

The city of Symphorian sprawled in a valley between this line of hills and towering mountains beyond. Eliska could see vehicles lining the streets, but she didn't see any people out and about. The whole city fell into a ghostly silence.

The four townspeople halted there and so did Anríq and Eliska. Her blood ran cold when she saw a massive cloud of Dark magic looming over the city.

It didn't collapse this Island nor did it threaten the city itself. The cloud just hovered there in a ring around the city's perimeter about a thousand feet off the ground. The cloud didn't descend even far enough to touch the church spire.

The setting sun shone just as beautifully on all the rest of the landscape. Whatever that cloud was, it only threatened the city and nothing else.

"It's been like this since the beginning," Brother Arsenault murmured. "Our magic-user tried to break the curse, but then he fell to the same plague and we've had no one since besides you two."

Anríq narrowed his eyes at the cloud.

Eliska cringed at the sight of it. It spoke to the Darkness inside her and not in a nice way. Symphorian wasn't suffering from a plague after all. That Dark force must be going after this city for some reason.

Just then, a cool wind blew across the hilltops. It tossed Eliska's cloak, Odael's curls, and Brother Arsenault's cassock in the breeze.

"We better go," Brother Arsenault murmured. "We don't want to get caught out here after dark."

They started forward. Eliska found herself migrating toward the city along with the rest. A feeling of impending doom gripped her when the party made it as far as the city walls.

Watch towers and battlements lined the walls where the Black Watch should have manned those posts.

A shield on the side of one of the watch towers bore the Watch's insignia, but no Watchmen stood guard. Nothing could protect Symphorian from the Dark force that really threatened it.

Anríq scowled all the way inside. The four townspeople surrounded him and Eliska on their way through the streets.

Only a few people showed their faces outside and everyone seemed to be in a rush to go somewhere or other. Not nearly enough healthy, able-bodied people kept the city going. How much longer could Symphorian hold out?

Night settled over the buildings and streets as the party entered the gates. The stars came out, but that Dark cloud never went away. It cast a pall over the whole place.

"We've been keeping the sick people isolated in the church," Brother Arsenault explained." "We didn't know if whatever was wrong with them might be contagious...."

"Is it?" Eliska asked. "How easily does it spread through the population?"

"We have no idea how it spreads or even if it spreads," the priest replied. "We haven't been able to find any connection between how or when people get sick. ...and now so many people are getting sick that none of us has time to figure it out. It doesn't seem to matter anymore where it comes from or how it spreads. We've all been working our fingers to the bone trying to cure everyone."

Eliska glanced up at the sky. "I don't think we have to wonder where it comes from."

Brother Arsenault halted in front of the church and pulled open a giant set of peaked wooden doors in the front.

They swung inward on a scene of mass death unlike anything Eliska could have imagined.

The people of Symphorian must have been the church-going kind because it was a big church. They had removed all the pews from the church's interior.

Sick people lay on blankets covering every square inch of the bare floor with more blankets spread over each person.

They sweated, trembled, and their teeth chattered all over the place. So many sick people packed the church that the few attendants had left only a few inches between one patient and another.

There must be close to five hundred people in this church.

"We have more in the rectory upstairs and in the gymnasium down the street," Brother Arsenault murmured. "We don't have enough space for everyone and more people keep getting sick every day."

Five women in white uniforms hurried from patient to patient. One woman carried a wooden bucket with steam billowing out of it.

She set the bucket down next to each person, ladled the steaming liquid into a bowl, and went through a painstaking process of lifting each patient on her arm and helping them to drink the liquid.

The process took forever. The patients trembled so badly that they got the soup all over their blankets. Some were too semi-conscious even to realize that she was trying to feed them.

Another woman went around trying with the same mixture of success to give the patients water.

The third went from person to person changing their blankets. She had to roll each person onto their side, scoot the old blankets away, arrange new ones under the patient, and then remove the old blankets for cleaning.

Eliska took a deep breath. "This is so much worse than I imagined."

"You wouldn't say that if you knew how many other patients we still have lying in the same condition all over town," Brother Arsenault husked. "Some don't even make it here or the other places we have set aside for them. They just stay in their houses with no one to take care of them."

She glanced up at Anríq. She had no idea where to even start.

He turned to the left and approached the very first bed. The person lying in it was another middle-aged man, but this one looked like a rough working man. He didn't keep his hair neatly cut and a scraggly beard covered his face.

Sweat saturated his hair and beard and he quacked with tremors that made the blanket ride down to his chest.

Anríq extended his hand over the man's chest and Anríq's hand started to shake, too.

Eliska took one more deep breath, but she already knew what she would find when she started trying to heal these people. Was she really ready to go that far?

Chapter 23

Anríq turned to the left and Eliska turned to the right. All the doubt went out of her mind when she saw a little boy lying in line with the other patients.

She walked over to him and stared down at him. He didn't shake and tremble. He was almost dead already, but not quite. He held on by a slim thread.

He lay perfectly still and ghostly white under his blankets. He already looked like a corpse. Eliska didn't even have to hold out her hand to know what was wrong with him.

She could have sent a healing flow of magic into him, but that wouldn't save him—not quickly enough.

Brother Arsenault came over to her. He must have figured out that he could talk to her instead of Anríq.

"Can you tell what's causing the disease?"

"It isn't a disease. The Dark is invading their souls. It's taking over the whole city. It will kill everyone if something doesn't stop it."

"*Can* you stop it?" Brother Arsenault asked.

She didn't answer. She hardly dared to touch this boy.

She already knew she could heal him and she could do it quickly enough to save him. There was only one way. She just had to take his Darkness on herself the way she took it from Barsali.

She would do it the minute she touched him. He was as good as dead if she didn't. It was that simple.

She didn't have to turn around to look at the hundreds of people behind her.

Now that she tapped the Darkness inside her, she felt all the other people lying at death's door all over this city.

Brother Arsenault told the truth about how bad it was. Almost three thousand people lay dying all over town.

They packed the gymnasium, the rectory, and a few other larger community centers farther away.

Hundreds more lay on floors and beds and couches in their houses.

She didn't dare to look up to see how or even if Anríq was trying to heal that man over there. She didn't need to know. No way could she let this boy die—or any of the rest of them.

She stuck out her hand and didn't let herself hesitate. She pressed her hand onto his chest and the Dark rushed into her in a death torrent.

This boy's name was Jeovin and she flashed into his memories.

She watched him playing with his sister and brother. She saw him wrestling with his brother and being extra aggressive. He let his naturally violent tendencies run away with him.

The memories sped up and he sat back on the floor watching his sister open a large box wrapped up as a gift.

She exclaimed and almost cried when she lifted a tiny grey kitten out of the box. She hugged it, petted it, and exclaimed over its tiny ears, tail, and paws.

The Dark burned into Jeovin's insides when he saw how much she loved the kitchen. He waited, bided his time, and stole the kitten when his sister was out of the house.

He took the tiny creature into an alley a mile away, put the kitten on the ground, and watched it toddle around for a while.

Then he drove a long marlinspike through its head and tossed the dead body down the drain in the side street.

He went home and went about his business as if nothing had happened.

He feigned ignorance when his sister came home and couldn't find her kitten. Their parents searched the whole neighborhood. No one ever found the body and no one ever found out Jeovin's secret.

The Dark invaded Eliska's soul. It spread to every part of her and left him clean and whole.

As soon as she removed the Dark curse, love and happiness overflowed his heart when he remembered his family. He fell into a peaceful sleep dreaming about what would happen when he went home to them.

She took her hand off him and buckled almost on top of him as all that Darkness overwhelmed her insides.

Every Dark memory of everything he'd ever done wrong, all his worst secrets and nightmares—they roiled inside her in a brutal tempest of pain, rage, and guilt mixed with resentment and sadistic fury.

She gasped in horror at everything running through her heart and mind right now. Cold sweat broke out all over her and she struggled to breathe.

"Are you all right?" Brother Arsenault asked.

She forced herself to stand up. "I'm....I'm fine. He's whole now."

"Oh, thank you!" The priest grabbed her hand and kissed it. "Bless you, my child. Bless you!"

She revolted at his touch, but she stopped herself from yanking his hand away. A sick feeling of cold dread burned a hole through her insides.

She turned away and saw the next person line. This one was a woman with a huge swollen pregnant belly sticking up from under the blanket.

Eliska stumbled on her way over there. What would it be this time?

She went down on one knee next to the woman and placed her hand on the woman's chest right above her heart.

A catastrophic wave of gripping fear seized Eliska by the guts. This woman didn't carry any Dark secrets—not like the boy over there.

This woman was the wife of the working man Anríq first approached. This woman suffered from crippling fear, first that her husband would die and leave her alone, second that something would happen to her unborn child, and also that carrying and giving birth to this child would kill her in the process.

Terror plagued this woman day and night, but she never told her husband or anyone else. She never confided even in the parish priest.

The Dark fear ate away at her on the inside and poisoned her child even before she gave birth to it.

Eliska didn't sense anything physically wrong with either of them. The woman's own fears turned Dark and robbed her of all hope and pleasure.

Eliska gritted her teeth. Sweat trickled down her forehead and stung her lips and eyes, but she refused to give up.

She'd already committed herself to this path. She couldn't go back, especially not for someone like this woman. Did the Dark invade her and cause her to develop this fear—or did the Dark just prey on a fear this woman already had?

It didn't matter because Eliska couldn't let the woman die—or her child die.

Eliska pulled the Dark out of her. This patient took a lot more effort because there were two of them.

The woman's fear terrified her unborn child. The child was a girl and she developed a pathological fear of the day she would finally be born into the world.

She suffered from nightmares about something terrible happening either during the birth process or afterward. She didn't want to get born or face such a terrifying world. Eliska couldn't stand to leave either of them in such torment.

She worked harder and harder to suck out all that Darkness. When she finished, she slumped over the bed shaking all over. Brother Arsenault wasn't here. He'd crossed over to check on Anríq.

Anríq still stood over the working man, the pregnant woman's husband. Anríq drew symbols on the man's body and placed items from his bags around the man's bed and on top of him.

Eliska saw at one glance exactly what Anríq was trying to do. He was driving the Dark out. He knew better than to take it on himself.

Her head swam when she tried to stand up, but she pushed herself to the next bed when she saw a frail old man trembling all over. He kept whimpering and sobbing in his sleep.

She knelt down next to his bed, touched him, and flashed into his memories. He experienced the same loop of nightmarish memories from his childhood of being beaten by his father and stuck with pins by his mother.

Eliska went through the cycle again and again. The boy endured these tortures almost every day for years before he got old enough to run away from home.

The man started sobbing uncontrollably when she pulled the Dark out of him. She couldn't take the memories away, but she broke down the veil of fear and shame enough for him to actually feel how much his parents hurt him.

She stayed with him longer than she needed to just to make him feel better. She flooded him with her magic to offer him a little more healing.

She really did swoon when she finally took her hand off his chest. She had to sit there fighting back the cold before her head cleared enough to move on to the next patient.

Eliska only had to swivel around to look at the person in the next bed.

This one was another mother with three young children crowded against her under one blanket. They had all either passed out or fallen asleep with their arms around her.

Eliska put her hand on the woman's chest and jolted in alarm when her magic connected to all four patients at once. These four were even farther gone than Jeovin.

The woman had lost her husband when a building collapsed while she'd been pregnant with her youngest son. She had to raise these children on her own since then.

Fear and desperation drove her to work harder than she should have. She stayed up until the early hours of the morning sewing and doing laundry for people around Symphorian to earn enough money to keep her children fed and housed.

Eliska ran through their memories of the mother propped up in bed with her children cuddled against her. They lay in exactly the same combination of positions as they lay on the church floor right now.

She talked to them, laughed with them, sang to them, petted them, and showered them with more love than Eliska could stand. Just watching them and feeling the love between them brought tears to her eyes.

The Dark threatened to tow her down into a sea of endless horror. The woman and all her children hovered on the very brink of death.

Eliska fought and struggled to pull them back, but the Dark proved too strong. It almost pulled Eliska down with it. She couldn't save them no matter how hard she tried.

She broke free just in time for the Dark to completely wipe out the woman and all three children. Eliska jolted back to her senses still sitting on the church floor.

Anríq worked on the other side of the room going from patient to patient. He wouldn't be able to heal them fast enough before more people died. He took too long to go through the process of protecting himself and them.

She glanced down at the woman and her children. They lay in the same positions as if they were asleep. No one would ever disturb them again. They would stay locked in their loving embrace forever.

A hot, salty tear streaked down Eliska's cheek at the sight of them. She understood that love now.

She left them there and moved on to the next bed. The momentum and certainty of what she had to do took over.

She didn't think about it anymore. She had to save these people.

She could carry the Dark for all of them. Her magic would protect her from it. Even if it didn't protect her, it belonged to her. She already was Dark. What did a little more Darkness mean to someone like her?

Better for her to take it and leave these people whole and clean to live their lives. It was the least she could do for them and the rest of the world.

At least she found a way to make up for all the wasted years she spent wandering the Coil with no purpose in life.

Chapter 24

Eliska passed to the next patient's bed. A businessman in a nice suit lay under the blankets. No one had bothered to change him out of the clothes he was wearing when he got sick.

The man's wife and three children lay in the beds beyond his. He had two sons aged fourteen and eleven and a nine-year-old daughter.

The minute she touched the father, she plunged into another nightmare scene of him violently attacking his wife and children whenever he felt the need to let off some steam.

He enjoyed venting his energy on them for no other reason than that it gave him a feeling of power to do it.

He liked the look of terror in his wife's and daughter's eyes. He used to like the see that look from his sons, too, when they were younger.

Now he enjoyed seeing that fear distorted into rage. His sons hated him, but they couldn't stop him from doing it anyway.

Eliska went through a split second of doubt about whether she should heal this man at all.

The next instant, she planted her hand on his chest and took it all—all the rage, all the power, all the brutal, vindictive, careless glee he felt when he did it.

He was no different from Jeovin. She really didn't care anymore if someone deserved to live or not. Who was she to decide that?

For some reason, this church made all these patients equal. She didn't come here to decide who should live and who should die. She would gladly have saved Aline's life if Eliska only had a chance to.

Eliska didn't care if someone insulted her in the worst possible ways. She didn't care if someone deserved to live or if they would continue to live a decent life after this.

She healed the man and then worked her way down the line to heal his wife, his sons, and his daughter.

She went through the whole scene of years and years of violence as each one poured out their memories into Eliska's soul. She took it all one brutal punch and kick after another.

The sons fantasized about killing their father. Their own Darkness made them violent.

They vented their frustrations on each other, their sister, and other children they knew.

Eliska started to see a pattern between Jeovin, these older boys, and the father. One memory blended in with another.

All these people—they were all one person. All their memories got jumbled in her mind. She couldn't keep track of where one person ended and another began.

She saw herself going through the same memories...or were they just nightmares? Did they ever really happen?

She flashed back and forth between the old man getting beaten by his father as a young boy....to the sons....to the father getting beaten by his father.....

It never ended. She was each of those people. She felt all their emotions. She felt every sensation.

She finished healing the little girl and flopped across the girl's chest trying to keep track of all the pictures in her head.

The townspeople's good memories got mixed up in there, too. She saw their smiles, felt their hugs, their kisses, and their overpowering love for each other.

That love cracked her heart in half. She couldn't contain it all—not the way she could contain the Dark.

She never dreamed anyone could love another person so much—but hadn't she loved the children like this?

She jolted back to her senses when someone touched her shoulder and said her name.

She reared away from the girl to find Anríq bending over her. "Eliska? Are you all right?"

"Huh?" She looked all around her trying to remember where she was and even who she was. "I'm fine."

He used his finger to pull a sweaty lock of hair out of her face. Then he did the same thing where her hair plastered to her neck. "You should slow down. Don't heal people so fast. Pace yourself."

"I'm fine." She turned to the next person. "Are you going back over there?"

She glanced across the church. She couldn't tell from here how many people Anríq healed—like it mattered.

He answered her, but she didn't hear what he said. Another wave of memories wiped out all awareness of the church around her.

She couldn't even tell anymore which of the patients the memory came from or if it came from any of them. Maybe she just imagined it.

She scooted to the next bed. An elderly woman lay on it with her hand sticking out from under the blanket.

She held hands with an equally old man in the next bed. No one had tried to take their hands apart.

The sight of them holding hands did something to Eliska. She had to give them back to each other. Anyone who felt that kind of love for another person definitely deserved to live.

She started with the woman just because she happened to be lying closer. Eliska accessed both of them through their joined hands.

The man had been abandoned on the streets as a toddler and dragged himself up by pure grit and hard work. He and the woman had four adult children living in this city—all with their own families.

The woman had been the daughter of a wealthy aristocrat in Symphorian.

Her father threw her out on the street with nothing but the clothes on her back when he found out she fell in love with a poor laborer from the wrong side of town.

These two had been married for sixty years and still loved each other as much as the first day they met.

Eliska almost broke down crying when she felt how much they loved each other. She had to take their Darkness just to give them a chance at whatever years they had left.

They spent their free time spoiling their children and grandchildren. The two old people showered their grandchildren with love. The old man lived a second life through the young ones and got back the joy and innocence he lost in his youth.

Healing him broke Eliska's heart, but she didn't stop until she left him clean, whole, and glowing in the beauty of the family he worked so hard to build.

She kept working steadily for another four hours before Anríq came back to find her.

"Come with me," he told her. "Brother Arsenault is taking us to the house where we'll stay."

She stumbled out of the church and almost tripped over the patients. The attendants had moved out the people Anríq and Eliska healed and brought in new people.

Eliska's vision blurred looking at them all. She couldn't keep track of every detail of these people's lives and she didn't want to.

She also didn't keep track of the details of the house she and Anríq were staying in. She stayed upright just long enough to find the bedroom.

She toppled onto the bed and passed out, but she suffered from nightmares of all those memories twisted together.

She went through years of torturous desperation as the little boy surviving on the street. She suffered the worst grief, shame, and humiliation when the girl's father threw her out of the house because her sweetheart was too poor.

People spit on her when they saw her around town after that. They even did it after she was a married woman with her own children.

They spit on her in front of her children, but she explained it all to them by saying that those people didn't understand what a prince their father was.

Eliska woke up in the middle of the night and stumbled out of the house. The city lay in darkness....or was it Darkness? She couldn't tell the difference anymore.

The house Brother Arsenault gave her and Anríq attached to the back of the church. The two buildings shared a wall with a long corridor connecting them together.

She walked outside, around the church, and found a water faucet built into the church wall. She'd spent too much time in Tenby not to recognize the tap.

She turned it on and stuck her head under the flood. The water chilled and soaked her hair. Water soaked her clothes when she straightened up, but she didn't mind.

She stood there swaying for a minute as more memories and nightmares washed over her and through her. She saw them whether she kept her eyes open or shut.

Her awareness of where she was kept blurring into different scenes, both of what she'd seen in the church and elsewhere.

Those memories got mixed up with Barsali's memories and a few other random hallucinations she didn't recognize.

She stumbled back upstairs and passed Anríq's room on the way to her own bed.

He lay curled up on his side on top of the bed. He had his shirt, weapons, and bags off.

She stopped in the doorway to stare at him while he slept. Was he having nightmares, too?

Memories of the Barbarians' camp flooded her. She went through a torrent of memories she'd never sent before—and yet she recognized them.

She saw Anríq as a little boy running to catch up with his much older brothers. She saw him as an older boy trying to learn to use his magic to heal people.

Then she went through the whole torturous process of getting attacked, beaten, threatened, and eventually shunned when he left the tribe and his father turned his back on Anríq.

More memoirs swamped her awareness. They came from other Barbarians....and other people in this city....healthy people....and more people from farther away in the Coil....Tenby people...Middleborough people....

She blundered back to her room, tried to sit down on the bed, and missed.

She landed on the floor and crawled back onto the bed. She lay there panting hard while the room spun in circles around her.

She was still lying there in a fever when Anríq came for her the next morning. He sat down next to her and raked his fingers across her sweaty forehead to comb the hair out of her eyes.

"Slow down," he told her. "You'll make yourself sick if you keep going like this."

"I can't let anyone else die," she mumbled. "I already lost four of them yesterday."

She had to sit on the edge of the bed before she pushed herself to her feet.

She held herself together on the way to the church. She didn't want Anríq to see how much this Darkness affected her.

Once they got there, they split up the way they did yesterday. He took the left side of the church while she took the right.

She started on a man who had already lost his wife and three children to this curse. He actually fought back when Eliska tried to take the Dark from him. He tried to keep it so it would kill him, too.

He raged against her efforts to try to save him. Then he plunged into grief-stricken despair when she succeeded and he remembered what he lost.

She dragged her miserable way through all his memories and the torment of watching his loved one die before his eyes. The grief poisoned him and let the Dark in so he became cursed, too.

He burst into tears, turned his back on her, and refused to look at her when she finally finished taking the last shred of Darkness out of him.

She tried to send him some healing magic through his back, but he spun around, lashed out to punch her, and bellowed at her to leave him alone.

He cursed her as a witch and roared for the whole church to hear that he wished she was dead in his wife's place.

Eliska backed away. Brother Arsenault moved in with some of the attendants and removed the man from the church.

Everyone else stood around staring, including Anríq and the other attendants. Then the hum of activity returned and everyone went on as before.

Chapter 25

One patient blended in with another. Eliska healed another family of five, but she couldn't keep track of their memories. Everything got mixed up with the memories of people she'd already healed.

She was just starting on another elderly couple when a mother stumbled in carrying a child less than two years old.

The mother held the little boy in his arms, cast a desperate glance around, and charged Eliska. "Please...." the woman begged. "Please ....you have to save him....He's dying!"

Eliska only nodded, but she couldn't put her hand on the boy's chest while his mother held him so tightly. She put her hand on his head instead and plunged into another scene of unspeakable horror.

The woman had been one of five survivors of a town razed by the Corsairs.

She'd witnessed the bloody slaughter of everyone she knew when the Corsairs cut down men, women, and children without mercy.

She only survived by getting buried under piles of bodies and pretending to be dead.

All of that translated through her child.

Eliska took all their Darkness and wound up taking all the Darkness from the slaughtered town, too—and from the Corsairs—and from everyone else who survived. It all flowed into her through an unbroken channel of Darkness.

Was the cloud up there above the city feeding all this Darkness into her? Was it taking her over? She couldn't stop it.

The woman broke down in tears after Eliska took her hand away and said the boy was whole and only sleeping now.

The woman actually went down on one knee, kissed Eliska's hand, and thanked her with tears pouring down her cheeks.

Eliska turned away feeling sick. She could barely stand to look at the woman. Eliska knew way too much about this woman now.

Eliska went back to healing everyone else. She worked her way down the rows of patients one bed at a time. She didn't even try to keep track of their memories, but some of them stuck out anyway.

She came to a boy of about ten. He would have reminded Eliska of Anthane except that this boy had black hair instead of sandy-blonde like Anthane's.

This boy was awake when Eliska got to him. His frightened eyes darted in her direction.

"Who are you?" he gasped.

"My name is Eliska. I'm here to help you and hopefully heal you."

"Don't," he whispered. "It will hurt you."

"Better me than you." She sat down next to him. "What's your name?"

"Kasir," he half-whispered. "You don't want to see."

She couldn't look at him. "I've seen worse. Believe me."

She raised her hand to touch him, but he managed to lift his arm and block her. "They're all gone," he whispered. "I'm the only one left."

Her eyes shot to his face. "What do you mean?"

"They all died. I watched them die. I'm the only one left alive."

"Who?" she asked. She didn't want to know.

"My mother and father and brothers and sisters. They got sick in our house. I was there. I watched them die one by one."

Eliska couldn't listen to this anymore. She carried too many horrors in her head already. "Then it's all the more important that we save you." She raised her hand again.

He shot out his arm and knocked her hand away. "Don't!" his features pinched and he forced himself to look away. "Don't look. It's too awful."

"It will be worth it to me if I save you. I can't just sit here and let you die."

"You should," he muttered. "It would be for the best."

"It wouldn't be for the best. You could have a full life in front of you. You could save other people or do some good for someone. Besides, if you die, then you'll make me Darker than I already am."

He glanced in her direction. He had the eyes of a child, but they brimmed with a depth of profound understanding she couldn't remember seeing in anyone so young.

Did he understand what she didn't say—that she was already Dark? Taking his Darkness wouldn't make that much difference in the grand scheme of things.

One person's Darkness didn't amount to much. A whole city full of Dark power? That was another matter.

She didn't tell him that, though. She clasped his hand and eased his arm down as gently as she could.

"I have to save you," she murmured. "That's what I'm here for. That's all I'm here for."

He didn't fight her again and he passed out when she tapped his memories.

She let herself slip off into another delirium so she wouldn't have to witness all the nightmarish horror of him watching his father, mother, and siblings die one after the other.

She tried not to feel his grief and terror as he took care of each one. He worked himself into an exhausted fever trying to save them all when he was only a little boy himself.

That exhaustion and terror let the Dark in for him, too. He might have survived if not for that.

She drained it all away and left him sleeping peacefully in his blankets.

The attendants followed her all day. They had to work fast evacuating all the people she healed and bringing in new ones to take their places. Was there any end to it?

Anríq worked through the crowd much more slowly on his side of the room. She made sure not to look at what he was doing.

She sure hoped he wasn't watching what she was doing, but she already pretty much knew he was.

The poison built to an unstoppable torrent churning inside her. She didn't even make it until sundown before she couldn't take anymore.

She stumbled out of the church, down the corridor, and into the house where she stayed with Anríq. She buckled onto her bed and sat there shivering with her head hanging down on her chest.

Her teeth chattered and cold sweat soaked her clothes. She couldn't even summon the energy to lie down.

The mattress compressed next to her when someone sat down on the bed at her side. It could only be one person. No one else would have come in here.

"You're making yourself sick." Anríq pressed his hand to her forehead. "You can't keep taking all this Darkness."

"I can take it," she croaked. "My magic is strong enough to contain it. These people can't. They'll die if I don't."

"You'll die if you keep going like this."

She had to summon all her effort just to shake her head. "I'll be okay. I'll heal these people. Then I'll be able to recover."

"And what if you don't?"

A spasm stopped her from answering. Her closed eyes gave her a bird's-eye view into the Dark recesses of her own soul. She could take it. She could contain it. She could survive it.

That was the problem. It was her. She belonged to the Dark now. She always had belonged to the Dark. She just didn't want to admit it even to herself.

"Quentienne invited us to have dinner with him tonight," Anríq went on. "Stay here and get some rest before then. Don't go back to the church."

"I have to. More people will die if I don't."

She tried to stand up, but her legs wouldn't support her. She bounced back down on the mattress.

"Lie down and get some sleep," he told her. "If you feel better later, you can go back. Don't go back there now. I'll go and treat the more serious cases."

She didn't have the energy to argue with him. He worked much more slowly. He might not be able to get to the more serious cases in time to save them all.

A hundred images flashed before her eyes of whole families wiped out by the Dark. She's lost more than one after the woman and her three children.

She even lost some poisonous, violent families even after she took their Darkness. That happened way too often. She took their Darkness, poisoned herself, and the patients died anyway.

Anríq stood up, swiveled in front of her, took hold of her shoulders, and pushed her down on the bed.

She wilted under the pressure.

He draped the blankets over her, tucked her in, and left her there in the blissful silence, but nothing could stop all these pictures from marching through her head.

They blended with her own dreams and memories. She couldn't tell anymore whether she was awake or asleep.

Chapter 26

Eliska and Anríq walked down the Symphorian city streets to a massive house at the far end of town.

The house stood several stories taller than the church itself. Giant crystal windows covered the house's front wall. Peaked turrets stuck up from the roof and sprawling gardens lay behind the wrought iron gate.

The rest of the city lay in deathly silence. This city had even more sophisticated machinery than Tenby, but none of Symphorian's wonders were working right now. The whole city had ground to a halt.

Anríq pushed open the gates and stood back to let Eliska in. She struggled to keep her eyes open. Memories, secrets, and nightmares taken from the townspeople kept clouding her mind and blocking her awareness of where she was.

This only lasted for a few seconds before she swam back to consciousness. She didn't stop walking, so Anríq didn't notice anything.

She told herself that, anyway. He must have noticed. He was too astute not to.

He closed the gate behind her and they continued up the broad marble steps to the front door. He knocked on it and Quentienne opened it from the inside.

"Come in, come in!" he exclaimed. "All the servants are down with the plague, so it will just be the four of us tonight. Come in!"

He ushered the pair into a lofted foyer.

The place reminded Eliska of the Lake Country orphanage—or what the orphanage would have been in its prime.

Beautiful statues, oil paintings, tapestries, chandeliers, and plush carpet covered every inch of the grand house, but even this palatial residence sounded unearthly quiet.

Quentienne showed Anríq and Eliska into a massive dining room lined with suits of armor, flags embroidered with heraldry, and even more tapestries and paintings everywhere.

A long table with forty chairs ran down the center of the hall. Brother Arsenault was already there waiting for them.

He came forward to shake hands with both of them. "It's such a pleasure to welcome you. We're all so grateful you're here."

Eliska changed the subject by pointing at a red flag hanging near one of the suits of armor. "Do you know what this symbol means?"

"I've never seen it before," Brother Arsenault replied. "I mean, I've seen it *here*, but nowhere else. "

"That's strange, don't you think?" she asked. "You would think it would at least be shown or mentioned somewhere."

He shrugged it away. "I can't tell you that. Maybe Quentienne knows. This house has been in his family for generations."

"I don't know where it comes from, either," Quentienne replied. "The flag was there when I was small and it's been there ever since. I don't know where half the stuff in this house came from. It's all been handed down for as long as anyone could remember."

Eliska let it go. She didn't tell them about the Chivalric Order of Custodians.

For all she knew, the last knights died outside Tenby. They might be extinct by now.

"Come sit down!" Quentienne waved to the long table. Place settings sat in front of every chair, but the steaming trays of food only occupied one end of the table.

Quentienne pulled out the chair to the right of the one on the far end. "You sit here, Eliska. Anríq can sit next to Brother Arsenault."

Eliska sat down and rested her staff against the table next to her.

Anríq sat down in the velvet chair next to Brother Arsenault, but Anríq didn't take off his weapons, either.

Quentienne sat at the head of the table, but his presence didn't cast an imposing atmosphere over the place. This meeting felt comfortable and intimate despite the grand room.

Quentienne served everyone and talked about what Symphorian had been like before the plague hit. Brother Arsenault chimed in with details whenever he felt like it.

The three men started eating and Quentienne served wine to all four of them.

Eliska stared down at the food on her plate and pushed it back and forth with her fork. The thought of putting food in her mouth made her sick.

Quentienne kept mentioning names she knew.

She knew them as patients she'd already healed and she also knew them from her memories taken from neighbors, relatives, and even enemies of the people he mentioned.

Flashes of memory winked into her mind and then hovered before her eyes in a continuous stream of imagery.

She knew more about these people than Quentienne would ever know. She knew their deepest, darkest, deadliest, most closely guarded secrets.

The stream of pictures and the flood of emotions overwhelmed her mind. Her eyes lost focus more than once. She couldn't keep track anymore of how often she lost awareness of where she was.

She snapped back to her senses when someone said her name. "Eliska?"

She looked up. "Huh?"

Brother Arsenault frowned at her. "Are you feeling okay?"

"I'm fine. I'm just tired. I guess I just need to get some sleep."

"I was just wondering why you can heal people so much faster than Anríq can," Quentienne told her. "You've healed five times as many people."

Her eyes darted to Anríq. He stared at her across the table. His eyebrows twitched together in the center, but even his face became fuzzy and indistinct for a few seconds before she dragged her eyes back into focus.

She tried to shrug it away. "He has his own methods for doing things as you must have seen. The Servants develop their own ways of healing. They learn on their own, so each Servant does it differently."

"I don't see you using any method at all," Brother Arsenault remarked. "You just touch the person and they're healed. It's remarkable—miraculous, even."

"It isn't miraculous." She pushed back her chair. "Would you please excuse me? I really need to go lie down. I need to reserve my energy for tomorrow. Thank you for your hospitality. I'm sorry I'm not very good company right now."

"Not at all." Quentienne stood up. "I'll walk you out."

Eliska stumbled out of the houses. She mumbled through the last rushed goodbyes and thanks to Quentienne before she hurried back to the church.

She had to stop more than once to collapse against a wall and let her head spin. She panted hard. Her head throbbed with fever, but the rest of her felt ice cold.

She somehow made it back to the house, crawled into bed, and sank into unconsciousness.

She woke up in the middle of the night to find Anríq bending over her. He used something from his bags to draw on her neck, arms, hands, and feet.

She drifted out of consciousness once before she came back to her senses enough to talk to him. "I'm sorry....I had to leave...."

"You're in trouble, Eliska," he murmured. "The Dark is taking you over."

She shut her eyes and turned her head away, but he didn't stop working on her.

"You should change your methods of healing to drive the Dark out instead of taking it on yourself," he told her. "It will take longer, but at least you won't poison yourself."

"I can't let anyone die," she husked.

"Even yourself?"

She tried again to tell him that she wouldn't die, but right then, another flood of memories and overpowering emotions swept her out of her mind.

She tossed and turned in a fevered hallucination all night. She had nightmares in her sleep that didn't end when she jolted awake.

She even tapped the memories and phantoms haunting the healthy people in this city.

She snapped wide awake from a nightmare about Brother Arsenault getting locked in a cellar as a boy.

His father fed Arsenault and his three sisters on a few thin scraps of bread and water each day while the father hoarded his money for himself.

He invested it to build his wealth and refused to buy clothes or food for his children.

Arsenault got caught stealing food from a local grocer. The grocer had already noticed Arsenault stealing in the past and didn't say anything.

The man let Arsenault get away with it so he could take the food home to his sisters, which they ate in secret so their father wouldn't find out.

This time, though, the father spotted Arsenault from across the street, dragged the boy home by the hair, and locked him in the basement for a month with no food at all.

Arsenault suffered hallucinations and nightmares the whole time about what was happening to his sisters on the outside.

He wasted away to a skeleton and would have died, but the grocery got suspicious when the boy didn't come back to steal food. The grocer called the constable who raided the house and found Arsenault on the verge of death.

The local authorities removed him and his sisters from their father's custody and took them to the church where they were adopted and raised by the priests.

Chapter 27

E liska bolted straight upright in bed staring all around her before she remembered. She was still inside Brother Arsenault's memory of his father locking him in the cellar.

The cellar's damp stone walls blocked her from seeing anything outside. She went around the room again and again clawing at the stones and trying to find a way out, but she never found any.

The impenetrable darkness of the cellar took root in her soul and never left her, not even when Arsenault became a priest himself.

She floundered back to reality and stumbled out of bed. She needed air. She needed to go outside at least to convince herself that she still could.

She made it as far as the hall outside her room before her legs gave out. She crumpled to the floor and lacked the strength even to push herself up on her arms.

She must have drifted away in another river of memories before because she came back to reality to the sensation of Anríq picking her up. He lifted her in his strong arms and carried her back into her room.

He laid her on the bed and sat down next to her. He pressed a cold cloth to her forehead and ran it down her cheeks. "What do you see?" he asked.

She tried to shut her eyes, but that didn't block out the memories anymore. They overflowed her ability to contain them. She could barely choke out the words when she said, "You don't want to know."

"Don't go back to the church," he told her. "Or if you do, let me teach you some different ways of driving out the Dark so you don't take it on yourself."

She didn't tell him that she already knew how to drive out the Dark. That wasn't the problem.

Taking it was too easy. The Darkness already inside her magnetized the patients' Darkness with such a stronger pull.

Dark attracted Dark. It wanted to enter her to make her wholly Dark like itself.

She felt him touching her and doing things to different parts of her body. She dragged herself back to her senses just long enough to feel him pressing against her stomach.

She did her best to turn it into a joke even though she already knew he didn't mean anything by it.

"Be careful," she croaked. "Lanara will get jealous."

His eyes darted up to meet hers before he went back to what he was doing. She cringed under that look.

"Sorry," she muttered. "I shouldn't have said that. I know you don't think that way."

"Think what way?" he asked.

"About women. You don't think about getting with anyone. That's part of the Servant's vow, isn't it?"

"You're confusing the Servants with the Black Watch."

A lightning bolt went off in her mind when she realized what he just said. Her eyes flew open and her head snapped around to stare up at him. "What?"

"The Servant's vow isn't a vow of celibacy or chastity or whatever you call it."

She gasped out loud. "You mean you....you could.....?"

"It's happened before. Some Servants travel in pairs and even marry each other and have children together."

Her jaw dropped. "Why didn't you tell me?! Why did you let me think....?"

She broke off and blinked as the puzzle pieces clicked into place.

He brought his wet rag up to her face. The sensation of it passing down her cheeks sent a shiver through her—and not the kind she'd been suffering from with the nightmares.

He wiped the rag over each of her eyes one after the other and then across her mouth before he started wiping down her neck.

That sensation—that slow, deliberate, intimate touch....

All this time, she'd been telling herself it didn't mean anything. She always told herself he couldn't because he was a Servant.

He read her mind, dipped his eyes to his hands working over her, and raised them to lock on her.

"I didn't tell you because I needed to be sure you took the Servant's path for yourself and not so you could be with me," he murmured. "That's what you did, isn't it? You took the Servant's path."

She tore her eyes away. She couldn't stand the way he was looking at her right now.

"I'll never be a Servant like you," she choked. "You're so much better than I am."

"You are a Servant. You're acting as a Servant right now with these people. You're sick in this bed because you're giving them everything you have. You're serving all of humanity."

She couldn't answer. She'd always dreaded what would happen when he found out about her taking the Servant's path. She couldn't face him.

She would never be the kind of Servant he was. She could only ever hope to approximate his goodness and selfless dedication.

Even thinking of herself as a Servant made her too ashamed to look at Anríq. She couldn't call herself that. She wasn't good enough and never would be.

"Why didn't you tell Lanara and the others that we were together?" he asked.

She couldn't answer that, either. She would never get together with Anríq—not ever. She wouldn't want to poison him with her Darkness.

She would probably never get together with anyone. She never even thought about it before she met up with the Black Watch.

One of these days, she would lose Anríq, Yann, and Marine the same way she lost Wesh and the Watchmen.

Then she would go back to wandering alone. Serving and healing would give her the only relief from this curse.

"Aren't you even going to talk to me?" Anríq asked. "You've never been this quiet before. You've been touching me and helping me all this time. Don't tell me you're going to turn away from me now because of this."

She couldn't even bring herself to look at him. "Actually, I was thinking about Yann. He's jealous of you because he knows I like you."

"He has nothing to be jealous of," Anríq replied. "I have nothing to give you besides the wanderer's life."

"I already have that."

Now he was the one to turn away. He dropped his rag in a bucket of water on the floor by her bed. "He's a good man and he cares for you very much. You couldn't ask for better than that."

"You're a good man and I know you care for me very much," she pointed out.

"At least he has a profession." He stood up and went back to his old business-like ways. He pulled the blankets over her and tucked her in before he left the room.

She faded out of consciousness again. The memories of dying people wiped out what he said about the Servant's path. It might as well have been a celibate path for all the good it would do her.

She would wander alone with no one. That was her service—to keep this poison isolated inside herself. She could carry it. No one else had to find out about it.

She must have fallen asleep again—or maybe she slipped into a coma.

She floated back to awareness in deep darkness. A faint light glimmered out in the hallway and she heard Anríq and Brother Arsenault talking out there.

"She's dying," Anríq murmured. "I can't save her."

"Can't you heal her the way you heal people in the church? Is it the same curse?"

"She's taken on the Dark from all the people she saved. I don't do it that way. That's why it takes me so much longer. I have to go through a series of protections to drive the Dark out. I tried to tell her to do it that way, but she wanted to save as many people as possible."

"Isn't there anything you can do?" Brothers Arsenault asked. "More than two hundred people are alive because of her."

"I would kill myself if I tried to help her. It's too Dark and too deep. Her magic is so much stronger than mine—and she doesn't think she deserves anything else. She might even think she doesn't deserve to live. The Dark might have poisoned her as far as that already—and she still thinks she's going to keep going."

"We can't just let her die!' Brother Arsenault exclaimed.

"I don't see how we can stop it now," Anríq murmured. "I can't touch this. I don't dare to."

Chapter 28

E liska rested her hand on the church threshold and looked in at exactly the same number of people. They lay in rows sweating, shaking, and trying to stop their teeth from chattering. At least half had already fallen unconscious.

Anríq turned off to the left and went to work. That left her to turn to the right.

She halted at the first bed she came to. A woman lay under the blankets and she didn't move even to open her eyes. It was the mother of the young child Eliska saved earlier—the woman whose town got wiped out by Corsairs.

Eliska gulped down a wave of nausea. Where was this woman's child—the child Eliska risked so much to save? She couldn't leave that child motherless.

Eliska rested her hand on the woman's chest and jolted so hard she almost lost contact with the woman.

The Darkness raged inside the woman's innermost being, but it wasn't Corsairs marauding across the landscape. It was Darklings.

They stormed all over the countryside tearing towns apart, devouring people, and destroying whole cities in their path.

Eliska dropped into that landscape and fired her staff at the Darklings. They turned on her thundering to shake the Earth. They all converged on her.

She darted here and there shooting her magic at any Darkling that got too close.

She couldn't stop long enough to draw the Dark out of this woman. Eliska had to work her hardest just to hold the Darklings at bay.

Without warning, the ground imploded beneath her feet. It sucked down into a vast Dark vortex pulling everything into it, including the Darklings.

That Dark power took hold of Eliska. It would drag her all the way down into the Dark if she didn't fight back.

She slammed her staff into the ground with all her might and jerked back to full awareness on her knees by the woman's bed in the church.

Eliska stared down at the woman's still body. She was dead. The Dark took her and almost took Eliska.

Eliska staggered away from the woman and halted next to another bed. This patient was an elderly man with a scruffy white beard and bushy white hair. He still looked strong and muscular in his shoulders despite his many wrinkles.

A middle-aged man knelt next to the bed holding the patient's hand. The younger man looked up at Eliska through eyes overflowing with hopeless despair.

"You have to save him! You have to bring him back!" the younger man pleaded. "I'll do anything! I'll pay any price. Just tell me what I have to do to save him from this."

Eliska blinked at the younger man. It was the father she healed on her first day in this church—the father who brutalized his family.

A sickening wave of memories smeared through her mind. Her eyes bleared under the Dark wave as she remembered everything. She replayed this man's memories of his own father beating him as cruelly as this man beat his own sons—maybe even worse.

Now this man knelt by his father's bedside begging some stranger to save the man who tormented him and made his life a living hell.

She already knew what she would find when she placed her hand on the father's chest, but she did it anyway. What right did she have to judge anyone? She already saved the man. His sons might grow up to be as violent as he was.

None of that concerned her. She served all of humanity—all of it.

She would have healed the Corsairs who razed that woman's town. Eliska would have healed anyone, no matter who they were. She would have healed Brother Arsenault's father the same way she healed Jeovin.

The Darkness poured out of the old man and enveloped her mind. She floated away in a sea of cruelty, sadistic power, and gleeful enjoyment in other people's suffering.

She lost awareness of where she was. She came back to her senses lying on the floor. Anríq, Brother Arsenault, and the middle-aged father bent over her talking, but she couldn't hear them.

Darklings raged behind them, loomed over the three men, and lashed tentacles through the church, but for some reason she couldn't figure out, the Darklings didn't attack. No one else saw them.

Their roars drowned out whatever the men were saying. She saw their mouths moving, but she couldn't hear anything over the noise in her ears.

It sounded like a mixture of Darkling roars and waves crashing on rocks. ...or maybe it was the sound of explosions when Layers collapsed. Was she in the Layers?

Maybe the vision of Anríq, Brother Arsenault, and the church was all an illusion.

Maybe she was already completely Dark and floating in a Dark Layer somewhere that convinced her she was still here.

She woke up later lying alone in bed. Sick cold welled up in her stomach and stung her throat.

The room whirled when she tried to sit up. She swayed sitting on the bed for a while, but she couldn't stay here.

The visions of people hurting each other and even killing each other—Darklings marauding the landscape—Corsairs attacking and turning into Darklings.....

All those images got mixed up in her mind. She lost count of how many times they changed. Were they even real?

She blundered out of the room, sprawled in the hallway outside, and crawled to the stairs. This house stifled her. She had to get outside.

She collided with a few different walls and even fell over the furniture on her way to the kitchen. The back door opened into a courtyard behind the church.

She grabbed a bucket from under the water faucet and barely positioned the bucket under her face before she puked into it. She didn't stop.

Sick poison forced its way out of her guts. She shut her eyes trembling all over as wave upon wave of nausea consumed her. She couldn't move even to raise her head.

Her hair hung into the puddle of puke. She couldn't unclasp her fingers from the bucket to move her hair out of the way.

She retched a dozen more times before she let her sweaty forehead fall on her arm.

She didn't take her head out of the bucket. Another wave would come soon. She didn't want to waste her energy moving when she needed to come back here in a minute.

She wavered out of consciousness and back into the Dark Layers—wherever they were.

Faces grimacing in malicious fury—children screaming and cowering in terror—bodies torn apart—they all got mixed up in one swirling vaporous soup of dreamlike surreality.

Darklings surged out of the shadows and sank back into the shapes of people. Each surge brought a fresh rush of foul poison from her stomach.

It stung her tongue and she spat it into the bucket. She tipped her body against the door frame to stop herself from falling off the steps into the gutter.

She didn't know how long she sat there in quivering misery.

Would it always be like this from now on? Would she ever come back to normal? She didn't even know what normal was anymore. That word didn't apply to her.

She pried her eyes open and strained to look around to her to find out if it was day or night, but she couldn't see well enough even to tell that.

She leaned back with a shaky sigh. She should probably go back to bed, but at that moment, another brutal wave of nausea gripped her. She doubled over the bucket as her whole body spasmed with convulsions.

A fountain of rotten, stinging, putrid bile poured into the bucket and she spat it out gasping for breath. She couldn't open her eyes.

Just then, a hand touched her back. Of course he found her.

"I can't let you go back to the church," he murmured. "You'll die if you don't stop."

"I.....I....have to....."

"Are you trying to kill yourself? Is that what you're trying to do?"

"I'll....I'll make it....." She broke off when another torrent of puke ejected out from her mouth.

His finger traced the side of her face to pull her hair out of the way. He tucked it behind her ear and held that lock of hair there to stop it from falling into the bucket again.

His touch felt unimaginably good, but nothing would stop the Darkness. It took over everything. She swam in a world of memory, death, and tragedy all poisoning her from the inside.

The memory of the woman hiding under a pile of bodies while the Corsairs razed her town and killed everyone else—the torture of that memory came rushing back when Eliska remembered that the woman was dead. Eliska took that Darkness, but she couldn't save the woman.

Faces of people she couldn't save haunted her out of her mind. She burst into tears and puked again. The pain of spasms in her middle stopped her from feeling the true depth of anguish over all those people's deaths.

Anríq's hand kept running up and down her back, squeezing her neck and shoulders, and petting her hair while her body revolted against all this rot and horror inside her.

She couldn't contain it anymore. He was right. Not even her powerful magic could take all of it—not without it destroying her utterly.

She crumpled over her bucket and let her fevered brow fall on her arm again. She floated in the memories until she no longer existed.

She must have fallen asleep because Anríq woke her up. "Let's get you back upstairs to bed," he murmured.

She broke down crying again for no reason she could think of. He always treated her so kindly even when she was completely beyond saving.

He would always take care of her no matter how Dark she became, but he was just doing his job.

He helped her stand up, took the bucket away from her, and supported her as far as the stairs. She trembled all the way there and kept either sobbing or startling when she saw Darklings coming out of nowhere.

They lunged for her and bared their fangs at her only to change into snarling faces of violent people attacking someone weaker than themselves—maybe even someone they loved.

Anríq picked her up again without asking and carried her the rest of the way upstairs.

He put her in bed and then, like some kind of miracle, he climbed onto the bed next to her, curled up against her body, and put his arms around her.

He pulled her head down onto his chest and ran his fingers through her hair. He didn't move while she shivered and whimpered in between jolting from one reality to another.

She forced herself to drag herself back to some half-measure of sanity. She had to stay conscious just for a few more seconds.

"Anríq...." she whispered.

"Yes?" he asked.

"Promise me.....promise me you won't take it.....Promise you won't take the Darkness to save me....."

He didn't answer for a minute. Of course he must have been thinking that. It was the only way to save her.

After a few seconds, he turned his head, pressed his nose and mouth against her hair, and whispered. "I won't. I promise."

She collapsed immediately. The relief of knowing he would be safe.....she could finally release herself in that.

He would be all right as long as he didn't take the Darkness on himself. She could endure anything as long as she spared him from this.

Chapter 29

E liska woke up alone the next morning. Sunshine streamed through the window—or it would have if the Dark cloud up there didn't block out so much of the light.

She went through the same torturous process of dragging herself out of bed. She had trouble seeing where she was going.

She made it back to the church and paused on the threshold looking out at the rows and rows of patients.

Anríq knelt over one of the beds working on a youngish man with a goatee.

She didn't have to set foot inside the church to feel all the Darkness boiling away in each of those people. It formed a matching black tide sweeping toward her from all the patients.

Their memories, fears, nightmares, and secrets stabbed into her brain. She shut her eyes and rested her forehead on the doorjamb, but nothing would stop it.

She couldn't even summon the magic to protect herself from it. The magnetic power of Dark to Dark drew it all to her. She didn't have to go near the patients or even set foot in the same room with them.

She inhaled all that Darkness into her, but it just kept coming. Would she even survive this? Did it even matter anymore?

She couldn't stop herself now even if she wanted to—which she didn't. The Dark became her and it wanted more Darkness from any available source. It needed it. It hungered for it.

Right then, the church doors exploded off their hinges. Ogost charged in from outside, turned right and left, and spotted Anríq who happened to be nearest the door of all the able-bodied attendants.

Ogost rushed Anríq, grabbed his arm, and pulled him toward the doors. Eliska couldn't hear what Ogost was saying. She didn't need to.

Debris and swirling vapors whipped back and forth across the church entrance just beyond the doors. Pelting wind caught household objects and even vehicles off the streets.

They tumbled in the hurricane with Dark vapors slashing and crashing against windows.

The sound of breaking glass, exploding houses, and distant screams got caught in the howling shriek of wind.

Anríq rushed outside with Brother Arsenault and the other attendants right behind them. Eliska's eyes floated half-shut. She didn't have to leave the church to see exactly what was going on out there.

She stumbled down the aisle, tripped over a few patients, and slammed her shoulder into the church entrance doors before she hauled her eyelids open enough to see it for real.

The Dark cloud hovering over the city had built to a massive, towering column rising as far as the eye could see.

It wiped out what little blue sky had been there before Anríq and Eliska came to this church.

The cloud revolved in a fast-moving vortex of Dark Layers collapsing on top of each other. The mass of shadow up there kept gathering in strength and snatching people and objects off the ground.

The minute Eliska got her eyes open, the cloud swooped to the east and compressed on one side of the city.

What had been a cloud stretched and covered that whole half of the countryside. It formed into a wall of Darkness moving in on Symphorian even as the vortex tore the place apart from above.

Brother Arsenault raised his hand in front of his face to protect his eyes from flying splinters and broken glass caught in the wind.

Anríq stormed out into the streets and unhooked his club to face down the Dark Layer. He wouldn't be able to defeat it on his own.

Eliska couldn't summon the strength even to push herself off the door jamb. She could barely keep her eyes open.

That was the moment when she realized she didn't have her staff. She must have left it upstairs in her bedroom. She'd been too out of her mind even to remember to bring it—not that she would have been able to do anything with it if she did bring it.

Anríq flexed his knees and raised his club over his shoulder for the first strike. The Dark Layer consumed the sky and cast the city permanently in shadow.

Townspeople ran screaming for shelter, but nothing would save them from this.

Eliska's eyelids started to sink. When she forced them open one last time, she saw the Layer rushing down on Anríq. It would swallow him in seconds.

She had to save him—and everyone else. Her life was already over. She was as good as dead. She might as well go out with one last act of service.

She raised her hand. She had nothing else with which to fight the Dark, but she couldn't fight it. She couldn't fight herself. She didn't want to.

She raised her hand and the vast depth of Darkness in her guts blasted out of her hand.

She summoned every trace of power she had—and in that moment, she tapped the Darkness itself.

She trembled at the sheer colossal power of it. She'd taken so much of it these last few days.

Her own terror, rage, hatred, and cruel violence fed it and made it even more poisonous if that was even possible.

It took her over, and in that moment, it exploded her magic out of all proportion.

She never let herself use Dark magic before. She never dared to. She lived in fear every day of what would happen if she went there.

Now the dam burst and she unloaded all of it on the Layer. A channel opened between the Layer and the Darkness inside her.

The two forces met in a deafening thunderclap that exploded the whole world—or maybe it only seemed that way to her.

The Layer imploded into an even tighter, Darker, more unstoppable flood of pure evil.

It streaked across the landscape, stabbed into her hand, and turned the whole world Dark before it wiped her out completely.

Some time might have passed, but she couldn't tell.

She became aware of herself floating in dim vapors staring at a sea of Darklings.

They seethed and roared at her, but they didn't attack.

She used her Dark power to manipulate them. She could turn them in any direction and direct their tentacles to slash where she wanted them to slash.

She could even indicate by a mere thought when she wanted one of them to roar and which other Darklings she wanted them to roar at.

Dark forces flashed into existence in the Layers, took form, rushed her, and vanished at her slightest whim. She could direct them anywhere, too.

The limits of her awareness showed her the Layers of the Coil collapsing and taking out towns, cities, Islands, and whole populations. She even saw the Voyant floating through some of them and wreaking destruction everywhere he went.

She watched from a distance. She could have sent these Darklings to any Layer to attack and kill anyone she wanted to attack and kill. She could have sent them to wipe out whole worlds, but she didn't.

She just turned them, directed them, and made them dance to her thoughts. She didn't want to get involved with anything or anyone outside this Layer.

One of the Darklings turned on another, roared, and lunged for it to tear it apart with its teeth.

She blurred in a sheet of Darkness, let herself flow into the Darkling, and unleashed all the fury and murderous outrage in her heart to tear her enemy apart.

She let all the horrible memories out of their box. She became the father attacking his son at the same time that her awareness split into the other Darkling confronting her.

She became the son attacking his father, first to defend himself, and then to release all the locked-up fury that had been building over years of mistreatment.

She let all of it free in a moment of pure violence. The two Darklings tore each other limb from limb until their Darkness drifted away in specks of shadow to rejoin the rest of the Layer.

Eliska reformed a dozen yards from where she started. She'd been floating in this Layer since....she couldn't exactly remember when.

She played out all the horrors of her memories through these Darklings.

She became a Corsair cutting women and children apart. She became Jeovin killing small creatures and hiding their bodies.

She became whole armies of Darklings destroying Islands and devouring populations in her path.

In the end, those Darklings just disappeared into the Coil along with all the other Dark forces. They were nothing. They weren't real and yet they were real because all those things really happened.

Darklings released from the Layers to maraud and destroy Islands—they were all real. They left dead bodies strewn across the countryside. Each of those people had been real.

The memories, secrets, and nightmares of everyone they consumed joined the endless flow of pictures and emotions.

They passed through Eliska just long enough for her to become aware of them before they vanished and became nothing but shadows winking in the Coil.

They reorganized themselves out there and faces emerged between the vapors. She recognized families from the church—some of whom she'd saved and others she didn't.

Their faces swelled out of the Layers, twisted in different expressions, looked at each other, and went through different scenes from their memories before the images evaporated.

She even accessed the memories of people who hadn't been in the church at all. One bright orange vapor took the form of a middle-aged woman who worked as an attendant in the church.

The woman held a crying baby in her arms and tried to rock him while she talked frantically to Brother Arsenault in a rushed undertone. "I don't know what to do! The mother's dead and the healers are too busy working on everyone else."

"Give him to me. I'll take care of him." Brother Arsenault held out his arms to take the child.

The minute the two adults touched each other to transfer the baby from one to the other, the baby stopped crying.

Brother Arsenault looked down and then both adults burst into a flurry of putting the baby on the table and trying to figure out what was wrong with him.

They whirled around him in a frenzy, but the baby had already stopped breathing.

Brother Arsenault snatched the body off the table and raced off to the church, but by the time they got there, Anríq told Brother Arsenault that it was too late.

Chapter 30

Eliska didn't see herself in the vision of the baby dying—because she wasn't there. She must have been upstairs asleep or passed out somewhere.

A familiar voice spoke up behind her back. "It wasn't your fault. You saved as many as you could."

"You shouldn't have come," she snapped over her shoulder. "You don't belong here."

"Neither do you." He waited. "Aren't you going to turn around and look at me?"

She didn't move. "Leave me alone," she growled over her shoulder. "I belong here. Just leave me here where I belong. I'm beyond saving."

"You don't have to be. Come back to the church."

"There's nothing there for me," she muttered. "I'll only poison everyone—the same way I would poison you. Go on with your work. You're too good. I'll stay here and hold the Dark. It won't touch you."

He didn't answer for a minute. She shut her eyes and counted down the seconds before he went away. She really didn't want him around—especially not here.

He didn't belong in any Dark Layer. He didn't belong anywhere near the Dark.

She really hoped he was back there deciding that she really wasn't worth saving—or maybe that he would finally realize what she was trying to do.

She couldn't contain the Dark the way she thought she could, but she could at least occupy it here. She wouldn't magnetize it to herself out there.

She would stay here with it. Then it wouldn't need to go out there and go after all these other people.

She stiffened when he took another step closer to her from behind. His presence sent a shockwave of tension through her. What was he going to do?

He promised not to take her Darkness and now she knew he couldn't. It was too big for him to do anything about it now.

He adjusted his position in a way she didn't see.

Out of nowhere, he slipped his hand against her cheek and turned her face. That touch caused another instinctive reaction. She couldn't fight him. She didn't want to.

Whatever he did must be right. She'd been telling herself that from the beginning. She could only come close to being as good as he was.

He pressed his hand into her cheek and irresistible gravity made her melt into his hand when he turned her around to face him.

He raised both hands and cupped her face in his big, strong, rough hands. His blue eyes burned down at her from directly above.

Very slowly, he bent down and kissed her—just once—before he straightened up and went back to staring into her deepest soul.

"You're a Servant, Eliska," he murmured. "You don't belong in here by yourself. Your place is out there with the people who need you. You saved all those people. You saved the whole city, but they still need you. The Coil is still unstable and saving those people means finding a way to stabilize it. You couldn't stay here alone while all those people are still in danger. You're one of the few people who can actually save them. You have to come back to save them even if it hurts you to do it. That's the Servant's way. You sacrificed yourself for them. Now you have to do it again. You were made for that. You won't be able to do anything else."

That kiss—his words—even him holding her face like this—it made no difference at all. The same pictures kept flooding her mind no matter what. They never went away. Nothing would make them go away.

They did something, though.

In the end, she couldn't tell whether it was his kiss, his hands, his eyes, or his words. None of them changed anything—but something changed.

She couldn't help the world by staying confined in these Dark Layers. She really wished she could.

That was the problem. Staying here made it easier for her. It didn't make it easier for the rest of the world.

She didn't understand that—unless it worked the same way as Anríq breaking his vow of silence.

It wasn't the Servant's way and yet he became more of a Servant by breaking these rules.

Staying here and keeping the poison isolated from everyone else—it was the Servant's way. She did it for them—for all the people out there.

And yet, somehow, in ways she didn't understand, she became more of a Servant by taking the poison out into the world.

She didn't know why, but he was right. She had to go back—not for herself, but for them.

The nightmares blurred together in a rapid streak of pictures all blended together—children, parents, generations of violence, whole populations killing and being killed—their collective sea of memory became hers.

She drifted back to her senses, but she wasn't in the Dark Layer anymore. She lay on the bed in the house behind the church. Anríq lay by her side with his arms around her.

He had his shirt off and her head lay on his big chest.

She must have fallen asleep with her arms around him, too. She felt his skin on her hands, arms, and face. She smelled him in ways she never smelled him before.

She registered a split second's realization of where she was, who she was with, and why.

The next instant, the same stream of images raced across her mind and in front of her eyes, but these memories didn't belong to anyone else. They were hers.

She recognized dozens of faces—faces of people she knew and met in the Coil—people she either couldn't save or didn't even try to save.

She recognized people she never met but only watched from afar—people torn apart by Darklings—or torn apart by other people—or destroyed by their own inner Darkness—or attacked by people.

She saw the Corsairs wipe out towns—and she did nothing to stop it.

She could have. She could have stopped it all with one wave of her staff, but she didn't. She turned her back.

She turned her back on children beaten and murdered, helpless men and women brutalized, entire populations enslaved or sucked into the Dark.

She could have saved so many of them if she only tried. She didn't try. She didn't care to try. She turned her back on them and went her own way—to protect herself.

In most cases, she didn't even do it to protect her own safety. She did it to protect herself from feeling anything—about anyone.

Their faces came back to haunt her now. Those crimes—those deaths—that suffering—it never bothered her before.

Now a matching torrent of Dark emotion boiled up out of her soul for each of those people.

She didn't have to access their memories or the terror, rage, humiliation, and injustice that they felt in their last moments.

In some cases, they were still feeling all of that when their attackers left the victims alive to carry these nightmares for the rest of their lives.

She didn't need to remember what they remembered or feel what they felt.

She remembered what she remembered and felt what she felt. She remembered everything—right down to the smallest detail.

She remembered every body, every drop of blood, every shifting Layer of the Coil inflicting mass death on thousands or millions of innocents.

She didn't remember them until right now.

Tears sprang to her eyes, and once they started, they wouldn't stop.

She remembered how she felt. She remembered watching all of that and feeling absolutely nothing.

She didn't care—about anyone or anything—least of all herself.

She watched. She remembered. And she did nothing.

She didn't care to do anything. She turned away and went off alone for no reason at all.

She couldn't stand the shame of her own actions. The tears kept coming and so did the memories.

She buried her face in Anríq's chest and tried to hide from it, but it would never go away—not as long as she lived.

This must be why she had to come back from the Dark Layer—so she would see this.

She would never be able to live this down. She could spend the rest of her life wandering the Coil as a nameless, faceless Servant. She could spend every day of her life helping other people.

She would never remove the stain of this crime. That was the true poison—not all the Darkness she took from those sick people.

Nothing would ever take this poison away from her because she could never bring those people back. No one could go back in time and make her protect those people. Those memories remained imprinted on her mind forever.

The pain poured out of her in hot, bitter tears. They formed pools in the clefts of Anríq's muscles, but he didn't try to wipe them away.

Neither did she. She had no right to feel this pain or shed these tears. Those people were the ones who suffered. She was the one who made them suffer as surely as if she killed, maimed, and mutilated them herself.

She had no right to feel sorry for herself or hide herself away or to protect herself—not ever again.

She owed them this. She owed them so much more.

They deserved more than she could ever give in her lifetime in some small, pathetic attempt to make up for her colossal failure.

Anríq's arms closed around her and he kissed her hair, but even that galled her beyond endurance. She didn't deserve him, but she already knew that. She didn't even deserve his comfort.

Chapter 31

E liska woke up alone and stared at the empty place in the bed next to her. Anríq wasn't here and neither were his clothes, bags, or weapons.

She stretched out in bed, ran her fingers through her hair, and sighed.

She stared up at the ceiling and watched the endless train of faces, pictures, and phantoms flickering in front of her eyes.

They didn't go away. Of course not. They would always be there, but at least she could stay lucid now.

Staying lucid only made it harder, but she no longer gave herself the option to turn away.

That time had passed for her. She had to look and see. She had to face the true magnitude of her error.

All the years of her life leading up to this point—they had all been one catastrophic mistake—the mistake of protecting herself from other people. She couldn't hide from it anymore.

She would have to stay lucid from now on. She didn't have a choice about that. She would have to keep her eyes open and see all their faces, all their torment, all their horrific deaths and abuses and suffering.

She would see them when she was awake and when she was asleep. She would see them in her private moments. She would carry the stain of their blood as her Servant's mark. No one had to give her any other.

No one else ever had to acknowledge that she even was a Servant. She knew. She would never be able to get off this path even if she wanted to.

She didn't want to. This was her only hope. It was the only reason she was still alive.

She knew that now. She had no other life. She might as well end it right now if she even thought about doing anything else.

She dragged herself off the bed and sat on the edge of the mattress staring down at the floor. Every inch of her body and mind hurt.

She felt how weak she was—but only physically. Her body felt bruised and shaky. A soft breeze would have knocked her over.

Her magic was as strong as ever if not stronger. This Darkness raged inside her. It wanted to find an outlet through her staff or through her hands.

It wanted her to use it to destroy. It would never leave her alone.

It would nag her every hour of every day. She would have to work extra hard to contain it so it didn't escape from her control.

She didn't care about that and she no longer worried about being able to control it.

She could use the Dark power itself to control it. She could just turn the Dark power on itself.

She could use the Dark to fight the Dark. It was the only weapon strong enough with which to fight it. She understood that now in ways she never understood before.

That didn't matter because she knew what she had to do. She got to her feet and picked up her staff.

She didn't wobble this time, but she had to be careful putting her weight on her legs. Every step hurt, but not because she was sick or injured. *She* hurt. Her innermost soul hurt.

She set off walking down the long corridor heading back to the church. She didn't have the luxury of being weak—not when people needed her. She better toughen up if she wanted to face all the dangers out in the Coil.

She picked up her pace and her spirits lifted on the way there. The effort and attention of using the Dark to counteract the Dark itself—it gave her a new kind of energy. She could do this.

She could do it better than she should have been able to.

Her being took to the Dark, but that didn't matter because she would use it for the right reasons.

She stopped on the threshold and looked through the door into the church. It was empty. The townspeople hadn't moved the pews back into place. Was everyone dead?

She tiptoed inside and her footsteps echoed off the walls. The broad, empty floor rang hollow.

That sound sent goosebumps up her arms. She kept looking around for the people she should heal.

She would have been able to heal them so much better now. She could control the Darkness. She would be able to heal thousands of them and maybe even engulfed another Dark Layer. It would only make her stronger.

She stopped in the middle of the church trying to get her brain to accept that no one was here. Where was everyone?

She didn't want to face it if they were dead—as if their memories weren't bad enough already.

She stopped there and turned around. She found herself facing the altar with all its finery and symbolism. She didn't know exactly what they meant, but standing here looking up at it did something to her.

What if it meant something? What if it actually meant what all these people seemed to think it meant?

Standing here exposed the Dark inside her more than anything. This whole thing—this church—the altar—the symbols—the statues—they all saw.

They all recognized her for exactly what she saw. They saw the Dark, but they also saw her as a Servant.

They saw the road in front of her....and somehow, them seeing it made it okay. She was doing this for them and for all the people who needed her—both past and present.

A confused tempest of emotion gripped her in front of the altar, but before she could move, the church door swung open. The hinges creaked and then the door banged when Anríq's footsteps crossed the empty floor.

"There you are," he exclaimed. "I didn't know you were awake."

"I am," she replied.

He cocked his head to study her. "You look better. How do you feel?"

She shrugged it away, but she didn't avert her eyes. She didn't have to hide anything from him. "About the same, I guess, but at least I'm not throwing up anymore—and I don't seem to be in any danger of collapsing."

He waved behind him toward the open church door. "Come outside into the fresh air. It will make you feel better."

She didn't see how anything would ever make her feel better, but she didn't want it to. Her feeling better wasn't the point.

She followed him to the door, but she couldn't stop herself from looking all around the church for all the people who weren't there. "Where is everyone?" she asked.

"I'll show you." He stepped outside and stood aside to give her room to pass through the door Then he shut it behind her.

She stopped there on the steps staring at the city. The Dark cloud no longer hovered in the sky overhead. Morning sunshine streamed into streets full of people going about their daily lives.

A man in a muddy work apron pushed a wheelbarrow toward a half-constructed brick wall. A boy pushed a hoe back and forth in another wheelbarrow to mix the mortar for the bricklayer.

A woman with flour all over her arms came out of the bakery across the street. Vehicles rumbled past the church and all the machines chugged and churned and bleeped and whizzed everywhere.

Nearly everyone she saw wore either dirty work clothes or fancy expensive attire like the dress Odael wore and Quentienne's suit from that very first evening.

Anríq stepped out onto the church steps next to Eliska. They stood there watching for a long time while she took in the whole scene.

"You healed the whole city," Anríq told her. "They're all back to normal now."

A few people noticed them standing there. People stopped work to stare back.

She could no longer deny that they were staring at her. Anríq must have been out here before he came back to the church.

All the townspeople stared at her. The wave of stillness and silence spread outward from the church as more and more people realized she was here.

Anríq squeezed her arm to nudge her forward and guide her down the steps. Quentienne and Brother Arsenault hustled out of some corner and rushed the pair.

"You're awake!" Brother Arsenault exclaimed. "We didn't know if you would make it."

"I did," Eliska mumbled.

Quentienne waved behind him. "Come to my home."

Anríq didn't give Eliska a chance to answer. "We'll move on, now that Eliska is healthy enough to travel. We came here to heal your people and we've accomplished that. Now it's time for us to go."

"At least stay and share a meal with us," Brother Arsenault insisted. "We haven't had a chance to properly express our gratitude—for everything you've done."

"That won't be necessary," Anríq replied. "We're just glad everyone is feeling better. Come on, Eliska."

He took her arm again and turned her away. They headed off toward the road that brought them here.

They left Quentienne and Brother Arsenault behind, but it still took a long time of walking between all those people's staring eyes before Anríq and Eliska made it out of town.

Everyone turned to watch her walk past. No one made a sound.

She squirmed under their gaze. She didn't do anything special. What was one city in the cosmic scheme of things?

It didn't come close to tipping the scales against all the hurt and dead people on the other side—the side that counted against her.

She didn't explain herself to Quentienne and Brother Arsenault. She saw herself standing in silence while Anríq spoke for her.

She'd been doing that for him all this time. Now their positions reversed. Did that make her a Servant?

Someday, she would fall completely silent. She would only speak when she needed information about what people needed her to do and who they wanted her to heal.

She would press her hands together and say, "I will serve." Then no one would expect her to say anything else.

She and Anríq passed out of town into the blessed silence of the countryside. They continued for a few minutes and climbed the same hill where they first looked down on the city.

They both stopped there to look back. The sun glowed on the Symphorian in a peaceful aura of domestic activity. A hum of noise drifted out on the breeze.

"Can you find Yann now?" Anríq asked.

Eliska opened her Coil projection.

She didn't wait for Anríq to put his hand under hers to add his magic to hers. She expanded the image and showed the golden lines by herself now. She didn't need his help.

He didn't comment on it. He didn't ask where she got the extra power to do this.

She pointed to one of the lines. "There he is. He and Marine are still together in a stable island."

"Let's go find them. I don't want them wandering around the Coil unprotected if we can do anything to help them."

Eliska shut her hand.

Before she could move, a shifting Layer of something like cloud passed between this hill and the city in the distance.

The cloud covered the city and Symphorian vanished behind the mist. She didn't hear any rumble of changing landscapes or the crack of earth breaking as Darklings came out.

Anríq watched in silence at her side before he murmured, "It might not be gone. It might just have moved."

She nodded and he turned away. She followed him down the other side of the hill heading somewhere else.

Chapter 32

Yann tumbled through multiple Layers and smashed into something solid. It held him for a second, but he couldn't even see where he was. Too much pelting slashes of vapor and Darkness surrounded him.

The next instant, the surface gave way and he crashed through a sea of fire scorching him all over.

He screamed, curled into a ball, and threw his hands in front of his face, but the searing heat threatened to roast the flesh off his bones.

At that instant, Marine collided with him and they both plummeted into another abyss of vast, churning chaos.

He struggled to orient himself and then they both splashed through a sheet of freezing cold water before they landed on the ground again.

Yann had half a second to catch his breath before the ground underneath him heaved out of position. It rolled and undulated in waves.

He dug his fingers into the surface to hold himself in place, but it didn't pitch or toss or explode. It just kept rolling and undulating in gentle waves traveling back and forth across this Island.

He couldn't call it a landscape or a countryside because it wasn't any of those things. It didn't have any trees or bushes or houses or roads. It didn't even have grass.

He couldn't recognize the surface underneath him. It didn't look like any kind of floor he knew. It wasn't tile or wood or even pavement or earth.

It just looked like one giant expanse of some kind of smooth, solid substance.

He flattened himself to the swells and tried to look around. The swells sank to his right and he caught a fleeting glimpse of Marine before the swells rose between them and cut off his view.

That one instant told him all he needed to know.

She cowered between the swells shrieking, snarling, gnashing her teeth, and darting furtive glances and outright murderous glares at things he couldn't see.

He looked away....and then looked back. She saved him just now. He wouldn't survive in the Coil without a magic-user to help him.

He didn't see Eliska or Anríq anywhere. Marine was all he had left. She was his one chance to get out of this.

He pushed himself up onto his hands and knees to go over to her, but the landscape reacted to his every move.

It heaved higher to pitch him onto his sides. He rolled only to get knocked somewhere else by another swell.

He flattened himself again until the heaving stopped.

He tried four different times to get onto his hands and knees. The same thing happened every time.

The landscape responded to his efforts by throwing him down, tossing him farther away from Marine, and actively working against his efforts to rejoin her.

Yann couldn't ignore it any longer. The landscape was working against him. Was it his enemy? Did he really want to start thinking of the Layers that way? Why not?

He considered the Coil a neutral force of random chaos and mindless destruction, but that was before Middleborough collapsed and he and the Watch got thrown into the Coil with no way out of it.

Too many recent collapses coincided with the party's movements. They seemed to follow him around and collapse things at the worst possible time to put him in the most danger.

This must be the Voyant's way of attacking Yann. He couldn't explain it any other way.

He decided not to crawl over to Marine. Instead, he pulled and dragged himself along the floor without pushing himself up.

He maneuvered between the swells and even used them to navigate closer to her.

She didn't see him so he used her lunatic screeches to guide him to her.

She didn't flatten herself to the floor. She huddled in a ball between the swells, but they didn't react to knock her down. Maybe the landscape sensed that she wasn't a threat to it.

Voyant's attack on the cloud tower left Marine as bedraggled, tattered, and filthy as ever. Yann couldn't recognize anything about the nice dress she had been wearing when the group left Tenby.

Those days seemed like a hundred years ago.

He swam into the same nest of swells and dared to sit up in front of her. "Marine...." he gasped. "Where are we?"

She shrieked at him, lunged for him, and bared her teeth in an animal snarl.

He jolted away and raised his hands to hold her at bay. Her teeth closed in a vicious snap just inches from his face, but at that moment, he caught a glimpse of her making eye contact with him.

She was still in there somewhere. She might be communing with the Dark, but she was still the same person.

She jerked away, turned sideways, and looked off across the landscape in another direction.

Yann sank back against the swells and stared at her. The floor didn't toss him around or try to throw him down.

He surveyed what part of the sky he could see from down here. At least nothing came to threaten him here.

He could just sit here for a minute and think. The swells kept rolling and swaying underneath him, but his mind cleared enough to realize that he wasn't in any immediate danger—not yet.

Marine kept pivoting from one direction to another, muttering, snarling, shrieking, and yowling.

She snapped her teeth at invisible enemies—or maybe she was actually friends with these Darklings. He didn't want to think about it.

He checked the landscape for the hundredth time and then studied her. Could he somehow get through to her?

She said she could commune with the Dark whenever she wanted to—so what was stopping her from coming out of it to talk to him.?

He sat forward, scooted nearer until he sat right in front of her, and tried again. "Marine....can you hear me?"

He didn't know what he expected, but of course he didn't get a response. She didn't acknowledge him.

He took a deep breath. "I know you can hear me....."

He didn't know if she could hear him or even understand him, but he had to talk to someone. She was the only person left for him to talk to.

"We have to find out where we are....and meet back up with Anríq and Eliska....." His voice vanished into the silence.

The feeling of silence bearing down on him from all sides—he couldn't stand it.

"I know you're doing this to fight the Voyant, Marine," he blurted out. "We can't fight the Voyant here. We have to travel to another Layer or at least meet up with Anríq and Eliska. They can help us. We can't fight the Voyant on our own with just the two of us. This is your mission....Help me. I can't do this by myself."

He choked on the words, but right then, she turned in his direction.

She made a fraction of an instant's eye contact with him before she looked away.

She didn't gnash her teeth or snarl or shriek at him this time nor did she try to bite him.

She just looked at him and acknowledged him before she went back to muttering over there with her shoulders hunched. That instant of eye contact confirmed what he already knew. She could hear him and understand him.

He straightened up. He wasn't alone. He could do this—somehow.

He dared to slide a few more inches closer to her. "I don't have the magic to shatter this Island. You'll have to do it. Do you know where we are? Can you figure out how to get us to an Island where we might be able to find something?"

He couldn't imagine what they would find. If his friends and companions were right about the Voyant coming after him, then he would be dead in a matter of minutes. He wouldn't be able to fight the Voyant.

He didn't want the Voyant to recruit him and make him into a magic-user, either. Yann just wanted to get to some stable Island—preferably one where Marine would get her sanity back. Then he'd at least have someone to talk to.

He would even have been willing to get her back without her magic. Her help and company would have been worth the sacrifice, but maybe she didn't see it that way.

She didn't respond to his request—not at first. She stayed over there muttering and growling and letting off the occasional screeches that sounded like pain.

He cast one last hopeless look around the landscape. What would he do if she didn't take them somewhere else? He wouldn't be able to find food or water in a landscape as barren as this—and he couldn't stand up even to explore the place.

A buzzing noise caught his attention.

He turned around and realized that she actually was doing something. She placed her hand on the floor next to his knee. The vibration came through her palm.

She vibrated the floor faster and faster until it trembled. The tremors became so violent that the Island couldn't hold together anymore.

He realized what she was about to do, grabbed his glaive, and tried at least to get onto his knees so he would be ready when he fell through into the Layer below. He really hoped he didn't fall into some Darkling's open mouth.

The vibration built to a deafening pound. It spread outward and stopped the whole landscape from rolling.

She didn't stop. She put her other hand on the floor next to her to make the vibration increase even more.

"Get ready, Marine!' Yann yelled over the noise.

Cracks forked across the floor jutting away from her hands. They spread underneath him and Marine. How much of the Island would she destroy to get the two of them through to somewhere else?

Right at that moment, five people walked over the nearest swell behind Marine. The people included a middle-aged man, a woman, and what looked like three teenagers—two boys and a girl.

They looked straight down at Yann and Marine.

"Wait!!" Yan bellowed, but it was too late.

The cracks exploded outward and the floor buckled with an ear-splitting crash. Yann and Marine plummeted through along with a whole bunch of blocks of whatever substance made up the floor.

The five strangers wheeled off somewhere else while Yann and Marine fell straight down into another landscape. They couldn't have fallen more than fifteen feet.

They crashed down in another Island, but this one looked like its sky covered the landscape thousands of feet overhead. That shouldn't have been possible.

Yan didn't have time to think about that. He hit the ground, rolled, and bumped over something just as it erupted out of the ground.

He tumbled onto his back still crushing his glaive in both hands.

The thing that burst out of the ground shot over him, curved downward, and he found himself staring up at a spiky dragon head as the creature arched its neck to glare down at him.

The creature opened a mouth studded with fangs and spat a jet of fire at him.

He barely had time to hurl himself out of the line of fire, but more of these dragon heads sprouted out of the ground all around him. They knocked him here and there no matter where he rolled.

He took a split second to recognize that he actually was in some kind of countryside this time. Grass, bushes, and a few sparse trees grew out of a landscape of flat, short, green grass.

He didn't see any other animals, but he did see dozens upon dozens of these dragon heads bursting out of the grass.

Fortunately for him, they only made it six or seven feet out of the ground. They never got any taller nor did they seem to have any bodies attached to them.

A flash of light and a burst of magic caught his attention. The blast came from Yann's left and plastered the first dragon that threatened Yann.

His head jerked that way and the dragon head roared in fury. It spun around only to take another magical bombardment in the face from Marine storming across the landscape.

The sight of her electrified Yann. He shot to his feet swiping his glaive at all the dragons.

People walking around in this landscape seemed to antagonize the dragons. They shrank back under the ground if no one went near them. Entire sections of the landscape looked like normal, harmless grassy areas with a few bushes and trees.

The instant someone set foot on a patch of grass, the movement triggered the dragons to attack.

Their heads rose on swaying, sinuous necks. The dragons bared their teeth, hissed, and spat fire at the unsuspecting intruder.

A dozen people fought for their lives all over the landscape. Yann couldn't tell from here if these were the same people he just saw in the undulating landscape.

He didn't have time to check before more dragons erupted out of the ground to surround Marine.

She stood up straight, shot out her hands one at a time, and unloaded magical bombardments on any dragon that threatened her.

She couldn't hit so many of them. She could only keep them at bay as they all surrounded her. She couldn't get out of that circle.

Yann barged over there, but he had to fight his way to her. More dragon heads burst out from under the grass all around him.

They would have surrounded him, too, He couldn't let that happen.

He slashed his glaive at them, severed their heads, jabbed his glaive into their eyes and mouths, sliced their throats, and did anything possible to damage them.

The headless necks withdrew underground, but they always seemed to regenerate in a few seconds—or maybe new dragon heads grew to replace the old ones.

He didn't know and he didn't care. He fought his way between them and carved a path to where Marine stood.

She didn't see him until he stabbed a dragon head from behind. It had been about to torch her, but he impaled it through the skull and skewered it to the ground.

She spun around ready to shoot him in the face with another magical explosion. Her eyes locked on his. She was back. She had her sanity.

A flushed smile lit up her features, but she couldn't stand there smiling at him. She whirled the other way and went back to shooting the dragon heads as fast as she could.

Yann sprang into the circle while he swiped his glaive at another five dragon heads attacking from behind him. Marine backed up against him.

Her body sealed against his spine. She kept jolting every time she unloaded on the dragons.

"Break the Layer!" he yelled over his shoulder. "We gotta get out of here!"

"What about those other people?!" she yelled. "They aren't magical!"

Yann took a split second to glance in the direction of the other poor travelers trapped in this Island. He couldn't take more than a split second and he couldn't see enough from here to make a decision.

All five of them fought with regular melee weapons. None of those people used magic.

Before Yann could come to any decision about what to do, a different explosion went off somewhere. He didn't see where it came from or what caused it before the Island collapsed underneath him.

Marine screamed, lunged for him, and strapped her arms around his chest. He barely had time to grab a hold of her and slash his glaive at the dragons about to slaughter him before he and Marine plunged out of sight into a world of chaos.

Chapter 33

S tinging Dark vapors cut Yann's face and battered his body. Heavy
blows hammered him all over. He couldn't see anything in this
place that would hit him.

He swiveled himself around, hugged Marine tighter against him,
and tried to cover as much of her with his own body as he could. The
blows got worse. They would break bone any second now.

Just then, the two travelers broke through another curtain of millions of tiny needle pricks and landed in a bed of deep, long, tangled
grass.

It cushioned their fall. Yann and Marine broke apart and tumbled
down on top of what felt like a mattress.

Yann sprawled there panting hard. He had to continually remind himself that he still had his glaive just in case something went
wrong—when something went wrong.

Trees surrounded the area and he heard water trickling somewhere.
He didn't want to trust that anything in this place might not pose a
threat.

He scrambled onto his knees and crawled over to where Marine lay
face down on the grass.

He gripped the shoulder of her frilly dress. "Marine...." he croaked.
"Are you okay....?"

She exploded off the ground, reared away from him with a frightful shriek, scuttled backward, and crashed into a tree trunk a few yards away.

Yann froze staring at her in shock. She grimaced, slashed her teeth at him and other things he couldn't see, and her wild eyes rolled all over the place.

He wilted in defeat and sank onto his ankles. Damn it. He lost her again.

He really wished he could find an Island where she just stayed sane. If he ever found a place like that again, he would just stay there. He couldn't deal with her coming and going like this.

He needed her. That was the truth. He needed one person in this crazy world who knew him and whom he knew—someone he could talk to—someone who understood his situation. She was his only lifeline.

He glanced around...and froze when he saw creatures in the nearby tree branches.

Something that looked like a striped version of a marmot ambled along one of the branches.

The creature only made it a foot before it morphed into a huge snake slithering over the same branch.

The snake wrapped its coils around the branch, created a loop to lower itself to a branch below it, and changed into a round ball of spikes with two cruel eyes glaring out of it. This creature didn't have any arms or legs at all.

It rolled along the branch and embedded its spikes in the bark to anchor itself so it wouldn't fall off.

Yann swallowed hard. Different creatures all over these woods kept changing into different creatures before his eyes. Were any of them dangerous? Were all of them dangerous?

Right then, another much smaller dragon pelted down from the high canopy. This one couldn't have been bigger than a medium-sized dog. It pounced on the spiky creature, seized it in its claws, and tried to lift off with it.

The spiky creature turned into another dragon and counterattacked the first dragon. They started fighting right there among the trees until something that looked like a horse rose out of a nearby branch.

The horse emerged from the bark itself. The horse hadn't been there until right that minute.

The horse only stood a foot tall. It set off cantering down the branch to intercept the two dragons. The horse's palomino mane and tail streamed out behind it.

It launched off the branch and changed in mid-air to become a completely different animal.

The horse flattened itself into a giant pancake with greyish-green scales all over its flat, two-dimensional body.

The pancake didn't seem to have any eyes or any other facial features. It definitely didn't have any arms, legs, or mouth.

Neither of the dragons noticed the pancake until it slapped into them, wrapped itself around both dragons, and took them to the ground.

The dragons shrieked, but the pancake completely enveloped both of them, wrapped its thin body around them, and smothered them underneath itself.

The dragons' muffled screams drifted from inside along with bubbling, hissing, simmering noises that made Yann's skin crawl.

The pancake contracted around the two dragons and compressed them. A few jerks of movement jutted the pancake's outer skin to show where the dragons just had been.

In a matter of minutes, the pancake shrank too small for the dragons to still be in there. This thing must be digesting the dragons.

Marine's voice startled Yann out of his wits. "Don't worry," she chirped. "They aren't harmful to people—only to each other."

He whipped around from right to left trying to find her. He spotted her huddled under the same tree.

She hunched there with her knees drawn up to her chest. Her greasy hair hung over her eyes and she glared into the trees while she muttered, snarled, and curled her lips in feral grimaces.

He blinked at her. "Um....Marine....?"

"We should keep traveling," her voice told him. "We should keep searching for Anríq and Eliska so we can meet back up with them."

Her voice didn't come from her. He was staring straight at her when she said those words. Her mouth didn't move and she didn't look at him—but her voice sounded perfectly sane.

He glanced around. "Um....where are you?"

Her high-pitched musical laughter echoed through the woods teeming with all these bizarre creatures.

"I'm right in front of you, silly!" she exclaimed. "You can see where I am...."

"Then how are you talking to me...from over there?" He pinpointed where her voice was coming from.

It came from a creature sitting in the branches above his head. It would have looked like a bird except that it didn't seem to have a head or legs, either.

The body seemed to consist of a feathered ball with no other features Yann could see besides two clawed feet holding onto the branch.

"I'm using my familiars to talk to you," Marine told him. "I'm communing with the Dark...."

"Do you have to do that *now?*" He tried not to sound too resentful about it. "Can't you just act normally?"

"I'm trying to find out where we are and how we can get back to where we got separated from Anríq and Eliska."

"We got separated from them in a chaos Layer," Yann pointed out.

Her voice drifted to him from another snake crawling up a nearby tree. "Oh, yeah. I forgot about that."

"Can you tell where we are?" he asked. "Can you find a way to get us to a safe Island?"

"We're in a safe Island now," she replied. "I told you these creatures don't harm humans."

Yann's eyes skimmed the woods. Her voice kept switching from one creature to another. "You'll have to forgive me if I don't believe that," he muttered.

"Don't worry so much!" she exclaimed. "Everything's gonna be fine!"

"Yeah," he rumbled. "Tell me another one."

She burst out in laughter again. He should have resented her laughing over this danger, but he was too happy to hear her voice—her sane voice. At least she was here with him.

"Do you know this Island?" he asked.

"No, I've never been here before."

"Then how are you using all these animals as familiars? Shouldn't they be....you know....familiar?"

She wouldn't stop giggling. "You're so funny, Yann!"

"Sorry," he mumbled. "I'm not magical. I don't understand."

"Never mind!" she lilted, but her voice sounded so warm and friendly that he could just imagine her beaming at him with that rosy glow shining out of her cheeks. "I'm using the Dark to channel my voice through these creatures. You don't need to understand anything else."

"So....where do you want to go?"

"Follow the creatures. They'll show you."

Yann stopped dead in his tracks. The woods in front of him looked like a vast nightmare-scape of dangerous, deadly creatures all attacking each other, trying to eat each other, and changing into every other kind of creature imaginable.

"You...you want us to go....in *there?*"

"It's the only way," she told him in a much more businesslike tone. "Come on. Let's go."

She scampered in front of him—her body did, anyway. This would be the first time ever that she took the lead or showed anyone anything. She always hung back when she traveled with the Black Watch.

She darted into the woods, scuttled a few dozen yards in front of him, and stopped to hunker near a different tree trunk.

She didn't look up at all the creatures and horrors lurking just inches above her. Any of them could attack her, wrap itself around her, and start digesting her—or Yann.

He gulped down a wave of nausea at the thought, but he couldn't stay here by himself, could he?

He swiveled his glaive in front of him to stab anything that so much as looked at him the wrong way.

He inched into the trees, but she turned out to be right.

All the creatures standing, sitting, slithering, rolling, and squirming all around him—they stared at him to watch him pass, but they didn't attack.

He kept jumping from one side to the other to point his glaive at them, but when they still didn't attack, he eventually lowered the weapon and just walked along looking at everything.

"How do you know about this place if you've never been here before?" he asked no one in particular.

Marine's voice came from behind him to the right. He didn't have time to turn around to see where it came from.

"I don't know anything about this place," she told him. "I'm just communing with the Dark forces to talk to you through them."

"How did you know these creatures don't hunt humans?" he asked.

"I can sense their intentions through the Layers."

He shut his eyes and shook his head. "I don't get it. I really don't."

She burst out laughing again—or her voice did. Her body stayed over there crouched under a tree. She didn't even look at him when he walked past her heading in the same direction.

"You aren't as much of an imp as you think you are," she told him.

"Oh, yes I am! I'm the biggest imp there ever was. I don't have a magical bone in my body. I don't even know how it works."

"Maybe the Voyant wants to change that," she pointed out. "Maybe Eliska is right and that's why he's looking for you."

"I doubt that." He squirmed and changed the subject. "If he wanted to recruit someone, he would recruit you or her."

Marine gave a little sigh of something like either contentment or approval. "She really is something special."

"She says exactly the same thing about you."

Marine snorted. It came out as a sneeze from another ball of fluff, but this one hung by a glistening strand of some kind of mucus. The goo oozed from a branch and held the ball of fluff suspended ten feet off the ground.

"She's everything I wish I could be," Marine exclaimed. "She's strong, brave, sensitive, beautiful...."

"You're all those things, too," he pointed out. "When you clean yourself up."

She burst out laughing. "Yann! I'm hurt! How dare you say that to me?!"

He found himself chuckling. Her sense of humor always put him at ease.

"You sure are beautiful when you clean yourself up and act normally." He tried not to wrinkle his nose at the crazy girl writhing and convulsing nearby. "I wish you could be like that all the time instead of......"

He broke off. He didn't want to offend her by saying what he really thought of her when she looked like that. At least he could talk to her right now.

"Maybe when we defeat the Voyant and this is all over, I won't have to commune with the Dark anymore," she suggested. "Maybe I'll be able to go home to the Hallowed Vales, marry a prince, and live happily ever after the way I'm supposed to."

Yann cocked his head. He would have studied her if she had been the one talking to him right now. "Is that what you want?"

"Of course! Isn't that what every princess wants?" She laughed. "I'm a princess. I grew up in a palace eating off golden plates and drinking out of golden chalices. I need a man who can keep me in the lifestyle to which I'm accustomed." She exploded in laughter. "That's so silly, isn't it?"

He tried to smile at her—or the empty piece of air her voice came from. "I'm sure you can find a handsome prince to give it to you. Any guy would be lucky to marry you."

"Aw!" she exclaimed. "That is such a sweet thing to say."

He forced himself to look away, but that only made him look back down at her squatting in the dirt. "Anyway, it's going to be a while before we find a way to defeat the Voyant."

She sighed and her voice settled to a normal tone. "You're right. I don't see how we can ever get out of it."

He hesitated and then blurted out. "Why do you have to commune with the Dark, anyway? Why can't you just...you know....walk next to me normally and talk to me yourself?"

"I will," she told him. "I just need to search for a while first."

"What are you searching for?"

"I search the Dark Layers for any information I can find—and also for any sign of the bolus of knowledge."

"But you never find anything in the Dark Layers," he pointed out. "What's the point of even doing it?"

"I haven't found anything yet, but I might. I don't want to miss anything."

Chapter 34

Yann and Marine continued through the woods for a few hours. Her voice kept him company along the way and they kept their conversation light. They didn't talk anymore about defeating the Voyant or what would happen when they did.

All that talk about Marine marrying a handsome prince made Yann's blood boil. He would never be a prince eating off of golden plates or drinking out of golden chalices.

Marine would never be more than a friend to him.—not that he knew what the hell he wanted out of life anyway.

Her remarks brought up all the old questions. Why did he even care if she married a prince if Yann planned to take an oath to the Black Watch?

He wouldn't take the oath because he wasn't a member of the Watch. He didn't even know where the nearest outpost of the Watch was located nor could he find it even if he did know.

He could wind up wandering the Coil forever. Then the question of finding a girl and settling down would become a non-issue.

He had enough to worry about just keeping himself alive right now.

"Ooo, look!" Marine exclaimed. "I see the edge of the trees ahead."

Yann spotted open fields out there.

"How can we meet back up with Anríq and Eliska?" he asked.

"I don't have a way to navigate in the Coil the way she does. I guess we just have to wait until Eliska finds us instead."

Marine broke off with a gasp when the two of them stepped out of the trees. The fields beyond these woods extended down to a river.

Yann didn't have to go near it. He could already tell from miles away that it was a Dark river.

Enormous wolves paced back and forth on the other side of the river. They guarded a magnificent city with clouds of flying vehicles circling enormous buildings. The noise of activity floated on the breeze even at this distance.

"That's it!" Marine gasped from behind Yann's back.

"What is?" he asked.

"The White Spire!" she breathed. "That's it! This landscape—it must have restored itself—unless we're in another illusion Layer."

"What are you talking about?" Yann asked.

"Eliska and I—we came here together when we got separated from you and the rest of the Watch—but this Island didn't look like this. Some kind of firestorm torched the city and killed everyone in it. All the buildings had been destroyed and fire razed the whole landscape. Only the White Spire was still there—and we saw the Voyant going into it. Eliska and I tried to break in more than once, but we couldn't even cross the river. The Voyant set up too many magical defenses."

"How do you think he restored the city?" Yann asked.

"I don't know...or maybe he moved the White Spire to another Layer."

"How could he do that?" Yann asked. "How could he move an entire building?"

"He's a powerful wizard, Yann," Marine sneered. "And the White Spire is magical. It can appear in any Layer of the Coil where he wants it to appear."

"Well, if you and Eliska couldn't break into it, then we won't be able to." Yann turned away. "If you don't want to take us to another Island, we should probably find a place to spend the night."

A different voice spoke up from the woods behind Yann. This sounded like the congested, nasal voice of an annoying little man "Your friend could break into the spire."

Yann whirled around fast trying to see who spoke to him this time. Marine crouched near some tangled tree roots. She didn't look up.

The creature that spoke to Yann actually did look like an extremely ugly, shrunken, wrinkled little man.

A pendulous, oversized belly and folds of loose skin hung all over its naked form. The creature only stood ten inches tall and perched in the crook of a branch.

Its enormous head distorted into an oversized jaw with two fangs sticking upward from the lower jaw. Heavy, bony brows darkened the small, fierce eyes.

"How do we break in?" Marine asked from another direction.

"Your friend isn't magical," the little wrinkled man replied. "The Voyant's defenses won't work on him. The Voyant is protecting himself from powerful magic-users, not some imp with a death wish."

"Yeah," Yann muttered. "That's me all over."

Marine burst out laughing again. "You really would go in there, wouldn't you?"

"Why do you want me to go in?" he asked. "I wouldn't be able to tell you anything."

"You can see what he's doing," Marine replied. "You might be able to find out his plans."

Yann snorted. "Now I know you're crazy. You're too crazy to know what the hell you're doing."

"Come on, Yann!" she pleaded. "Please? We've been trying to break into the White Spire all this time...."

"Who's we—apart from you and Eliska? Did the Guardian Templars try to sneak into the spire?

"The Guardian Templars never even found the Layer with the spire in it. Please, Yann? You'll be my hero for life if you do."

He made a face. "For whatever that's worth."

She laughed. "How about a big kiss from me? Is that enough of a reward?"

"A kiss on the cheek? No, it isn't. You kissed Anríq on the cheek just for making you dinner."

"Don't tell me you're jealous of Anríq!" she countered.

Yann looked away. "Fine. I'll do it. Just tell me what to do."

"You have to cross the river, climb the tower, and look inside it."

"You mean it doesn't have a front door I can just walk into?"

"Well, look at it," she exclaimed. "It doesn't have an outer door."

Yann studied the White Spire. She was right. From what he could tell, the outer cylindrical structure had been constructed of white marble rising to a pointed turret at the top.

A brilliant white light shone from four windows facing outward from the highest peak.

"That's where you'll find the Voyant," Marine told him. "That's where we saw him enter last time."

"I sure hope you're right about this," he murmured and took a step forward.

He advanced into the open fields between the trees and the Dark river.

He held his breath waiting for something to happen, but he was still too far away from the spire. He could just imagine the mayhem that would ensue when he finally got there.

The wolves paced faster as he got closer. They curled their lips back from their fangs, growled at him, and raised their hackles in tall, threatening spikes.

Yann gripped his glaive tighter and stopped on his side of the river. It oozed in its bed as black and ominous as the river that wiped out Eliska's awareness. It nearly killed her.

Wesh said it wouldn't affect an imp the same way if it affected Yann at all, but he still didn't want to go near it.

The temptation to impress Marine won the day. He dropped his glaive on the other bank, took a deep breath, dove in, and extended his arms above his head to swim to the other side.

The instant before his feet left the ground, an almighty boom went off in the air halfway across the river.

He didn't see what caused it, but at the same instant, a long vine of some plant shot out of the bank behind him.

More projectiles erupted out of nowhere. They came out of the ground and some even soared across the countryside from the woods behind him.

They all bombarded whatever that was in front of him. He didn't see anything, but there must have been something there for these things to bump into.

Vines, grass stems, twigs, rocks, dirt clods, and even tiny whizzing creatures bombarded some kind of magical surface right in front of Yann. All that stuff bounced off what looked like another watery magical pool.

The vines smashed and pounded the surface. The tiny creatures morphed and changed their shape every few seconds. They bounced off the surface only to spin the other way and dive in for another assault.

A torrent of projectiles whistled past Yann, assaulted the pool, and it detonated in his face. He was already leaping off the bank and he wound up diving straight through the breach.

His arms and head broke the surface and he plunged into a deep, black ocean of pure Darkness.

Gripping cold shut off his eyes, nose, and mouth. He couldn't tell anymore where he was or if he was going in the right direction.

He only knew he had to get out of this river as soon as humanly possible.

He struck out with his arms and legs to swim for the farther shore. God only knew how he would fight the wolves.

His lungs burst trying to hold his breath. He didn't dare to open his eyes—and then he broke the surface.

He didn't swim along the surface the way he would have in a normal body of water. The Dark river didn't function that way.

He wound up swimming straight up and broke the surface heading out into the open air.

The Dark ooze fell away from him instantly. It didn't soak his clothes, hair, or skin the way it soaked Eliska. Every droplet vanished and left him as clean and dry as he could possibly be.

He kept stroking his arms even as he swam through open air. He wound up standing on the bank with a foot of the Dark ooze around his calves.

He walked up on the other bank so he stood right in front of the wolves, but they didn't attack him.

Another epic surge of projectiles and flying creatures of all sizes converged across the countryside and enveloped the Wolves.

They shrieked and roared in fury trying. They whirled and snapped their jaws both to get away from the attacking debris and also to bite it back.

Yann didn't understand any of this. He only knew he had a straight run to the spire—for as long as the opportunity lasted.

He sprinted between the Wolves, made it to the spire's outer walls, and started climbing.

Mysterious shapes curled out of thin air and raced for him. Curling tendrils of light and what looked like disembodied strings of scaly flesh cracked and whipped all around him.

Then the projectiles and rapidly transforming creatures from across the river showed up to defend him here, too.

He couldn't look at what they were doing. He grabbed the wall and started climbing.

The white marble wall offered plenty of hand and footholds, but he kept flinching and cringing every time some magical battle broke out inches away from his head.

Random objects smashed into the stone on either side of his face. Creatures splattered there and some exploded in magical bursts, some small, some large.

Concussions kept going off behind him. He had no idea how any of this was happening. He couldn't stop now to figure it out.

Chapter 35

Yann climbed higher toward the turret at the top of the White Spire. The noise coming from behind him escalated to a thunderous roar.

Some of the explosions and crashes pounded his back and shoulders. He had to stop climbing more than once to tighten his hold so he wouldn't plunge off into the wolves' mouths.

The projectiles left the wolves alone as he climbed higher. The projectiles followed him up the spire's falls so these magical forces could defend Yann on the way up. If he fell, the Wolves would be all over him in seconds.

He took one last deep breath and pushed himself to climb the rest of the way to the turret. He grappled for a fingerhold on one of the four windowsills.

He pulled himself up just enough to peek over the side.

The windows looked in on a single room fifteen feet wide. It was completely empty except for the Voyant himself.

He glowed with the same golden halo. Everything else about him looked the same way Yann remembered from their previous encounters.

The Voyant raised his hands in front of him and created a much bigger, more detailed projection of the Coil than the one Eliska used.

The sight set off Yann's alarm bells. Eliska was the only person who could make that projection. Everyone said so. Anríq, Wesh, Marine—none of them could do it.

Was there a connection between Eliska and the Voyant? Was he.....?

No one knew who her parents were. Was he her father? Was that why he wanted to find her?

Yann forced himself to pay attention. The Voyant used magic radiating from his hands to distort the Coil in different shapes. He flexed his fingers to compress different Layers and make them collapse on top of each other.

The sight ignited Yann's fury. This bastard was manipulating the Coil right now—right here in front of Yann's eyes.

The Voyant buckled certain Layers and destroyed Islands with all their defenseless inhabitants trapped inside them. The Voyant didn't know or care who he killed in this sadistic game of his.

Yann gritted his teeth to climb the rest of the way into the turret. He didn't know what he would be able to do against the Voyant, but Yann had to try something.

He glanced over his shoulder to see if all the magical projectiles, creatures, and mystery weapons were still hanging around. Could they defeat the Voyant? Yann doubted it.

The minute he thought about them, he heard a different kind of silence The creatures, projectiles, and spikes no longer revolved around his head.

Yann froze when he saw Marine hovering a dozen yards away from him. The whips, tentacles, and magical forces that had been trying to attack him now went after her instead.

She floated there with her back to him while she fired magical pulses at all those assaults.

The creatures and projectiles swirled around her trying to fight the Voyant's defenses, too. Some of the creatures bore an uncanny resemblance to the familiars Yann had just talked to out in the forest. She must be the one doing this.

She fought back to stop all those forces from coming near Yann, but she couldn't hold them at bay.

They overpowered her, and right then, the Voyant soared past Yann's head and plowed into Marine full force.

She shrieked and writhed in midair, but she didn't fall. She tossed and contorted as magical concussions and starbursts flashed all around her.

The Voyant's hallow surrounded her, but Yann didn't see the Voyant himself. He must have vanished again and left his power here to destroy Marine in his place—or maybe this was another of the White Spire's defenses.

Yann stared at the scene in mounting horror. His fingers and his feet were starting to get tired from holding onto the spire walls. He would have to climb down, but he wouldn't be able to get back across the river without her protection.

He couldn't wait any longer. The sight of her in danger triggered an instinctive reaction.

He wrenched himself around and hurled himself off the spire with all his strength.

He launched himself into open space and slammed into her the way he did in the Layers.

He didn't know how or even if he would be able to save her, but she'd saved his life too many times for him to just leave her like this.

The impact tore both of them out of the halo. They plummeted straight toward the wolves, but the blow also set off a bone-crushing eruption that tore the whole Layer part.

The fabric of reality surrounding Yann detonated in his ears. He shut his eyes, tucked his head, and willed himself to hold onto Marine no matter what. He didn't risk this much to save her just to lose her again.

He braced himself for the wolves to attack and for the crash landing when he and Marine hit the ground. Falling from this height would break every bone in their bodies.

He wound up burying his face in Marine's neck where it met her shoulder. He clamped his arms around her to keep her with him .....and then they struck a surface underneath them.

They didn't break any bones. The surface bounced, undulated, and then sank under their weight when Yann and Marine both fell back down on it.

His eyes popped open and he looked up just as another bouncing wave heaved them into the air. It sank the same way and Yann stared all around him at a completely different Island.

A different combination of trees, bushes, and animals lived here. None of them looked like any of the familiars from the last Island. None of the creatures here transformed into something else.

The creatures didn't look anywhere near as dangerous, either—which was a good thing because Yann no longer had a weapon. He dropped his glaive by the Dark river and didn't get it back.

The whole landscape bounced and swayed in gentle, rubbery, undulating waves. Every move Yann made translated into a pouncing ripple spreading outward from where he sat.

Marine got his attention by giggling. He jerked around and found himself staring at her grinning up at him. She giggled again and bounced her weight on the grass underneath her.

It raised and lowered her in an easy rhythm in time with her bounce. She pressed her hands down on the grass to make the ground do the same thing. Then she did it harder to make Yann bounce.

Yann blinked at her as the truth sank in. She was perfectly sane again. He would recognize that mischievous glint in her eyes anywhere.

He forced himself to look around. "Now where are we?"

"At least we aren't fighting the Voyant anymore," she remarked.

"Are you okay? Did he hurt you? You sounded like you were in pain."

"I was—but I'm okay now." She bounced the grass and giggled again. "This is fun."

"Don't start, okay?"

Her eyes widened and a smirk spread across her mouth. "Don't start what? I would never start anything."

He made a face at her. "Now I know you're planning something."

"Planning? I'm not planning anything."

Yann tried to stand up. "Let's find out where we are and find a place to spend the night."

"No way!" she yelled. "I'm gonna have some fun. Come on, Yann!"

She shot to her feet and started bouncing along the surface in big, hard jumps. Each jump made the landscape surge in higher and higher waves.

She used the momentum to propel herself high into the sky and whooped with glee. "Whoo! This is great! Come on! Have some fun for once! You never do! You're way too serious!"

"Come down here now!" he snapped. "You're gonna break your neck!"

She exploded in laughter. "You're just jealous because you can't let your hair down! Come on! You'll never get another chance like this.

Isn't it bad enough that we're in a war against the Voyant and the Coil is collapsing around our ears? Wheee!"

She turned a somersault in midair and then did a backflip. She didn't seem to notice or care when her dress fell above her knees and showed her underwear.

"You're crazy!" he yelled after her.

"Yeah!" she shrieked. "Come on! We can be crazy together. Besides, we can travel faster this way!"

He frowned at her, but her childish laughter infected him the way it always did.

She got all tangled up in her own skirts and missed her bounce. She fell down on her back and oofed when the fall knocked the wind out of her, but she immediately got to her feet, laughed, and started jumping again.

The sight of her having so much fun snapped something in Yann's being. She was right. They would probably never get another chance to enjoy themselves like this—not anywhere as safe as this. This was by far the safest island he'd seen.

He threw caution to the wind, flexed his knees, and jumped. He bounced higher and higher.

She exploded in laughter when she saw him joining in. "Yay! Isn't this great? Watch this!"

She turned another triple backflip, bounced, and then did another layover to the front.

"Now you're just showing off!" he told her.

She squealed with glee. That sound sent a tendril of fire through his insides. He wanted to make her laugh like that.

He bounced closer, timed his next jump, and collided with her.

He sent her sprawling, but she just bounced up again. "Hey! You cheater!" She shrieked and laughed again.

"I'm gonna take you down, Marine!" he told her. "You can't get away from me!"

She screeched with laughter and started bouncing away from him across the landscape. She had to be careful to avoid trees and a few rock outcroppings.

He bounced after her and found himself gasping with laughter. This really was fun. He almost caught her a few times. Her screams of fake terror only made him laugh harder.

She made it as far as another forest before she turned around to face him. Her eyes flashed with mischief and high color lit up her cheeks. He couldn't remember her looking more beautiful.

He bounced toward her, but she dodged, grabbed him by the jacket, and threw him away. He had to bounce for a few more minutes before he got near enough to take his revenge.

He pretended to just enjoy bouncing at a distance from her. He waited until she turned around.

She used her bounces to gain altitude so she could see the landscape beyond the woods. She made her last mistake when she turned her back on Yann.

He launched himself at her, grabbed her, and body-slammed her into the ground with all his weight.

She screamed again and then burst out laughing when the force of his bounce hurled both of them into the air. They both somersaulted away from each other, but she retaliated instantly.

She landed on all fours, propelled herself up, and tackled him. They both crashed down on top of each other and fought for dominance.

She turned out to be a lot stronger than he realized. She pinned him, but he bounced her off, took a few more bounces on his knees, and brought her down with a grunt before he pounced on her and sat on her.

He sat on her back bouncing up and down while she squealed with laughter. "I'm gonna get you for this, Yann!" she shrieked. "Mark my words!"

His sides ached with laughter. "Where's that kiss you promised me?

"Did I say kiss? I meant kick. I'll kick you up the backside as soon as I...."

He burst out in fresh laughter. "You won't go anywhere until you offer complete surrender. Admit it. I beat you."

"You bastard!" she roared and laughed again.

Without warning she flipped him off. He didn't see how she did it. She didn't use magic. She must have used the stretchy landscape.

She tumbled him off, landed on top of him, and shoved his face down into the bouncy surface of the grass.

She toppled off and collapsed against one of the heaving swellings while she caught her breath.

Yann tried to get up, but he wound up sinking back against another bank nearby. He beamed at her and she beamed back. "So who was the winner?" she panted.

"Let's call it a draw. We're supposed to be allies here."

She laughed again. "Deal."

He looked around more seriously. "The time here is the same as the Island where we saw the spire. We should find a place to spend the night."

"We probably shouldn't bounce inside that forest," Marine pointed out.

"What did you see beyond it?"

"More farmland....and a few towns and cities. The landscape doesn't seem to bounce over there."

"Let's go check it out."

She smirked at him. "Now aren't you glad you did this?"

He found himself grinning back at her. "Yeah. Thank you for encouraging me. Let's go."

She bounced the grass underneath her. "It would be a lot more comfortable to sleep here than on the solid ground."

He got to his feet and held out his hand to her. "I'm sure it isn't what you're used to back at your father's palace."

He helped her stand up and tried not to notice the feeling of her velvety hands touching his. He let go immediately so she wouldn't think he was trying to hold her hand.

They entered the woods and the canopy immediately darkened the way. The leaf cover exaggerated the growing shadows of dusk.

Yann and Marine held onto the trees to stop themselves from bouncing into the branches, but the bouncy nature of this Island diminished more and more the farther they went.

The landscape completely solidified by the time the travelers made it to the other side of the woods.

Marine stopped at the tree line, gazed out at the countryside falling into night, and sighed. "It was bound to end sooner or later."

"It's too bad we can't see where this Island is in the Coil," Yann remarked. "We might be able to come back here one day."

She smiled up at him—and this time, she gave him a full, warm smile of pure understanding. "Maybe Eliska can help us with that. We should find her."

"Not tonight. Come on. Let's make camp and get comfortable. We'll need sleep for tomorrow."

Chapter 36

Yann gathered a bunch of sticks and Marine used her magic to ignite them into a fire. The two travelers worked together to hunt a biturong for their supper.

He found himself gazing at her in the firelight. Every minute he spent with her increased the feeling that she was something beyond rare and precious—something completely out of his reach.

"I saw some towns and cities in the distance when we were jumping around," she told him after they finished sucking the juice off their fingers.

"You told me."

"One of those cities has a Temple of the Guardian Templars," she added.

He looked up. "Really?"

"They might be able to tell us something we don't already know. They might even know where the bolus of knowledge is."

"But if they have a functioning Temple, they wouldn't need the bolus of knowledge," he pointed out. "They'll already have all the knowledge there in the Temple."

She burst into a huge grin and her cheeks colored. 'You're so smart! Why didn't I think of that?"

He turned away to stop her from seeing his cheeks burning, but she must have been able to see them anyway. He and Marine only sat a few feet apart.

She turned back to gaze into the flames and sighed. "I wish Anríq and Eliska were here."

"I'm surprised her magic isn't enough to overcome the Voyant," Yann remarked. "Everyone keeps saying how much more powerful she is than everyone else. Even Wesh said that."

Marine murmured under her breath without looking up. "I don't wish she was here because of her magic. She has something—something more powerful than magic—something that can't be covered up with jokes and games."

Yann didn't want to talk about Eliska—not in front of Marine. "I'm sorry I didn't find out anything when I looked into the spire. I guess we'll just have to guess what he's doing."

"I saw enough while you were there. You got both of us close enough for me to see what he's doing."

"You did?" Yann frowned. "So what is he doing?"

"He's attacking the Barbarians. I didn't see anything more than that before he came after me."

"Why don't you, Anríq, and Eliska combine your magic to break into the spire? Would the three of you working together be enough to get you inside?"

"Maybe, but there's no way to completely eliminate the Dark, not even if all the magic-users in the Coil worked together. The Dark is part of the Coil. The Coil can't function without the Dark."

"So what's the solution?" he asked. "What chance do we have?"

"The only thing we can do is stabilize the Coil. That means taking out the Voyant and replacing him with someone who will rule the Coil benevolently. We don't have to go looking for the Voyant because he's already looking for us. We just have to find the person he wants—or the person he's trying to stop."

She looked up at him and the expression on her face made him look away. "That isn't me. I can't become the Voyant. I'm nothing."

She shrugged it off and settled back on her elbow. "We'll ask the Templars about it. They might have more information about who the person is."

He found himself studying her more closely, now that he didn't have to worry about her looking at him like that.

"Would you mind showing me the route to the Temple?" he asked. "In case you lose your mind tomorrow or something like that?"

She only laughed at him. "I guess I can't argue with that."

She picked up one of the sticks he'd gathered for the fire and scrawled a crude sketch in the dirt by her knees.

"There are two mountain ranges out there—here and here. They come together in a pass—here. There's a good-sized city there—not as big as the one we just saw—but good-sized."

"Why do you think the cities don't have the Guardian Temple?"

"That city we just saw had a church instead. That's their thing."

"Are the two incompatible with each other? I don't know enough about either."

"Didn't you have a church in Middleborough? Don't tell me all you people were heathens."

"No, we didn't have a church. No one could afford to support one."

She sighed again and gazed into the flames. "I used to hate going to church when I was growing up. We all had to dress up in our fanciest clothes. I used to joke to my brother that going to church was more of a fashion show than anything else. All the local dignitaries had to see us sitting there in the royal gallery box for five hours straight while the…."

"Five hours!" Yann gasped. "That sounds awful!"

She laughed at him and her eyes twinkled. "I'm sure I told myself it was a lot more awful than it was. My mother loved going to church. She would always come out of the service glowing. She couldn't wait to go back there every week."

"What is it like?" he asked. "What do they do?"

"They sing...and recite passages of scripture....and the priest gives a sermon.....and then everyone takes communion."

"What's that?" he asked.

She waved it away. "It would take too long to explain."

Now it was Yann's turn to gaze into the flames. "I'm sure your prince will understand all about it. You and he can go to church in all your finery with all your little princes and princesses. Then you can make *them* sit there for five hours straight."

She laughed again. "I can't wait."

He found himself beaming back at her. Her vivacious nature made him want to joke around and make her laugh some more.

She didn't look away when he stared down into her dark, glistening eyes. He would really have liked to make a move on her, but all this talk about princes and finery stopped him.

He eventually broke eye contact, stood up, and dusted off his hands. "Stay here. I'll gather some tinder to make you a bed to sleep on. I'm sure it won't be up to the standard you're used to, but it will be better than sleeping on the ground."

She only smiled at him more broadly. "I'm sure it will be wonderful because you made it for me."

He turned bright red and went out into the shadowy forest alone. He worked a lot harder to build both a shelter and a bed for her than he would have if she hadn't just given him that compliment.

He finally constructed a large leaf hut with a thick cushion of leaves inside it. He laid a mat of dry grass over the top to make it as comfortable as possible.

She watched from the fire without a word. He finally waved his arm in a sweeping bow toward the hut entrance. "Your boudoir is prepared, Your Majesty."

She burst out laughing. "My father would throw you in the dungeon if he knew we were going to sleep in there together tonight."

Yann's cheeks burned again. "Don't tell him."

"I wouldn't feel safe without you there to guard me." She flashed him another brilliant smirk, crawled into the hut, and curled up on her side.

Yann hesitated until she got into a comfortable position. She folded her arm under her head.

This position showed off the gentle sweeping curve of her hip dropping down to her waist and rising back up her ribs to her shoulder. Her dark hair spilled over the straw mat underneath her—the mat he made for her.

He took another deep breath, crawled inside the hut, and lay down on his side facing her.

He rested his head on his elbow planning to watch her fall asleep. He just wanted to look at her and bask in the glow of how beautiful she was—both inside and out.

Her eyes floated open as soon as he got into that position. She gazed up at him with so much overflowing meaning hidden in those eyes.

He found himself getting lost in them and he didn't look away. He didn't move any closer and neither did she.

In a little while, her eyes floated shut, but he stayed awake. He stared at her angelic face for a long time.

He wouldn't get another chance to bounce and play with her in that springy landscape.

He probably wouldn't get another chance to look at her like this. He just had to take the chance now. Then he would be able to remember this later after he lost her again.

Chapter 37

Marine sighed again when she and Yann left the forest for the open farmland. "I guess the vacation had to end sooner or later."

He found himself drifting closer to her. He didn't touch her or take her hand or say anything, but yesterday brought them closer together.

They walked in silence for most of the day as the city in the distance got closer. She didn't really need to show him that sketch of how to get there. He would have been able to find it without her help.

The landscape started out harmless enough. It spread outward from the two travelers in a carpet of green. Livestock grazed along the roadsides—and none of these animals changed their shape or even acted like that was a possibility in this world.

Everyone in the surrounding hamlets and villages went about their business. No one paid any attention to the travelers.

The day wore on, but it became more obvious with every passing hour that all was not right in the city up ahead.

Curtains of Dark magic kept sweeping out of the sky, descending on the city, and wreaking havoc.

Funnels and tornados of debris and wreckage ejected out of the streets. Pieces of buildings collapsed before Dark vapors drifted back into the atmosphere.

"I don't see any Layers collapsing up there," Yann pointed out. "I wonder what's going on."

"The Dark is attacking the city," Marne pointed out.

"Is there any way to stop it?"

"The city has magical defenses. Magic-users live there. They're trying to hold off the Dark, but it doesn't always work."

Yann squinted up at the sky and around at the landscape. "We don't see as many Darklings anymore. Have you noticed that? They don't come out as often or attack the way they used to."

"What do you think it means?"

"I don't know. I would have thought the Darklings would become more aggressive, more violent, and more common as the Coil destabilizes. Now it seems like the landscape itself is becoming more aggressive and violent—kind of like those waves tried to knock us over. Collapses seem to target us. It's almost like the landscape itself is turning against us."

"I wonder if it's like that for everyone or just for us.....or you."

He glanced over at her, but she gave no sign that what she said meant anything.

He let the subject drop.

He and Marine had a long hike to the city. That gave them plenty of time to observe the Dark forces assaulting the city.

"The attacks are definitely deliberate," he remarked. "Did you see that way that one shadow came down and retreated? It didn't blow along with the wind."

"I wonder what it is about this city that the Dark wants to destroy."

He stopped in his tracks, and without thinking about it first, he took hold of her wrist to pull her to a stop. "Don't commune with the Dark, Marine—not here. I need you to stay sane."

She only smiled at him. "I won't be able to commune with the Dark here. I wouldn't be able to find out what I want to know from the Templars if I went out into the Dark. Besides, the Temple blocks Dark magic. You don't have to worry about anything."

He ran his hand across his eyes. "Thank goodness for that."

She didn't try to take her arm out of his grasp. "What's wrong?" she asked. "Does it bother you that much when I go out into the Dark?"

"It didn't before, but now you're the only person I have left. If you go out there, I'm alone."

Her face pinched in sympathy and shared pain. "I'm so sorry! I didn't even think of that!"

"It isn't like I even need you to protect me—which we both know I do. It's just....It's a lot nicer when I can talk to you about everything."

She burst into a huge, beautiful smile. "It's much nicer when I have you to talk to, too. I would much rather be here talking to you than out there with the Darklings."

"Stay in touch with me once we get inside the city. Don't disappear into the Temple and leave me wondering what happened to you. Okay? Keep me updated on what you're doing and what you find out—like you did in Tenby."

She pressed his hand deeper into her arm. "I will. I promise. If I find out anything, you'll be the first to know."

They went on in silence after that. Marine's behavior gave Yann some assurance, but not very much.

More and more Dark forces drifted out of the atmosphere, blew through the city causing mayhem and destruction in their wake, and retreated back into the clouds.

Those forces snatched up anyone who went outside, tore them apart, and in some cases, carried them away into the shadows up there. Those people didn't come back.

The city itself became more distinct as the pair got closer. From a distance, the city looked like the towering metropolis of glass and steel where Yann and Marine saw the Voyant in his White Spire.

This city had some very tall buildings, but not as tall. It didn't have flying vehicles, either.

A hefty stone wall four feet thick surrounded the city's outer perimeter. "My God!" Yann gasped. "They have the Black Watch on guard!"

"This is great!" Marine exclaimed. "You should join them."

Yann's throat constricted when he saw uniformed Watchmen patrolling the wall.

They noticed him and Marine, too, aimed their weapons out at him, and bellowed down from the top. "Halt! Stop there and state your business!"

Yann raised his arms over his head and yelled back. "My name is Yann Dilnao! I'm a Watchman from Middleborough, a town that was lost in the Coil. My father Yvan was Commander of the Watch and we escaped with six other Watchmen—all of whom fell to the Coil. I'm the last one left! This is my friend, Marine. She's a member of the Guardian Templars! She's here to consult with them about how to stabilize the Coil and possibly save your city from the Dark! You can see we're both unarmed!"

The Watchmen held a hasty conversation up there.

"What's your rank?" the same man yelled down.

Yann took a deep breath. "I'm underage, so I haven't taken my oath yet—but my father raised me in the Watch my whole life. I've fought Darklings more times than I can remember—and my friend and I have been surviving in the Coil ever since. If you let me in, I'll join the Watch and stand on the wall with you. We've been looking for you for weeks."

The Watchmen had to talk about that, too, but in a minute, they opened the city gates to let Yann and Marine inside.

This city had a different style of gate from the ones in Tenby. An absolutely gigantic stone blocked a tall arch constructed into the defensive walls. The men behind the gate had to activate a series of counterweights to raise the stone.

It thumped back into place as soon as Yann and Marine entered. No one could get through that. The only other way inside the city was over the wall itself—or straight down from the sky.

The arch formed a small room inside the wall. The room opened into a huge courtyard full of Watchmen.

Four Watchmen surrounded Yann as soon as he and Marine stepped through the gate. Yann recognized one of the men as the guy who challenged him just now.

Yann would have been worried if he still had a weapon, but the Watchmen didn't hold him as a prisoner.

The first guy grabbed Yann's hand and shook it way too hard. "We're so grateful that you're here! I'm Maximil Rishar and this is Oran Sylvestre. Welcome to Savaré."

"Which of you is Commander of the Watch?" Yann's eyes darted down to the man's collar.

Yann froze when he saw the plain black band around Maximil's neck. Maximil wasn't wearing any pips there—not a single one. Neither was Oran.

"We don't have any rank," Maximil explained. "The Watch Commander recruited us from the general population. I was a shipping clerk. Oran here was a freight laborer. All of us standing the wall right now are recruits. The Watch Commander was just training us when we suffered an attack...."

"What kind of attack?" Yann asked. "Was it Darklings?"

"We...." Maximil glanced at Oran and then looked down at the ground. "We don't know what it was. None of us has any experience with this. We only took up arms the day before to join the Watch. None of us has even sworn the oath. We didn't plan to. We're family men—and then the Watch Commander and all his men got killed on the wall. We're the only ones left."

Yann gulped. "So....none of you has any experience.....at all?"

Maximil shook his head. "You're the most experienced man here. Would you....would you take over.....please? We need a Watch Commander—someone who knows what they're doing—someone who knows what we can expect to face out there."

Yann cast a glance into the courtyard behind Maximil's back. Two dozen Watchmen stood around listening to the conversation—or at least all those men wore Black Watch uniforms.

None of those men had any pips on their collar, either.

Yann's one lonely pip—the pip that marked him as so inferior to the others—it looked downright regal now.

Marine distracted him by touching his arm. "I'm going to the Temple. I'll see you soon."

He glanced at her in time to catch her eye before she hurried away through the streets.

"So...will you?" Maximil asked again. "Will you take command of us? We don't even know if our defenses are strong enough. We don't know what we should be preparing for."

Yann compressed his lips. He'd already gone through this once at Tenby. He knew the drill.

He threw back his shoulders. "Yes. I'll take command of you."

Maximil burst into a huge, trembling smile and his lower lip quivered. "Thank you so much! You don't know what this means. Please....come inside. We'll show you everything and explain what we've been doing—but we've all been in such disarray since the Watchmen died."

"I understand," Yann replied. "Show me your defenses."

Maximil led the way out of the arch room and into the courtyard. All the Watchmen stopped what they were doing to stare at Yann.

This city had most of the same machinery he'd seen in Tenby and then some. They had a different kind of screen in each house and he saw people working on them in different ways—ways he didn't recognize.

He ignored that and turned his attention to the defenses themselves. The city followed a different construction plan than the wall and the gate. They must have been constructed in ancient times. The city was too advanced with too many strange machines.

The wall turned out to be much thicker than Yann initially suspected. The Savaré wall didn't use scaffolds or ladders to climb up to the defensive positions.

Stone staircases had been built into the wall's interior. Maximil led Yann right inside the wall itself, up the stairs, and they came out on a stone ledge built behind the parapet.

The Watchmen stood on this ledge where the wall's bulk protected them from anything attacking from the outside.

Savaré didn't have rocket launchers or rifles or any other kind of guns the way Tenby did.

Yann was starting to wonder if Tenby might have been completely unique in the whole Coil for the kind of weapons its people used.

The wall couldn't protect Savaré from the Dark forces coming down from above. Nothing could.

Yann climbed onto the ledge and the assembled Watchmen moved out of the way to let him through.

The minute he got there, another Dark vapor drifted down from the sky—except that it didn't drift. Its movement looked too deliberate.

It lashed down at the city, struck another tall building, and detonated the spire rising into the clouds. The top ten stories exploded and rained rubble and broken glass into the streets below.

Yann and all the Watchmen ducked for cover. Yann put his arms over his head.

"It happens all the time," Maximil told him.

"So you haven't seen any Darklings?" Yann asked.

"*We* haven't," Oran explained. "We don't know what the Watch Commander and the other Watchmen faced before they recruited us."

"Did you serve in the last battle—the one that got them killed?" Yann asked.

Maximil shook his head. "The Watch Commander wouldn't let us fight. He said we needed more training or he would only be sending us to our deaths. He made us take shelter with our families—and when we came out, the Watchmen were all dead."

"Did you find their bodies?" Yann asked. "Did they die here or did they get taken to the Dark Layers?'

"They were here," Oran murmured. "They looked like they'd been flayed alive."

Yann narrowed his eyes at the countryside beyond the wall. "It might be Darklings or it might not be."

"What are we going to do?" Maximil pointed up at the sky. "How do we defend ourselves against *that?*"

"What shelter do you use for your civilians?" Yann asked.

"We have reinforced underground basements under most of the residential buildings," Maximil replied. "All our people have orders to take refuge there in case of an attack."

"You have magical defenses, too," Yann went on. "Show me where they are and what they're supposed to be doing."

Maximil and Oran exchanged glances. "Um....I don't know anything about that."

Yann frowned. "My friend is a magic-user. She said you had magical defenses—and magic-users helping defend the city."

The two Watchmen glanced at each other again. Neither of them answered.

Yann pursed his lips. He was starting to see the magnitude of the job in front of him.

He couldn't leave this city defenseless. These men didn't even have a Watch Commander.

"What defenses *do* you have?" he finally asked.

"Well....we have the wall...and our weapons...."

Yann didn't even have to look. These men had axes, swords, glaives, and a few maces. That was it. It wouldn't defend this city against anything, especially not anything Dark.

"Does this city have any magic-users in it at all?" Yann finally asked.

"We have a few different healers and spellbinders."

"Go get them," Yann ordered.

"But....they'll all be busy at this time of day. They all have professions."

"Tell them they'll all be dead along with everyone else in town if they don't come right now." Yann pointed out at the Dark vapors sweeping down. "Those strikes will get bigger and stronger. We needed defenses and we need them now."

Chapter 38

Yann lifted down a lantern from the shelf and left the storeroom in the Savaré Black Watch's headquarters. The Watch used the bottom story of one of the larger buildings nearest the wall.

Maximil and Oran waited for Yann to finish inspecting the Watch's supply of weapons. "So?" Maximil asked. "What do you think? Will it be enough?"

"I won't know that until the next attack. I didn't come to see if it will be enough because it will just have to be. I just wanted to see what you have."

Yann left the room. The lantern and the room used some kind of strangely powered lights like the ones in Tenby.

He led the two men out of the storeroom and halted on the stairs. "Where do you men stay? Do you have rooms in this building?"

"No, we...." Maximil and Oran exchanged glances again. They did that a lot whenever Yann asked them a question.

"We all have families," Oran blurted out. "We go home every night.....but we can stop doing that if you really want us to."

"No, you can keep doing it—as long as you realize you'll be on call around the clock in case something happens."

Yann walked past them to the stairs and climbed up to ground level. The headquarters consisted of the Watch Commander's office and a bunch of other multipurpose rooms.

"Did the other Watchmen live upstairs?" Yann asked. "Where are the bedrooms?"

Maximil opened and closed his mouth a few more times. They had rooms upstairs—but we'd like to give you and your companion your own apartment. We wouldn't feel right about you staying here. The Watchmen's rooms are....well, let's just say they're small and poor. They aren't good enough for a Watch Commander."

Yann took a breath to argue—or at least to explain that he and Marine weren't together.

He decided to give it up. "All right. Show me where you want me to stay."

The two men led the way outside. More Watchmen crowded the courtyard staring at Yann as he walked past. Everyone in Savaré did that no matter where he went.

The Watchmen led Yann to a different building, through the lobby, and into a moving box that carried them up three flights to the building's top story. These moving boxes would have terrified Yann if he hadn't already gotten used to them in Tenby.

Maximil opened the door or a magnificent apartment crowded with countless machines. Yann recognized some of them. Others he wouldn't have been able to understand if he studied them for a million years.

The apartment consisted of a giant living room bigger than the entire house the Watchmen stayed in during their time in Middleborough.

Trays of pre-prepared food covered the huge table with six chairs sitting around it. The apartment also had a kitchen similar to the one in the Watch's Tenby house.

The living room adjoined a huge terrace overlooking the city—just in case Yann needed something to remind him of the Dark forces descending from the skies.

Four palatial bedrooms exited the living room. This apartment would have resembled Costico's palace if not for all the machines everywhere.

Yann realized in that moment that the previous Savaré Watch Commander couldn't have lived here. He wouldn't have had a family or anyone else who needed so many bedrooms. He must have stayed in the headquarters building with the other men.

"Thank you very much," Yann exclaimed. "I'm very grateful for your hospitality."

"We're all so relieved that you're here, Watch Commander," Maximil replied. "None of us knew what to do before you came. Your arrival is the answer to our prayers."

Yann only nodded. "I'll meet you and the men out in the courtyard first thing tomorrow morning. Continue with your established rotations until then."

"Don't you want to change anything?" Oran asked.

"Not until I see exactly what you're doing and I can't do that now. Good night. Sleep well."

Yann stopped short of actually shutting the door in their faces. He waited for them to leave before he shut it, got himself something to eat, and collapsed on the couch.

This was a fine turn of events—getting himself instated as Watch Commander—again.

He didn't let himself think about what his father might have thought about that. The situation on the wall looked bad enough. Yann didn't see how he would be able to save these people from any-thing—no more than he had been able to save Tenby.

He bent over the tray of food and picked up what looked like some kind of sandwich.

A thin kind of bread cake surrounded shredded meat, cheese, and vegetables with some kind of sauce leaking out of the edges where someone had cut the sandwich in half.

He took one bite before Marine breezed in. She had changed her clothes and probably taken a bath at the Guardian Temple since he saw her last.

She attacked the food in wolfish bites. "This is fantastic!"

"I guess the townspeople brought this here to welcome us," Yann remarked.

"I'm not talking about the food!" Marine mumbled with her mouth full. "I'm talking about the computers! This place has the most advanced technology! I haven't seen this stuff since I was an initiate."

Yann looked up. "They do? Are you sure?"

She burst out laughing, choked on her food, and some of it came out of her nose. She had to wipe her eyes and clean herself up before she could go on.

"What do you think that is?" She pointed across the room at what looked like a picture on the wall.

"Um....it looks like a painting of a landscape."

"It's a computer, silly! You really need an education."

"Watch it!" he snapped. "I got plenty of education."

"Well, you're about to get some more. Watch this."

She went over to the picture and tapped on it. It vanished and brought up a completely different screen.

Yann floundered in confusion watching her swipe the screen back and forth, tap on different pictures to open different pages and documents, and then shut them before she did something else.

"Does this help us?" he asked. "Does this have anything on the Voyant?"

"*This* doesn't, but it lets me access all the Templars' records in a fraction of the time. If the Templars know anything, I'll find it."

Yann sank back down on the couch. "I'll believe it when I see it. We've followed too many dead ends already."

"But don't you see?! The information must be out there somewhere! We just haven't found it yet."

"Uh-huh. You let me know when you do. Until then, I need you to send some of your Templar friends down to the wall to create a magical barrier to keep out the Dark vapors."

She straightened up and blinked at him with a bulge of food sticking out of her cheek. "Doesn't the Watch already have that?"

"They don't have any magical defenses. They might have before, but they don't now. They don't have squat as far as I can tell."

She gaped at him. "Are you serious?"

He nodded. "These men are just family men and businessmen. None of them is a real Watchman. They barely know how to hold a weapon. They only got recruited a few days ago."

She stared at him with her eyes hanging out before she managed to swallow the food in her mouth. "Wow. That's terrible."

"It isn't their fault. The Watch got wiped out during the last attack."

She went back to eating. "So what's attacking? Is it Darklings or just Dark forces?"

"None of them can tell me. None of these men have ever fought before—either Darklings, Dark forces, landscape collapse, or anything else. They're completely untried and untrained."

"I'm so sorry," she exclaimed. "You really have a herculean task in front of you, don't you?"

"You don't have to be sorry for me. I'm just sorry they don't have anyone more qualified to call on. I'll do my best, but they need a real Watch Commander."

"You're as real a Watch Commander as they're likely to get. If they haven't faced anything, then someone with your experience will be perfect."

"I meant a more seasoned officer like my father—or any of the other Watchmen. They all had years of experience fighting the Darklings."

"A more seasoned officer like your father still wouldn't be able to protect these people from this," Marine pointed out. "We need Anríq's club and Eliska's staff for a situation like this."

"Well, we don't have either, so we need the Templars to step in and fill the gap. Can I count on you to recruit them?"

She smirked at him across the table. "You bet. I'll do whatever I can to help."

"So how are things at the Temple?" he asked between mouthfuls. "Did they welcome you back with open arms? They certainly improved your wardrobe."

She laughed. "They didn't welcome me back with open arms because, unlike you, I'm still just an initiate. The Temple is packed to the rafters with Brothers, Masters, and initiates more skilled and experienced than I am. I'm nobody to them."

"Are they letting you access the information you need? Are they keeping you out of the library?"

She burst into another smirk. "That's where the computers come in. I can access what I want through them."

"I don't want to know what you're doing. Just tell me when you find the information."

"I will." She got to her feet. "Do we need to have another wrestling match to decide which rooms to take?"

He laughed and his cheeks flamed. "Something tells me that wouldn't be a good idea in here."

"We could put a bunch of mattresses on the floor. Then we wouldn't hurt each other—or at least I wouldn't hurt you."

He couldn't stop laughing. "Pride goes before a fall, young one. You can choose which room you want. I'll take the dregs."

She joined in the joke and disappeared into one of the bedrooms. She didn't shut the door.

He flatly refused to look in that direction. He didn't want to see whatever he might see of her getting ready to go to sleep. He'd already seen enough last night in that leaf hut.

Chapter 39

Yann paced up and down the wall observing the Watchmen practicing with their weapons down in the courtyard. They drilled the strikes and combinations he taught them. They just needed practice—a lot of practice.

He cast one flinty glance out at the fields beyond the wall. That countryside looked so harmless and serene yesterday when he and Marine came to Savaré.

Now he noticed something strange. The shadows lengthened from the forest at sundown yesterday. They didn't recede as far as they should have when the sun came up. The Dark vapors hanging over the city hovered a little lower and a little Darker.

The Dark forces never attacked outright—not with such power that they could wipe out the city—but they would attack in force eventually. The Dark powers would continue to gather until they laid this city to waste the same way they destroyed Tenby.

He stationed five magic-users around the wall to erect a magical barrier like the one that protected Middleborough.

Yann had to spend at least an hour explaining to these people exactly what he wanted. None of them had any experience with any kind of defense. They never needed it before.

Now they wove an intricate net of magical fibers into a vast dome to protect the city.

The process took way too long. They'd lifted the dome twenty feet above the wall. That wasn't nearly high enough to protect the city from the Dark vapors attacking from above.

The longer Yann watched, the more convinced he became that this really was another attack. Those vapors didn't strike at random.

Whoever was doing this wanted to make it look random, but it wasn't. The vapors really did come after the city for the one express purpose of inflicting damage on the buildings.

Yann gave orders for everyone to evacuate the taller buildings. This wreaked havoc on the population because Savaré didn't have enough space for all these people.

The population had to go through another flurry of reorganization. Yann got roped into supervising and giving orders to everyone on what to do.

He wouldn't have been able to tolerate it if everyone didn't keep showering him with gratitude for doing this. No one mentioned that he was the youngest person involved in this.

Maximil came up to him just then. "If you follow me, Watch Commander, I'll show you the field hospital."

Yann went with him. No one called Yann by his name in this city. Hardly anyone knew it besides Maximil and Oran.

The three men descended to the street and turned off toward a different building. Yann didn't know what was in it, but just then, Marine came down the street.

"Oh, good, you're here," Yann exclaimed. "I was hoping you could take a look at the barrier. Some of the magic-users are leaving gaps in the fabric. I need you to close the holes and correct them so it doesn't happen again."

"Sure," she replied. "Show me where."

He led her to the north side of the wall where one young man was weaving the fabric of the barrier too thin.

Marine placed her hand next to his. Magic streamed from her hand, spread outward, closed all the holes, and the barrier shot up another fifty feet right away.

"That's amazing!" some nearby Watchmen breathed.

"How did you do that?" the young man asked.

She only smiled at him. "Try to weave it a little tighter. We can't have any holes or we might as well not have a barrier at all.

She turned to Yann. "Could you please come to the library with me? I want to show you something. It's important."

"Okay," he replied. "Let me just take care of a few things and then we'll go."

He returned to the courtyard and gave new orders for the next group of Watchmen to train.

He had to go through the group and show them exactly which maneuvers to practice because the men didn't remember what he taught them the first time.

"Your wife is a powerful magic-user," Maximil remarked on their way back across the street.

"My...." Yann almost asked who Maximil meant and to correct him about Yann not having a wife.

Yann changed his mind and bit his lip to stop himself from grinning. These people thought he and Marine were together.

Yann's stomach flipped at the thought—but it would never happen. She was a jewel—someone else's jewel.

No way would she ever turn her head for some common Watchmen.

He wasn't even a Watchman. He was nothing. He was a homeless wanderer just like Eliska and Anríq.

Yann and Marine headed across town together. "What did you want to show me?" he asked on the way.

"I think I found what we're looking for," she murmured under her breath. "I can't be sure, but I think I found it."

He looked up. "Really? What is it?"

"I have to show you. I don't dare to tell you without showing you."

The excitement in her eyes stopped him from asking. If she thought she found the answer, then it must be something big.

She climbed the long granite steps to the Guardian Temple. He'd never just waltzed through the front door like this, but no one stopped her.

The two friends filed through dozens of halls. They all looked remarkably similar to the empty halls the travelers found in the cloud tower—the obvious difference being that all of these had hundreds of people in them.

Initiates and students ate, studied, talked, discussed, and the Brothers and Masters took classes full of pupils all seated at their desks.

They read from books, but they as often worked on computers at almost every desk. The Brothers and Masters used computer screens to display diagrams and text in front of their classes.

Yann's head spun trying to take it all in, but none of this seemed to interest Marine.

She returned to a different kind of library—a library with not one single book in it.

Five long tables ran the length of the room. A bunch of initiates sat at the tables working on more computer screens on the surface. No one looked up when Marine walked in.

She found a place at the far end of the lefthand table, pulled a computer screen toward her, and showed it to Yann—like he would somehow be able to understand what was on it.

"Okay, here we go," she whispered.

"Did you access the forbidden library from here?" he asked.

"I didn't have to. I didn't think I would and I was right. I found the information in the regular archives. It turns out that the Voyant Mendicat isn't as secret as we thought."

Yann frowned. "Then why haven't we found this before?"

"Probably because we were researching the Voyant instead of the King in the White Spire."

She did something to the screen and changed the document that appeared on it.

"Do you remember what we talked about in the cloud tower?" she asked. "You asked if there was any correlation between the instability cycles and the Voyant taking over as ruler when the old King dies."

"So is there?'

"Yes. They correspond exactly—and take a look at this. This is an old legend about the succession of Kings."

He frowned at a list of names. "This is the same list we saw in the genealogy. It lists all the births and deaths we saw there. I don't understand what this is telling us that we don't already know."

"This is a much more complete list. Look. This one includes birth and death dates for Queens who were married to the Kings—and even some who weren't."

"How could they be Queens if they weren't married to the Kings?"

"That's what I'm telling you. They became Queen by another method—and some of these Queens never married at all. Look at this."

She scrolled the page down.

"These queens here didn't have children, so the Throne went straight to the current Voyant—and look. Every single listing for the Kings, Queens, and successions from father to son—or from mother to son—they all include the following inscription. 'He took the Shard of Hotha from the Sacred Shrine and entered the Hall of Light to become King'."

"What does that mean?"

"Look." She changed the page again. "This is an artist's picture of the Hall of Light."

She rotated the computer in his direction. A prickle went up his scalp when he looked down at an image of two people—a man and a woman.

The characteristic golden halo surrounded both of them—and the purple-pink glow radiated outward from their chests.

A magnificent garden sprawled to the edge of the picture. Light blasted from every plant, bench, fountain, archway, and stone in the garden.

"This purple thing must be the Shard of Hotha," Marine whispered. "Whatever it is, it has to do with the succession of Kings in the White Spire. Whoever becomes King has to take the Shard."

"Then we're looking for the person who will succeed the King and take the Shard," Yann pointed out. "That's the person who will take the Throne away from the Voyant and bring stability to the Coil."

"Exactly," Marine replied. "These dates indicate the last King died without an heir. The Voyant took over—which started this current instability cycle."

Yann frowned again. "Wait a minute. Why couldn't the Voyant just take the Shard himself? Is it linked to the King's bloodline or something? Is that why a new King can't rise unless he's a direct descendent of the old King?"

"I don't think so. Look. I found this." She brought up more drawings of the couples—the ones Yann and Eliska saw in the tunnels under the maze Island. "Don't you remember? The Voyants always come in pairs—but what if these aren't the Voyants? Look. These couples are wearing crowns. They can't be the Voyants—and they all have the Shard. They *both* have the Shard. There must be two of them—two Shards of Hotha."

"But we've already seen individual Voyants with the Shard."

Her face lit up and she pointed at him. "Aha! That's the thing! The solo Voyants with the Shard coincide with instability cycles. The way I see it, the two partners both have to take Shards—and look at this list here. It lists what the records call affiliates. Each ruler has an affiliate—a companion of sorts. Some are Kings and Queens. Some are brothers or friends or other relatives. Some are even random strangers from entirely different races who didn't know each other beforehand."

Yann's jaw dropped. "So.....so anyone can take the Shard—like...literally anyone?"

"Not anyone. Two people have to take both Shards—one for each person. One of them becomes King—or Queen if it's a woman. The other person becomes the affiliate. If one dies and no one else takes the second Shard, the instability cycle starts."

Yann raised his eyebrows. "That sounds complicated."

"It isn't as complicated as it seems. See? The last King in the White Spire was Yimichi Ocuron. His queen was Hubua Ocuron. She was his affiliate until her death. She died more than twenty years before he did. His second affiliate was Noleron Kupuro—the man we currently know as the Voyant. The King's death started the instability cycle."

"So Yimichi Ocuron died without an heir."

"It looks that way."

"So why didn't the Voyant just find someone else to take the second Shard? Did he keep the second Shard a secret so he could keep ruling by himself?"

"I don't think so. If we're right about this, he would have become King the minute he found an affiliate to take the second Shard. I can't explain why he hasn't found another affiliate. It doesn't make any sense—but it sure looks like he's going to great lengths to find one specific person."

"Maybe it has some link to the bloodline that we don't know about."

"I don't see how it can. I found confirmation of what Anríq already told us. Both Yimichi Ocuron and Noleron Kupuro were Barbarians before Yimichi became King."

Yann gasped. "That isn't possible!"

"I know, but I'm telling you the truth. Neither of these men had a drop of royal blood. There is no way they could have been related to the previous line of Kings."

"How did Yimichi become King, then?" Yann asked.

"I wish I knew. As far as I can tell, he just appeared out of nowhere, took the Shard, and blammo! He became King, married Hubua, and she became his Queen when she took the second Shard. The records indicate all of that happened at exactly the same time."

"This doesn't really solve the mystery, does it?" Yann pointed out. "If anything, it just makes it more confusing."

"At least we know what the Voyant wants and who he's looking for."

"We just don't know how to find the person. If you're right that it could be anyone, then there's no earthly reason he should be looking for one person. He can take anyone off the street."

She gazed down at the pictures of the Kings and Queens, each with the Shard of Hotha radiating in their chests. "I almost wish I could ask him."

"Sorry. You're out of luck there."

She sat back and smiled up at him. Her eyes widened when she looked up at him. "There you go. You told me to tell you if I found anything."

He realized how close he was sitting to her in this quiet laboratory. "Thank you. This is huge."

"Do you need anything else from me?"

"Actually, I do. I need magic-users on the wall who can help us fight whatever comes for us."

"Don't you already have that?"

"We need more. We need people who can actually fight Darklings—or any other force that comes. Magic-users could hold off instability and save all our lives."

Her smile slipped and she glanced away. "That's going to be difficult to sell to the Masters."

"Is there a way you could take me to talk to them?"

"I'll try. Wait here."

Chapter 40

Marine left Yann sitting in the library. He kept his hands in his lap so he wouldn't feel tempted to touch something and maybe break the Templars' equipment.

After a few minutes of waiting, his curiosity got the better of him. He swiped the screen in front of him and ran through the pictures, documents, lists, and texts she found.

It was all there. He found himself staring at the two glowing figures holding hands in the Hall of Light.

All Marine's conclusions made sense to Yann. Too many of these pictures showed couples, each with a Shard burning in their chests. There had to be two Shards.

The Shards sure did seem to bring the two people together—and one of the partners dying triggered an instability cycle—unless the surviving partner found another affiliate to take the second Shard.

This really was an amazing piece of research—and Marine didn't even have to access any forbidden library to find it. It was all right there in the public record.

Everything about the King in the White Spire was public record exactly the way she said it would be.

Historians and accountants followed every King around day and night to document everything the King did and said.

Just then, Marine came rushing back. "They said yes!" she whispered. "They want to see you as much as you want to see them!"

"Who?" he asked.

"The Masters! Come on!

She grabbed his hand and towed him back out into the Temple's labyrinthine corridors.

Yann caught some of the pupils and initiates glancing at his uniform, but no one stopped him.

Marine led the way up a bunch of flights of stairs. Maybe the Guardian Templars didn't have the moving box—which made no sense at all considering they had computers and God only knew what else.

She finally pushed open the doors to another massive library—this one full of books. Yann didn't see a single computer anywhere.

A bunch of aging men stood at the end of the room. They all wore Templar tunics embroidered with crosses and the men all turned around to face Yann when he entered.

"You asked to see us, Watch Commander?" a white-haired old man asked.

"Yes, Master. Thank you for seeing me. I wanted to ask you if you would be willing to recruit some of your most powerful magic-users to help us defend the city against the Dark. We don't know what will come against us, but the Watch doesn't have the defenses to handle it without magic. The five magic-users we have out there erecting the barricade won't be enough. We need everyone you can possibly spare. The survival of the whole city depends on it. I wouldn't ask otherwise."

"Yes, of course, Watch Commander," a much younger Master replied. "We understand completely and we'll be happy to cooperate."

Yann froze. "You will? I wasn't expecting that."

"Why weren't you expecting it?" the oldest Master asked. "The survival of the city depends on it as you said. What would you like us to do?"

"Um...." Yann glanced at Marine. "Do you know how to fight? I'm so sorry for my ignorance. I've been around a different class of magic-users and I don't know what skills you have."

"We know how to fight the Dark—and Darklings." the oldest Master replied. "When would you like us to come out? The Dark isn't attacking us now—not in that way."

"If you have some time, I would appreciate it if you could send some more powerful magic-users to erect the barricade as quickly as possible. The city is too big and five isn't enough. We're still suffering attacks from the Dark vapors because the barricade isn't high enough."

The oldest Master scratched his chin and frowned. "I see. That is a problem, isn't it."

"Once the barricade goes up, I don't see any reason for you to stay outside the Temple. Once the attack does start, I would need you to fight whatever it is that comes after us. If Darklings assault the wall, then I would need you to station magic-users around the perimeter to defend the wall. If they come from the Layers, then you should probably distribute yourselves through the city to fend them off.'

"We understand, Watch Commander," the younger Master replied. "We will do as you ask. Give us five minutes to round up our people and we'll erect this barricade right away. We can't afford any more delay."

"Thank you," Yann exclaimed. "I'm very grateful for your help."

"Thank you for coming to see us," the oldest Master replied. "Please don't hesitate to call on us whenever you need our help."

Yann turned away to leave the room....and paused. He turned back. Should he?

"Was there something else, Watch Commander?" the younger Master asked.

"You know....it would be really helpful if all of your people got involved in this. The more the better. Your order is best suited to fighting the Dark. I'm sure you understand the need for it now that the Coil is becoming more unstable by the day. You should be out there combating the Dark—not locked away in your Temple. Excuse me for saying so, but you could have protected the city long before I showed up here if you only got involved sooner. Like I said, the more people you bring out, the better. I don't see any reason for anyone to stay behind, not even the youngest pupil. That's just the way I see it. Thank you for your time, Masters."

He got out of the room as quickly as possible before one of them torched him with their magic for the audacity to say something like that.

Marine broke down in stifled giggles as soon as they left the room. "You are such a champion, Yann!" she snickered.

"What did I do? I just told them to defend the city. What the hell are they thinking—hiding in there when people are dying in the streets?"

She beamed at him. "You really told them. I'm so proud of you! You're a hero."

"Hardly," he muttered.

She took his hand again and led him out of the temple and back to the courtyard. Everyone saw them together.

"Will you go back to the Temple now?" he asked.

She nodded. "I suppose I'll get recruited with everyone else."

"Be careful, okay? Don't let anything happen to you."

Her cheeks glowed. "I'll see you later at the apartment."

"Okay."

Yann saw himself standing right in front of her. Some forgotten impulse told him to kiss her right now—but not in a passionate, romantic way.

The whole sequence of events seemed to call for him to give her a very light, casual peck—almost as if they really were an established couple parting for their day's work.

He didn't do that. She squeezed his hand and murmured. "Bye," before she hurried away.

He watched her go trying to understand this feeling in his stomach. He really wanted to kiss her, so why didn't he?

It didn't have anything to do with her being a princess and him being a Watchman. That was just stupid.

She liked him. He already knew that. She liked him as much as he liked her. She was probably waiting for him to kiss her. In fact, he would bet on it. So why didn't he?

He didn't want their first kiss to be a quick, light, casual peck on the street in front of the wall. He wanted it to be special—as if it could ever come to anything. Why did he even think about kissing her?

He turned back to the wall and went on with his business.

Maximil escorted Yann to the field hospital. It occupied the downstairs floor of a different building, but it didn't have any patients in it right now. Everyone who got hurt in the last battle had either recovered and gone home or they were already dead and buried.

Yann turned his attention back to the defenses, but the more he saw, the more hopeless it appeared.

The five local magic-users managed to raise the barrier another ten feet while he had been gone. This would never work.

The Watch didn't have any kind of projectiles or catapults or anything to fight Darklings. The Watch didn't even have bows and arrows—much less the archers to shoot them.

These men would be lucky to stay alive in the next battle. The previous Watch Commander had been dead right to hold these men back and send them down into the basements to keep them alive.

Maybe Yann should do the same thing.

He couldn't do that. These men were all he had to fight whatever might be out there.

If Dark forces came for the city from the upper Layers, no amount of fighting would hold those forces off. They could wipe the city completely out of existence before anyone raised a weapon to defend themselves.

A possible Darkling attack didn't look much better. The Watchmen wouldn't be able to stop Darklings from getting inside the walls and then it would all be over.

Chapter 41

Yann stared out at the landscape beyond Savaré while he made up his mind what to do next.

A commotion behind him made him turn around.

His stomach dropped when he saw a hundred men marching toward him up the street. Every single one of those men wore a grey tunic embroidered with a gold cross.

Yann stood rooted to the spot watching all those Templars coming toward him. They narrowed their eyes, clamped their lips shut in grim determination, and strode up the street without looking left or right at anyone.

The three Masters Yann had just spoken to led the crowd—all except for Marine. She walked in front of those three heading straight for the courtyard.

She stopped right outside it, pointed at different Templars, and then swiped her finger at the surrounding city neighborhoods.

"Master Regin, you and your Brothers will go up to the wall and erect the barrier as quickly as possible. Master Prismael, you take your group to the center of town and defend the top of the dome from Dark vapors dropping from above. Master Tregre, you'll go through the Watchmen and give them the knowledge they need to use their weapons properly."

The Templars split up. Marine went through the group directing everyone to their tasks.

The younger Templar who'd just negotiated with Yann took thirty men to the wall.

Master Regin and his Brothers fed massive torrents of magic into the barricade. It started to rise much faster and curved upward into a glistening dome to close over Savaré.

Another thirty Templars climbed up onto the wall and went down the ledge talking rapidly to each other.

Marine came over to Yann. "What...the hell....are you doing?!" he whispered.

"They're assigning themselves places on the wall. As soon as the next attack starts, those thirty will come over here and stand the wall along with the Watchmen." She raised her eyes when she saw him staring at her. "What? This is what you asked for, isn't it?"

He couldn't answer. This was too amazing.

The rest of the Templars went from man to man in the Watch. Each Templar pressed his hand to each Watchman's forehead.

The Templars left the Watchmen blinking in stunned disbelief. Then the Watchmen looked down at their weapons.

"The Watchmen should be able to fight now" Marine explained. "We're giving each of them the knowledge they need—and the experience gathered from the Temple archives."

Yann gulped hard. "You didn't have to do this."

"Of course we did." She beamed at him. "You made quite an impression on the Masters. I knew you would."

She darted in and gave him a quick kiss on the cheek before she hurried away.

Yann stared at everything trying to get his brain to accept what was happening.

Half of the Masters descended the wall, returned to the main street in the middle of town, and fired a jet of magic straight up at the apex of the barrier dome.

They knit it together and closed it just as another thread of Dark vapor dropped out of the sky. It lashed and cracked across the barrier, but the barrier stopped the thread from sinking any lower.

The thread went ballistic. No one could fail to see the thing deliberately attacking the barrier and trying to break through.

The thread didn't just drift around nor did it leave when it failed to penetrate the dome. The thread stayed there snaking all over the barrier.

More Dark filaments dropped from the sky. None of those threads were there before.

They hit the dome and squirmed all over it trying to get inside. The Templars and townspeople stood out on the sidewalk watching it.

"This is it," Yann murmured. "It's starting."

He barely got the words out before a thunderous crack barked across the countryside. It came from the forest—the same forest where he'd just been watching the shadows growing by the hour.

The forest itself heaved out of position. All the shadows between the trees, bushes, and roots ejected off the ground and formed a Layer swooping down on the city.

More Dark vapors dropped out of the sky. They forked and slithered all over the dome trying to break the barrier.

Master Prismael and his group fired their magic upward to bolster the dome.

Word raced through town from mouth to mouth. More Templars charged the wall facing the approaching Dark Layer.

Marine lunged in that direction to join them, but Yann held her back. "Don't go up there!"

"I have to!" she yelled back. "I have to help them!"

"It's too dangerous! I don't want anything to happen to you. If you get hurt, I have no one. Do you understand that? You're all I have left!"

She burst into another beautiful smile. He experienced another overpowering impulse to kiss her right now. Now would be the perfect time, but she broke away. "I'll help the townspeople get into their shelters. Does that satisfy you?"

He took his hand off her arm. "Yes. Thank you."

She charged away into the city streets, but the townspeople already knew the drill. They rushed to certain buildings all over town.

Yann hadn't gotten a chance to review Savaré's underground shelters, but that was one aspect of the city's defense he didn't really worry about. It was the only defense that had been doing its job lately.

Master Regin's group never got a chance to descend from the wall. They crowded the western side facing the Dark Layer.

All the Templars fired their magic into it and forced it to a stop. The Layer shuddered and deep groaning booms echoed out of it as it tried to continue its march toward the wall.

Yann stormed through the Watchmen. "Everybody up on the wall and stand your posts! Keep an eye on the perimeter in case Darklings come after us. Oran—go down to the storeroom and bring up every spare weapon you can carry. We're going to need them."

Yann climbed up to the wall and went man to man making sure everyone knew what he was supposed to do and where he should stand.

The Templars kept a few Brothers in reserve just in case the Layer got the jump on them. In a few minutes, even they came back.

Yann glanced down at the street to make sure Master Prismael's people were still holding up the dome.

Yann's heart turned another somersault when he saw Marine returning with even more Templars—young ones this time.

She had to yell to make herself heard over the noise of bombardment—both from the Dark vapors overhead and the crash of explosions coming from the western wall.

Everyone in the whole city yelled at once. Yann couldn't hear Marine, but he did see what she did.

She directed some of her people to help Master Prismael, some to the wall, and others to different places around the city.

Yann couldn't pay attention to her anymore. Oran raced across the street just then carrying an armload of weapons. Yann grabbed a new glaive—a much better glaive than the gypsy one he lost at the White Spire.

He climbed up to the wall just in time.

The Layer held off—or rather the Templars held it off. Marine's group of younger Brothers, initiates, and even pupils added their magic to the steady stream of power flowing outward from the wall.

The Layer rumbled louder, but it couldn't advance.

"We need to find a way to break it!" Yann yelled to Master Regin.

Master Regin narrowed his eyes at the Layer and nodded. "Leave it to me. I know what to do."

Yann didn't ask what Master Regin was going to do. Whatever it was would be something magical which was outside Yann's wheelhouse.

Master Regin went down the line of Templars yelling into their ears. Yann raised his glaive. Whatever the Templars did to defeat that Layer would release all the gathering Dark powers standing against this city.

Yann didn't see anything here that would make the Voyant or the Dark turn against Savaré, but maybe they didn't need a reason. Maybe the instability itself sent these forces to destroy the city.

Master Regin stepped back. All the surrounding Watchmen sensed something about to happen. They faced outward across the fields ready for anything.

Yann counted down the seconds until Master Regin bellowed, "NOW!!"

Yann didn't understand what the Templars did. From his perspective, they just kept bombarding the Layer with magic to hold it at bay.

They must have done something because a colossal wave of energy surged down the beam, smashed the Layer, and shattered it into a million pieces.

All the tiny fragments of Dark energy burst apart and a hurricane wind slammed into the barricade. Enough Templars already stood down on the streets feeding their magic into the dome. It held, but only for a second.

All the wisps of Dark energy that made up the threatening Layer blasted apart and turned into thousands upon millions of tiny gnashing monsters—each one no bigger than a coin.

They hurtled on the wind to slam into the barricade. It flexed under the assault—and then all those Dark forces started chewing their way through the barrier.

The Templars on the wall reacted instantly, rushed the field, and plastered their hands against the magical surface to fortify it. Yann raised his glaive and stabbed the blade through the barricade.

He impaled one of the creatures and it screeched in fury before it shattered into another cloud of even smaller fragments. These splattered in droplets all over the barricade and started burning their way through it.

Yann stabbed again and again. The barricade stopped the Dark forces from clinging to his blade when he pulled it back inside.

The Watchmen copied him, charged the wall, and stabbed time after time, but no one could stab the droplets.

Yann heard people yelling behind him, but mostly he heard the crackle of Dark vapors snaking and hissing all over the top of the dome. Were they breaking through right now?

He couldn't look to see how well the Templars were holding off the Dark forces. The surface in front of him started to thin as the droplets and a million gnashing teeth chewed their way closer to Yann's face.

He burst into a frenzy stabbing anything and everything he could see. The Watchmen fought all around him doing the same thing.

Too many droplets and tiny burrowing creatures covered the barricade just at the edge of the wall. They blacked out any view of the countryside beyond that thin film. How much longer could the barrier hold?

Without warning, the barricade detonated in Yann's face and sent him flying. He hurtled off the wall and slammed down hard on his back in the street right outside the courtyard.

He heard the evacuating men, women, and children screaming not far away. He grabbed his glaive and launched himself to his feet, but at that moment, an unstoppable hurricane of black hit him in the face and chest.

The Dark flattened him instantly and he went down hard before it covered him completely.

Chapter 42

Yann startled awake out of a sound sleep. His eyes darted everywhere trying to see those Dark forces. He had to destroy them before they destroyed him.

Splitting pain tore him apart in his chest, back, and stomach. He winced and froze there. He didn't even want to lie down in case he hurt himself again.

"Easy," Marine murmured. Her soft hands came to rest on his chest. "Lie down. You got hurt in the battle, but you're going to be okay. Just lie quietly while I finish healing you."

Her touch acted on his deepest instincts. He collapsed back on the bed and realized he was in his bedroom in the apartment in Savaré.

She sat on the bed next to him looking as magnificent as ever. Her dark hair swept forward around her face and her deep eyes glistened down at him.

He forced himself to relax and then a rush of warmth flooded his body. He had his shirt off and her hands lay right against his bare skin.

He collapsed in relief as the pain faded away. "Thank you!" he gasped. "Oh, my god!"

She chuckled. "You took it hard that time. You've been unconscious for two whole days. I've been working on you all that time and you only just regained consciousness."

He dragged his eyes open to look at her, but the sensation of her touching his chest blocked out everything else.

She sat on his bed touching him in ways he never imagined she ever would. This moment sent a surge of excitement through him.

"What happened?" he asked. "What happened to the city?"

"The Templars drove back the Dark. None of that would have happened if you hadn't recruited the Masters. You saved everyone."

He groaned and looked away. "How many people got hurt when the barricade went down?"

"A lot of people got hurt, but no one got killed this time. The Templars have been going through the city healing all the injured. They've reestablished the barricade and it's holding off the Dark vapors. All of this is thanks to you."

"I don't want thanks."

She smiled down at him with so much heartfelt understanding and admiration—and her hands kept migrating all over his body. She touched his chest, shoulders, and down to his stomach.

Her beauty overwhelmed him the way it always did, but the light in her eyes shining down on him alone—he couldn't keep his hands off her.

He raised both arms and let his hands fall on her arms where they extended down to his chest. He allowed his fingers to wrap around her biceps and then follow them up to her shoulders.

He slipped his other hand behind her back and down to her waist. He allowed himself to feel her for the first time—really feel her.

The intoxicating reality washed him away. He was touching her like that. He was touching her the way he always wanted to.

She burst into another huge, blushing, beaming smile and giggled. She lifted her hands off his chest, leaned back, and started to turn away. "Okay! Now I know you're feeling better."

He grabbed her wrists harder than he should have and immediately fought himself under control to soften his grip. "Wait!" He steered her hands back down onto his stomach. "Don't stop, Marine......don't stop."

He sank deeper into the mattress and pressed her hands into his skin. He couldn't pretend to use magic, but he tried to let a flow of some warmth stream from his hands into hers and through them into his body. Her touch felt mind-blowingly good.

She blushed again, but she didn't pull away.

Her hands drifted over his skin and he knew now that she was touching him like that, too. She did it on purpose. She wasn't trying to heal him—not the way she did before.

She traced every inch of his chest, shoulders, sides, and stomach. Then she inched up to his neck and finally touched his face.

He let himself float in the majesty of her beautiful face and the bottomless depths of her eyes.

He ran his hand up her spine and combed his fingers through her hair. He laid his hand against her cheek and passed his thumb across her lips.

Jesus, he wanted to kiss her so bad, but waiting like this and just looking at her almost satisfied him more than that.

She didn't stop touching him back. She didn't hide from any part of him, not even the hungry look on his face that told her how much he wanted her.

He ran his hand down to her slender neck. He didn't know what part of her he would touch next, but right at that moment, she turned her head and kissed the palm of his hand as it passed her mouth.

She did it quickly, lightly—almost jokingly, but that one kiss broke the chain holding him back.

He threaded his fingers into her satin hair, cupped the back of her neck, and pulled her down.

Their lips met in a velvet kiss that didn't end. His other hand glided around her back and guided her body down on top of his. She settled into him so perfectly.

Her lips lit his world on fire. His arms closed around her, exactly the way they should have held her all along.

He didn't keep track of where that kiss began and ended. It didn't seem to matter anymore because she was here with him now.

She sank on top of him, and naturally, effortlessly, she rolled aside and settled into his arms at his side. Her hair spilled across his shoulder and she merged with him there.

He shut his eyes and sank into the feeling of holding her. The emotion and beauty radiating from her shattered his world. Nothing would ever be the same after this.

He must have fallen asleep because he woke up hours later and felt her still lying there. Her arms wrapped around his bare chest and her ribs expanded and contracted under his hands.

She stirred in her sleep and let out a tiny peep of a sigh before she started to move. She squirmed once. Her body felt immaculate in his arms. A ripple of tension traveled down her torso and legs where they touched his side. He felt everything through her dress.

He adjusted his hold on her and she woke up the rest of the way—or partially. She sighed, took a deep breath, and moved her head back. Her hair fell over her face when she rested her head on his shoulder instead of his chest.

He used his other hand to finger-comb her hair away from her face. She didn't open her eyes. God, she was so beautiful!

He had to kiss her again. Her lips responded instantly and she came to life, but she still didn't open her eyes.

She wrapped her arms around his neck, pulled him in, and her mouth opened in a full, succulent kiss. Their tongues danced in a sea of bliss that electrified Yann to his core.

He rolled over to face her. Her body felt thin, small, fragile, and unimaginably appealing, but he wanted something more from her than that.

He just wanted to feel her lying here next to him kissing him and then falling back into his arms.

He never wanted to stop feeling this. He would almost have been willing to continue fighting the Voyant forever just to keep her here.

Chapter 43

Yann squeezed Marine's hand and gazed down into her eyes. "Behave yourself out there today or I might have to discipline you in my capacity as Watch Commander."

She laughed, blushed, and dipped her eyelashes. "I wouldn't want that."

He bent in and kissed her once before the doors opened to let them out of the moving box.

He didn't let go of her hand when they walked out of the building to enter the Savaré city streets. He only let her go when they got closer to the wall.

Yann split off to the right to rejoin the Watch. Marine went left and rendezvoused with a bunch of Templars waiting for her.

Yann climbed up the wall and passed down the ledge to check the defenses.

Master Regin's Templars occasionally fed their magic into the barrier forming a dome over the city, but the magic-users didn't have to do it very often. The barrier was stronger enough—or it seemed to be.

Shadows still hovered over by the forest. They surged outward at sunset and sunrise, but the Dark didn't come any closer.

Occasional filaments of Dark vapor drifted out of the sky to crackle on the dome, but they never put it in danger the way they did before.

"What are they waiting for?" Maximil muttered in Yann's ear.

"They did this before," Yann replied. "They held off for days before they hit us."

"Why?" Oran asked. "It isn't like they have to gather their forces or anything. They can strike whenever they want."

"They can't be waiting for us to gather our forces, ether," Maximil pointed out. "We aren't getting any stronger or weaker by waiting."

"I don't claim to understand the Dark." Yann glanced down at the courtyard.

Marine directed the Templars to different parts of the wall. She also went through the assembled Templars in the city streets. They would be the ones to bolster the dome's highest point when it needed it.

He heard her giving orders to the much older Masters and Brothers. They all outranked her, but they listened to her and obeyed her without question.

Yann waited for her to finish. She left with the Templars assigned to the wall.

Yann went down there and intercepted her. "Could you come up to the wall for a minute, please?" he asked. "I need to ask you something."

She smirked at him. "What—in front of the whole Watch? How could you?"

"Cut it out," he told her. "I want to get your opinion on why the Dark forces don't attack now. What are they waiting for?"

She smiled at him in that way that made it impossible to resist her, but she was right. They kept their growing relationship private—if they even had a growing relationship.

So he kissed her a few times. They slept in his bed with their arms around each other, but she never took her clothes off and neither did he. Neither of them suggested taking it any further.

He still hadn't technically violated any oath because he hadn't taken one. What would he do if he had to choose between Marine and the Watch?

Then there was the question of getting her father's approval. Yann could just imagine how that would go.

He didn't take things any further because he didn't want to face any of those questions. He just wanted to appreciate the time with her.

He couldn't even do that with Savaré under threat.

She followed him up to the wall. All the Watchmen moved out of her way. They started out giving the Templars a wide berth, but that evaporated after the last assault.

The Watchmen kept a healthy distance between themselves and Marine now—much more than they did with any other magic-user.

Yann found himself hovering at her side. He wanted to be near her in case anything went wrong, but he also saw himself the way everyone else on the wall saw him acting.

He stood much closer to her and followed her movements the way he would if they really had been a couple.

He should have stopped that. He should have made it clear to everyone that he and Marine were just friends—but they weren't anymore.

He had to admit that to himself. They'd crossed into uncharted territory. They weren't friends. He didn't know what they were, but it wasn't that.

"Can you find out what the Dark forces are doing—without losing your mind?" he asked.

"I don't think so." She squinted toward the forest and then up at the sky. She pointed at the vapors. "The veil is getting thinner. See? You can see Layers coming through. The Dark must be trying to either collapse this Layer or take it over."

"What can we do about that?" Maximil asked.

"We might be able to convince the Templars to go outside the dome and carry out a preemptive strike against the Dark. They would shoot their magic up into that breach." She traced her forefinger across the clouds where Dark vapors blew back and forth in the wind.

"Could they close the rift?" Yan asked. "Is that what you're saying?"

"The alternative is sitting around waiting for the Dark forces to attack us first. They got inside the barrier already. They can do it again. I think we can all assume they'll continue to escalate until they wipe this city the same way they wiped Tenby."

Maximil and Oran both gasped. "Wipe it?! Are you serious?!"

She only nodded. "We've seen it time and again."

"What did we ever do to them?" Oran asked. "We're good people. We do the right thing. We never did anything to deserve getting our whole city wiped out."

"It's nothing you did," Yann told him. "No one deserves that. This is just the Coil's instability playing havoc with Layers and Islands. There doesn't seem to be any pattern to it. It's happening everywhere."

"The instability could be causing that breach," Marine suggested. "The breach could be letting in the Dark. I suppose we have no reason to think the Dark created the breach just to come after Savaré."

"Good. Go tell the Templars to meet me so we can talk about this preemptive strike of ours. You can brief them on what's involved and then we'll all meet up to decide if we really want to carry out a plan like that."

She beamed at him and hurried away. Yann turned back to study the forest. Maximil and Oran both watched Marine go.

"You're lucky to have her," Maximil murmured.

"Huh?" Yann looked at him. "Who?"

"Your wife. She's beautiful, kind, and she obviously worships you."

Yann looked away again. The Watchmen always referred to Marine as Yann's wife.

He didn't see her worshiping him—not at all. She smiled at him, but she smiled at everyone. She acted exactly as warm and affectionate toward him now as she did before they started kissing.

He distracted himself from thinking about that by surveying the whole area. For some reason, the shadows deep in the forest gave him the most concern.

He couldn't explain why they concerned him more. The Dark wisps descending from the upper Layers posed a much bigger danger.

Maybe their crackling sounds across the dome tricked him into thinking that.

So much water had passed under the bridge since he left Middleborough—and even before that. He'd fought the Dark too many times to be fooled by crackles, sparks, and flashing lights.

The Layer that would have completely consumed the city during the last battle—it came from the forest. That wall of Dark threatened Savaré more than anything.

Those wisps up there did pose a threat, but a lot more Dark power lurked out in the forest. Yann just couldn't see it as clearly right now.

Once the next attack started, that Darkness would rise out of the trees and form a much bigger force than anything else around here. The Dark Layer would have consumed Savaré completely without the Templars holding it back.

He strode down the wall checking on them. Just as many Templars manned the wall now as during the last battle. They certainly took their new job seriously.

Yann didn't turn around when he heard Marine talking to the Templars down in the street.

The Templars who had given the fighting skills and knowledge to the Watchmen now went through the city repairing buildings. The Templars checked and bolstered the reinforced basements where civilians sheltered during assaults.

Yann concentrated on the wall itself. The Watchmen acted much more confident now. They paid more attention at their posts.

They also seemed to have organized themselves into some kind of command structure without any input from him.

Maximil and Oran reported to Yann. He gave them orders and the two men transmitted what he said to the other Watchmen.

He turned away from the wall to go down to the ground. He wanted to check on the weapons supplies—not just of the weapons the townspeople already had.

He wanted to start manufacturing new ones and hopefully get the Templars involved in fashioning some kind of projectiles.

Yann wouldn't be able to reproduce the rockets they had in Tenby, but maybe the Templars could come up with the next best thing—something magically propelled or something like that.

Marine would be able to help him with that. She knew about the Tenby rockets. She could explain it to the Templars.

Then again, Savaré had advanced technology. Maybe they had more than they let on—or maybe they just didn't realize what they had.

Yann headed down the wall to the stairs when a shout went up on the wall behind him. One glance showed him the Dark shadows rising out of the forest exactly the way he'd just been imagining they would.

At the same time, the Dark vapors struck the dome much louder just then.

The breach in the upper Layers widened and a cloud of shadows poured through the veil to envelop the dome. They blocked out the sunshine in seconds.

The whole city erupted in noise behind Yann's back—and not from the thousands of vapors attacking the dome at the same time. Yelling voices echoed across town as everyone ran everywhere at once.

Marine yelled for the Templars to add their magic to the dome. Templars who had been working on the buildings charged to the wall and crowded in with their comrades.

The Dark emerging from the forest looked like nothing Yann had ever seen before. It erupted from far out in the countryside.

It might have been another wave of instability except that it came straight for the city. It had to be a direct attack. It just took a different form.

Giant spikes stabbed out of the trees, ruptured the soil, and the spikes even stabbed into each other. Each spike jabbed upward fifty feet pointing in a different direction.

Yann couldn't tell from here what the spikes were made of. They might have been made out of the bedrock. He couldn't think of any other explanation since they came from underground.

What they were made of didn't matter one bit. More and more spikes ejected through the soil, crashed into each other, and kept growing into a massive wall of pure black. If they started out as stone, they merged together to wipe out all light coming from that direction.

Those spokes shattered tree trunks and buried the forest within seconds. The wave crawled across the landscape coming closer.

"Fire!" Master Regin bellowed.

Chapter 44

The assembled Templars fired their magic at the Dark Layer rising to the sky. The wave of black spikes merged with the Layers breaking through from above.

The Layer spread north and south as far as the eye could see. It curved inward to encircle the city of Savaré from both directions.

Yann tightened his grip on his glaive. This was the first time he'd faced the Dark when he couldn't fight anyone or anything. The Templars had to do everything.

They fired their magic through the barricade to bombard the Layer. It stopped five miles from the city, but the Templars couldn't stop the Layer from growing. It just kept getting bigger.

A deep, deadly rumble reverberated through the ground, up the wall, and into Yann's legs. How long would the Templars be able to hold off the Dark?

The crackling noise of all those Dark vapors on the dome drowned out every other sound.

The constant sizzling sounds blended into a sea of noise. Templars from Master Prismael's group fired into the dome from below to stop those vapors from breaking through.

The noise escalated to the boom of distant thunder—except that it wasn't nearly distant enough. The Layer trembled and the Dark power cracked. It rumbled all the way up to the sky and jolted the ground hard enough to rattle the city.

Without warning, a loud crack like gunfire blasted through the air overhead. Yann glanced up and his worst nightmare came true when the barricade collapsed. All those Templars working together couldn't hold it back.

It broke at its highest point, started to peel down to the ground, and all those Dark vapors swarmed inside.

At exactly the same instant, the Dark Layer outside overcame the Templars' best efforts to stop it. The Layer rushed inward to surround the city.

It swooped across the countryside crawling closer by the second. It would get here in no time. Yann and his fellow Watchmen wouldn't be able to fight it without magic.

The Templars fired again and again. Master Prismael's group bombarded the vapors and barely managed to slow them down, but nothing could stop them.

Nothing Master Regin's group did had any effect on the Layer at all. More spikes rocketed out of the ground on the Layer's forward edge.

Monstrous shapes, mouths full of gnashing teeth, and undulating bodies surged through the Layer just below the surface.

They didn't form enough to take the shape of actual Darklings—not any Darklings Yann and his men would be able to fight.

At that moment, something moving very fast streaked across the sky above the city wall. Yann barely had time to see Marine shoot off the ground and dive through the breach in the dome. It kept dropping. It no longer offered Savaré any protection.

She blasted over the falling edge and into the sky above the city. She stopped there hovering a hundred feet off the ground, spun around, and flung her arms and legs out to both sides.

"NO!!"Yann bellowed, but it was too late.

More Dark filaments fired from her fingers and her feet. Even hair blasted outward in a spiked crown around her head and more Dark vapors shot from the end of every strand.

Those threads radiated in every direction and caught all the vapors invading the city. Every Dark vapor streaking downward to attack Savaré whipped around and slithered back in the opposite direction.

They all converged on her. More of her lines struck the Dark Layer and pulled its Darkness toward herself.

The vapors collided with her and surrounded her in a million lashing, stinging, burning sparks. She roared too loudly for that voice to come from anything human—and then the Darkness from the Layer hit her, too.

It poured into her through her hair, her skin, her eyes, her fingers, and every other part of her.

It surrounded her in a spinning ball of flashing flame.

No one inside Savaré moved to intervene. Yann didn't know if the Templars *could* intervene. It looked like Marine was doing this all on her own.

She left the city completely safe from the whole attack by taking it into herself.

The ball of Darkness around her swelled to a corona of Dark power. It blazed with light, but at the same time, it throbbed with Dark shadows and rippling flame.

More faces, monsters, and gruesome shapes materialized out of the swirling mass of energy.

Vapors slashed her dress to ribbons and went to work on her hair, skin, and body. The Dark threads snaked all over her, whipped against her, and cut her to shreds.

Yann gulped down a wave of sick cold. He couldn't even help her. No one could—or could they?

He glanced over at Master Regin.

Yann froze when he saw the Templars working hard to erect the barricade again.

The Templars on the ground charged back to the wall and joined their comrades to knit the protective dome back over the city—now that none of the Dark forces threatened Savaré anymore.

Yann couldn't argue with that. He didn't want to distract the Templars from concentrating on the barricade in case something else went wrong.

Yann didn't point out that Marine was outside the dome. She must have planned it that way from the beginning.

The blazing inferno hid her naked body from everyone inside the city, but it couldn't hide the pained grimace on her face.

Her features twisted in agony as the Dark forces attacked her, merged with her, and their Darkness joined with her own magic.

Yann couldn't tell anymore if the Dark forces even were attacking her or just communing with her. Was there any difference?

Her lips curled back from her teeth in a feral roar of pure furious determination—and that grimace changed her features.

Her face morphed into something hideous—something like a Darkling.

Her teeth erupted too long and her cheekbones and eyebrow ridges swelled. Her body contorted into a monstrous shape.

The next moment, an almighty boom exploded outward from the center of her body. The burning sphere of Dark energy detonated and Marine plummeted to earth.

Yann burst out of position. He threw his glaive down right there. He didn't care if he faced the Darklings barehanded.

He had to shove through dozens of Templars to get off the wall and back to the archway leading outside.

Master Prismael grabbed him to hold him back. "Don't go out here, Watch Commander!" Master Prismael yelled in Yann's face. "You can't go near her! She's a Darkling! She's gone over to the Dark! You saw her!"

"I saw her save this city!" Yann bellowed back. "She is not a Darkling and she did NOT go over to the Dark. Get your hands off me!"

Yann threw an elbow to shake off the old man's hold. Yann would have thrown a punch or maybe even done something a lot worse.

He wouldn't leave Marine out there—not after she just saved the whole city from certain destruction.

The Dark forces would have reduced this city to a smoking pile of rubble if she hadn't pulled them away in time. No one had to explain that to Yann.

He charged to the gate, but on the way there, his fevered brain remembered one thing.

She was out there stark naked in front of the whole city. Every man of the Watch could see her.

He snatched a blanket from one of the storerooms and rushed to the archway. "Open it!" he ordered the Watchmen standing around.

No one moved for a second. The men on watch stared at him. Then they glanced at each other.

"Open it!" he snapped a little louder.

"But....she's a Darkling," one of them stammered. "If we open the gate, she could get in here."

He opened his mouth to bellow at them for their stupidity, but he didn't have time for that.

He dove for the counterweight and pulled the rope to release it. The counterweight sank to the ground and pulled the gate stone upward to open it.

Yann advanced outside more slowly. He had to cross the field to where Marine went down.

He had no idea what he would find. He might find her burned to death or cut to shreds by all those vapors.

She wasn't dead. Part of him almost wished she was when he saw her crouched on the ground. She snarled, hissed, and yowled at empty air.

She jerked from right to left snapping her teeth at invisible Darklings.

The vapors had burned her all over her body. They even burned all her hair off.

A mat of bubbling black burns covered her scalp, neck, back, and every other part of her that he could see.

She whipped around and screeched at him. Her wild, crazed eyes glared at him exactly the way they used to when she lost her mind.

Her long hair no longer hid just how insane her face had become. Yann stopped there and stared down at her.

Blood and blisters covered her body. Would she ever be able to heal from this?

He wouldn't be able to heal her. He wasn't even sure if one of the Templars could do it—or if they would be willing to do it.

They better not start making a stink about her being a Darkling—not after she just saved all their lives.

Yann took another step forward, but he stopped when she curled back her lips and gnashed her teeth at him.

"It's okay, Marine," he murmured. "You're okay. You saved the city. Everything is going to be okay. Let me help you. I won't hurt you. I promise."

He raised the blanket. He would hurt her by putting it around her, but no way in hell would he leave her out here.

A hundred eyes watched him from the wall. All the Watchmen and all the Templars who just thought so highly of her—none of them hurried out here to take care of Marine.

She turned her back on him when he took the last step to her side, draped the blanket over her shoulders, and wrapped it around her. It might hurt her, but at least the Watchmen wouldn't see her body totally exposed.

Yann squatted down next to her and found himself putting his arms around her.

"Everything is going to be okay," he murmured as much to reassure himself as her. "You'll come back from this. I know you will. Come inside. I'll take you somewhere you can rest."

She didn't face him. She kept jerking and jumping in his arms. She spun one way and the other snarling and shrieking at nothing.

He couldn't wait any longer and he didn't trust her to walk back to the gate.

He straightened up and scooped her into his arms. He expected her to fight him.

She didn't stop twitching, but she huddled in his arms and her yowling noises quieted to low mutterings and even some whining. She must be in a lot of pain.

Maybe the pain itself drove her out into the Dark. He couldn't possibly know that and he really didn't give a crap about it anymore.

Chapter 45

Yann carried Marine back to the gate. A bunch of armed Watch-men stood around watching him come closer. Maximil and Oran were there.

All the Watchmen raised their weapons as he got nearer as if she might attack them for some reason.

He barged straight past them and didn't look sideways at their weapons. He stormed into the archway. "Close the gate," he snapped over his shoulder.

"What are you going to do with her?" Maximil asked.

"I said close the gate!" Yann fired back. "Don't ever make me repeat an order more than once."

He marched off back to his apartment building. He couldn't deal with these people right now. He didn't want to hear anyone call Marine a Darkling. No way.

He kicked open the apartment door, carried her into his own bedroom, and laid her on the bed. She curled into a fetal ball, but she didn't lie down. She crouched there the same way she did out in the fields.

She kept jerking and spitting and growling the way she always did when she communed with Darklings, but she made a split second of eye contact with Yann—just once.

"You'll be okay," he told her. "We'll bring you back from this. I promise. You'll be safe here. Don't worry. You're safe now. No one will bother you."

She didn't respond, but he didn't need her to. She could hear him. She was still in there.

Someone had to take care of her. No one else would do it, but he couldn't leave her hurt and in pain like this.

He sat back and watched her for a minute before he decided what to do. He wouldn't be able to stay in here and keep an eye on her around the clock. He would have to go back out to the wall.

What would happen during the next assault?

The Dark forces would keep building in strength. The next assault would be worse. Savaré wouldn't have Marine around to save the city a second time.

He got to his feet, went into the living room, and brought back a bunch of food the townspeople left for him and Marine to eat. The townspeople brought in a constant supply so Yann and Marine never ran out.

He put one of the plates on the bed next to her and she attacked it in wolfish, greedy mouthfuls. She crammed the food into her mouth too fast, got it on her cheeks, and wiped the excess off by passing her wrist across her mouth.

Yann studied her. She must be really hungry. Maybe communing with the Dark took more energy than he realized. How would he know?

He went out to the kitchen, brought back a pitcher of water and a glass, poured her some, and handed her the glass.

She snatched it out of his hand hard enough to splash the water on the bed. Then she guzzled the contents and barely waited long enough for him to pour a second one before she pounded that, too.

He left the water on the bedside table. She attacked the food in rabid handfuls. He didn't need to stay here for this.

He went back outside and stopped on the sidewalk to look around. The Templars were just putting the finishing touches on the new dome.

Whatever Marine did, no more Dark vapors descended from the upper Layers to attack the dome. She didn't seal the breach. No one could do that.

Yann looked straight up through the hole at Layers churning, seething, and collapsing on top of each other up there. How long would it take before they collapsed this Island, too?

He couldn't see the shadows in the forest from here. He would have to go up to the wall for that, but he didn't care about that right now.

He climbed up there, retrieved his dropped glaive, and found Master Prismael, Master Regin, and Master Tregre all working together to knit the barrier into a tighter mesh.

"I need one of you to come with me and heal Marine," Yann blurted out.

"No one can heal her of the Dark," Master Regin replied over his shoulder. He didn't stop what he was doing.

Yann pinched his lips to hold back fury. "She went into the Dark to save the whole Coil," he snapped. "She went into the Dark under orders from Templar Masters just like you, so don't you dare start blaming her for this. She just saved the whole damn city. If one of you doesn't come right now to heal her, I'll take her out of town and the rest of you can rot here for all I care. Doesn't any of you have a shred of decency? Why the hell have I been working my tail off to defend if you can't even help us when we need it?"

The other Templars bowed their heads in shame, but they didn't stop working on the barrier.

Only Master Prismael stopped what he was doing to turn around and face Yann.

"I won't be able to heal her from the Dark. It would be too dangerous for me to take the Darkness on myself. It would corrupt my magic and turn me Dark, too."

"I'm not asking you to take her Darkness," Yann countered. "I'm asking you to heal her injuries. That's all. What is so difficult about that? Hasn't she earned even that small consideration from you—from all of you?"

Master Prismael sighed. "You're right, Watch Commander. I'll come."

Master Regin actually stopped what he was doing and turned around to block Master Prismael from going anywhere. "No, Master! You can't do that!"

"You foul piece of trash!" Yann barked. "How dare you?!"

Master Prismael raised his hand. "The Watch Commander is right. Healing Marine's injuries won't put me in danger and she has earned that much from us and a lot more. Lead the way, Commander."

Yann stalked off to the apartment building. He had to force himself to wait for Master Prismael. This better not turn into a regular problem.

He led Master Prismael back to the apartment. Yann put his glaive by the door so Marine wouldn't see him coming near her with a weapon.

She hadn't moved since he left. She'd devoured all the food on the plate and drunk the entire pitcher of water. She really must have been hungry.

Master Prismael halted on the threshold and stared at her in abject horror when he saw the way she was acting.

"My God!" he husked. "What in the name of Heaven happened to her?"

"She's communing with the Dark," Yann explained. "She's been doing this since I first met her."

Master Prismael spun around fast. "Are you serious?! And....Templar Masters.....made her....do *this?*"

"That's what she said. They set out to defeat the Voyant Mendicat and they got Marine to commune with the Dark to find out what he was doing. She goes out of her mind when she does it. Other times, she comes to certain Islands where she's sane. It's hit and miss. I guess she went a little too far out there this time."

Master Prismael gasped, "My God!" again and passed his hand across his eyes. "What were they thinking sending an initiate to do *this?*"

"It doesn't seem to harm her," Yann replied. "She comes back to her senses eventually. She doesn't seem to suffer from any ill effects."

"I would never send *anyone* to commune with the Dark—not ever!" Master Prismael whispered. "I wouldn't send a trained Master with decades of experience, let alone an untrained initiate!"

Yann waited for him to say something else. "So....can you heal her—physically, I mean? You don't have to bring her back mentally. She can handle that on her own."

"Oh. Of course." Master Prismael stepped the rest of the way into the room.

Marine kept her back to him when he approached the bed.

He hesitated again, but he eventually worked up the courage to place his hand on her back where the blanket covered her.

He sent a flow of magic into her from behind. She didn't move or turn around. She didn't stop muttering, growling, and hissing to herself.

The flood of magic swept up her scalp, cleared away all the cuts and blisters, and left smooth pink skin in its place. Her hair grew back, but that was all.

Master Prismael lowered his hand, opened his eyes, and took a step away. "It's done. She's whole—physically at least."

"Thank you," Yann murmured. "I'm grateful."

Master Prismael's old eyes darted up to meet Yann's. "We're the ones who are grateful—to both of you. I'm sorry for my fellow Templars' behavior. I'll speak to them and tell them to continue as before. "

Yann mumbled, "Thank you," again and showed Master Prismael out of the apartment.

Chapter 46

Yann accompanied Master Prismael back down to the street and split off toward one of the reinforced basements.

It was empty, now that the townspeople were returning to their normal activities.

Yann went into one of the many storerooms attached to the basement. The people of Savaré had loaded the room with food stores, water containers, blankets, and other survival supplies.

They'd also laid in stacks of clothes of all sizes for every kind of person just in case.

Yann rummaged around and found a dress for Marine. It was much plainer than the ones she usually wore, but it was better than nothing.

He held it up to check the size. This dress consisted of a plain brown bodice and skirt in a thick, tight twill weave. Gathers made the sleeves puff at the shoulders, but that was the only decoration.

He took it back to the apartment. Marine was back to glaring at the world from under her hair, but at least it was clean.

Yann took a deep breath, removed the empty plate, and sat down on the bed next to her. "Here. I brought you this. Put this on."

He didn't wait for her to respond. He pulled the blanket off and slipped the dress over her head.

She didn't help him or acknowledge him in any way. He had to wrestle her arms into the sleeves and then turn her body in different directions to pull the dress down over her.

He pretended not to notice that he was seeing her naked body right in front of him. How many nights had he spent dreaming about her? Her body meant nothing to him right now.

She struggled when he tried to move her limbs into different positions. He had to use more strength than he wanted to when it came to pulling her hands through the sleeves.

Then he had to tug the two sides of the dress close enough to each other for him to button the buttons.

He finally finished and she drew her knees to her chest on the opposite corner of the bed.

He let out a shaky breath. How much longer would he have to deal with her like this before he got her back? Would he ever get her back?

He stood back waiting for something to happen, but she didn't acknowledge him again. What should he do now—leave? This was his bedroom.

He absolutely refused to move her to her own room. That would have been too cold even to consider. He wouldn't lock her away or keep her isolated just because of this. She deserved better.

He finally got himself some food and sat down on the other side of the bed. He considered trying to talk to her. She would be able to hear him, but he couldn't quite bring himself to do it.

He listened to her muttering and growling while he ate. He would have to leave this room sooner or later to go back on watch.

The sun went down outside. This apartment sat high enough off the ground for him to see the landscape beyond the wall. The shadows didn't come back and neither did the Dark filaments.

She must have driven back the Dark forces.

He was still sitting there when someone knocked on the door out in the living room. He went to see who it was.

He stiffened when he found Maximil, Oran, Master Regin, and Master Tregren standing out in the corridor.

Yann wouldn't have minded so much if the four men didn't come armed. He could already see where this was going.

"Watch Commander," Master Regin began.

Yann didn't even try to keep the ice out of his voice. "Can I help you?"

"Our scrying visions indicate a Dark force coming from this apartment," Master Regin went on. "Marine has gone over to the Dark. We have to drive her out of town. We can't have a Darkling inside the walls."

Yann narrowed his eyes at Regin and then shot a death glare at the other three. "Is that what you came here to tell me?"

Regin dipped his chin once. "If you interfere, we'll have no choice but to drive you out of town, too."

Yann picked up his glaive from the place where he set it against the wall earlier. He made no attempt whatsoever to hide it when he swiveled the blade to point at the four men. "If any of you wants to lay a hand on Marine, you better be ready to fight your way through me first."

"That isn't necessary, Watch Commander," Regin began.

"Apparently it is. She's injured—and she got injured saving all your lives. So you want to drive her out now, do you? I hope you're ready to kill me first because that is the only way you will ever go near Marine."

"She's a Darkling...." Maximil interjected.

Yann sneered at him. "Would she have saved your city from Dark forces if she was a Darkling? Use your heads."

"Then how do you explain Dark forces inside this apartment?"

"She communes with the Dark—and before you start jumping up and down about that, remember that she started doing this on the instructions from Templars Masters just like you." Yann glanced around. "Where's Master Prismael? He was here before and he didn't say anything about driving her out."

The two Masters glanced at each other. "Master Prismael doesn't approve of us coming here," Oran explained. "He doesn't agree that Marine is Dark."

"That's because she isn't," Yann snapped. "So I suggest you go down to the wall and bring back a bunch of other armed men if you want to fight your way inside this apartment."

"We don't need more men," Master Regin pointed out. "I can flatten you with my magic right now."

"Then do it," Yann fired back. "What are you waiting for?"

None of the four men moved except to exchange glances again. Filthy cowards.

Yann waited a few more seconds and then slammed the door in their faces. How dare they?

He took his glaive with him this time when he returned to the bedroom.

Marine had turned herself farther away from the door. Now she sat facing the big windows looking out over Savaré.

Yann rested the glaive against the wall on his side of the bed. He sat down, kicked off his boots, pulled off his jacket and shirt, and stretched out on his side on the mattress.

He rolled onto his side watching Marine. He didn't expect any response from her and he didn't get one.

She kept rocking, jerking, snarling, and biting. Her crazed eyes skimmed the room, out the window, and everywhere else other than at him.

He settled down to keep watch over her until he fell asleep. Maybe she would be able to get some sleep, too. He didn't see what else he could do.

He observed her frantic movements for a while, but he didn't see anything he hadn't seen a million times before. He started to close his eyes when he felt her weight shift on the mattress.

She tipped over and curled up in front of him. She must be tired.

He relaxed. He wouldn't have to watch her so closely if she fell asleep.

All at once, she blurted out the words, "Yann.....I need...." in between all her other gibbering and snarling.

His eyes shot wide open, but she just went straight back to growling and yowling.

"What is it?" he asked. "What do you need, young one?"

She struggled against whatever force made her keep acting like this. She broke into a few strings of English words before the spasms took her.

Her eyes flickered to his face and her eyebrows shot together in desperate pleading before the madness wiped out her expression.

Those brief snatches of lucidity breaking through—they wrung his heart. He raised his hand and ran his fingers through her hair.

"It's all right," he murmured. "Take your time. I'm not going any-where. You'll come around. There's no rush. I'm here. You can rest. I'll still be here in the morning."

She whimpered once and then slashed her teeth at his hand. He yanked it back, but only for a second. Then he went back to raking it through her hair. Touching her felt too good even if he couldn't fix what was wrong with her.

No one could. That was the problem because there was nothing wrong with her.

She sank back down on the mattress when she broke into another burst of words disconnected with snarls and grimaces.

"I need.....I was trying to tell you.....I need you to tell the...."

He waited, but whatever she was trying to say didn't come out any more clearly than that.

He finally put his arm down and closed his eyes. She went back to muttering and growling under her breath. She was still doing it when he fell asleep.

Chapter 47

Yann woke up with his arms around Marine. He didn't feel her crawl up next to him in the middle of the night. He must have put his arms around her instinctively, but he didn't want her anywhere else.

She still jolted and twitched every now and then. That must have been what woke him up—which meant she must have just woken up.

He raised his hand to rake his fingers through her hair. "How do you feel, young one?'

She twitched again. "I ...I feel...." She broke off in another snarl.

"You should probably stay in here today," he suggested. "The Watchmen and Templars...."

"I heard....." she murmured and screeched again.

Yann cringe. He really didn't want her to hear what they said about her. Now he would have to go outside and face them.

"Thank you," she blurted out and immediately went back to growling.

"Don't mention it. What else would I do? I wouldn't leave you out there."

"They would."

"Well, I'm not them." He pushed her off him and she sat up. She curled her knees to her chest the way she usually did.

He watched her struggle against her madness for a while. Watching her hurt.

He didn't want to see, but he made himself bear witness to her struggles. She did this for the whole city.

She saved millions of people. Keeping an eye on her and admiring her sacrifice was the least he could do.

He eventually sat up, pulled on his shirt, and went out to the living room to get her something to eat.

"Do you think you'll be all right to stay in here by yourself today?" he asked when he brought it back.

She took a long time of convulsing on the bed before she got her head clear enough to speak. "I just.....want to....I need to find out..... the Templars....."

"If you tell me what you want to know. I can ask them for you...."

Her eyes darted to the window. "Out there....."

"You don't have to go out there," he told her. "You're still fragile. You should stay in."

"What if.....the attack...."

"The Templars will handle another attack, but it looks like you drove the Dark back into the forest. We have some time before it comes back."

"And.....those men....."

He didn't have to ask which men she meant. "If they don't drop it, we'll just leave. I don't want you going through all this for people who don't reappreciate you."

Her eyes locked on him with unnatural clarity. "They appreciate you."

"That's exactly my point. You've done more for them than I have, so them appreciating me doesn't really mean jack, does it?" He leaned in and kissed her on the head just because. "Take it easy today and try to get some rest. You don't have to go out there unless you're feeling better."

"You mean...." She broke off in another snarl and she didn't come out of it this time. It took all her effort just to talk to him that much.

"No one is going to mess with you, young one," He put his arm around her shoulders and squeezed. He tried not to notice her jerking away from him. "Just concentrate on getting better. These people asked us to come here. We don't have to stay if we aren't welcome."

He took his glaive down to the wall and went about his normal business of reviewing the men.

The new dome protected the city—or the dome would have protected the city if there was anything there to protect the city from.

Yann reviewed the Templars on the wall, too. None of them asked about Marine—the bastards. None of them had the decency even to ask if she was feeling better.

Yann didn't see Master Prismael anywhere. Did the other Templars send him away—or drive *him* out of town? Yann really would have believed anything at this point.

None of the Watchmen challenged his orders or made any noise about Marine being inside the walls.

Yann made up his mind. He wouldn't leave unless these people gave him a reason to. He committed himself to defending this city and he would do it.

Their feelings about Marine didn't really mean anything. He was a member of the Black Watch committed to defending these people. They needed a leader, so he went through the motions of being the leader they needed him to be.

Maximil and Oran acted like they never accompanied Master Regin and Master Tregren to Yann's apartment. The two Watchmen went through their duties as normally as possible, too.

"How do you want to handle the next assault?" Maximil asked. "I saw Darklings coming out of the Layer last time. They'll probably break through next time."

"I was thinking we could come up with some magical weapons."

"Magical weapons—how?" Oran asked. "None of us has magic."

Yann made a face and waved at all the Templars standing around. "We have more magic-users here than any other Island I've seen." He turned to Master Regin. "What do you think about coming up with some magical weapons?"

"We're already using magical weapons," Regin replied.

"I don't mean those. I'm talking about projectiles. The last town I defended used propelled rockets to fend off Darklings."

Regin's eyes flew open. "Really? I've never heard of that."

Yann studied the man in front of him. Was Regin lying?

These people had a vast computer network connected to every other advanced city in the Coil.

Did Regin seriously expect Yann to believe that Tenby had rockets but none of these other cities had ever even heard of them? Please.

Yann let that drop. "What do you think about getting the Templars working on it? We have some time before the next assault."

"I guess we could," Tregren interjected.

"Get onto it," Yann ordered. "We could have bombarded that Layer last time when the Templars' magic failed."

The Templars gathered in a cluster and discussed the rockets in great detail, including how they should be constructed and how they should propelled.

Yann considered going back to either his apartment or the Temple library and looking up the rockets on the computer—or getting Marine to do it for him. These idiots better not be lying to him about their defensive capabilities.

Wouldn't Marine have found something in her research—like maybe a few hundred banks of artillery hidden right outside of town?

Yann pushed that thought away. She hadn't been looking for artillery because she'd been too busy researching the King in the White Spire.

He decided to ask her, but right then, a dangerous silence fell over the streets nearest the wall.

Everyone stopped what they were doing and stared in blank amazement when Marine came outside. She strode toward the wall.

Yann might have been the only person who knew her well enough to recognize how jumpy she still was, but she held herself together better here than she did in the apartment.

She tried to smile at the people nearest her, especially the Templars, but they only withdrew from her.

She burst into a huge grin when she saw Yann standing on the wall above her. He waved for her to come up and join him.

Her cheeks colored when she got to the top. "How are you?" he asked.

She nodded and brushed her hair out of her face. She looked as beautiful as ever. "I feel better. Thank you. How are things here?"

"The shadows are holding off." He pointed to the forest. "Can you tell from here if they're amassing for another assault?"

"They'll never go away completely. They aren't as strong as they were before, but they're still out there. They might take a few days before they come back." She looked up at the breach in the Layers above the Dome. "That's going to be a problem. "

"Could the Templars close the breach?"

"They would have to go outside the dome to do that." She bit back a smirk. "You could ask for volunteers."

He heard what she didn't say. If he asked anyone, he would ask Master Prismael. Even he might not be able to convince the other Templars to do it—not even for the city's safety.

"I was hoping I could talk to you about something," Yann went on. "Do you remember the rockets we had in Tenby? Could we do something like that here—or the magical equivalent?"

Her eyes shot wide open and she gasped in astonishment. "Why didn't I think of that?! It's brilliant!"

"The question is whether a projectile like that would work against these Dark forces. They worked against Darklings, but we aren't seeing Darklings here—not that kind, anyway."

She turned to Master Regin who happened to be standing closest to her. "We could create starburst spells and combine magic from more than one Templar behind each bust."

"What's that?" Yann asked.

She flapped her hands. "It's a flash of explosive magic designed to destroy something, but we would have to combine our magic to make it strong enough—and it would take some modification if we wanted to propel it somewhere to detonate at a distance from its launch point."

"Great!" Yann exclaimed. "When can you start?"

She turned back to Regin. "Gather up ten of your fellow Masters and we'll give it a shot. We'll fire out onto the fields over there and see how far we can shoot and still make a decent explosion."

"Are you saying you could increase the burst's firepower by combining magic from more than one Templar?" Yann asked. "Like you could keep building until it's strong enough to take out a whole Dark Layer if you had to?'

She wouldn't stop grinning. "Yes. I don't see any reason why we wouldn't be able to."

They both turned to Regin. He didn't move or respond during their discussion.

He still didn't move when Yann and Marine faced him. "Well?" Yann went on. "You heard what Marine said. Gather your Templars and let's do this."

Regin stared back at him and then glanced at Marine. Yann's temper started to rise, but Regin turned away before Yann could lose his composure completely.

Regin mumbled something to the Templars nearest him and then headed off down the wall to relay the order to every other Templars on the ledge.

Yann glared after the back of Regin's head, but Yann came back to reality when he smiled down at Marine. "It's great to see you up and around. I didn't think you would get back on your feet this soon."

Almost as if his words made it happen, she jolted just then. Her shoulders spasmed and she glanced over her shoulder at something behind her even though there was nothing there.

She squirmed. "Maybe I shouldn't have...."

"Of course you should have. We need you." Yann threw caution to the wind, put his arm around her shoulder, and squeezed. Everyone here thought he and Marine were already a couple, so why the hell not?

She smiled back at him, but plenty of uncertainty snuck into that smile.

The moment only lasted a second before they both checked to see how close Regin and the other Templars were to coming back to do their starburst experiment.

Yann and Marine froze in their tracks when they saw Regin leading the Templars to a different stairway farther down the wall.

Regin and all the other Templars filed down the stairs, passed inside the wall, descended to the ground, and walked away up the street.

They left the wall completely devoid of Templars. The dome glistened overhead, but the barrier wouldn't last long without the Templars protecting it.

Regin marched over to the Templars in the middle of the street—the Templars who bolstered the dome's highest point.

He said something to them and the whole mob of Templars filed through the streets heading back to the temple.

"Um....what just happened?" Marine stammered.

Yann clamped his lips shut. He had to fight himself not to lose his temper in the worst possible way. The Templars did not just leave the wall completely undefended. No way in hell.

Yann tore his gaze away from the retreating Templars. The Watchmen stared after the Templars in abject horror.

"You men space yourself out along the wall to fill the gaps," Yann ordered and turned back to Marine. "I need you to start thinking about producing some more melee weapons, too. It will be more important now."

He didn't say the rest. The Watchmen would need a lot more melee weapons without the Templars—like a lot of weapons.

Chapter 48

Y ann stepped into a warehouse in Savaré's industrial district. He didn't usually get a chance to come down here.

A bunch of sweaty, greasy, filthy workmen slaved over a long line of machines Yann didn't recognize.

Marine paced back and forth down the line giving orders to everyone. She was still speaking English and she showed no sign of slipping back into her madness, but he still didn't understand a word she said.

These workmen had set up the machines to produce battleaxes, swords, spears, glaives, and daggers by the dozen.

Marine used her magic—and recruited some of the most junior pupils in the Temple—to magick these machines to work extra fast.

The workmen went from machine to machine making adjustments. Another crew toiled at the end of the line to remove the weapons as soon as they came out the other end.

None of the workmen had a problem taking orders from Marine. Yann heard them calling her, "Ma'am," whenever they had to tell her something.

"How is it coming along?" Yann asked Marine when she finally made it over to him.

She beamed at him and pointed at the mounting pile of weapons. "You can see how it's coming along. How many do you want us to make before we have enough?"

"I don't know if we'll ever have enough. If the Templars don't come back, we'll have to fight the Darklings hand to hand—and if the Darklings don't come, we'll be screwed." He lowered his voice. "I guess I can't send you to go talk to the Templars a second time, can I?"

She fought her lips under control and tried to smile, but she failed. "You better go. If they don't listen to you, they definitely won't listen to me."

He nodded. Of course he already knew that.

He really didn't look forward to dealing with the Templars again. He really never wanted to lay eyes on them again after what they did.

He left her there and went back outside. He didn't go to the Temple.

He should have done that immediately, but he went back to the wall instead. He needed to think about it before he decided how to deal with anyone from the Temple.

Pure habit made him glance over the wall toward the forest. He didn't expect to see anything.

He probably wouldn't have noticed anything different, but his senses had become overly tuned to the slightest change in any Dark force no matter where it came from.

The forest itself didn't look any different. The spikes that ruptured the trees apart last time left the forest perfectly intact when Marine expelled the Dark from the landscape.

The shadows between the trees looked just a little bit darker—hardly any different, but just enough for Yann to notice it.

He froze to the spot starting at it.

The sun was going down. Did the dusky light make the shadows look longer and darker than they were—or was something out there?

He turned around to give orders to the Watchmen nearest him.

Yann planned to order some of them to go meet up with Marine and bring the new weapons out to the wall.

He also planned to send someone to the Temple to ask if Yann could visit Master Prismael later that evening.

Master Prismael might not have any influence over the Templars anymore after he healed Marine.

Yann couldn't think of anyone else in the Temple to turn to. He definitely wouldn't ask Regin or Tregren. Yann didn't trust himself in the same room with either of them after today.

He stiffened again when he saw the Templars coming up the street. Regin and Tregren led a party of a hundred Templars—more than had been out here earlier.

Yann tightened his grip on his glaive—like he would be able to land a single blow on one of those wizards before they annihilated him.

Maximil snarled through gritted teeth behind Yann's back "What the hell do they want now—the traitorous wretches?"

Those words snapped Yann out of his trance. So he wasn't the only one who knew what the Templars did to this city by abandoning their posts.

Yann stalked down the stairs to meet up with the Templars in the middle of the street. Maximil, Oran, and fifteen other Watchmen went with him.

They lined up behind Yann. He stopped there and waited for the Templars to stop in front of him.

This was the last thing Savaré needed right now—an internal conflict between the Black Watch and the Guardian Templars. They should have been working together to protect this city instead of fighting amongst themselves.

Master Regin dipped his chin at Yann in the usual way. "Watch Commander."

"What are you doing here?" Yann snapped. "You made your position pretty clear when you abandoned the wall."

"I'm sorry you see it that way, but we never had any intention of abandoning the wall."

"And yet that's exactly what you did. If the Dark attacked this city while you were over there powdering your noses, we would all be dead now. What do you think I'm doing out here—playing games? What conclusion was I supposed to draw when I asked you point blank to build up our defenses for the next assault, but instead you took all your Templars and walked away and left us to guard the wall alone? If you don't plan to defend this city, maybe you should leave Savaré right now. We don't need traitors like you around here.'

"We have no intention of abandoning the wall or the city, Watch Commander," Regin replied with exaggerated patience. "I had to consult the other Masters to find out about fulfilling your request about the propelled starbursts."

"You didn't need to take every single Templar off the wall to do that. You're making an excuse. Maybe you think I'm too young and stupid to see what you're doing, but you're mistaken. If you care about this city at all, you'll get back up on the wall and resume your posts. That's more important than any weapon. I shouldn't have to explain this to any of you."

A murmur went through the assembled Templars. Yann really didn't care if he offended them. How dare they try to get away with such a flimsy excuse?

Regin only nodded again. "You're right, Commander. We'll do it as you say."

"You're damn right you will. I'm the one responsible for the safety of the whole city—not you. You and your dogs here made a big stink about Marine being a Darkling, but she's the one who has done more than you have to save this city—a hell of a lot more. Now get back to work or pack your bags and get out of town. Don't let me see you away from your posts again unless you get my permission first."

He heard himself snapping at much older men—much more powerful men. To hell with them.

He made them shoulder their way past him. Then the Watchmen made the Templars shoulder their way through the whole Watch before they made it back to the wall. Bastards.

Yann watched them go. Then he went up to the wall and breathed down all their necks to make sure they stood their posts the way they were supposed to.

He didn't give them a minute's peace—and he sent men to bring up the weapons anyway.

He couldn't rely on the Templars anymore. He would ask Marine about the starburst weapon—and about recruiting some of her much younger magic-users—people who wouldn't be so concerned about following someone else's instructions.

The sun kept sinking. His gaze kept darting toward the forest. The shadows kept lengthening. They stretched into the fields and extended their claws toward Savaré—or did Yann just imagine that, too?

He started to turn away when a crash startled him from the west. He spun around and automatically raised his glaive.

Sure enough, his worst nightmare came true when all those crawling, clawing fingers of shadow kept spreading over the fields. They stretched much farther than they should have considering the time of day.

"Here it comes!" he roared down the wall. "The next assault is starting! Stand your posts! Prepare to repel another assault!"

The Watchmen took a minute before they realized what he was talking about. Those shadows didn't look like anything threatening—not at first.

Shouting voices traveled from mouth to mouth down the wall in both directions away from Yann's position.

Yann took his eyes off the Dark for a split second to glance up at the breach in the sky. The Layers didn't come through and no Dark vapors descended to assault the dome from up here.

His throat went dry when he turned back to face the western fields. The fingers crawling across the grass shot away impossibly fast. They covered the field in no time, hit the wall, and snaked up the stone to the magical barrier.

The Templars leapt in, planted their hands on the barrier, and poured their magic into it to make it stronger.

The Dark squirmed, wriggled, and crawled all those grasping fingers up the dome's edges.

The shadows climbed higher and higher and formed a solid sheet of Darkness covering the dome. The Layer blocked out the sunset until it enveloped the dome all the way to the top.

More Templars fired into the dome from below, but the pressure building from outside became too great for even the Templars to keep the dome intact.

The dome trembled and then rumbled under the weight of some unbearable force. Yann couldn't see anything outside that might be causing it.

The Templars shuddered from the effort of holding back the Dark. A few older Masters bellowed and then some unseen force hurled them away from the barrier. Each man down weakened the city's defenses more.

Chapter 49

Yann stormed down the wall yelling orders at the Watchmen to arm themselves and be ready to defend the city by any means necessary.

They wouldn't be able to. He saw that already.

Horrific shapes of faces, Darklings, and bizarre nightmare-scapes undulated in the sheet of black covering the dome.

Those faces leered and grinned inches away from the Templars straining to hold back the Dark. The Watchmen scrambled to distribute their new weapons.

Yann sent a silent cruse on the heads of all the Templars who abandoned the wall today. They could have created their starburst weapon without going anywhere. Then maybe this city would stand a chance at survival.

Yann turned around at the gate and came striding back, but everyone already knew everything they needed to know.

He planted himself in his usual spot and rotated his glaive forward to make his last stand.

At that moment, Marine rushed past him from his right to his left. She passed behind him running down the wall. She must have come up the stairs.

He yelled out, "Hey..!" but she was already rushing farther away.

She ran to a spot on the wall. He didn't see what made her stop.

She faced the barrier, raised both hands, and stuck them through the field. Her hands vanished into the Darkness on the other side.

Then she took another step forward—a step closer to the barrier. Her arms vanished up to the shoulder.

"NO!!" Yann roared and lunged for her.

She glanced back only once, made eye contact with him, and plunged the rest of the way through.

He raced to the spot, but she was already gone. She completely vanished into the Dark Layer outside the barricade.

Whatever she did produced an instantaneous effect. A massive force sucked all the Darkness away from the barrier. That invisible force left the dome perfectly intact and glistening with brilliant magic.

The Dark that made up the Layer zoomed away as far as the forest before it exploded to a massive size—even bigger than it had been when it covered the dome.

The Dark compressed into a ball and then morphed into dozens of shapes before it formed a gigantic image of Marine as a Darkling.

Yann barely recognized her hideous features. Giant fangs sprouted for a mouth that was way too big for her. Dark swirls and fiery sparks erupted along her scaly skin. Tentacles lashed all around her.

She seethed right and left in the air two hundred feet above the forest. She roared to shake the landscape. Every part of her huge body contorted, undulated, and twisted as she changed shape before Yann's eyes.

His stomach turned at the sight of her. He couldn't remember ever seeing a Darkling as disgusting as this, but it was still her. He could still recognize just enough of her features. It was her.

She erupted to something almost as big as Savaré itself. Her deafening roars rattled the buildings and windows even from this distance.

Her tentacles whipped and slashed the air. She hit some of the trees underneath her, cracked their trunks in half, and swiped sideways to clear the landscape.

Whatever Dark force took her over tossed and yanked her back and forth for a few torturous minutes. No one on the wall moved or even breathed watching this.

Then, without warning, she exploded into a million, billion Dark wisps of vapor. They all ejected outward in a colossal burst of Darkness before they smashed inward and crashed in on her with a deafening boom.

She turned back into her normal self. She wasn't a Darkling anymore—and none of the other Dark forces were there anymore, either. The shadows Yann saw earlier no longer haunted the forest.

The Dark released her that high off the ground and gravity yanked her down hard. She plummeted into the trees and vanished.

Yann spun away and stormed down the stairs back to the arch. He didn't even bother to tell the Watchmen to lower the counterweight.

Yann hacked his glaive at the release rope and barged outside into the growing dusk.

He only made it thirty feet away from the wall before the gate stone fell back into place behind him.

He paused there for a second to listen as that fatal thump resounded through the earth under his feet. He didn't even have to ask what it meant.

He set off across the fields still holding onto his glaive. At least he had that. He would walk away from this cursed city with a glaive—and Marine. He didn't need anything else.

It took him a long time to find her, but she made it easy by yowling and growling a lot. He had to stop to listen before he heard her. Then he followed the sound of her voice.

She crouched in the crook of some gnarled tree roots. The assault shredded her dress and disheveled her hair back to a mass of stringy tangles, but at least the Dark didn't burn her this time.

Yann slumped onto the ground nearby and watched her. She did it again. She saved that ungrateful city for the second time—and for what?

Never again. He made up his mind then and there. He wouldn't take her back there for all the money in the world.

The Watchmen and the Templars wouldn't let him take her back inside the city anyway and he didn't want to. He would never let them insult her again. They didn't deserve her.

He got over his disappointment pretty soon and scooted over next to her. "It's all right," he murmured. "I'm here. You're safe now. You don't have to go back there. We'll just spend the night here and then we'll go somewhere else in this Island. It seems stable enough as long as we keep away from Savaré. I'll get a fire going and see about finding us something to eat. We'll be safer here than we were in the city.'

He couldn't be sure of this, but he had to say something to reassure her. He didn't want her to think he forgot about her just because she lost her mind again.

She was still there. She was still the same beautiful, wonderful, caring person he admired so much.

He admired her even more after the sacrifice she just made for a bunch of strangers. She proved herself. If that didn't convince the Templars, nothing would.

He got to work gathering sticks and starting a fire. It took a while. He didn't have Niyazi's skills, but eventually, Yann built up a small blaze. It cast a glow of light and warmth into the night.

He actually felt better out here. This forest gave him a sense of peace he didn't feel in the city.

He would have thought the Dark would lurk and oppress everything out here, but he actually felt the opposite.

Leaving Savaré lifted a weight off his shoulders and not because he no longer cared about the city's safety.

He listened to the night insects deeper inside the forest shadows. This forest didn't feel Dark at all. It actually felt comfortable.

Marine sat on the other side of the fire with her back to him. Her snarling, hissing, and spitting noises actually flooded him with relief. He had her. He could lose everything else as long as he still had her.

He would take her somewhere else. She would get her sanity back even if for just a little while.

He would still lose her. Something would always happen to take her away from him, but she would always be there. He never doubted her heart.

After a little while, she stopped growling and curled up on her side by the fire. She curled up facing the flames so he could see her face while she slept.

If they'd been in their apartment in Savaré, he would have run his fingers through her hair and rubbed her arms and back until she fell asleep. He might even have curled up with his arms around her and slept like that.

He didn't do it now. He didn't need to do it. Just looking at her was enough.

He went so far as to cover her with his jacket before he returned to his place to watch her.

Her features cleared when she fell asleep. Her cheeks and forehead relaxed.

She turned back into that angelic princess who overflowed his heart with emotion just from looking at her.

She was so beautiful, but that beauty shone from the inside. She was priceless beyond words.

Chapter 50

Y ann woke up when Marine roared right next to his head. He jolted upright and had to take a few deep breaths to calm down when he saw her crouching nearby.

He breathed a sigh and looked away. "Don't do that! You scared me!"

"I'm sorry!" her voice replied from the branches above his head.

He looked up. He didn't see any creatures that could act as her familiars.

He did see a ball of vines clinging to the branch. "Um....you didn't say you had familiars here."

The vine ball shivered and its leaves fluttered. "Sometimes I can use them and sometimes I can't depending on which Island I'm in." She laughed. "This is fun! I like talking to you through familiars."

He grimaced at her body sitting huddled under a nearby tree. "I like it better when you're here with me."

"Where are we going today?" she asked.

"How should I know? I don't know anything about this Island. You know more than I do. Did you see anything on those computers of yours?"

"I didn't get a chance to study any maps of the area. Let's go back to that road—the one we were on when we came here."

"That's the road leading to Savaré," he pointed out.

Her voice dropped. "Oh, right. I forgot."

"Let's strike off north," he suggested. "This forest seems safe enough for now."

"You're right!" she exclaimed. "I like it here."

He found himself grinning at her even though she wasn't here.

He didn't know how to tell her body to come. Then he realized he didn't have to. Her consciousness spoke to him through her familiars.

He started walking north. She followed while her familiars talked to him along the way.

He made it as far as the tree line and cut parallel to it so he wouldn't go near Savaré.

"I can just imagine what the Templars would say if they could see you talking to me through familiars," he muttered.

"They shouldn't have any problem with it," she replied. "They were the ones who taught me how to do it."

"Why are these Templars so cut off from your order? It doesn't make sense that each order doesn't know what every other order is doing."

"I agree it's a silly way to run things. I didn't realize they were so cut off and insulated from each other—not before this happened."

"Master Prismael said he wouldn't send a trained Master into the Dark the way Brother Matherus sent you."

"Then I guess it's better that people like Brother Matherus were the ones who went to war against the Voyant. Those fools in Savaré didn't even think to use their magic against the Dark until you asked them to."

"Yeah," Yann murmured. "It does seem strange."

They came to the northern edge of the forest where it joined up with easier, more open country.

Marine's voice transferred to some bushes nearby. Her voice kept jumping from one plant, animal, and object to another.

"I wonder where we are," she remarked.

"It's too bad you couldn't combine your magic with one of the Templars to use Eliska's Coil projection."

"I don't think anyone in the Temple knows how to do that."

Yann stopped in his tracks. "Really? I had no idea it was so rare."

"She has incredible magic. She can do things I've never seen anyone else do. That projection might be one of a kind."

Yann found himself looking all around him. "I wonder what happened to her and Anríq. I hope they're all right."

"I'm sure they're saying the same thing about us. If I know anything about them, they'll be more concerned about us than they will be about themselves. They'll be especially concerned about you."

"Why do you think the Voyant hasn't come after me again?"

"Maybe he did. Maybe he sent those Dark Layers to capture you."

His head whipped around. "Do you really think so? Do you think all of that was because of me? Then why was the Dark attacking Savaré before I got there?"

"Maybe the Dark was attacking Savaré before you got there and then the Voyant stepped in and doubled down once he realized he could capture you there."

Yann snorted. "Or maybe the Voyant isn't after me at all."

"He's after someone," Marine pointed out.

Yann fell silent. He didn't ask how he and Marine would be able to find the person the Voyant was looking for.

Yann and Marine wouldn't have to go looking for the person if Yann *was* the person.

He didn't want to think about that, so he set off across the fields. Marine followed a dozen yards behind him, but her voice kept pace with him jumping from familiar to familiar.

He forgot to think about this. She sounded the same way she always did. It started to feel normal to do it this way.

Her body kept dropping back, falling behind, and then scampering to catch up.

He didn't keep track of that, either. He didn't turn around each time to make sure she stayed with him. He just assumed she would meet up with him eventually.

"It would be nice to know if we could find another town or city," he remarked.

"It would be even nicer if we could find out beforehand if the town or city was under attack from Dark forces," she countered and laughed.

He joined in with the joke. "You're right. Let's stay away from those from now on."

Her voice shifted forward to a shrub a few feet in front of him and to his right. She started to say, "How far do you want to go before we try again to....?"

At that moment, a fully developed conifer tree crown ejected from the level grassland. The tree tore the shrub apart and kept growing taller and taller.

Marine screamed just as more giant trees blasted out of the soil all over what had once been open fields.

Yann lunged away from them, but they spread too fast. They overtook him.

He charged back to Marine and grabbed her with both arms around her shoulders. "Hold on! The landscape is collapsing!"

She screamed again as more trees erupted into a massive forest—a much bigger, taller, darker forest than the one the pair just left this morning.

Yann turned one way and then another trying to find a way out, but the trees blocked him in on all sides.

Shockwaves blasted through the ground underfoot. They ricocheted outward from Yann's position, tossed the trees off the ground, and they slammed down before they threaded their roots back into the soil.

He floundered to keep his balance and to hold onto Marine at the same time, but they couldn't stay here. One of these trees would bounce out of position and squash the pair any second now.

"Come on!" he roared and pulled Marine forward.

He took off running through the landscape trying to find his way out of this, but he didn't see any end to his forest. The trees might have changed the entire Island in a matter of seconds. Then what would he do?

He ducked his head and tried to cover Marine to protect her from falling branches. He had to dodge right and left to save both of them from trees ripping out of the ground and then slamming down with bone-crushing force.

Her weight fell against him and he guided her where he thought they ought to go, but he still didn't see any way out. He and Marine could be trapped here.

"Hold on, Marine!" he yelled, but right then another tree tore out of the ground on his left.

He dove to the right to squeeze through a gap between two trunks.

He ran full force into something solid and realized a split second later that it was a person.

Yann gasped in shock. "Anríq!"

Anríq's eyes popped open in a mirror image of Yann's expression. "Yann! We found you!"

Yann didn't have time to ask how Anríq found him. The forest kept tearing itself apart all around them.

Anríq swiveled backward and raised his club, but at that moment, Eliska dropped from high up in the sky.

Yann didn't see her before she plunged between him and Anríq and slammed down on the ground. "Hold on!" she bellowed.

Yann tightened his grip on Marine. He couldn't let her go for anything.

Eliska swung her staff around her head and unleashed a torrent of magic that circled the four travelers. Yann experienced an unstoppable inward magnetic force that squashed all four friends together. Then she spiked her staff into the ground and shattered the Layer.

It buckled and the four friends pitched into a weightless void full of chaos vapors, but this Layer didn't have any gravity. The travelers just wound up floating there and not going anywhere.

The same force held everyone together so they didn't fall apart.

"Where have you been?!" Yann asked. "We were worried about you."

"We were worried about you!" Eliska countered.

"I told you so!" Marine's voice chirped from somewhere nearby.

Anríq and Eliska looked around everywhere. "Um....what are you doing?" Eliska asked.

Marine laughed. "I'm using familiars to talk to you."

"Familiars!" Eliska snorted. "What is that? Besides, there's nothing here."

"The vapors are here."

Yann studied Anríq and Eliska, but they seemed unhurt. "How do we get out of this if you can't shatter the Layer and we don't fall into another Island."

"I can take us to another Island," Eliska replied. "Just give me a second."

She opened her Coil projection, but it looked nothing like the one Yann had seen her use before to navigate the Coil.

This one expanded to four times the size. Gold and silver lines traced through it heading in different directions.

She could expand and contract different Layers and blow them up to show more detail. She even showed little details of the landscapes inside each Layer.

She located the Layer in which the party floated right now. "All the Layers around us are collapsing. We'll need to travel a long way before we find a stable Island."

"How do we do that?" Yann asked.

"We should try to find an Island where we can get more information about the Voyant," Marine's voice replied.

She shrieked at the same time—or her body did. The shriek came out of her mouth. The voice came from somewhere above the traveler's heads.

Anríq and Eliska both spun around trying to look everywhere at once. Yann found their behavior odd at first. He had gotten used to this during his travels with Marine.

"What do you have to do to take us there?" he asked Eliska.

She concentrated on her projection. "I say we just go to any stable Island for now. We can worry about where to go after that once we're on solid ground."

Chapter 51

E liska said, "Hold onto each other," again even though none of the other three friends could possibly let go of each other even if they wanted to.

She swept her staff in another circle around the group, surrounded everyone with another brilliant ring of magic, and then did something to make it burst outward.

That explosion shattered the Layer and the whole party tumbled into a completely different Layer where Yann couldn't see anything.

He definitely would have gotten separated from the others if Eliska's magic didn't bind them together. He tightened his grip on Marine, but he also felt Anríq's bulk and Eliska's much smaller frame squashed into the cluster, too.

Eliska fired a flare of light from the end of her staff, but Yann couldn't see anything in this Layer apart from his three friends.

They plunged through, broke what felt like a flimsy sheen of silk, and fell into a completely different Layer.

At least this one had light. The friends could see where they were, but Yann immediately wished he didn't.

The four friends bounced down onto a giant web of springy, stretchy fibers as thick as Yann's leg. The web must have been a mile wide with thousands of fibers all connected into a lattice.

Yann tried to sit up, but some kind of sticky glue stuck his arms and legs to the fibers.

One glance around the area told him all he needed to know. A massive spider as big as a house perched at the center of the web fifty yards away. It turned around and fixed its many eyes on the four friends.

"This is bad," Yann muttered.

Eliska circled her staff around the friends again, released the binding spell, and also did something to unstick the glue holding them down. "Come on! Get up! We gotta get out of here."

"How?" Yann asked. "There is no way out. Just shatter the Layer and send us somewhere else."

"If we fall out of this Layer, we'll fall into another collapse. I know another way we can get through this into a safe Island. Follow me."

She grabbed Anríq by the wrist, pulled him to his feet, and took off balancing down the fibers.

Yann picked up Marine, grabbed her hand, and followed. They had to teeter on the fibers which turned out to be thinner than they seemed. A bottomless void full of swirling chaos vapors dropped away underneath the web.

Yann missed his footing more than once and fell through up to his hips. He had to slow down to stay on top.

The spider tiptoed out onto the web. Every step the travelers took made the web bounce and shudder underfoot.

The spider darted forward, stopped, and then darted forward again. Eliska sidestepped out of line and glanced over her shoulder. "Keep going!"

"Where are we going?" Yann asked.

She pointed across the web. "There's another Island over there! Keep going and you'll run into a brick wall. Anríq can break through the wall with his club. You'll be safe over there. Go!"

She shoved Yann and Marine forward. Anríq kept running along the fibers. He could run the fastest of everyone here. His size didn't slow him down.

Yann pulled Marine along with him. She ran well and didn't slow him down, but she couldn't talk to him here.

He didn't give himself the option to look behind him to see how close the spider was coming.

Just then, Marine stumbled and one of her legs fell through the web. She screamed and then thrashed trying to free herself. Her madness stopped her from thinking clearly about how to correct the situation.

Yann turned back to help her—and his blood ran cold when he saw the spider closing on Eliska.

She stood her ground and bent her knees with her staff raised. The spider darted for her, shot out another fiber to catch her, and she deflected it with another magical blast.

Yann hesitated for a second to watch her. Her magic seemed to have exploded beyond anything he ever remembered her using before.

Each of those blasts ejected a colossal torrent of scorching energy. Everything she did with her magic caused a bigger effect than before.

Marine wriggled and brought his attention back to her. He hauled her back onto the web and steadied her. "Are you okay?" he panted.

She howled and writhed away from him. That was the only answer he was likely to get.

He took her hand and went on more slowly so she didn't fall again, but he couldn't stop himself from looking back at Eliska.

The spider fired dozens of threads from all directions. She parried them at mind-blowing speed. She shot here and there in a whirlwind.

All her blasts combined into a curtain of magic around her. The spider couldn't touch her.

It tried to skirt her to come after the other three friends. She unloaded on the spider and hurled it back toward the center of the web, but she didn't hurt it.

The spider screeched in fury, charged her, and she did the same thing again. She still didn't harm it.

She threw it back again and again. Each time, it bounced off the web, landed on all its jointed legs, and rushed her while it showered her with fibers.

She repelled them all easily, and on the last charge, she hurled the spider all the way back to the other side of the web.

She stayed where she was aiming her staff at the creature, but the spider didn't rush in to attack her the same way.

It jumped back onto its feet and stopped there to study her across the web.

The two adversaries eyed each other in matched hostility, but the spider didn't come back. It tiptoed forward and resumed its place at the center of the web. It never took its eyes off the party even for a second.

Eliska didn't budge for a minute. Anríq's shout got everyone's attention. "I'm there! I'm at the wall! Come on, Eliska! Come now so we can break through!"

She glanced in his direction before she went back to narrowing her eyes at the spider. She backed away, but she didn't let her guard down.

Yann and Marine ran the rest of the way to Anríq's side. He stood in front of a towering brick wall. It extended as high up as Yann could see and plunged all the way out of sight in the chasm below.

Anríq unhooked his club and tapped it on the wall, but not hard enough to damage it.

Eliska inched backward all the way across the web. She didn't turn her back on the spider even once.

"Do it now!" she called over her shoulder when she rejoined the ground. "We'll fall through, so I'll have to bind us again."

Anríq took a step back, raised his club, and all his muscles swelled when he swung it at the wall.

It smashed into the surface with a deafening boom and the wall crumbled from the impact.

Another hurricane force snatched the friends through the breach into a howling chaos Layer slashing and shrieking with Dark vapors and flying debris.

Yann tried to pull Marine closer. He never let go of her hand while they were on the web.

Eliska magicked the friends together in another binding spell, but only for a second before they landed in another completely different landscape.

This one looked remarkably similar to the Island where Yann and Marine had been trying to save Savaré. This Island had all the same kinds of vegetation.

The group landed in another grassy field near a good-sized country town, but Yann saw right away that something was seriously wrong with this place.

People walked back and forth over the whole landscape, but none of them made eye contact with the travelers or each other.

No one spoke. No one conducted any kind of business. Everyone just wandered around in a dazed trance.

Yann sat up and watched them for a second. "What's wrong with them?"

"This could be an Island of the lost," Eliska suggested. "I've seen it before. The instability wipes out the people and leaves them alive. See? Everything else about the town looks normal. Let's go take a look."

"Wait a minute!" Yann exclaimed. "You can't go in there!"

"No one will mind. They won't even see us." She got to her feet and dusted the grass off her clothes. "Are you coming? I'm hungry. They'll have some food we can take."

"Take?!" Yann fired back. "You're just going to steal it?!"

"They won't care. Come on."

She pulled Anríq to his feet again. She didn't do the same thing for Yann.

He was beginning to see a pattern here, but he didn't argue. He helped Marine up. She howled and screeched as much as ever.

Eliska turned out to be right. None of the townsfolk paid the slightest attention to the travelers.

Eliska went into a grocer's shop and helped herself to whatever she wanted. A few different people wandered into the aisles while the group was there.

The locals ambled around, bumped into things, and shuffled off somewhere else without seeing a thing.

Eliska loaded her bag with fruit, bread, cheese, cured meats, and even a few boxes of sweets. Then she got to work stuffing Anríq's bags with food, too.

"Are you sure about this?" Yann murmured and shrank away from another man stumbling up the aisle in his direction.

The man wore work clothes and a carpenter's apron. Not a hint of life flickered in his dead eyes. He looked straight through Yann.

Eliska and Anríq stepped out of the man's way to let him pass.

"It's fine," Eliska repeated. "Who would we pay? There's no one here."

Yann searched the store, but she was right about that, too. No one stood behind the counter on the side wall. Yann didn't even see anyone nearby who might be the shopkeeper.

Anríq didn't stop her from putting food into his bags. If he didn't protest, maybe it was okay after all.

Marine didn't follow the group into town. Yann went outside to see where she was and spotted her sitting huddled on a nearby porch.

Eliska must have decided that she had enough food. She and Anríq left the shop at the same time and the party set off across the countryside.

They ran into the same problem everywhere they went. This Island certainly had a healthy population—at least physically.

No one interacted. No one worked. No one did anything other than just walk around staring blankly in front of them.

The scene was really starting to unsettle Yann. Yann found it impossible not to cringe whenever one of the lost people came near the party.

He walked back to take Marine's hand again. "Stay with us," he told her. "I don't want you to get lost."

A sheep in one of the nearby fields giggled from his right. "You're such a prince, Yann!"

He made a face. "Your future husband would get murderously jealous if he heard you talking like that about a penniless Watchmen."

A cow on the other side of the road burst out in Marine's characteristic musical laughter. The sound made Anríq and Eliska jump.

"Be quiet, Marine!" Eliska whispered.

"What's wrong?" Marine asked. "It isn't like I can wake these people up."

"Can't you do anything for them?" Yann asked. "Isn't there any way to heal them?"

"What's wrong with them isn't wrong with them," Eliska explained. "I mean...what's wrong with them is wrong with the whole Island. There is no way to heal them. The instability is affecting the whole Layer. That's what makes them act like this."

"And you've seen this before?" Yann shuddered "This is awful."

"At least they're still alive," she pointed out. "The landscape could shift and they could come out of it."

"Really?"

She shrugged. "Anything is possible."

"So you haven't seen that? You haven't seen a landscape shift and bring them back to their senses?"

"No, I haven't seen it, but anything is possible in the Coil."

Chapter 52

Eliska took some of the food out of her bag, broke it into pieces, and handed it to Anríq. He took it from her and ate while they walked down the road.

She gave some food to Yann next, but something in the way Eliska and Anríq acted set off his alarm bells. Yann couldn't put his finger on it because they had always acted like this since they first met.

She took some bread and cheese out of her bag, stuffed the cheese inside the bread, and held it out to Marine.

She snatched it and crammed it into her mouth grunting and snarling in animal madness.

Eliska stared at her in horror, but then, Marine's voice spoke up from a fencepost behind them. "Thank you, Eliska! This is delicious."

Eliska gaped at Marine with her mouth open. Marine—or Marine's body, at least, kept stuffing the food into her own mouth way too fast.

She got crumbs in her hair and squashed all the food into her cheeks before she even started chewing.

Then she glared at everyone with those wild haunted eyes. Her gaze darted back and forth across the landscape from under her curtain of filthy hair.

"Has she been like this the whole time you've been together?" Eliska asked.

"No, not at all," Yann replied. "She was really helpful and involved in...."

He broke off. He didn't want to talk about what happened in Savaré.

Anríq got their attention just then. "There's a house up ahead. We should stop there."

The party approached the house in silence. Eliska pushed open the door to a neat little stone cottage.

It sat a dozen yards back from the road with perfectly maintained pastures full of livestock all around the house.

Yann didn't see a single flaw in the fence. A thriving vegetable garden grew near the front door. Whoever owned this house even grew flowers.

Fresh flowers stood in a vase in the center of the table in the house's main room.

"This landscape must have collapsed recently—like maybe in the last day or two," Yann pointed out. "Everything is still too fresh."

"I doubt it," Eliska replied. "It could have collapsed anytime."

"Then why is everything so clean? None of the food has had time to go bad."

She shrugged that away. "It just happens that way. I brought us here because this Island is stable. It's been like this for a while—years, I would say."

Anríq passed her, went over to a bed in the corner of the main room, and started taking off his bags and weapons before he sat down on the bed.

"This is a good place," he remarked. "We should stay here—but not for too long. The instability would start to affect us and we could wind up lost like all the rest of these people."

The friends spread through the house—or at least Yann and Eliska did. Marine hunkered in a corner between two walls and turned her face away so she wouldn't see anyone. She kept muttering to herself over there.

Yann and Eliska searched the house. It had two bedrooms, one on each side of the main room, plus the extra bed in the center. It sure looked like Anríq was claiming that one.

Eliska went to the big stone fireplace. It covered almost an entire wall of the main room.

She took some sticks out of a basket by the hearth, arranged them in the grate, and used her magic to ignite them.

The crackling sound gave the house a cheerful atmosphere compared to the wasteland of lost souls wandering around outside.

"It sure does feel strange to stay somewhere like this after all those fancy machines, Yann pointed out.

Eliska looked up. "Did you stay somewhere with machines?"

"We were in a city. Where were you?"

She bent over the fire to add more sticks to it. "We were in a city, too."

Yann found himself studying her. He'd been too busy earlier to notice how much she'd changed.

She looked the same, but she didn't act the same. It didn't show while she had been working to get the group to safety. Now he couldn't unsee the evidence right in front of his eyes.

She kept zoning out, staring into space, and then shuddering, clamping her eyes shut, and shaking her head like she wanted to get something out of her mind.

Dark circles ringed her eyes—or maybe they were just darker now than they had been the last time he saw her.

Marine's voice spoke up from a shelf of decorative plates above the fireplace mantel. "How long should we stay here?"

"If we're right about the Coil becoming more unstable with every passing day, then this Island will collapse eventually, too," Yann replied.

Eliska didn't look up. She kept her head down and stared into the flames before she clamped her eyes shut again.

Yann sat down at the table and watched her from behind. Had she lost weight in just the few short days since he and Marine got separated from Anríq and Eliska?

She looked bonier in a deathly, skeletal way. Her face looked drawn and pallid. Yann didn't like what he saw in her at all.

He glanced over at Anríq and found Anríq staring back at him. Anríq's direct blue eyes transmitted the message loud and clear. Something was wrong with Eliska. Yann just couldn't figure out what it was.

It started when she and Anríq went to take those children to the orphanage—or maybe it started before that.

Now the sight of her alarmed Yann. Was Eliska dying? She certainly looked like it—so why didn't Anríq heal her of whatever was wrong with her?

Anríq broke eye contact first and turned away to rummage in his bags. He pulled out all the food she gave him to carry at the grocer's shop.

He stacked it all on the table where anyone could help themselves, but Yann didn't feel like eating.

Eliska left the room and came back carrying an armload of firewood even though it wasn't cold nor was night coming.

She stacked it all by the hearth and then sat down at the table across from Yann. The impression of her as a skeleton barely keeping herself alive struck him as even more pronounced, now that he faced her head-on. God, she looked awful!

"So what was this city like?" she asked. "Tell me all your adventures."

"I wouldn't go so far as to say we had adventures, but Marine did find out some important information about why and how the Voyant is causing all this instability."

"Really?" Eliska looked up. "How is he doing it?"

"Do you remember those purple glows we saw in the drawings of the Voyants? It turns out they aren't the Voyants. They were wearing crowns—and the purple things come in pairs just like the Voyants."

"What does that mean?"

"Those purple things are the Shards of Hotha. There are two of them. When a person takes one of the Shards, he becomes King in the White Spire—or Queen if it's a woman. Then a second person takes the second Shard. The records call this second person the affiliate. They act as a kind of companion to the King and the two Shards work together to stabilize the Coil. If one of the partners dies and no one takes the other Shard, the instability starts."

Eliska frowned. "Wow. I never would have thought of that."

"The Voyant is just a single person carrying one of the Shards. We couldn't figure out why he just doesn't give the second Shard to another person. Marine says any random person can take it. Most of the affiliates have been Queens to their respective Kings, but the affiliate can also be a relative, a friend, or even a total stranger. We don't know why the Voyant is allowing all this instability to happen while he goes searching across the countryside for one particular person."

"So the person doesn't have to be a blood relative of the previous King?" Eliska asked.

"No, not at all. Anríq was right about the last King and the Voyant being Barbarians. There's no blood relation between them and the previous line of Kings."

"That's really strange," Eliska remarked.

"So basically someone has to take the second Shard," he finished. "That's the way to stop the instability cycle. It doesn't have anything to do with defeating the Voyant."

"Then why does the Voyant keep attacking? He keeps attacking not just us but everyone else. It looks more like he's trying to kill us than capture us or recruit us like I originally thought."

"I can't explain it," Yann replied. "Marine thinks he's looking for one specific person. Brother Matherus said the same thing and I agree. We just have no way of knowing who it is."

"That makes no sense," she countered. "If he wants someone to take the Second Shard, then it doesn't matter who he gets."

Yann spread both hands. "I don't understand it any better than you do." He turned aside and called over his shoulder. "It's too bad you didn't get to spend more time in the library. You might have been able to track the person down."

Marine's voice came from the basket of firewood this time. "Oh, please! Not more time in the library!"

Yann laughed.

Eliska jumped out of her skin and her eyes flew open.

Yann didn't understand at first why she should act so shocked about Yann and Marine talking to each other like this. It was the same way they'd been talking to each other all along.

He read a different reaction in Eliska's startled eyes—a reaction that didn't have to do with the change in her.

Her eyes darted from Yann to the dishes on the shelf to Marine hunkered down in the corner.

He realized in that moment the startling contrast between the way she looked and the way he was acting.

He actually felt happy to be joking around with Marine. He didn't care that she was out of her mind as long as she could still talk to him.

The cloud hanging over Eliska cooled his enthusiasm, especially when he spotted Anríq watching them again.

Anríq's constant vigilance cast a pall over the room. Anríq's presence radiated protective threat over her. He knew something was wrong and he kept watch for anything that might make the situation worse—even if it came from Yann.

Now Yann was the one who looked away first. He couldn't look at Eliska anymore. The sight of her made his skin crawl.

He got up and pretended to search the house again. Footsteps outside drew his attention to the window overlooking the vegetable garden, but it was just some of the lost people blundering around.

He changed the subject. "What about you two? Where have you been and what have you been doing since we got separated?"

Anríq and Eliska exchanged glances before she shrugged that away. "Like I said, we were in a city. It came under assault from the Dark and we did what we could to save everyone before we got separated from them, too."

"Was it another Darkling attack?"

"No, that was the weird thing about it. Darklings never came. It was mostly just Dark Layers and Dark forces trying to envelop the city."

Yann frowned. "That's strange. It was the same in the city where we were. The Darklings never came."

"I wonder if it means anything," Marine's voice added from a different part of the room.

"Will you stop doing that?!" Eliska gasped. "Just speak normally."

"I am speaking normally," Marine replied.

Yann laughed again, but he stopped himself when he saw Eliska's reaction. She didn't appreciate Marine's sense of humor at all, which was strange considering how close they were before this happened.

"Can't you make your voice come from over there?" Eliska pointed at Marine's body.

"I have an idea." Yann got to his feet, carried his glaive into the corner, and stood it against the wall next to Marine. She snarled and snapped her teeth at him before she turned away. "Use that as a familiar. Then everyone will be happy."

"Great idea!" the glaive squealed. "I should have thought of that."

"Stick with me and you might learn a few things," Yann replied.

Now she was the one who laughed and Eliska reacted the same way. She jumped and her eyes flew wide open again. What in the world was wrong with her? Why did she keep jumping and staring every time someone laughed?

His attention must have made her uncomfortable because, in a few minutes, she left the table and went back to staring into the fire.

As soon as she did that, she went through the same cycle of zoning out, jumping, shuddering, shutting her eyes, and trying to shake whatever it was out of her head.

She sat with her back to Yann, but he couldn't stop watching her in horror. He didn't want to think about what might be wrong with her. He would just have to ask Anríq, but Yann couldn't do that in front of her.

Something definitely happened to her—something other than trying to save a city from the Dark.

Anríq looked fine—at least physically. He acted concerned about Eliska's condition, but other than that, Yann couldn't tell anything different about him. Anríq certainly seemed healthy enough.

Chapter 53

E liska jolted out of a sound sleep. It took her a long time to realize that she even was awake. The nightmares kept parading in front of her eyes the same way they always did.

The same endless onslaught of death, violence, and bloodshed played out in rapid succession. One nightmare blended in with another.

She jolted from Arsenault's basement to the village sacked by Corsairs to another city torn apart by Darklings and back to the house with the violent father beating everyone just for looking at him the wrong way.

She flickered between unborn babies living in terror of being born to their mothers poisoning their neighbors' food to wealthy misers swindling penniless widows and leaving them to starve.

The nightmares all blended into each other until the moment when they stopped on one particular scene. It was a memory of the children's journey to the orphanage in the Lake Country.

This memory came from Thaddi. It happened before Eliska met up with the ground when four adults led the party and used their magic to try to protect the children.

The party had started off with two women and two men. The other woman was named Lisana and the man was Harol.

Both had been powerful magic-users who didn't share Aline's hostility to teaching the children magic—or letting them enjoy themselves in any other way.

The children had been camping in another mountainous Island when Harol caught a juvenile rock hyrax. He used his magic to tame it and gave it to Thaddi as a pet.

Thaddi carried the creature for over a week. Thaddi protected the animal from countless landscape collapses and Darkling attacks by hiding the hyrax in his shirt.

Thaddi spent evenings around the campfire feeding the hyrax tidbits of his own food. Harol found this amusing and teased Thaddi about it.

The other children became enamored with the hyrax, too. They used to gather around the little creature every evening. Thaddi got to be the one to decide which of the children could pet the hyrax in which order.

Then came the inevitable day when the Island collapsed and Darklings rampaged across the countryside. Harol lost his life defending the rest of the party.

Aline waited just long enough for her, Lisana, and Athanes to get the children to safety in another Island.

Then she used her magic to rip the hyrax out of Thaddi's shirt, pinned the creature to the ground under her hand, and fired a magical pulse to kill the hyrax in front of all the children.

Eliska's collective memory from all of them gave her a front-seat window into the full depth of Thaddi's grief, but he couldn't show it in front of Aline.

He let a few tears trickle down his cheeks, but that was all. He didn't want to give her the satisfaction of letting her see how much she hurt him.

Overwhelming grief crushed Eliska's insides. She struggled to hold back tears and fought to sit up in bed, but the anguish overcame her best efforts to hold it back.

Thaddi never had anything. He'd been orphaned as a baby and left in the care of strangers for the rest of his life.

The hyrax was the first thing he ever really loved—and he loved Harol for giving it to him. Thaddi cherished the hyrax as his one enjoyment in his empty life. Now even that was gone.

Eliska also got a ringside view into the surge of sadistic power Aline felt when she killed that wretched creature. She simmered with resentment every day Thaddi carried it around, but Aline didn't dare to act as long as Harol was alive.

Then, just when Eliska tricked herself into thinking the memories couldn't possibly get any worse, the memory switched to Vidal.

Eliska tried to sit up on the edge of the bed, failed, and retched on the floor when she saw the things his parents made him do in their rituals. She might even have screamed when she saw how bad it was.

She got so consumed with the memory that she couldn't be sure if she even made a sound. She might just have choked on the tears pouring out of her chest.

Grief, shame, horror, and rage tore her apart. She couldn't hold back the tears anymore. She broke down completely when she felt all the torment he'd been carrying around all these years.

She buried her face in her hands, but that only brought up more and more images from his past. Poor Vidal. He tried so hard to stop her from seeing. He would have been heartbroken if he lived long enough to find out what Eliska had really become.

Now she couldn't stop herself from seeing it all. He carried as much Darkness as she did if not more.

Yann lay asleep in the next room. Eliska fought herself under control just enough to keep silent, but she wound up sobbing anyway.

She could never tell Yann what really happened to Vidal—or how he died—not ever. She would carry that secret to her grave.

She heard movement out in the main room. She tried to stop crying in time, but she didn't manage it before Anríq stepped into her room. He wasn't wearing his vest.

He sat down on the edge of her bed, leaned close enough to see her in the dark, and raked his fingers through her hair to pull it off her damp cheeks.

"Did you have nightmares again?" he whispered. "It's all right. I'm here. You're safe. You're in the land of the lost with me and Yann and Marine."

His kindness gave her permission to fall apart all over again. His soft voice and strong fingers always made her feel safe, but he could never take the nightmares away.

She couldn't tell him about Vidal, either—not the full truth. Anríq already knew too much.

He put his arm around her shoulders and pulled her against him. Her head fell on his shoulder and she let the sobs crack her soul in half.

No one else would grieve for Vidal or Thaddi or even Harol. He at least tried to give the children some nice experiences even if he couldn't do much.

She was still crying hard when she heard movement in a different part of the house. It didn't come from the main room where Marine lay curled up on the floor in front of the fire. The sound came from the other bedroom.

She sat up and Anríq took his arm away immediately, but she didn't get her sobs under control before Yann appeared in the doorway. "What's going on?" he whispered. "What's wrong?"

"Eliska had some nightmares," Anríq replied, "but she's okay now."

Yann frowned at Eliska in the shadows. He could see plain as day that she wasn't okay now nor would she ever be.

She couldn't fail to notice him studying her earlier this evening. He must have seen how much she changed since he last saw her.

She didn't want him to see, but she couldn't exactly hide it, could she? She carried it stamped into every cell and bone in her body.

Yann took a few steps closer. He could see her clearly now. He could see her crying her eyes out over a bunch of people who were already dead.

His scrutiny tore down her defenses the rest of the way. Her face screwed up in misery. She couldn't stand the way he was looking at her with a mixture of horror and devastation that some mysterious disaster had brought her so low.

Anríq got to his feet right away. "I'll clean this up," he murmured and left the room. He had to walk around Yann to get through the door.

A minute later, Anríq opened the house door, came back with a bucket of water, and started cleaning up the puddle of puke by the bed.

Yann glared down at him and Eliska. No one moved or spoke for a second before Anríq threw the dirty rag back in the bucket and went outside.

Eliska kept her head down so she wouldn't see Yann standing there. She really wished he would leave, but instead, he sat down on the bed in Anríq's place.

Yann went through the same routine of combing his fingers through her hair to keep it out of her face.

"I know I won't be able to do much," he half-whispered in her ear. "In fact, I probably won't be able to do anything, but if I can, I will. I would do anything I could to help you. You know that, right?"

The strain in his voice pushed her over the edge all over again. Of course he would care enough to do something if anyone could.

Yann cared as much as Anríq did. She didn't question that, but she could never tell Yann what really happened—not all of it.

Oh, what was she even thinking that? She would never tell him any of it. She had to protect him from it the same way she had to protect everyone else.

He put his arm around her shoulders and kissed the side of her head. She had forgotten how good he felt—how good it felt to know he was there and that he cared.

She didn't forget. She stopped herself from thinking about it because she didn't know if she would ever see him again.

Him sitting next to her like this and showing her as much care and tenderness as Anríq—she couldn't stand it. He wouldn't if he knew how truly poisonous she was.

He would, though. That was the thing. He would probably give it even more.

He would guard her and protect her and take care of her—and he would do absolutely anything to make it better. She never doubted that for a second.

She couldn't even speak to him. She would never be able to find the words to tell him anything—not even one word. That was the worst part. She just had to sit here and live with it.

The memories just kept on coming. They switched every few seconds, streamed into each other in a rapid blur of pictures and hallucinations, and stopped on other memories of other people.

She relived their worst experiences along with the torrential cascade of emotion that made the images all the more torturous and soul-crushing.

He sat next to her for a long time with his arm around her shoulders while she poured out all that grief and pain through her tears.

He didn't go away. He didn't try to distance himself from it.

After what might have been hours, he stood up and pushed her down on the bed. "Lie down," he whispered.

He tucked the blankets around her and stroked her hair a few times before he kissed her on the temple.

"I'm going to see what Anríq is doing and then I'll come back to check on you," he murmured. "Try to get some rest. I'll be right in the next room."

Chapter 54

Y ann slipped out of Eliska's room and headed for the house door leading out into the yard. His fury erupted the minute he got away from her.

He found Anríq at the water pump in the backyard. "What the hell happened?!" Yann demanded in a rushed whisper. "What the hell is going on with Eliska—and don't you dare stand there and tell me there's nothing wrong with her! She looks half dead and she keeps jumping at the slightest sound."

Anríq straightened up and leveled Yann with a brutal stare. It wasn't Anríq's usual understanding gaze.

"Well?" Yann snapped. "What happened? I know she wasn't in the best shape when she left, but Jesus! I would have thought you would try to protect her—and now look at her!"

"I did everything I could to protect her, Yann," Anríq breathed. "There are some sicknesses I can't heal."

Yann's jaw dropped. "So she's sick?! She's sick with something incurable?"

"No, nothing like that."

"What is going on with her, then? Tell me the truth."

Anríq compressed his lips, flared his nostrils, and scowled. "I know you're asking because you care about Eliska, Yann, but I can't tell you."

He started to turn away. Yann's last shred of composure snapped. He lunged for Anríq, grabbed his arm, and yanked him back. "Don't you dare walk away from me! Tell me what happened to her!"

Anríq kept his voice low. Both of them did. He tried to keep his voice calm and steady, too, but a distinct note of hopeless desperation crept into his tone no matter how hard he tried to hide it.

"I would tell you if I could, Yann," Anríq murmured. "I really wish I could, but Eliska would probably kill me if I did. I don't mean she would just get really angry. I mean she would probably really turn her magic on me and kill me. She's much more powerful than I am. I wouldn't be able to defend myself. If you care about her as much as I know you do, you'll help me try to take care of her. That's the best either of us can do right now. Maybe she'll tell you herself one day. I don't know. That's up to her. I would be violating her trust if I told you in her place. I'm sorry if that hurts you. I love you like a brother, but telling you would hurt her more and I just can't do that. She's hurt enough already as it is."

Yann gaped at him in stunned horror. This was so much worse than he suspected—even though he'd already begun to suspect the worst.

He had to swallow the lump in his throat before he could make himself heard. "So....is she dying?"

"No, nothing like that."

The answer didn't satisfy Yann at all. He had to look away. "It would almost be better if she was. I can't stand seeing her like this."

"Don't say that," Anríq replied. "As long as she's alive, there's always a chance we might meet a magic-user strong enough to heal her."

"What magic-user would be strong enough to do that?" Yann fired back. "You better not be talking about the Voyant."

"I don't know of any magic-user strong enough to heal her, but there must be someone somewhere. As I said, there's always hope as long as she's alive. That's what I hold onto at least. I wish I could tell you something else."

Yann passed his hand across his eyes. This was beyond anything he let himself imagine.

What could possibly be bad enough to make Eliska turn against Anríq?

She didn't turn against him because he didn't violate her trust. He wouldn't do that. Now Yann understood why.

Yann looked up to find Anríq studying him with a different expression on his face. It was Anríq's pained, understanding expression—the one he got when he wanted to help someone and couldn't.

Of course Anríq couldn't violate Eliska's trust by telling Yann what happened. Yann would have been furious if Anríq did something like that to him.

Yann nodded. "Okay, man. I understand. I'm sorry I asked."

"You don't have to be sorry, Yann. I know you care about Eliska as much as I do. I know you only asked because you want to help her."

"Of course I do!" Yann snapped. "How the hell can I watch her suffer like this and not do anything?"

"Unfortunately, there's nothing any of us can do for her. I wish there was."

"So she just has to live with it—possibly forever?"

"I'm afraid so. This will be much harder for her than it will be for us. I have to remind myself of that every day when I start to pity myself for watching her suffer. She....."

Anríq broke off and looked away.

Yann saw the wheels turning in his friend's head. Anríq had been about to tell Yann something—something Eliska probably didn't want Yann to know.

"Okay, man," Yann murmured. "I understand. I won't ask again."

"No one is sorrier than I am that this happened," Anríq went on. "I would have done anything to stop it."

Yann opened his mouth to ask again what exactly did happen, but he stopped himself in time. That was the mystery.

He really didn't know if he could stand to watch her struggle like this, but he essentially had no choice—not if he really cared about her.

Anríq finished wringing out his rag. He tipped the last drips of water out of his bucket and stood there holding it under one arm. He stood there waiting for Yann before they both went back inside.

Yann turned away first and Anríq followed him back into the house. Anríq puttered around the main room putting the bucket away and hanging up the rag to dry by the fire.

Yann went into Eliska's room. She lay there with her eyes closed, but he saw right away that she was still awake.

He rubbed her shoulder, bent over, and kissed her on the head. "Do you think you'll be able to sleep now?"

She nodded without opening her eyes. "Thank you both. I'll see you in the morning."

He left the room, but he left the door open. Anríq sat down on the bed across the main room. He would be able to hear if Eliska woke up in distress again.

Yann returned to his own room and left his bedroom door open, too. He sat down on the bed and looked out through the door at Anríq sitting on the edge of his mattress. Anríq didn't lie down right away.

He sat up in silence for a long time. Yann couldn't have closed his eyes for anything.

He strained his ears for any disturbance coming from Eliska's room, but she didn't make a sound.

He wasn't sure if he wanted her to fall asleep or not. She needed rest. She needed rest really bad, but she would probably have nightmares again if she did fall asleep.

He racked his brain for a way to help her, but he was just an imp. If Anríq couldn't help her, no one could.

Anríq was right about one thing, though. There had to be a magic-user somewhere in the Coil with the power to heal her.

Was that the Voyant?

Yann's fury exploded off the charts. The Voyant killed Yann's father. Yann would destroy the Voyant the very first chance he got—but what if the Voyant could heal Eliska?

Which would Yann choose—revenge or the chance to heal her? Revenge wouldn't bring his father back.

Yann eventually stretched out on the bed and stared up at the ceiling for a long time. Anríq didn't lie down. Did he plan to stay up keeping watch all night?

Yann should have done the same thing, but he eventually fell asleep still puzzling over the whole thing.

Chapter 55

Eliska woke up early the next morning. Everyone else was still asleep.

She went outside and ran her head under the water pump. The freezing water made her feel better after last night's ordeal.

She wrung the water out of her hair and explored the farmyard. She found a henhouse with a bunch of eggs in the nests. She carried them back to the house just as Anríq started to stir.

He rolled onto his side and pried his eyes open to squint at her. "You should be asleep."

"So should you. Stay there. I'll make breakfast."

"Since when did you become so domestic?"

She laughed at him, lifted down the heavy cast-iron frying pan from the wall, built up the fire, and rested the pan in the coals.

She sliced some of the cured meat from yesterday into the pan and started cutting up the leftover fruit and cheese. "We should go back into town and get some more supplies."

"Maybe we should have a conversation first about how long we plan to stay here." He sat up and started getting dressed. "I already know what Marine is going to say."

"You mean going after the Shard of Hotha? Maybe we should get some more information before we do that—like maybe find out where the hell the Shard even is."

He shot her a grin. "Details."

She smiled back at him. She felt better, now that she actually did something. Sitting in one place made her think too much.

She fried the meat and then fried the eggs in the fat. Yann came out of his room while she was setting the table.

Both boys went outside and came back with their hair wet.

"Don't you think you should take a bath?" Yann asked Marine. "Anríq could hold you down and I could scrub out your hair under the pump."

Marine's laughter came from somewhere near the ceiling. "You wouldn't dare to manhandle a lady like that! I'll tell my father!"

"Lady—you?" Yann snorted. "Have you seen yourself lately?"

She only laughed. Eliska found herself shaking her head over their interaction. He could tease Marine and make her laugh in ways no one else could.

Eliska studied him across the table while they ate. Something happened to him in the last few days, too. Watch

He grew in confidence when he took over as Commander in Tenby.

Now that confidence shot off the charts. Yann wasn't a boy anymore. He was enough of a man to stand up to Anríq and tell everyone else what to do.

"So what's the plan?" Yann asked while they ate. "Are we going hunting for the Voyant and the Shard of Hotha or are we going to lie low and wait for him to come looking for us?"

"We don't know where the Shard is, but we do know where the Voyant is," Eliska pointed out. "He's in the White Spire. Too bad none of us can get inside it."

"I can get inside it," Yann blurted out.

Her head shot up fast. "You what?"

"Marine and I tried it while were alone together. We were walking through an Island and we came to a city with the White Spire in it."

She gulped down the food in her mouth. "You did?"

He nodded. "There was a Dark river in front of it and a bunch of huge wolves guarding the place. One of Marine's familiars suggested that I try to get inside the spire because the Voyant's magical defenses wouldn't work on me."

"And....did that work?"

He nodded again. "She and her familiars used their magic to defend me. I swam across the river and then all the familiars attacked the Wolves so I could get through."

She gawked at him with her jaw on the floor. "What did you do?"

"I climbed the spire walls and looked into the Voyant's little room at the top."

Her mouth opened and closed a few times, but no sound came out.

"Anyway, I saw him manipulating the Coil and making certain Layers collapse. Then some of the other defenses overcame Marine's familiars. She stepped in to help me out and draw them away, but she also wound up driving the Voyant out. They got into a fight....."

Eliska gasped and her hand flew to her mouth.

"I saw the Voyant attacking her and I had to do something, so I dove on top of them and slammed into the ground. The Layer collapsed and we fell through into a different Island."

Eliska gulped down her mouthful and shook her head over her plate. "That's amazing."

"Why don't all three of you try it together?" he suggested. "You and Marine might not have been able to do it alone, but Anríq could help you—and your magic is so much stronger now."

Her head shot up and a shiver went up her scalp at those words. "What?"

"Your magic," he repeated. "Your Coil projection is way bigger and more detailed—and all your magic seems to be enhanced. I don't know what happened to you, but it definitely made you more powerful—like you needed it or something."

He tried to smile at her. She cast her eyes down at her plate. She didn't want him to know about the Dark making her magic more powerful, but he couldn't exactly miss it, could he?

She pushed her food back and forth across her plate. She wanted to puke again.

"You should eat something," he told her. "You're skin and bones."

She didn't look up. So he knew. Of course he did. He put his arm around her last night. He must have felt how fragile she was—like he couldn't see it with his own eyes.

She felt his eyes drilling into her from right across the table. Anríq didn't come to her rescue—probably because he was thinking exactly the same thing.

They would work together now. They would work together to take care of her.

Why did she think it would be any different? They were friends and they both cared about her. They wouldn't let her get away with anything.

Yann didn't say anything else until she put a forkload of eggs into her mouth and started chewing. Then he filled a bowl with food and took it over to Marine. "Don't tell your prince about this, either," he told her.

She laughed. "The list is going to be really long by the time I finally marry him."

"Who are you talking about?" Eliska asked. "What prince?"

"It's just a joke between us." Yann sat down and started eating again. "So what do you say to you three trying to break into the White Spire?"

"You would have to come with us, Yann," Anríq interjected. "The three of us could fight the defenses while you make a break for the spire the way you did before."

"But you would have to actually get inside this time," Marine added. "You would need to get inside and look around for the Shard."

"How would I do that if the Voyant is there?" Yann asked. "He would kill me—or capture me."

"If he's already trying to capture you, he's trying to capture you to give you the Shard," Marine pointed out. "That's what we want—for someone to take the second Shard."

"I don't like the sound of this. I don't want to go into the spire alone if he's going to be there."

"Then maybe we can draw him out," Anríq suggested. "Maybe all three of us fighting the defenses will be enough to engage him while you make a play for the Shard."

Yann squirmed in his seat. "I don't want to take the Shard—especially if the other counterpart is the Voyant."

"Wait a minute," Marine interjected. "The records stated that the King in the White Spire took the Shard of Hotha from the Sacred Shrine to enter the Hall of Light. That's how he becomes King. We don't know where the Sacred Shrine is."

"It might be in the White Spire," Eliska suggested.

"But we don't know for sure that it is," Yann pointed out. "We should probably find out before we go running off to confront the Voyant."

"So how do we find the Sacred Shrine?" Marine asked.

"Maybe you should have stayed in the library a little longer," Yann replied over his shoulder.

Eliska turned to Marine and realized a second too late that she was about to consult a crazy person to get some useful information.

Eliska went through a flurry of confusion about who to address her next question to.

"Um.... You know how you got that book out of the library in the cloud tower—the book with the original genealogies of the Kings?"

"Yeah?" Marine replied from the opposite side of the room. "What about it?"

"Could you do that again?"

"I would have to be in the library to do it," Marine replied. "We don't even know where the library is from here."

Eliska glanced around at nothing. "Could you come here....please? I might be able to find it if you help me."

Eliska didn't expect much, but as soon as she asked the question, Marine scuttled across the floor in a crouch. She scampered under the table where the other three friends couldn't see her.

Marine extended one hand above the tabletop and held it there. Eliska couldn't really ask for more than that. At least Marine was helping her.

Eliska created her Coil projection. She hadn't noticed how different it looked before she and Anríq got separated from Yann and Marine.

Now Eliska saw the projection through their eyes. It revolved on its own and details of landscapes, people, and lines of direction streaked through the image.

She concentrated on the task in front of her, placed her hand over Marine's hand, and directed Marine to move her hand underneath Eliska's. "Now," Eliska instructed. "Do it now."

Marine sent a flow of energy into Eliska's hand.

"Try to find the information we need," Eliska told her. "Search the Coil the way you searched that library."

Nothing happened for a second. Then the image pivoted and turned to its other side.

The picture expanded by itself to show another city—a big city teeming with people, vehicles, and machines even more sophisticated than anything the friends had seen so far.

Eliska gasped. "Is this even real? I've never seen anything like this in the Coil before."

"Where's the information?" Yann asked. "It might be one of the computers."

Eliska looked up. "You mean...you used computers?"

"Marine did it. I just watched. See if you can locate where in the city the information is. If it's on the computers, it might not show up as a single location."

Eliska expanded the image and blew up a view of the whole Layer. The city in question occupied a northern position in a beautiful land of sunshine, commerce, and prosperity.

All the people looked rich. They would have to be to fly all those airborne vehicles around.

A silvery line appeared on the image and she zeroed in on it. "It's here—in the Hall of Magical Learning."

"Are they Guardian Templars?" Yann asked.

"No, they belong to a different order. These people aren't magic-users. They're just librarians."

"So the information must be in a book," Yann pointed out. "Can you find out which one it is?"

Eliska looked away. "That would be a terrible idea."

He frowned. "Why?"

"I'll do it," Anríq interjected and stuck his hand between Eliska's and Marine's

Eliska didn't dare to look up at Yann studying her. Hiding the truth from him was going to become an increasingly thorny problem.

Anríq sent a flow of magic into the Coil projection and his magic joined up with Marine's. Eliska didn't have to do anything more than keep the projection open.

They expanded the image even further and the picture zoomed between mountainous stacks of books even bigger than the ones in the cloud tower.

"There it is." Anríq pointed to the book in question. "That will tell us where the Sacred Shrine and the Hall of Light are if it doesn't tell us where we can find the Shard itself. The book is in Section 85F, Shelf 1673."

Yann pushed back his chair. "Let's go."

Chapter 56

The friends put the little house in order. Eliska stood outside on the lawn, gazed back at the house with genuine affection, and sighed. "It sure is a nice Island. I wish we could stay here."

"After the war is over, you can get yourself a house just like this," Yann teased. "You can wear a long dress and a white apron and yell at your kids."

She snorted. "Dream on, pal."

He grinned at her. "We can all dream."

"So what are *you* going to do after the war?" she asked.

He made a command decision not to look in Marine's direction. "I don't know. I guess I'll see if I'm still alive when that happens." He turned away. "We have a long way to walk."

"We don't have to walk," she told him. "We can go to that Island and then I can magick us closer to the city. It will cut the journey in half at least."

Yann raised his eyebrows. "You could do that?"

She nodded and pretended to brush the hair out of her eyes. "It beats walking the whole way."

The others gathered around her. She created another binding spell to hold them together. Then she used her staff to drill through the lawn and sent the party falling through a dozen different Layers.

She and Anríq fought Darklings, but for some reason, the travelers didn't encounter nearly so many even in the Dark Layers.

The group fell toward a gigantic black ocean heaving below them, but Eliska fired her staff into it and it shattered like any other Layer.

The group splashed through the surface into the Island they were aiming for.

They landed hard in the back of a fast-moving freight transport vehicle whizzing along the road at high speed. The friends scrambled to sit up.

The vehicle's high-walled sides blocked anyone from seeing the four travelers. Wind whistled through the container's top.

Rolling countryside streamed under the vehicle falling behind as the landscape. Eliska created her Coil projection and located the party.

"We're less than ten miles from the city!" she yelled over the engine noise. "I say we jump out and approach the city on foot."

"Why bother?" Yann called back. "This vehicle will take us straight inside."

"It might take us to the other side of the city! Then we would have to hike all the way across it to find the Hall of Magical Learning."

Yann shrugged. "You're in charge here—not me."

She burst into a grin. "Since when?"

"Since day one. When do we jump out?"

She didn't explain anything. She wrapped all four of them in another binding spell, and in the blink of an eye, she transported all of them out of the vehicle onto the roadside.

"Tell me before you do something like that!" Yann gasped.

"I was just trying to make it easier for you. I didn't think you wanted to jump and maybe break a few bones in the process."

He looked away. Marine broke free from the binding spell and scampered onto the grass to put some distance between herself and the others.

Now Yann, Anríq, and Eliska could see the enormous city towering in front of them.

"It doesn't look quite so spectacular in person, does it?" Yann murmured.

"It looks kind of....dirty," Eliska whispered back. "It doesn't look anything like the other cities we've seen."

Yann didn't ask about the other cities she'd seen. "I guess we have to go in to find this book."

The party set off across the countryside. Marine hung back growling and muttering to herself. Yann had to stop himself from talking to her on the way.

The traffic increased the closer the friends got to the outskirts. The travelers passed between scattered houses and farms before the city wall came into view up ahead.

This wall stood fifty feet high—much bigger and more imposing than anything Yann had ever seen. This wall made Savaré look like a flower bed.

Men of the Black Watch patrolled the wall.

"They sure have a lot of Watchmen," Eliska murmured. Then she cracked a grin at Yann. "You won't be able to throw your weight around here."

"I won't throw my weight around because I don't plan to join the Watch—not here. We're here to find a book. Let's get this over with. As soon as we get inside, you can direct us to the Hall of Magical Learning."

"That should be interesting. I've always wanted to see a place like that."

Yann didn't answer. Maybe someone at the Hall of Magical Learning would know enough to help her.

Then he remembered. The people at the Hall of Magical Learning weren't magic-users. They were just librarians.

The group filed up the last street heading for the city gates. Crowds of people and long lines of different-sized vehicles clustered around the gate all waiting to get inside.

The friends joined the dozens of people waiting their turns to approach the gate.

The gate consisted of some kind of heavy metal plate. Each person consulted a pair of Watchmen standing on duty outside the gate. One of the Watchmen talked to people on foot. The other Watchmen talked to the vehicle drivers through their windows.

The Watchmen asked each person their business and either waved them forward, turned them back, or processed the person's request some other way.

Yann didn't see how these Watchmen were deciding who to let through and who to turn away.

When they left someone through, the person or vehicle approached the gate, but it didn't open for them.

The metal plate turned into a watery pool of magic. The person or vehicle passed through it and vanished behind the plate metal surface. No one could see anything going on behind it.

The four friends took hours to inch forward to the front of the line. The process took an eternity.

Vendors went up and down the line trying to sell food and trinkets to those waiting to enter. Yann was just starting to wish he had some money to buy something to eat when the four friends made it to the front of the line.

Three people separated the travelers from the gate itself. Yann was the only person wearing a Black Watch uniform not standing a post on the wall.

The Watchmen spotted him long before he got there. He also caught them checking out Anríq, but the Watchmen didn't show any sign that they knew who or what he was.

The person in front of the four friends was a little old lady carrying a chicken under one arm. She pulled up in front of the Watchmen.

She informed the Watchman on duty that she was here to visit her daughter who had just given birth. The old woman didn't explain what the chicken was for and the Watchman didn't ask.

He waved her past. Now nothing stood between the four friends and the Watchmen who would decide if they could enter or not.

Yann opened his mouth to explain the group's business, but at that moment, a squad of twenty Watchmen marched out of some hidden alcove in the wall.

They came out of somewhere near the gate. Maybe the magic hid the alcove, too.

The Watchmen formed into ranks pointing spears at the four friends. "Stay back, Darklings!" the lieutenant in charge bellowed.

Yann glanced around. He didn't see any Darklings.

"Be gone, Darklings!" the man went on. "Take a step closer and we'll kill you right here."

Yann, Eliska, and Anríq looked behind them. The enormous line snaked out of sight around bends in the road back there. Yann still didn't see any Darklings.

He and his friends looked at each other, shrugged, and shook their heads.

"Take your Darklings and leave," the Watchman on duty snapped. Then he waved behind Anríq. "Next!"

"Wait a minute!" Yann blurted out. "We have to go inside. We're here to consult with the Hall of Magical Learning. It's important."

The Watchmen leveled him with a critical eye. "You're a member of the Watch and your friend here is a Servant. You two are welcome to enter. These Darklings will have to leave. We don't allow their kind here."

He waved to one side. It took Yann at least another minute to realize that the guy was waving at Eliska and Marine.

"They aren't Darklings," Yann explained. "They're our friends."

"Then you can leave with them," the Watchman snapped. "You two can enter, but not with them."

The three friends studied each other again. Yann didn't ask why these Watchmen thought Eliska and Marine were Darklings.

Then again, the people of Savaré assumed Marine was a Darkling.

Maybe these Watchmen had a way of reading when someone got too close to the Dark. The Templars of Savaré did the same thing. They scried a Dark presence in Yann's apartment after Marine communed with the Dark.

He didn't understand why these people thought the same thing about Eliska. Maybe they detected Barsali's Darkness inside her. Hell, maybe she became Darker since she and Anríq got separated from Yann and Marine.

Yann wouldn't have been surprised if that was the reason. It would explain a lot about her behavior, the nightmares—all of it.

He pushed that thought out of his mind and drew his three friends to one side. "What do you want to do?"

"You two should go ahead and find the book," Eliska told him. "I'll take Marine out of town and wait for you there. I'll be able to find you."

"I don't like splitting up," Yann muttered. "Not after we just found each other."

"Finding this information is more important. Once you find out what's in the book, we'll compare notes. Then we'll be able to decide how to go after the Shard."

Yann didn't want to separate from either of the girls. He got a very bad feeling about this.

Chapter 57

Eliska backed away and Marine went with her. Yann and Anríq headed for the gate.

In a second, the two boys passed through the magical pool and entered the city itself. Yann couldn't see beyond the pool to the outside anymore.

He sighed and faced front. "Let's get this over with. I don't like them staying behind."

"Neither do I," Anríq snarled. "There's something wrong with this place."

Yann's head shot up. "You feel it, too?"

Anríq glared all around him and clenched his teeth "This is much worse than that cursed town we saved from Simion Mihaili."

Yann didn't answer. He didn't get the same creepy feeling from this bustling metropolis, but it didn't shine with the same idyllic glow as he remembered from Tenby.

Tenby might have been living under constant threat of annihilation from the outside, but at least it didn't rot from Darkness on the inside. No one in Tenby came across as Dark—because they weren't.

He couldn't quite pinpoint what was wrong with this place. Everyone in it went about their business. The machines, vehicles, and giant buildings didn't look wrong or out of place.

Eliska and Anríq were right, though. Something about the place felt dirty—and it had nothing to do with the city's appearance.

Yann and Anríq advanced through the streets heading for the Hall of Magical Learning. A few people approached Anríq and asked him to heal their sick relatives.

He stopped for a few minutes at each place, but he didn't stay. He healed each person one after the other, bowed to the patients' families, and left.

The feeling of oppressive rot and Darkness became more pronounced the deeper inside the city the boys traveled.

Yann paused across the street from the Hall of Magical Learning.

"It all comes from here," Anríq muttered. "This is the source of it."

"Do you still want to go inside?" Yann asked. "Did we really come all this way to pull the plug now?"

"No, we'll go in," Anríq decided. "We have to find out what's in that book."

Yann didn't want to go into the heart of such a powerful Dark force for any reason—not even to find information on the Sacred Shrine.

Anríq started forward, so Yann had to go with him.

The two boys climbed the steps and Anríq pushed open the entrance doors.

The boys stepped into one colossal chamber. The Hall of Magical Leaning didn't have any interior walls.

The stacks stood in massive shelves from floor to ceiling hundreds of feet high. People worked all over ladders and walkways everywhere Yann looked.

"Someone would have to be one hell of a librarian to work here," he murmured.

"You'll have to read the book for both of us," Anríq replied out the side of his mouth.

"I will. The question is how we find the book."

Yann got his answer the next minute when an old man in a floor-length grey cassock approached the two boys. The old man bore a striking resemblance to Brother Arsenault—only much older.

He smiled at Yann and then at Anríq. "Can I help you young men?"

"We're looking for a book," Yann replied. "Obviously."

The old man only smiled at him. "I'm happy to help any man of the Watch...and any Servant. My name is Earstine Mariad. If you tell me which book you want, I can get it for you."

"We don't actually know the name of the book, but it has to do with the Shard of Hotha, the White Spire, and the Sacred Shrine where the King takes the Shard."

"Ah, yes!" Earstine Mariad smiled more broadly. "I seem to remember...."

"The book we're looking for is in Section 85F, Shelf 1673."

Earstine Mariad only smiled. "Of course. I know exactly the book you mean. Wait here while I get it for you."

The old man turned away. Yann planned to wait until the old man passed out of earshot before Yann remarked to Anríq that this could take a while.

Earstine Mariad might have to hike all the way to the other side of the library and climb a million ladders before he found the right book.

Yann relaxed and looked around for somewhere to sit while he and Anríq waited.

Earstine Mariad turned his back on the boys, and just as fast, he spun around and erupted into a massive Darkling.

The library vanished in a blink and the Darkling lunged for the two boys.

Yann and Anríq both dove out of the way in time to avoid the creature's giant snapping fangs.

Yann stabbed out with his glaive, but he didn't have time to aim well enough to do any damage. He launched himself to his feet and took a flying leap to drive the glaive farther in.

The Darkling swatted him aside before he got anywhere near it. He tumbled a dozen yards away. He suddenly couldn't see any other people in the library apart from Anríq.

Anríq somersaulted the other way and rolled onto his feet grabbing his axe off his back.

Yann didn't have time to stand up. The Darkling plunged for Anríq first.

Yann dove for the creature and stabbed his glaive into the Darkling's neck, but the magic shimmering on the monster's tough hide deflected the weapon.

Yann had to come up with something else before this demon killed both him and Anríq.

Anríq swiped his axe and a deafening boom resounded through the hall when the weapon connected with the Darkling's head.

Yann couldn't wait any longer. He lunged for the Darkling's head to stab his glaive through the skull, but before he got there, the Darkling lashed its tentacle at him and swatted him across the floor.

He skidded backward and smashed into one of the bookshelves. The Hall of Magical Learning sounded awfully hollow with no other people around.

Anríq dove in on the other side and delivered another almighty chop for the Darkling's head, but the Darkling anticipated that, too.

A different tentacle snatched Anríq off the floor, raised him high above its head, and slammed him down full force.

Seeing Anríq in danger rocketed Yann to his feet. He charged the Darkling for the third time and slashed tentacles away when they tried to strike him.

He made it as far as the creature's head, but he couldn't get near enough to the eye to do any damage. He needed another strategy.

The Darkling must have realized that Anríq posed a much bigger threat to it than this puny imp with a toothpick for a weapon.

The Darkling turned on Anríq and delivered dozens of pounding blows one right after the other. Yann seized the opportunity while the Darkling's back was turned. He wasn't likely to get another chance.

He sprinted down the Darkling's long body to its hind enough, sprang onto the tail, and sprinted up the spiked ridge running the length of the Darkling's spine.

Yann didn't try to stab the creature down here. He wouldn't be able to stop it until he got to the head.

He had to slow down to fight more tentacles coming after him, but the Darkling was enjoying itself too much by attacking Anríq.

Deafening booms rocked the library every time the Darkling punched down on top of Anríq's body with brutal force.

Any second now, the Darkling would get tired of playing with its food, dive on top of Anríq, and devour him with all those teeth. Yann couldn't let that happen.

The Darkling reared off the floor when it felt Yann running on top of it. He wobbled to keep his balance.

He didn't allow himself to wonder about the damage this monster was inflicting on Anríq, but right then, when the Darkling turned its attention to getting rid of Yann.

Anríq pushed himself off the floor as soon as the Darkling left him alone. Yann couldn't tell from here how injured Anríq was, but at least he was still armed.

The Darkling tossed its head when Yann got near its neck. It almost threw him off.

He sprawled on his stomach and held onto the creature's spikes to keep himself on top. He couldn't let himself fall off. This was the safest place in the whole library right now and definitely the one where he would be able to do the most damage.

Anríq hauled back his axe to strike. Yann had to make his move now. The Darkling wouldn't be able to fight both boys at the same time.

He dragged himself a little higher by the creature's spikes, raised his glaive, and stabbed for the creature's eye. Yann flexed every muscle in his body and brought the weapon down with all his strength.

The glaive plunged three feet into the creature's eye just as the Darkling was about to engulf Anríq.

The Darkling bellowed to High Heaven, shot upward off the ground, and a catastrophic blow struck Yann from the side.

He tried to yank his glaive out, but it got stuck and then an unstoppable force sent him flying across the library. He hit another stack of bookshelves, slammed down on the ground, and lost consciousness.

Chapter 58

E liska headed out of town for the countryside she and her friends just crossed to get to this city. She didn't look back except to make sure Marine stayed with her.

None of the townspeople looked sideways at Marine. That on its own should have set off Eliska's alarm bells—and it did. Something wasn't right here.

She opened her Coil projection to check on the two boys. They inched through the city and made a few detours.

She found herself smiling when the projection showed small bursts of magic at each location. Anríq must be healing people along the way.

The two boys approached the Hall of Magical Learning, but she had to shut her projection when she and Marine got back to the road.

"Come over here, Marine," Eliska guided Marine to a grassy bank by the roadside—or Eliska tried to guide her. Marine didn't exactly cooperate.

In the end, Eliska sat down and waited for Marine to hunker down nearby. Eliska really wished she could talk to Marine—about anything.

Marine hadn't spoken through her familiars since the party arrived in this Island. Maybe Marine couldn't use her familiars here.

Eliska sighed and trained her gaze on the last bend in the road. The boys would come around that corner when they finished checking the book to find the Sacred Shrine.

Eliska looked down at her hand. She planned to open her Coil projection, but at that moment, a distant crash and a high-pitched shriek echoed across the landscape.

She didn't see anything wrong at first, but a second later, a surge of instability swept the landscape.

It started far out in the countryside in the direction the travelers came from. The surge took time to cross that much territory, but when it got here, it struck fast and hard.

Houses blasted out of position and came alive. The people surrounding Eliska and Marine all spasmed out of shape and torrents of wild magic poured from their eyes and mouths.

The whole world dissolved in chaos, but for some reason, the Island itself didn't break down. It just went insane all over the place.

Eliska jumped up and grabbed Marine, but the wave hit both of them, too. Marine convulsed every which way.

Her muscles spasmed out of control She wouldn't have been able to stand at all if her muscles didn't lock into position.

She screamed, but instead of sound, Dark magic blasted out of her mouth. It poured from her eyes and streaked from her fingers and hair.

Eliska ducked out of the way only to run into more people ejecting magical blasts all over the place. They exploded houses, hit each other, and tore up the landscape, but the Island still didn't collapse. Why?

Eliska didn't have time to worry about that. The Dark magic taking over Marine lifted her off the ground.

Eliska should have run from the Darkness taking over Marine, but Eliska couldn't do that. She couldn't let her friend fall to the Dark. Eliska had already lost too many people already.

She waited just long enough for the upheaval to jerk Marine the other way around. Marine turned her back on Eliska and Eliska dove in to tackle her.

She slammed Marine down on the ground just in time to avoid another barrage of explosive magic bursting through the windows of a nearby house.

Eliska didn't have time to raise her staff. She slapped her other hand down on the ground next to Marine and Eliska smashed the Layer with everyone and everything in it.

The Island disintegrated and everyone wheeled off into a Layer of pure Darkness.

That Darkness triggered a cascade in Eliska's soul and released all the Darkness she'd been working so hard to contain ever since the Symphorian church disaster.

The memories and nightmares erupted off the charts, but she didn't try to control the Darkness this time. This was her. It swelled inside her and fed her unimaginable power.

Marine regained her sanity instantly and rotated outward in Eliska's arms. "Look out, Eliska!" Marine yelled, shot her arm past Eliska's head, and fired at something behind Eliska's back.

One of the townspeople had drifted too close. This was another working man wearing grease-stained overalls. He had long hair and a thick beard.

He roared at the two girls and a fountain of Dark power shot from his mouth.

Marine fired an answering pulse from her hand, but it didn't deflect the gush of Dark magic coming from the man.

Eliska didn't have time to raise her staff or her hand this time. She roared back at the man and unleashed her own Dark power on him.

It exploded out of her beyond all proportion and smashed him far away across the Layers. A second later, an enormous house cartwheeled across the girls' path.

Eliska raised her staff. She could control the Darkness better this way, but the power built to such an epic pitch that she had to be careful.

She didn't dare to tap the full depth of the Darkness that had become her innermost being.

She fired at the house. It only detonated into a cloud of shrapnel, each piece alive and hellbent on destroying anything in its path.

All those scraps, splinters, and shards shot for the two girls.

Marine fired blast after blast to drive those projectiles off, but the two girls' combined magic still wasn't strong enough.

Eliska ejected another geyser of power from her staff, caught all those spikes in a huge net, compressed them into a ball, and fired it across the Layer to soar miles away from the girls.

Eliska didn't dare to slacken her guard an inch. She drifted a little closer to Marine.

Living houses transformed into monsters, people shooting magical blasts from every orifice, random vehicles caught in the upheaval—they all tumbled and flew through the Dark Layer along with Darklings and a bunch of other horrors Eliska didn't recognize.

Some of them might have once been people, creatures, or objects from one Island or another. Some instability or collapse must have transformed them into something totally unrecognizable.

"Stay close to me," Eliska growled over her shoulder.

"We have to find a way out of this," Marine murmured back. "Can you find out where we are?"

"We have to meet up with the boys. They were in the same Island with us. They could be trapped in this Layer, too.

"Can you find out?" Marine asked. "I wish I could say I'll protect you while you look, but it will probably be the other way around."

Eliska turned to smile at her friend over her shoulder.

Their eyes met and Eliska knew. Marine knew. Marine saw Eliska use Dark magic just now. Marine also saw just how much more powerful Eliska had become since Symphorian.

The warmth and sympathy in Marine's eyes made it okay. Marine communed with the Dark all the time. Why did Eliska think Marine would hold it against Eliska when she started doing the same thing?

Eliska opened her hand to consult her Coil projection. She traced the golden lines showing Yann and Anríq traveling from the Island of lost souls to the Hall of Magical Learning.

"Oh, my god!" Eliska breathed.

Marine looked over. "What's wrong?"

"The boys are in trouble! They're under Darkling attack. The library was a Dark Island. I knew there was something wrong with that place! Come on! We gotta help them!"

Eliska grabbed Marine again, but this Layer didn't have any solid floor or walls or ceiling. Chaos and vapor surrounded the two girls.

Darklings, people, and magically distorted houses flew through the Layer. Out of control blasts, forces, and explosions pummeled everyone and everything in one direction or another.

Eliska magicked herself and Marine across the Layer to where she saw the boys in danger, but when she got there, the Layer had already shifted the library somewhere else.

"What's going on?!" Marine hollered. "Why aren't they here?!"

Eliska consulted her Coil projection and followed the lines to two other locations in the same Layer.

"Something weird is going on," Eliska told her. "We might be in some kind of puzzle maze."

"How do we get out of it?"

"We don't. The boys are trapped in here, too. We have to go through the maze until we find the library with the boys in it."

"But...." Marine's eyes widened when she looked at the projection. "They could be dead by the time we find them."

"No, they won't be. Come on." Eliska grabbed Marine's hand and placed it on top of her own. "Add your magic to mine."

Marine poured her magic into the Coil Projection and Eliska expanded it. She might have been able to explode the maze by using her Dark magic, but she didn't want to endanger the boys any more than they already were.

The projection widened and zoomed in on the girls' current Layer. It showed Dark channels cutting between multiple Layers—each one Darker and more dangerous than the one before it.

Marine gave a little squeak of horror when she saw it. "Oh, no!"

"We're going in there and we're going to save those boys," Eliska growled. "We'll be all right if we work together. Just stay near me."

Marine nodded fast. "Just tell me what you want me to do."

Eliska dipped her chin one more time. She had to go now or she would lose her nerve.

She kept a firm grip on Marine's hand and magicked both of them into the first Layer of the maze.

It occupied another hurricane Layer full of unstoppable forces tearing everything to pieces.

Darklings thrashed, writhed in agony, and bellowed their heads off before tornado winds ripped their bodies apart.

They exploded in concussions that blasted the Layer into an even deadlier battleground of forces all fighting each other.

Marine screamed when the first blast hit her. Eliska ejected a ball of protection around both of them, but they couldn't travel like this.

"Hold onto me!" Eliska roared. "Combine your magic with mine! That's the only way we're going to get across. Come on! We gotta move! We don't have much time!"

Marine crushed Eliska's hand in a death grip, but Eliska didn't want her to soften it. They had to stay together in this if it was the last thing they ever did.

Marine's magic flooded Eliska and the shield of protection got stronger—just strong enough to keep the girls alive.

Eliska took off running through the Layer. The tempest of flying body parts, Dark vapors, and slashing forces whirled everywhere. She couldn't see any outer edge to this Layer, but her feet hit something solid when she ran forward.

Nothing but chaos and mayhem fell away underneath her. She charged across the invisible surface making for the other side of the Layer where she could break through to the next part of the maze.

She didn't have to use her staff to hold that field of protection in place. It radiated outward from her and Marine and gave them just enough shelter from the bombardment.

Eliska fired her staff to the right to drive off Darklings, random Dark shapes, and clouds of energy rushing the girls from her side.

Marine unloaded one barrage after another from her left hand to guard the pair on the other side.

Eliska swerved to avoid another three Darklings. They started out attacking each other and then a cloud of Darkness enveloped all three.

They contorted in surreal shapes that broke bone and tore the flesh from their bodies. Magic erupted from every wound and destroyed the Darklings faster than anything else.

One of the Darklings smashed down in front of Eliska. She sprinted around it dragging Marine with her.

More forces raced for the girls from all sides. Eliska's defenses seemed to attract the Dark powers like nothing else. The Darkness sensed someone resisting—and someone about to escape.

Eliska remembered her Coil projection. The entrance to the next stage of the maze was too far away. She and Marine would never make it.

A flock of Darklings came out of nowhere—ten on the right and ten on the left, but they didn't see the girls. The two flanks charged together with the girls trapped in the middle.

Eliska reacted on pure instinct and magicked herself and Marine to the entrance in the blink of an eye. The Darklings smashed together and shook the Layer before the girls plunged through into Darkness.

Chapter 59

E liska sat up and tried to look around. At least she was still holding Marine's hand.

Eliska transferred her staff to the hand she used to hold onto Marine's hand so Eliska could open her Coil projection. She didn't want to let go of either her staff or Marine.

"Are we still in the maze?" Marine whispered.

"Definitely. Why do you think it's so Dark? There's the exit. Come on. Get up. We gotta move fast."

"How far do we have to go?"

"Don't worry. I'll magick us there in case this Layer has any more dangerous things in it—I mean, *because* this Layer will have dangerous things in it." She grimaced to herself in the dark. "I should have thought of that first. Come on."

Eliska magicked herself and Marine to the exit and consulted her Coil projection again.

"The next Layer is another Layer of Dark chaos," she told Marine. "Stay with me and I'll try to get us across it as quickly as possible. Then we should be in the library."

Marine nodded. "And then we fight the Darklings."

"Right." Eliska took a deep breath. "Here we go."

She and Marine charged through the entrance and burst into another Layer of Dark chaos. At least this one had some dim greyish light coming from somewhere.

The girls could see more than they wanted to of even more Dark forces in fullscale battle against each other.

Darklings and distorted mountains, trees, monsters, and creatures slashed and tore at each other.

They pounded and bombarded each other with Dark magic. Their noise rocked the Layer.

The incessant bombardment didn't shatter the Layer because this Layer didn't have any walls or ceiling or floor to shatter. Only magic could break it.

Eliska didn't want to shatter the Layer. She just had to get across it.

She magicked herself and Marine through the battle to somewhere she thought the girls wouldn't get crushed by rampaging monsters.

The instant they landed, a giant grotesque man with misshapen bulges swelling from different parts of his body turned on the two girls and tried to grab them.

Eliska magicked both girls out of the way in time and came to rest somewhere else.

The instant they got there, a Darkling slashed its tentacle at them, pounded it down on whatever invisible surface the girls were standing on, and shattered it.

The two girls pitched off into the mayhem. Eliska magicked ten one more time and the same thing happened. All the Dark forces seemed to anticipate her. They got there instantaneously whenever she and Marine materialized in the new place.

Eliska lost her patience and magicked herself and Marine straight to the entrance to the next stage of the maze. This should be the magical library where Yann and Anríq were fighting for their lives against the Darkling.

Eliska plunged through the entrance without checking first. She and Marine materialized two hundred feet in the air above the library floor.

Shelves a mile high surrounded both girls and they plummeted with the pull of gravity to splatter on the floor below.

The Darkling reared onto its hind legs, let off a series of magical concussions from its skin, and turned on Anríq. He faced the monster with his axe raised.

Yann was just picking himself up off the floor across the room. He must have gotten hit and knocked down.

Marine screamed and floundered to hold herself up before she realized what was happening. Her magic caught her and she hovered in midair.

She immediately let off a torrent of Dark magic that caught the Darkling. The magic sparking and forking on its skin and tentacles started to flow upward away from it and streamed through the air toward Marine.

The Darkling howled in fury as Marine drained the Dark away from it to steal its power.

Anríq dove in to follow up her attack and rushed the creature from the side. He hacked his axe at the creature's head and a ground-shaking explosion blasted through the Darkling from the point of impact. Eliska couldn't wait any longer.

She let gravity take her, dropped from that height, and tightened her grip on her staff.

She channeled her Dark poison into the staff, landed full force on the Darkling's head, and exploded it to smithereens.

Its Dark power blasted apart into a million whisps of vapor that vanished into the air.

The blast shattered the Layer, hurled all the books away in a massive shockwave, and the library disintegrated in chaos before all that magic came sucking back in to crush the four friends.

The impact slammed Eliska down on the floor and all her friends tumbled down near her.

She rolled over choking to catch her breath. The others groaned and then jumped when a single book landed on the floor next to Eliska's head with a dull echoing thud.

The four friends stared at the book.....and then Eliska glanced around.

The library was empty—or rather the building that had been the Hall of Magical Learning was empty.

Not a single shelf, book, ladder, or scaffolds remained. The four friends were completely alone in the vast, empty hall.

"Um......I guess this is the book we wanted to find." Yann dragged himself onto all fours and crawled over to the book. He hesitated to touch it.

Anríq passed his hand in front of it. "It's harmless. It doesn't have any magic—good or bad. It's just a book."

Yann made a face. "Finally." Yann flipped the book open, turned the pages, and ran his hand down the first page. "Here it is. The White Spire."

"What does it say?" Eliska asked.

"Nothing. This is just the table of contents. This tells me which page to find the information on."

He turned a few more pages and read from a much larger block of text.

"Shard of Hotha.....Hall of Hight.....Sacred Shrine.....King's succ ession....blah blah blah.....This is all the same information we got from the Savaré Templars......"

Eliska and Anríq glanced at each other. Yann didn't notice.

He kept reading in silence for a minute. "Okay, here it is. This says the Sacred Shrine is definitely in the White Spire—so it follows that we would be able to find the two Shards there." He frowned. "Apparently the Hall of Light is in the White Spire, too, but I guess that makes sense since the King stays there after he takes the Shard."

"Can you find out anything that will help us locate the Shard inside the spire?" Eliska asked.

"There's nothing here. Hold on. I'll check something else."

Yann flipped back to the beginning of the book, ran down the table of contents again, and then turned to the very back of the book.

"This is a diagram of the White Spire's floorplan and interior lay-out."

"That's weird, " Marine remarked. "It shows the White Spire in a beautiful landscape. We saw it in a devastated land before."

All four friends crowded around to study the picture. Eliska traced the positions of throne rooms, bedrooms, kitchens, stables, and even interior courtyards.

"This is another magical puzzle like that maze Island," she pointed out. "We've seen the White Spire. It's a cylinder. It couldn't have all of this inside it—and it isn't even the same shape."

Marine frowned at the diagram. "I don't see anything labeled Sacred Shrine or Hall of Light. They aren't here."

"You're right," Yann replied. "Maybe they're magical, too."

"They would have to be if they house the Shard—or Shards," Marine pointed out. "I mean, these Shards are magical, so it follows that the process of taking the Shards from the Sacred Shrine, getting them embedded in your chest, and then entering the Hall of Light—all of that much be a magical process. You wouldn't just walk in the door, pick up some rock, and you're done."

Yann grimaced again. "Could you not use the word 'you' when you talk about that?"

She burst into a huge smile of pure affection when she looked at him. "Sorry. I'll try not to—but you get my point. Whoever takes this Shard will have to use magic—first to find it, then to take it for themselves, and finally to enter the Hall of Light to become King. That's what the records say."

"Then how can a non-magical person accomplish all of that?" Yann asked.

"Maybe that's where the Voyant comes in," Eliska pointed out. "Maybe you need the previous Voyant to escort you into the Sacred Shrine."

"I don't think so," Yann countered. "Everything we've seen so far keeps saying 'take the Shard'. Whoever becomes King has to actively seek the Shard. They can't just fall over and wind up with the Shard accidentally."

"So how do we find the Sacred Shrine?"

"Maybe that's the thing. Maybe we have to go looking for it."

"Isn't that what we're already doing?" Marine asked.

"We haven't looked for it yet because we only just found out that it exists. We've gone looking for the Voyant. We've gone looking for the White Spire and we've gone looking for information about all of them, but we haven't actually looked for the Shard itself or the Sacred Shrine. Maybe that's the point. Maybe we have to go on some kind of quest...."

"That would mean that one of us really actually wanted to take the Shard," Marine pointed out. "You keep saying you don't want to take the Shard and you don't want to be the person the Voyant is looking for. Maybe *you* wouldn't have to actively search for it or go on a quest to find it or use all your effort to take the Shard, but someone would have to." She looked around at Anríq and Eliska. "One of us might have to."

"I would do it," Anríq interjected. "I would do it to stabilize the Coil. It would save all these lives and everyone could live in peace."

"I hate to break it to you, but the Voyant isn't looking for you," Yann muttered.

"What difference does it make who he's looking for?" Anríq countered. "All that matters is that the person really wants to find the Shard and take it. Maybe that's why the Voyant is looking for one specific person—because he thinks this person would have a really good, strong, compelling reason to want to take the Shard."

"Well, I don't have a really good, strong, compelling reason to take it," Yann countered.

"Not even to save millions of lives?" Anríq asked. "Any of us would do that. I know you would."

Yann looked away.

Eliska stared down at the diagram in the book.

"I don't know where the Shard or the Sacred Shrine are, but I do know one thing," she murmured. "It's going to take all four of us working together to pull this off. We don't even know if we'll survive the process. If even one of us has a shot at taking the Shard, then all four of us should make the commitment to go on this quest. All four of us have to pledge ourselves to give everything we have to not just find the Shard but to take it even if we're the last one left who *can* take it. We don't know which of us that will be, so we all have to do it. We have to work together and fight together to make sure at least one of us gets there in the end."

The others exchanged glances.

Anríq nodded first. "I will serve. I'll give my best effort to finding it, and if I'm the last one, I'll take the Shard myself."

"Me, too," Marine added. "This is going to be dangerous. We'll all need to pull together."

"Do you agree, Eliska?" Anríq asked.

She nodded. "I'm in. I don't know if I'll be able to take the Shard, but I will if I can."

"What about you, Yann?" Marine took his hand and squeezed. "Do it for the Coil."

"I will," he murmured. "You're right. It's the only thing left to do."

"Let's go." Eliska stood up and cast one last look at the drawing in the book.

It showed her everything she wanted to know about the White Spire—except for the one thing she really needed to know.

The book couldn't help her.

"Can you find the White Spire?" Yann asked.

She opened her Coil projection and located the White Spire in another Layer. "It keeps moving around.

"It has to," Marine pointed out. "The Layers it appears in keep collapsing."

Eliska checked the Island where the White Spire appeared on the projection. It was another city Island like the illusion Layer where she and Marine first saw the Spire in the distance. The Island looked safe and inviting, but Eliska didn't trust that.

She checked the location and sent a blast of magic into the floor. It buckled and she magicked the party together as they pitched, zoomed, and sailed through dozens of Layers one after another.

They all collapsed as soon as the friends entered them.

Explosions of rock, whipping vapors, and torrential ice storms tossed the friends every which way until they broke through into a vast wasteland of scorched earth.

Even the stone-grey clouds overhead rumbled and rolled in a sea of coal-grey Darkness.

The White Spire stood in the distance. Eliska didn't see any Dark river near it or any wolves guarding it.

The spire had a burned look, too.

Millions of disembodied eyes hovered in the air all over the landscape. The eyes swiveled this way and that trying to look at everything that wasn't there.

A few of the eyes swiveled around to look at the travelers, but the eyes didn't focus their attention on anything for very long before they turned away to look at something else.

"Umm....what just happened?" Marine asked. "This isn't the Island where we just saw the spire."

"It might not be the same Island, but it is the Island with the White Spire in it," Yann pointed out. "It's right over there."

Marine cringed away from the eyes. "I don't like this place."

"This is a trap," Eliska murmured.

"How do you figure?" Yann asked.

"The Dark river and the Wolves are all gone. We're either in an illusion Layer designed to make us think the spire is here.....or the Voyant has completely changed his defenses. He didn't leave the spire undefended. I promise you that."

"Let's see what happens when we try to get near it." Marine started forward. "That will trigger the defenses if anything will."

She set off walking. Eliska didn't see anything else to do or any other way to get there.

She took a few steps to follow Marine. The boys did the same thing.

They only made it ten feet before the ground started to bubble and smoke underfoot. Marine teetered and her shoes started to sink into the soil as it liquified underneath her.

At the same instant, all the eyes turned inward and countless magical blasts burst from all the eyes.

Eliska dove for Marine and pulled her back onto solid ground at the last second, but those eyes kept bombarding anyone and everything, including each other.

Eliska didn't see any pattern to where or how they shot. Half the eyes just blasted off in no particular direction at all.

Stray shots peppered the ground and some of them hit Anríq across the back of his shoulders. He stumbled, roared, and pulled up his club.

Eliska ejected another shield of protection around the party, but she didn't act fast enough. Yann got caught outside the field.

Anríq swung his club swatting all those shots away. He bumped into Marine.

She added her magic to the fight and counterattacked against the eyes as much as she could. Anríq swung his club back and forth trying to deflect the shots coming his way, but he couldn't hit them all.

Marine had to duck under his arms every time he swung his club.

Eliska backed up to surround all four of them in her protection. She planned to gather her friends as closely together as possible before she shattered the Layer. The friends would have to find another way to the spire.

She looked around for Yann, and at that moment, a cluster of eyes spouted their magical bombardment at him alone.

She didn't understand it because she didn't see the other eyes targeting any one person.

She couldn't protect all three of her friends at the same time.

She dove out of place and lunged between him and the eyes to block the bombardment, but she missed her timing. The shot hit her hard and the Layer exploded around her ears.

Yann yelled something and he and Eliska fell through into another Island below. They slammed down on another beach—a gravel beach this time.

Eliska stumbled to her feet looking everywhere for the next threat that would come after her friends.

Her heart stopped when she saw Yann—and only Yann. Anríq and Marine weren't here.

"Anríq!" she roared. "Anríq! Marine!"

No one answered her. The waves whispered a gentle hissing lullaby when they rushed up the gravel and then pulled back into the ocean.

The more Eliska looked around everywhere, the more Marine and Anríq weren't here.

Yann straightened up, blinked, and realized why she was blundering around yelling for the other two.

He got to his feet and his eyes took in the emptiness of the surroundings.

She kept turning this way and that, but Anríq and Marine weren't here. They couldn't be gone.

She opened her Coil projection and Yann came over to look at it.

"No, no, no, no, no," she husked when she tried to trace the lines. They vanished in a sea of chaos. She couldn't find Anríq or Marine anywhere.

Yann's features pinched and he cast another hopeless glance around the beach. Eliska read her worst fears written in his eyes.

Anríq and Marine were gone. Now Yann and Eliska were alone together—maybe forever.

She gulped down a rising surge of desperate anguish. She couldn't do this—not without the one person who knew her the best.

Yann's voice shook when he finally worked up the nerve to say anything. "Do you remember what we decided in the library? We have to keep going. We have to find the Sacred Shrine so one of us can take the Shard. This is what we agreed on."

She fought back the tide of misery. Her mouth twisted up, but she didn't let herself break down. Anríq would continue with this mission if he was still alive anywhere.

He would want her to continue, too. She was a Servant. Even he called her that.

Yann put his arm behind her back and gently prodded her forward—somewhere. She didn't check the projection to see where they were going. They just had to keep moving forward—wherever this journey led them.

<u>End of Book 3.</u>

Keep Reading

C orrupted Coil Series: Book 4: Broken Cradle

Yann and Eliska are trapped alone in the Coil as it continues to disintegrate with ever-more dangerous instability threatening their lives. Things spiral out of control when the Voyant Mendicat attacks and tries to kill the two travelers. When unknown enemies come out of the woodwork, the ghosts of the past become the deadliest threat of all.

Eliska thinks this could be the answers to her prayers when she and Yann meet powerful magic-users who promise to heal her Dark Poison. These strangers will find out they got more than they bargained for when they tried to mess with her, but she'll have to face the shadow of her own tortured memories before she can truly break free. Will Yann be able to help her or will the destruction cost both their lives before they escape?

You can find it at your favorite book retailer.

Sign Up Once--Get all Theo Mann's free books including brand new releases

S ign Up Once--Get all Theo Mann's free books including brand new releases

With the Corrupted Coil becoming increasingly unstable and the human world torn apart by war, the Barbarians expects their Chieftain's sons to become his greatest warriors and take over his power after him.

When twelve-year-old Anríq's dormant magic comes to the surface, it will destroy everything he knows about his life, his family, and his future.

When those he most cares about turn against him, he'll have to find a new source of strength within himself and the allies to help him do what must be done before it's too late.

Sign up at www.theomann.com to read it for free

About Theo Mann

I write 70 books per year—and yes, before you ask, all these books are my original creative work. Nothing written under my name is AI-generated or ghostwritten because I write better than AI and any ghostwriter out there.

People don't read fiction for entertainment or to escape from reality. People read fiction to see their humanity reflected in another person's character and story.

This is my promise to you. When you read my books, you'll see your own humanity reflected in the characters and stories. I take this commitment to my readers very seriously. My books are an intimate form of communication between us. I would never disrespect my readers by turning that over to a machine or another writer. This is my bond between me and you as my reader.

I write 20,000 words per day as my daily work output. If anyone with a public platform would like to challenge me to prove this in a controlled environment, feel free to contact me on this website's contact page.

I worked as a professional ghostwriter for fifteen years. Now I'm on a mission to set a Guinness World Record by writing 700 books over the next ten years and 1400 books over the next twenty years, all originally written by me. See my website for the full book list.

I'm also the author of *Proof for the Existence of God* and the *Crimes Against Fiction* blog. You can find all my nonfiction work at www.crimes-against-fiction.com.

If you have a story idea, or if you would like me to explore a series in more depth, or if you'd like me to explore a character by writing a spinoff series about that character or world, leave me a message on my website's contact page. I answer all reader emails, so ask me anything, tell me what you liked and didn't like, and let me know where you'd like your favorite series to go. I would love to hear your ideas and find out what you'd like to read next.

Find out more at www.theomann.com.

Also by Theo Mann (so far)